Hench Western Adventures
Books 1 - 3

Hench
Blood Hoard
All's Jake

by

Joseph Parks

A PulpPerchPress (P³) Book

Published by PulpPerchPress (P³)

To get a FREE Hench short story
sign up for the Hench mailing list by going to:

JosephParksAuthor.com

Hench Books

Hench
Blood Hoard
All's Jake

CONTENTS

HENCH

Book One

JOSEPH PARKS

CHAPTER ONE

The Arkansas River shadowed Hench on his left as he rode into La Junta, Colorado. He was riding from Pueblo to Lamar, but stopped as dusk settled in on his second day out. It was a small junction town, with one leg of the Santa Fe Railroad heading northwest to Pueblo and another southwest to Trinidad. He rode his Appaloosa, named Speck, to the livery stables on the outskirts of the sleepy town. He was a short and hardy horse, a young gelding he'd come by a year earlier when his former horse grew too old to hit the trail any longer. Speck was a cream-colored horse with reddish-brown spots splashed across his body.

Speck taken care of, Hench moved on into the town proper, stopping at Walter's Saloon. It was a narrow place. To his left was a long shellacked bar handmade by Walter and his brothers. A dozen tables filled the rest of the place. Hench's worn boots clumped over the roughhewn wide gray floorboards. The place smelled of sweat, beer, and chili—the only food offered by Walter. The man himself, a bit over five feet tall with black hair slicked back, minded the bar. His real name was Rogelio, who had found his way here from Juarez some years earlier. Gabriela, his wife, minded the chili and the fire at the far end of the saloon. Hench made sure he caught Rogelio's eye then picked out a small table against the wall.

Hench removed his hat, once tan, now mottled with sweat and rain and dust over the years into a color approaching sun-dried horse dung. He dropped it on the table and slouched out of his tan canvas duster, which looked much the same color as his hat, folding it over the back of his chair. He would have liked getting out of his black leather chaps, but that could wait. Stretching his back, getting a few satisfying pops out of it, he smoothed out the front of his faded blue side-button shirt. His knees creaked as he settled into the chair. After bedding Speck, it was now dark out and closing in on ten o'clock. A couple of minutes later Gabriela appeared with a giant bowl of chili, a tin plate of crusty bread, a full bottle of rye, and a square of checkered cloth to wipe the chili off his face.

"How can you still be alive, Hench?"

"Lord only knows. It ain't like I'm goin' outta my way to stay above ground."

Gabriela chuckled and headed back to the bar.

With his boots on, Hench was almost five-nine. Graying and greasy dark brown hair hung to his shoulders. His mostly gray beard and mustache were getting a touch long, itching too much. It must have been close to time for his monthly visit to the barber for a shave and a bath.

He took a long slug from the bottle then dug into the chili, sopping it up with big hunks of bread and stuffing it into his mouth. Hench didn't know if the chili was actually any good, but after a long day on the trail, it tasted like the best you could get at Delmonico's. Not that he'd ever eaten at the restaurant or even been to New York for that matter, but to the best of his imagination, the chili rated just as high.

He drained half the bowl and half the bottle before coming up for air. He held up the empty tin plate so Rogelio could see it. Then he belched and looked around the saloon. Not very busy. There were still a couple of empty tables and maybe only half the bar was occupied. It was a quiet night.

Gabriela walked by balancing three bowls of chili topped with three tin plates of bread. She made the bread in the wee hours each morning. Hench had no idea when either she or Rogelio ever slept. She went to a table with three men who'd shown up after Hench had arrived. He didn't recognize them, but that didn't mean much as he only rode through the town on his way somewhere else. He dipped his head to eat some more chili when he heard the loud slap, a chair pushed back with force, and a man bellowing in anger and pain.

One of the men, probably young cowhands at one of the ranches in the area, had Gabriela by the wrist and was raising a fist to strike her. Hench moved fast, but Rogelio jumped the bar and arrived before he did. The cowhand was taller and definitely meaner-looking than Rogelio, but the saloon owner stood up to the cowhand just the same.

"Please, sir, do not disrespect my wife." There was some steel in his voice. He put his hand up to block the cowhand's fist.

Gabriela pulled against the grip. "Let go of me, pendejo!"

Rogelio didn't see it in time. One of the cowhand's friends rose quietly and grabbed the saloon owner from behind, wrapping him in his arms.

The first cowhand spit in Gabriela's face and raised his fist farther. Hench couldn't reach that fist in time so he grabbed a chair and flung it as hard as he could at the man's legs. The sturdy chair crashed into the back of the cowhand's knees. The man flipped back hard, smashing his head into the floorboards and pulling Gabriela off balance. She fell on top of the man. Her fists started smashing into his face.

Hench sped not toward Rogelio, but toward the third cowhand, who was up and coming around the table looking for someone to hit. He spotted Hench and came at him. When they were almost on one another, Hench slid to the right bringing his back arm up hard, his forearm striking the cowhand in the throat. The man staggered backwards gasping for air. Hench turned his attention to Rogelio. The man holding him seemed uncertain what to do with his two friends out of the fight.

Hench held up his hands, palms out. "Listen, there's no point in continuin' on. Let Rogelio go, collect your friends, and get outta here. Fight's over."

The man stared at Hench, still holding the saloon owner. Then Rogelio must have decided he'd had enough. He whipped his head back. He was shorter than the cowhand, which put the top of his head into the man's mouth and nose. The cowhand cried out and staggered back and Rogelio turned to hit him, but the cowhand recovered quickly, blood already flowing from his nose and a split lip. With a snarl he snapped his arm out, hitting Rogelio in the face. The saloon owner sat down, eyes wide and dazed.

Hench didn't wait for an invitation. He launched himself at the cowhand, striking him in the chest with his shoulder. The two fell to the floor, grappling one another. Hench tried to get some distance to throw a fist or two, but the man was strong and held Hench tight to him, nearly cheek-to-cheek. That wouldn't work out well for Hench if one of his two friends recovered enough to help.

"Hope you ain't fond of your ear."

"Huh?"

Hench sunk his teeth into the bottom part of the man's right ear.

"Son of a bitch!"

The man yanked his head back, helping Hench to pull a chunk free. Hench turned his head slightly and spit the earlobe into the man's face. His grip around Hench relaxed enough for Hench to push himself off far enough to deliver three shots to his face, Hench's arm moving fast like a piston on a steam engine. Then Hench rose to his feet. The man was still conscious but in a lot of pain with part of his ear missing, his nose broken, and probably spitting up a tooth or two.

Hench looked back at the other two cowhands. The one he'd hit in the throat was looking better, but the fight had gone out of him. The first cowhand, however, was in a world of hurt. Gabriela kept beating his face, which was slick with blood as were her hands.

"Whoa, Gabby, don't kill the asshole."

She stopped and looked over at Hench. "He grabbed my tit."

Hench paused for a second. "Okay, couple more."

She made the hits count. The man would be out all night and was probably concussed. Gabriela rose to a crouch and pulled his shirt out from his pants, wiping her hands on it. Then she turned to help Rogelio to his feet. He was still a bit shaky from the shot he'd taken.

Hench went to the man he'd struck in the throat. The man honked like a goose as he tried to get air in and out. He flinched away from Hench who grabbed him by the front of his shirt and hauled him in close. "Get your friends and get the hell outta here." Bloody spittle covered the man's face courtesy of his friend's earlobe.

The cowhand nodded and tried to move away, but Hench kept one hand on him. Hench pulled his silver badge out of the front pocket of his wool pants. The badge was stamped with COLORADO RANGER. "None of you are welcome back here. Ever. If you even glance inside I'll whip your asses again then lock you up."

He nodded and went to his friend whose ear was missing a piece and helped him to his feet. The man with the missing earlobe turned toward Hench. "It was just a little fight. Why you gone and bit my ear off?"

Hench wasn't going to answer him at first, but then he said, "I learned a lesson when I was young, in my twenties, always fight to win. No matter what."

The man shook his head and winced, his friend pulling on him. Hench watched them, hand resting on one of his black Schofield revolvers, as they dragged their unconscious friend from the saloon.

"It must be time for a drink," he said, turning back to his table and wiping the blood from his mouth with the sleeve of his faded blue shirt.

But he didn't make it that far.

CHAPTER TWO

Hench didn't make it back to his table at Walter's Saloon before a couple of pair of boots ran into the place. He turned, gun drawn and cocked in the same motion, expecting a stampede of the cowhand's buddies. The two men running in weren't armed and neither looked angry or vengeful. What they looked was excited. Rogelio was holding himself up at the bar, one of his customers looking at the welt growing on his face and chatting with him while Gabriela was already coming back out from behind the bar with a wet cloth, Hench assumed to clean up the bloody mess she'd made of the cowhand's face.

The men skidded to a stop by Rogelio and were jabbering over one another. The best Hench could figure was that something big had happened in town, and it wasn't good.

Rogelio held up his hands. "Slow down, amigos."

One of the men gulped air and then said, "It's Delilah, over at the Satin Perch. She got herself cut up bad."

"She been killed!" interjected the other.

Exclamations of shock and curiosity erupted in the saloon. Hench went to his table. He pinned his badge to his faded blue shirt, slid on his battered hat, draped his duster over his right arm, picked up the bottle of rye, and moved halfway between the front door and the men with the news.

The first one said, "You don't know she's killed."

"Sure do. Heard it from Emil. She's dead alright."

More exclamations and a hornet nest of murmurs as men discussed the news among themselves. Several immediately broke off and hurried outside. Hench followed behind. He was friendly with Madam Felicity, who ran the Satin Perch brothel and he'd known Delilah personally, or biblically as the case may be. Who'd want to cut up that girl? She was one of the sweeter doves, only stealing from him once. A growing stream of townsfolk swirled around him as they headed down the wide street. The brothel was a large two-story red-brick building several blocks down from Walter's Saloon. A crowd churned out front.

Hench took a long slug from the rye, then cradled the bottle in close to his chest and shouldered his way through. The inside wasn't any better. The parlor, resplendent in different shades of red and gold, was packed as well. Hench stepped up onto an overstuffed chair of crushed velvet to take in the entire room. He didn't see anything but curious gawkers. Jumping down, he shoved straight to and up the wide staircase opposite the front door.

At the top of the stairs, like following dozens of compass needles, he pushed in the direction of everyone's gaze. That led him to one of the two dozen private rooms in the building. A deputy sheriff stood in the doorway. He looked familiar, but he couldn't recall his name. He showed the man his badge. The deputy hesitated long enough for Hench not to care what his decision would be and he pushed his way through and into the room.

Delilah lay in bed naked and covered in blood. A body's worth of blood saturated the sheet beneath her in a red halo around her dead body. A man, visibly shaken, blood on him, wearing only underwear—no doubt hastily pulled on—sat in one of two wood chairs in the sparse room. The bed, and the dove, were on Hench's left, the two chairs were opposite the door on either side of an open window. A small one-drawer vanity with a mirror over it was across from the bed, a lit oil lamp on the top of the vanity. An intricately painted china wash basin was on the floor beneath the vanity, the basin's pitcher was in broken chunks on the bed.

The man was younger than Hench, maybe in his mid-thirties. Sturdy, with ruddy sun-bleached skin used to being outside all day. Doctor Rousseau had the other chair pulled up close so he could attend to the man. The doctor was close to Hench's age, somewhere in his forties. His skin was pale, his clothes were clean and pressed. His dark hair was just turning silver at the temples.

Sheriff Eugene Utley, a tall whip-lean man, was asking the man a question. Doctor Rousseau, one of two doctors in town, was patching up what looked like a pretty good cut on the man's arm. He appeared to have other cuts as well, but with all the blood it was difficult to see what was his and what might have been Delilah's. Hench stepped to the bed and disentangled a sheet from the rest of the covers and covered up the dove. Blood immediately bloomed through the white cotton.

"What'cha doin' here, Hench?"

Hench turned to the sheriff. "Just got to town. Was over at Walter's when I heard. This the killer?"

The man looked startled, already shaking his head. Not much of the blood on him could have been his, he was too alert for that much loss of blood. Utley shrugged. "According to Bertram here, he was with Delilah, *in the throes* so to speak, when Big Pat climbed through the window, drunk off his ass, and went berserk." Utley pointed to the knife on the vanity. "That's Big Pat's. I have deputies out lookin' for him."

"Why'd he leave his knife behind?"

Utley looked at Bertram. "Well?"

The man shrugged. "I don't know. He hit me from behind with that pitcher when I was, um, atop her. I was dazed after that. He ignored me and attacked the whore. When I snapped out of it and tried to get him off her, he cut me a few times and hit me," he motioned to some bruising on his face, "then people was bangin' at the door. He must'a dropped it durin' our scuffle, I guess, then got scared when people was poundin' at the door. He climbed back out the window."

"Big Pat say anything while he did all this?"

The man shrugged. "I don't remember if he did. I was pretty woozy."

Hench looked at Utley. "Know if Big Pat had some grievance with Delilah?"

"Not that I'm aware. Felicity is checkin' on the other girls and seein' that someone gets George over here." George was the town's undertaker.

"Sheriff!" The voice came from outside the window. A face appeared shortly after. It was one of the deputies. "Found Big Pat passed out in an alley down the way. Blood on him."

Utley nodded. "Well, there you go. Drag him to the jail, use a horse if you have to."

Hench had met Big Pat before. Not quite an outlaw but certainly a troublemaker. He was also huge and Hench had little doubt they'd need that horse to drag him to the jail. How'd they get him into one of the cells would be interesting to see.

The deputy disappeared and Hench went to the window and looked out to see a half-dozen large shipping crates stacked against the outside wall of the brothel. He went to the vanity and grabbed the oil lamp, returning to the window. Leaning out, the light showed the large wooden crates more clearly, which were burned with the name of a tool wholesaler. They must have come from the hardware and feed store next door. There was blood on the crates, giving some credence to the man's story.

"Terrance! What the hell are you doing here?"

Hench turned toward Madam Felicity. There were only a few people who got away with calling him by his given name. "On my way to Lamar and was stayin' over for the night. Just heard the news."

The woman glanced at the bed, her eyes brimming with tears. "I'm going to castrate Big Pat before I slit his goddamn throat."

"I'll hold him down for you, Felice," said Hench.

She was a handsome woman in her early forties by Hench's guess, but he'd never make the mistake to ask. She had unnaturally dark hair pulled and piled up on top of her head. She amply filled out a red satin dress with an improbably tight corset.

"Big Pat have a beef with Delilah?" asked Hench.

Sheriff Utley stepped closer.

The madam frowned. "Not that I'm aware. Big Pat's in here all the time, but despite his horrible disposition, I never had much trouble with him." She pursed her lips for a moment. "To be honest, I don't ever recall Big Pat being with Delilah. He'd seen all the rest of the ladies."

"What about this guy?" Hench hooked a thumb toward the man in the chair. "You know him?"

"Bertram? He's a regular. Comes in several times a month. Quiet."

Hench looked back at the bloodstained sheet in the shape of the dove. Why would Big Pat want to kill her? And it wasn't just a murder. He'd seen enough bodies to know that the knifing had been done with fury or lust behind it.

"Did she refuse to be with Big Pat? Maybe he felt slighted."

Madam Felicity shook her head. "Wasn't that way. Big Pat always asked for ladies by name, but never Delilah."

"Bert! Bert! Why won't you let me in? Bertram!"

Everyone turned to the door. A woman was trying to push past the deputy.

Madam Felicity whispered, "That would be Bertram's wife."

Sheriff Utley said, "Let her through, Manuel."

Hench whispered mostly to himself, "This should be interesting."

CHAPTER THREE

Becca Richardson rushed past the lowered arm of the deputy to her husband in the chair across the room. Doctor Rousseau had to sit back, holding a bandage above her head as she went to her knees and hugged Bertram.

"You ain't hurt bad, are you?" she asked.

Bertram grimaced as she wrapped her arms around his. "Just a bit."

She pulled back. "Dear Lord, I'm sorry. He'll be okay, Doc, won't he?"

The doctor nodded. "He'll be fine. If you could move back just a bit more, Becca, so I can finish up."

She sat back on the floor and watched.

The doctor frowned at her, looking at her right hand. "Now what'd you do to yourself, girl?"

"Oh, ain't nothin'. Burned it on a loaf pan this mornin'."

"Come by my office tomorrow and let me take a look at it. You have to be the klutziest girl I know."

"Yessir."

Utley whispered to Hench. "Now that's a good woman. My wife would'a been fit to be tied she find me at the Satin Perch—outside'a business."

Hench nodded, thinking of his own wife, dead now nearly twenty years. She'd have let him know her disappointment at him. But he never strayed during their short years together before she died in the winter of '68. He gave their house in Denver to family and rode off. It was the last time he'd had a place he called home.

He didn't like to dwell on such things so he moved about the room, looking more closely at the bed and the shards of china, he lifted the sheet covering Delilah, looking at the knife wounds. Why would Big Pat be in such a rage to kill this girl? Lowering the sheet, he walked over to the vanity and opened the drawer. It held some makeup, a metal syringe douche, with a tin of borax to kill sperm, and some laudanum. He pocketed the laudanum, which reminded him of the bottle of rye in his hand. He took a few more slugs from the bottle. Felice held her hand out. He passed her the bottle and she drank deep and long before handing it back. There wasn't much left.

"You look done in, Terrance," she said. He could have said the same about her. "Could I put you up for the night? Maybe have one of the girls give you a bath—lord knows you could use one."

That sounded better than good. He nodded. "Obliged."

"Sometimes," said Utley, "I think it wouldn't be so bad not havin' a wife."

Hench didn't say anything.

Felice turned toward the doorway. "Juanita!"

A tall dark-haired dove appeared and held her hand out to Hench. He didn't hesitate and moved across the room and took it. She guided him out of the room and down the hall.

Hench entered the sheriff's office a little after nine in the morning. Utley looked at him in surprise. Hench's beard had been cut back, his greasy hair was less greasy, his skin was clean. Even his clothes had been dunked in water and soap a couple of times. He'd left his duster back at the Satin Perch, the day was too warm for it.

"You look right smart there, Hench."

"Juanita refused service until I cleaned myself up a might. She took my clothes while I slept. Feels a little strange bein' in stuff so clean."

The sheriff's office was big enough for several men to make themselves comfortable. There were two desks, Utley sitting behind one of them, and a few hardback chairs scattered about. Utley was cleaning one of his two Colt Peacemaker revolvers. Six cartridges were lined up in a row on the desk. Hench approved. Taste varied, and some lawmen he knew kept the chamber under the hammer empty, but he'd come to believe that the sixth bullet could be the difference between lining up bullets on your desk or being one in a line of tombstones.

"Big Pat in back?"

"Yep. Help yourself." Utley reached behind him to a small wall-mount metal cabinet that was unlocked and pulled out a key ring with five keys on it and tossed it to Hench.

"Can I have his knife?"

Utley opened a drawer in his desk and pulled out the bloodstained knife. Not a Bowie, but about the same size—big and mean. Knife in hand, Hench looked through the keys and picked the most likely culprit and unlocked the heavy reinforced door at the back of the office. Four cells were in back, the heavy bars were anchored into the building's gray stone exterior. Only one cell had an occupant. Big Pat snored loudly. The bed was too small and the man's feet dangled off the end.

The cell took two tries with keys before he found the one that turned. He opened the door and stepped inside. Big Pat was six-five, and seemed to be almost that wide. He worked at the blacksmith, but he wasn't a smithy. Didn't have the talent for it. Or the brains. But he was good for moving heavy things. His head was mostly bald, but in a strange pattern as if God had decided only certain random spots should be bald or have hair. He slicked the whole mess back as best he could. He was an ugly ugly man. Hench figured Big Pat might be even uglier than himself.

He kicked the metal-framed bed hard. It didn't move beneath the man's immense weight. But Big Pat woke up. Or rather, he opened his eyes. He stared at the ceiling and blinked six or seven times before closing them.

Hench kicked again and yelled, "Pat!"

"What? What?" His booming voice echoed like thunder through a canyon.

"You awake?"

Big Pat blinked at him a few times, then he slurred, "They arrest you, too, Hench?"

Hench held up the knife. "This yours?"

Big Pat's eyes narrowed and he shrugged. Ponderously, he pulled his legs over and sat up. He rubbed at his face. "Looks like mine. Where'd you find it?"

"Stickin' into a little dove at the Satin Perch."

That jarred him awake. "What? Who?"

"Girl named Delilah."

Big Pat's face went white and he began to tremble.

Hench nodded. "Comin' back to you now? Man there said you was pretty drunk and based on how the deputies found you, I'd have to concur."

"What man?"

"He said you snuck into the room, knocked him silly, then made a pincushion out of the dove. Why'd you do it? She steal from you or did you catch somethin' off her?"

Big Pat started to surge up off the bed. Hench slammed a fist into his face. The giant bellowed and staggered to his feet, towering over Hench, swinging wildly. Blood flowed from his nose down over his chin. Hench ducked the swings and hit him in the crotch three times before Big Pat finally doubled over and crumpled back onto the bed, curled up like a gigantic baby, his hands cradling his oysters. Blood spilled from his face onto the coarse Indian blanket covering his bed.

In a hoarse whisper, Big Pat said, "I didn't do it."

"You have dried blood all over you. Your knife was in the room and it's covered in blood. You're gonna have to do a hell of a lot better than 'I didn't do it.'"

Big Pat tried to look down at himself, Hench assumed looking for the blood.

"Just 'cause you might not remember doin' it don't mean you didn't do it."

Big Pat didn't say anything, just grunted and held his balls. His face was purplish red and tears mixed with the blood on the blanket.

"Told you, I didn't do it." With a bit of effort, Big Pat rolled over on the bed, putting his back to Hench.

"You're gonna swing for this. Might as well tell me why you done it."

Big Pat didn't move or speak. Hench left the cell, locking it behind him, and went back out front, locking the heavy door at the back of the office.

"You heard?"

Utley nodded, reassembling his Colt. "Ain't the first murderer to say he didn't do it."

The front door of the sheriff's office was flung open. An older man burst in, thin as a rail with wispy white hair. He was dressed in Confederate field grays creased from sitting in a drawer or trunk. He glared at Hench. "You son of a bitch, heard you was in town."

CHAPTER FOUR

Utley loaded the bullets back into their chambers. "You two know each other?" He placed the gun back on the cleaning cloth on his desk and kept his hand on it, eyeing the old Confederate soldier.

"Yeah," said Hench. "I know Jeffry Donn ever since we took his unit prisoner at the Battle of Glorieta Pass in the New Mexico Territory durin' the war."

Utley frowned. "You was stationed in New Mexico?"

Hench shook his head. "I was a Colorado Ranger back then, too. Snot-nosed and twenty. Was pullin' duty in

Denver when the word came down. Rangers and regulars went on a forced march down to New Mexico to meet up with New Mexico volunteers and put a stop to the Rebs' incursions down there."

Jeffry Donn snorted. "'Put a stop?' You was damned lucky to win that battle."

Utley stood and holstered his revolver. "That was before my time in Colorado. What action was happenin' out here?"

"Rebs took Santa Fe and Albuquerque. They was—" started Hench.

Jeffry Donn spoke over him. "Command had us marchin' north to the Colorado Territory to take whatever gold or silver mines we could. I think they had plans to even send troops to California to use the seaports. Say 'to hell with you' to the damn Yankee blockade. Y'all were nothin' but cheatin'—"

"At the battle, a group of us was sent wide 'round to engage the Rebs' flank. We ended up capturin' their supply lines. Jeffry Donn, here, became our prisoner of war. But after the war this rebellious cur wouldn't leave, settlin' here abouts and causin' me angst."

"You just watch your back, Hench," said Jeffry Donn without any ire. "I'm still plannin' my revenge."

"Took their supplies so they had to retreat?" asked Utley.

"Cheaters!" yelled Jeffry Donn. "We was winnin' the battle. We was whoopin' you!"

Hench nodded. "Furthest West the Rebs ever got. Them not captured was forced all the way back to Texas after a while. I've had to put up with skirmishes with Jeffry Donn now for the past twenty-some years."

"Whooped your asses!"

Utley chuckled and headed for the door.

"Before you go, Utley," said Hench, "was wonderin' where your deputies found Big Pat?"

Utley frowned again. "Why's that?"

Hench shook his head. "Not sure. Just curious I suppose."

Jeffry Donn hooked a thumb toward the jail cells. "Big Pat locked up in back?"

Utley nodded.

"Good," he said, then yelled, "can't wait 'til they hang the devil! I'll be spittin' on his carcass!"

Hench suspected that was the general attitude in town.

Jeffry Donn said in a normal tone. "She was a good girl, that Delilah. You're gonna swing his ass, ain't you, sheriff?"

Utley opened the front door and started out, followed by Hench and Jeffry Donn. He said, "I'd be mighty surprised by any other verdict."

The sheriff led them across the wide dirt street, side-steppin' a fresh mound of green horse dung. "What brings you to town, Jeffry Donn?"

The old man shrugged. "Gettin' supplies. Visitin' friends. Nothin' special."

Hench said, "You don't live in town?"

"Naw. People get on my nerves. Got me a fine little cabin down the Arkansas River a bit."

The sheriff took them a few streets over to an alley. Utley stopped at the entrance. "Should be right in there somewhere."

Hench stepped into the shade of the alley, the Railyard Saloon on his right and Jim's Haberdashery on the left. He came upon the blood ten feet in. It was dried black in several patches in the dirt. Utley and Jeffry Donn followed behind.

"What are you expectin' to find?" asked the sheriff.

Hench shrugged. "Just piecin' it together in my mind. Still curious as to why Big Pat wanted to kill her."

"Weren't he drunk?" said Jeffry Donn. "That's reason enough for someone as mean as that asshole."

"Maybe," said Hench.

Utley said, "And maybe it was just a matter of time for him to do somethin' this mean. He and his boys ain't outlaws, but they all spent time locked up for a dozen different things. Two weeks ago, I had three of 'em locked up for a couple'a days for disorderly. Picked a fight with a crew drivin' cattle east. Always somethin' with them boys. Just a matter of time."

"And why's it even matter why?" said the older man. "He done it, right? Who gives a fig why?"

"You're right." Hench turned and left.

This time he got to finish his bowl of chili. Evening had come to the little town on the eastern plains of Colorado. Walter's Saloon was about as full as it'd been the night before, but the chatter was much louder. Everyone was talking about last night's murder. First time a dove had been killed in town. But Big Pat was locked away so no one was scared about it. No one was wondering who could have done such a thing and were they out there tonight waiting for someone else? These were all jabbers about trying to reason out how someone could kill such a pretty little thing—they'd have been only slightly more consternated if it'd been someone's wife or the schoolmarm. The details, however, were quickly turning into drunken tall tales. One tale had Delilah so cut up they had to use a wheelbarrow to shovel her into.

Rogelio and Gabriela didn't look too bad off after their own excitement the night before. Well, Gabriela didn't, though her hands were swollen and bruised from the beating she'd delivered. Rogelio had a goose egg on his cheek and a black eye nearly swollen shut, but he seemed to stand a little taller. He'd stood up to the cowhand, a much bigger man. Rogelio took the fight to him, even. Nothing to be ashamed about. The two seemed closer because of it. Hench caught them flirting with each other on several occasions like they were newlyweds. He couldn't blame them. Nothing like a good fight to roil up the juices.

He burped his appreciation of the meal, walked over to the bar and dropped down two silver dollars, and walked out into the night with his half-empty bottle of rye. He'd left his duster over at the Satin Perch. The spring weather was too nice for it. He looked up and down the street. Several people were trading saloons in the guttered light of oil lamps hanging outside various establishments. Sighing, not sure where he was headed, he started walking slow. Maybe he'd go back to the Satin Perch to bed down for the night. After losing a day he needed to be on the trail for Lamar at dawn.

There was the hum of voices hidden away within saloons. The clatter of a piano or the smooth playing of a guitar. Crickets sang their night songs to one another. A coyote yipped somewhere on the outskirts of town. The moon was high and bright. He could afford to take a little time to enjoy the evening and finish his bottle on the way. He stopped for a moment in front of a horse trough to look at the moon's reflection. He kicked it to watch the ripples scatter the bright disk. Then someone hit him hard in the back, felt like they put their shoulder into him.

A split-second before being hit he thought he heard someone coming up from behind and he was about to turn, but now he pitched forward into the trough. The water was a shock of cold as he was submerged to the bottom. He tried to push himself up, but the attacker lay on top of him, holding him under, even jamming a hand down hard on the back of Hench's head. The air had been knocked from him by the hit and his lungs were already beginning to burn.

CHAPTER FIVE

Hench was wedged into the bottom of the horse trough. It wouldn't take much time to drown, the air already knocked from him. He couldn't move his arms enough to get a good enough purchase to push himself up. He tried to twist and buck, but that just wedged him in all the tighter and used up what little precious air he had left. His lungs burned like someone had shoved torches down his throat. However, there was mud on the bottom that slicked his right arm enough to slide it slowly beneath his body.

He wanted more than anything to take a breath. Get a little air into his lungs. One quick gulp of the invisible stuff. He forced himself to just think about his arm. Keep it moving before the final darkness fell over him. Get it just a little farther. A little more. What little air he had seeped from his nose. Then he felt the handle of his left-side revolver, forced his hand around it.

The burning in his lungs seemed to set his whole body on fire. His head buzzed like it was filled with hornets. He coughed, his faced pressed down tight into the mud. Air went out and water came in. He convulsed. But the gun came free of his holster. He slipped his ring finger against the trigger. His convulsions helped turn him slightly. Not enough to raise the gun between his left arm and the trough, so he pressed the barrel against what he hoped was the fleshy part of his bicep and pulled the trigger.

In the small space of the trough under the water the gun sounded much like dynamite exploding inside his head. But then the weight of the man was gone from his back. Hench lurched to his knees, dropping the gun, puking up water, chili, and rye, and pulling out the gun on his right side. He spun and fired at the back of someone disappearing into the darkness. His heaving lungs and stomach wracked his body and the shots didn't come close to the target. The man was gone.

Several men poked their heads out cautiously and a few minutes later Sheriff Utley, wearing his long johns, holster, and boots, came running up. By that time, Hench had managed to drag himself out of the trough and lay in a swirl of mud. He couldn't stop coughing and he let Utley help him to his hands and knees so his head was at least facing down while he tore up his lungs and throat. Several more minutes and the coughing started to subside.

When he was breathing more than coughing, Utley said, "What the hell?"

Hench, his voice hoarse, explained what happened.

"You didn't see who done it?"

Hench shook his head. "I got a lot of people who wouldn't mind seein' me dead, but the timin' has me figurin' either the cowhands from last night or one of Big Pat's gang."

Utley started to help him to his feet, but Hench hissed. "Careful. Got a bullet hole in that arm."

"The man shot you?"

"Shot myself."

Utley didn't respond.

Hench said, unable to get much above a whisper, "Ask if anyone saw who done it."

Utley turned toward the curious onlookers and called out loudly, "Who was it that done this to the ranger? Anyone see him?"

He was met with silence. Hench suspected at least a few of them knew who it was but were being cowards— or maybe they hated Hench as much as the attacker.

Hench turned to the trough and picked up his bottle of rye bobbing on the surface. Some muddy water got into it but he didn't care and took several big swallows.

"Watch your back, Utley. If this *was* Big Pat's gang they might be lookin' to put us both down so's they can get him outta jail."

The two walked slowly down the street, Hench dripping water, his boots squishing with each step.

"You still leavin' in the mornin'?" asked Utley.

"Hell no."

"Didn't we just clean you up?" asked Madam Felicity, raising a painted eyebrow. "You are quite literally a drowned rat."

Water dripped over the finished dark brown of the floorboards. Hench started to strip.

Madam Felicity stepped closer. "Is that blood?"

"I got shot. But it went through."

"Jesus Christ. Emil!" A few moments later a tall soft man appeared. Hench knew him to work around the brothel where needed. "Go fetch Doctor Rousseau, tell him he needs to sew up a couple of bullets holes."

Emil hurried out the front door.

"And don't you dare get naked in my parlor!"

Hench stopped undressing.

"Juanita!"

The dove from the night before appeared. She looked at the madam and both women just shook their heads.

Doctor Rousseau pulled thread through the gap in Hench's arm. Hench grunted but didn't show any other pain. The bullet hadn't exactly gone through his arm, but skirted the outside creating a furrow that required stitching.

The doctor said, "You're lucky it happened like this. If you had fired even an inch farther into your arm you could have shattered the bone, deflecting the bullet, and you'd be lying dead at the bottom of that trough."

Hench didn't have anything to say to that. He looked up at Madam Felicity and Juanita. "Where does Big Pat's gang like to hang out?"

The madam said, "You think it was one of them?"

"More'n likely. Even if it ain't, no harm askin' 'em a few questions."

The doctor chuckled. "'A few questions?'"

Hench said, "Talkin' and knockin' heads together is all the same to me."

Juanita said, "One of the men, Señor Gary, told me once he and some friends took over the Winters casa. He asked if I'd like to come over and help them clean it up."

"Did you?" asked Madam Felicity.

"Of course not. I'm not loco."

"Winters?" asked Hench.

The doctor said, "Old abandoned place maybe a mile out of town. Next to the King Arroyo."

"I'll find it," said Hench, pushing himself up on the bed, tugging at the thread.

"Whoa, there," said the doctor. "Maybe you should get a good night's rest and let this at least start to heal."

"Tie it off, Doc. They tried to kill me once, I ain't hangin' 'round waitin' for 'em to try again."

CHAPTER SIX

Hench got dressed in dry clothes from his saddle bag, but there was nothing he could do about his boots. He'd just have to squish for a while. He wore his duster, in case he ended up staying out through the night. Spring nights in Colorado got cold.

It wasn't that late, but he still had to wake the boy at the livery stables to get Speck. After saddling his horse, he slid his Spencer carbine lever-action rifle into its scabbard. Then he rechecked his two black Smith & Wesson Schofield Model 3 revolvers and mounted. He headed south out of town. The moon lit the way in polished silver. The land was flat in all directions save for random burrs from a ditch or slight ravine. Scrub grass covered it all, greening now with spring rains but it would turn yellow come the summer drought. Dark shadows grew beneath small clumps of trees and shrubs, marking a creek or some other water source in the otherwise arid land. Off to his right some horses neighed back and forth. Another house or ranch.

He turned off at a small trail, nothing more than wagon ruts. According to the doctor this would take him to the Winters house. Another copse appeared before him, marking the edge of the King Arroyo. A dim yellow light could be seen through the trees. He left the trail and skirted around south of the house. He tied up Speck to a tree and eased off him. He took his rifle and started in the direction where he'd seen the light.

It was an odd-shaped house that loomed in the dark. It looked like a deformed dog lying down, an exaggerated hump for its shoulders. He'd seen no sign of a lookout. Except for the one flickering light, the house looked abandoned. Someone was here, but it certainly wasn't Big Pat's entire gang. Hench didn't hear any horses, no muffled sounds of voices. He moved toward a side door. Peering in, the moon showed an empty mud room. He turned the handle and pulled gently. It was unlocked.

He set his rifle down against the outside of the house and then pulled off his boots. In moist socks, he picked up the rifle and slipped inside. His socks were quiet over the floorboards, but unfortunately enough of the boards creaked that if anyone was paying attention, they'd now be on alert. But he wasn't about to stop. He moved through the house attempting to find the light he'd seen from the outside. The house was large and sprawling enough that he took a few wrong turns, ending up in rooms, some bare and some with bedrolls. He saw enough bedrolls to feel confident that Big Pat's men were using the place.

He left one such makeshift bedroom and turned down a hall and was finally awarded by a splash of light at the end of it. He moved more slowly. There was always the chance there had been a lookout and he was walking into an ambush. At the end of the hall he crouched and looked around the corner. He'd found the lamp. It was sitting on an old wood crate. The room looked empty. Probably a family room back when the Winters lived in the house. To the right was a table and at least a half dozen chairs. He crouched like that and just listened, waiting to hear someone whispering or even just breathing hard. But all he heard were the crickets outside.

Hench rose and stepped into the room. A shadow moved out of the corner of his eye. He ducked and turned toward it, bringing the butt of his rifle up. It drove into someone's gut as something whipped through the air above him, thudding loud into the wall behind Hench. The breath huffed out of the shadow as his cry of pain came out as a weak gurgle. Hench whipped the butt higher and smashed it into the man's face. He went pinwheeling backwards, crashing into the chairs and a table and falling hard. Hench stood and pointed the rifle at him while looking around the rest of the room. No one else was coming out of the shadows.

"Stand up easy. You so much as twitch and you'll have a hole in your chest. Let me see your hands."

The man untangled himself from the chairs and stood up. He had a three-foot long log in one hand. He was bare-chested, his chest heaving to catch his breath, a white dressing was wrapped around his shoulder. There was no holster around his waist.

Hench poked his rifle toward the man's shoulder. "That a bullet hole? You get that earlier tonight?"

The man didn't say anything, but he looked plenty scared. He should have. It took all Hench's will not to pull the trigger. This must have been the man that dunked him in the trough.

"You can let go of your pecker now."

The man looked confused for a moment then dropped the log.

"Where's everybody else?"

Again, no answer, but his lips seemed to twitch up in a slight smile. Hench looked around the room again. Still no moving shadows. No sounds of men causing floorboards to creak. Hench walked over to the oil lamp and picked it up, still keeping aim with the carbine in his other hand.

"Okay, show me to your room."

The man looked confused again.

"Move!"

The man walked to the hall that Hench had come out of. The man didn't have on boots either. The two padded back down the hallway and the man stopped outside a door.

"In here," he said.

"Go on."

The man went in followed by Hench. He lifted the lamp a little and looked around. There were two chairs in the room. One was draped with clothes and the other had a holster hanging from it, the gun lying on the seat of the chair. Hench went to the chair with the clothes and set the lamp on the floor. He felt the pants and the shirt hanging from the chair. They were both damp.

"You're the asshole what tried to drown me."

The man didn't say anything, still looking scared.

"Get on your shirt and pull on your wet boots. I'm takin' you in." Hench tossed him the shirt hanging on the back of the chair.

The man caught it and put it on. Then he stepped into his boots, pulling and stamping them to get his feet all the way in. He put his hand on the back of the other chair, next to his empty holster. Hench turned his back on the man and stepped toward the doorway. He heard the sound of metal against wood, he spun around and fired a shot into the man's chest. The man looked more shocked than scared. The gun, now in his hand, fired wide. Hench cocked and levered the rifle and fired again. The man took a few steps back, into the wall, and then slid to the floor, his chest spilling blood, the wall behind him streaked with blood.

Hench left the body where it fell to leave a message for the rest of the gang. He rooted around for a big enough blanket and spread it out on the floor of an empty room. Then he went through the house gathering everything he could find and piling it onto the blanket. The only guns he found were those of the man he'd killed. But he had their bedrolls and extra provisions. He'd thought about just setting fire to the place but decided he wanted them to find the dead body of their comrade. A fire could be put off as an accident.

Outside, he put on his boots and pulled the blanket to the King Arroyo, walking into the middle of the stream and letting the blanket go. Spring runoff was high and fast enough to carry most of it away. He trudged out and made his way back to Speck. The horse's ears flicked back and forth, listening to something, his body tense. Coyotes or maybe something bigger. Hench pulled himself into the saddle, keeping his carbine out. They made their way out of the tress and Hench guided Speck wide of the wagon ruts leading to the main trail in case what the horse heard was the return of the rest of the gang. But it wasn't any of those things. After getting back out to the main trail he heard the distant pops of gunfire.

The slight smile on the dead man's face returned to Hench when he'd asked where the rest of the gang were. "Sweet crickets." He kicked Speck into a full gallop back toward town.

CHAPTER SEVEN

The gunfire continued all the way back to town. It wasn't a constant barrage. Hench figured a siege of sorts. Big Pat's gang were spread out around the jail taking potshots more than anything. And who was in the building? This time of night there probably would have just been a single deputy to keep watch over Big Pat. If they were smart—he stopped right there. If they were all as addlepated as Big Pat himself, they might have started the siege without knowing they were only going up against one deputy. But maybe Utley had somehow been alerted and he had himself and his deputies inside the building defending it.

Speck covered the distance in a couple of minutes, though it felt to Hench like far too long of time. They rode hard through the outskirts of town and Hench didn't pull up until he was two blocks from the jail. He dismounted and went up to the main street, removing his hat and peering around the corner. It didn't take long to locate where a couple of Big Pat's men were holed up, shooting at the jail. He put his hat back on, cocked the hammer on his carbine, levered a cartridge into the chamber, and went around the corner moving quickly. He heard other shots that came from behind the jail. There was no door back there, but the sheriff certainly wouldn't want anyone coming up to the back wall with dynamite or a team of horses to try and pull the bars free from the windows.

Hench went a half block down and then crouched into a doorway. Across the street and up at the next corner was the shadowy outline of a man lying on the ground beneath a wagon. Hench aimed, but the shot would be a lucky one. He didn't want to tip his hand until he knew he could take one of them out. He hurried across the street, to the same side that the shooter was on. He stopped in the deep shadows of another doorway looking at the opposite corner that was diagonal from him. He waited there a full minute, but no shots came from that corner. Of course, that didn't mean someone wasn't there.

He left the doorway and moved forward in a crouch. The man beneath the wagon fired another shot with his rifle. Hench glanced at the jail. The lights were out. Was the man shooting at anyone or just wasting bullets? He wouldn't be surprised if they were all just shooting to shoot.

Hench edged up to the corner. He could see the man clearly, spread flat on the ground, rifle at his shoulder. He decided not to shoot him. Instead, he set his rifle against the wall and pulled his knife. Easing out into the street, he went down on all fours. The man stared straight ahead and squeezed off another round then levered his Henry repeating rifle. Down the street another shot echoed between the buildings. Hench crawled right up next to the man and tapped him on the hip.

"What is it?" said the man, turning.

The man's eyes went wide and he started to swing his rifle around. Hench launched himself, driving his left forearm into the man's throat, pinning him back to the ground. Hench slid the knife upward into the man's gut, near the breastbone. The man tried to scream, but Hench had his throat closed off. He assumed he hit the heart because the man struggled for just a few moments before going still. Hench then turned him back face down and rearranged the rifle so from a distance it would look like the man was still in position. He lay there next to the dead man, waiting for others of his gang to fire off rounds and reveal their hiding places.

The next closest man was about halfway down the block. He'd be difficult to get to—unless. Hench took off his hat and duster and then peeled of the man's coat. Grabbing the man's hat, Hench crawled out from under the wagon and put the dead man's hat and coat on. He retrieved his Spencer carbine from against the wall, and then he moved forward. He was now facing the jailhouse, more or less. He couldn't see any movement in it. It would be almost comical if the place turned out to be empty, except for Big Pat sitting in a cell in back, but that didn't explain where Utley and the rest of his deputies were. They would have been out here in the dark picking off Big Pat's men like Hench was doing. No, they must have been in there. Probably keeping a lookout, but otherwise waiting for the men to run out of ammunition or get hungry or just get bored and wander off.

Hench stayed crouched as he went along the front of buildings, more afraid of Utley or one of his deputies taking a shot at him. The man Hench was going after knelt behind a water trough. Hench stopped right behind him in the shadow of an awning, the man never turning.

He whispered, "Hey," his rifle at his side.

The man turned his head and squinted at Hench. "Gil?"

"Yeah."

The man looked confused. "What'cha doin' here?"

Before Hench could reply, or shoot him, another man appeared farther up the block running out into the street. Something sparkled in his hands. A lit stick of dynamite. The man ran toward the jail, pulling his arm back to throw. Hench raised his rifle and took aim.

"Whoa, there, Gil, that's Tommy."

Hench fired. Tommy stumbled but kept moving. Within a second Hench cocked the hammer, levered the carbine, and fired again. Tommy tumbled to the ground. At the same time, Hench dove to his right, cocking and levering the carbine as the man in front of him spun around and fired. The bullet missed as Hench rolled and then sprawled his body out, landing flat on his stomach, the rifle at his shoulder. He fired and missed as well.

The thing with such close-range gun play was that the man who stayed alive was the man who could calm his nerves enough to cock the gun and aim true. That wasn't nearly so easy to do as the body's instinct was to run or at least flinch out of the way—nerves jangled, causing problems with coordination. The man at the trough made a fatal mistake, but it wasn't intentional. His body betrayed him. His nerves took over and when he levered his rifle, his right hand pulled the stock of the gun down, the barrel rising into the air. That meant it would take him time to aim—only a second, but it was more than enough time for Hench to both cock the hammer and lever in another round while keeping the rifle aimed at the man. Hench's bullet hit him in the throat. Hench cocked the hammer, levered in another round, and fired again, hitting the man in the chest. He was dead before he finished collapsing to the dirt.

Before the echo of his second bullet died out, he scrambled forward toward the water trough. He shoved the dead man to the side and hunkered down next to his corpse. He pulled the magazine tube from the butt stock of his carbine and slipped in four rounds to replace the ones he'd fired.

The stick of dynamite went off. Rocks pinged against the building wall behind him. Something wet landed nearby, some piece of Tommy. Hench waited another couple of seconds then rose above the edge of the trough, looking for Big Pat's gang. With everything going on there was a chance they had no idea where the shot came from that took down Tommy or that he'd killed two of the gang. He wondered how many men were left out here. Juanita seemed to think there were about ten men in the gang, but were all of them willing to attack a jail, let alone a sheriff and his deputies?

Then a man jogged toward him from up the street. He had a revolver in his hand and was whispering loudly, "John! Hey, John!"

Hench assumed that was the dead man lying next to him. Hench said, "Yeah?" trying to imitate John's voice.

The man wasn't fooled. He raised his revolver toward the water trough. "Who's there?"

Hench rose to a knee. The man gawked and fired off two rounds before getting the revolver lined up. Hench kept his carbine low, he couldn't waste the time to bring it to his shoulder, and fired. The man gasped and dropped to a knee, giving Hench time to cock and lever his carbine and even raise it to his shoulder and fire. The man dropped. Even if all ten men were involved, they were now down to six. Though Hench didn't take that number as gospel.

Someone yelled out from down the street, "Robert?"

Hench tried again. "Yeah!"

There came a muted, "Damn!" and then soon after the sound of horses galloping away.

Now Hench had to decide if all the gang had gotten the word to retreat. Or were they smart enough to try a ruse, sending a few men off and leaving others behind to pick him off if he tried to get to the jail?

CHAPTER EIGHT

Hench stayed put at the water trough. He had nowhere to be and was in no hurry to be there. His carbine lay across this lap, cocked and levered. He had no doubt he could out wait Big Pat's gang if that was their play. For all he knew they were all long gone, but he saw no point in risking his life to figure that out for sure. And he'd spent many nights hunkered down waiting for some asshole or other to make a slip up. Of course, Hench wasn't expecting the slip up to come from Sheriff Utley.

One of the deputies yelled from the jail, "You still out there?"

Hench screwed up his face. What kind of question was that? What was Utley playing at?

"We got us a hurt man in here. We're willin' to let Big Pat go if you let us take him to Doc."

Was that true? Then Hench realized it was Utley who was hurt. Unconscious. He'd never let one of his deputies do something so lamebrained if he was awake—he'd certainly never give up a murderer in the bargain. Hench waited for a reply from Big Pat's gang, but none came.

"Okay, I'm comin' out! Don't shoot!"

"Damn." Hench scrambled to his feet and hurried into the shadow of the building. This could turn into something ugly in a couple of seconds. He moved farther down the block, in the original direction he'd come from, then turned back around, risking a move out away from the wall of the building to try and cover the street for the deputy. He had his carbine at his shoulder and was aiming down the street, but he kept sneaking looks to his left, in case any of the gang who had been behind the jail suddenly emerged from the side street.

Then the front door of the jail opened about a foot. A white handkerchief appeared on the end of a metal rod. The deputy waved it. Hench didn't see any movement in the street—or more importantly, in the shadows on the edge of the street.

Then Deputy Manuel eased his head out. "Don't shoot!"

But there were no shots fired. Hench thought the gang was too undisciplined not to try a potshot at the deputy—or at himself. He felt fairly certain by this time that they had all left, but he didn't let down his guard. Manuel came out farther, half-flinched as though expecting to be shot any second.

Manuel saw Hench for the first time, but didn't recognize him in the dead man's coat and hat. "Don't shoot!"

Hench didn't say anything. Manuel pushed the door open farther and Deputy Tyler backed out holding onto the corners of a blanket. The blanket emerged and sure enough, Sheriff Utley was sprawled on it. The third deputy—Jacob, maybe?—appeared on the other end of the blanket. Hench stayed where he was, covering the street. The deputies, probably still not recognizing him, stopped and stared at him.

"Go already!" he yelled.

The deputies hustled down the street toward Doctor Rousseau's office and home. Hench followed at a distance until he saw them get safely to the doctor's door and bang on it. A light came on a moment later and then the doctor appeared. At that time, Hench hurried up to them. Manuel tensed, but then he finally recognized Hench.

"Sheriff Utley's been—"

Hench talked over him. "You two stay here with Utley and keep him and the doctor safe. Manuel, come with me. We're heading back to the jail."

As Hench turned, Utley suddenly reached out and grabbed his arm. Hench bent toward him to hear. Utley whispered through bloody teeth, "'Bout time you showed up."

Hench smiled and then turned away, jogging back to the jail with Manuel.

Inside the sheriff's office, Hench lit a match and looked around. There was a disturbing amount of blood on the floor. "How bad is it?"

Manuel shrugged and shook his head. "Enough to scare us into giving up Big Pat. They attacked him at his house. He got away and came here, I'm not sure how. He was shot at least twice. We heard the shots and me and Tyler came running. Jacob was already inside here keeping watch. We didn't know what was going on, but then we were surrounded and stuck in here. I was so scared the sheriff would die on us. So scared."

"Grab blankets and hang 'em over the windows so we can light a lamp."

Manuel went to work. Hench bolted the front door and then went to the metal cabinet and grabbed a set of keys. He unlocked the door to the cells and pushed it open. In the dim moonlight, Big Pat looked up at him. "Sheriff dead yet?"

Hench walked up closer to the cell. "Was hopin' one of the bullets might find you in the dark."

"No luck."

"They comin' back?"

Big Pat shrugged. "How would I know? Didn't know they was gonna try to break me out. Now that's some good friends."

"Yeah, you can all swing together. I guess that ain't no big deal for you, you can only die once, right?"

A light appeared up front casting enough light over Big Pat to see his scowl.

Hench said, "Weren't enough for you to kill Delilah, you had to try to kill Utley, too?"

"Neither one was my fault."

"What, you stuck a knife into Delilah about twenty times by accident?"

Big Pat sat up. "They done that to her? No foolin'?" There was a hitch in his voice.

Hench furrowed his brow. "Quit your play actin'. It was your knife. We have a witness right there in the room."

"Who? Who was with her? Tell me!"

There was no mistaking the hurt and pain in Big Pat's voice. Hench took a step forward. "What the hell ain't you tellin' me?"

"Who was it? Who was in the room with her?"

Were his eyes glistening or was that just the way the light struck them?

"You know who was in that room because you were there." Hench's voice turned cold, almost shouting, "You took that big knife of yours and cut that pretty little girl up so bad that she was nothin' but a bloody lump of raw flesh. Couldn't even tell who it was anymore. They had to shovel her into a wheelbarrow to carry her out. And you know a girl like that don't deserve no decent burial.

Hell, they should'a just scattered her out back the brothel and let the buzzards take her away."

Big Pat lunged up from his bed and slammed into the bars, reaching an arm out to try and grab Hench. The man was sobbing.

In a quiet voice, Hench said, "Who was she to you?"

Big Pat slid down the bars until he was squatting on the floor, his face pressed up against the bars, both hands holding the bars as though he was holding someone. His body rocked back and forth as he cried.

Hench knelt. "Who was she?"

"She was my sister."

CHAPTER NINE

"Why the hell didn't you say that earlier?"

Big Pat said, "Who was there?"

"Goddammit, you could be free right now if you'd just told us."

"Horseshit. Utley'd never have let me go."

"How come nobody knows she's your sister?"

"You're joking, right? Look at me. Some asshole makes up a story about me and Utley locks me right up. How do you think folks would'a treated her if they knew she was my sister? Made her promise never to tell no one."

Hench stared at him for several moments before Big Pat said, "Go to Hell."

Hench went back out front.

"Do you think the sheriff will be okay?" asked Deputy Manuel.

Hench stared at all the blood on the floor of the office. It seemed like as much blood as drained from Delilah.

"Hench?"

"Hmm?" He turned to the deputy.

"Is it the sheriff? You think he's going to die?"

Hench was confused. "The sheriff? What are you—oh, I'm sure he'll be fine," lied Hench. "I was thinking about something else. Look, I gotta go check on somethin'. Lock the door after me and don't open it for no one but me or the other deputies."

Before he left, he went to Utley's desk and opened a couple of drawers before finding and pulling out Big Pat's knife. He slipped it into his gun belt. Cocking and levering his carbine, he left the office. He waited outside until the door locked behind him. There was no movement on the street. The locals were afraid to come out, which was smart, and he was confident Big Pat's gang had left. He walked diagonally across the street to the wagon. Bending down, he pulled out his hat and duster and rid himself of the dead man's belongings, tossing them under the wagon.

He headed back to Speck, turning down the street where he'd left the horse. As he approached, the horse neighed and pricked up his ears. Hench heard the footfall as well and he whirled toward it.

"Whoa there, Yank. It's just me."

"What the hell are you doin' skulkin' around here in the dark?"

"Heard the shootin' and come took a look," said Jeffry Donn. He wasn't wearing his old field grays, but a pair of tan dungarees and a white shirt. "Saw your horse down here so hung 'round 'til you got back. I'm guessin' Big Pat's gang tried to break him out?"

Hench nodded.

Jeffry Donn shook his head. "What a bunch of numbskulls."

Hench nodded again, he couldn't agree more. "Unfortunately, they shot Utley. He's hurt pretty bad."

"Sweet Jesus. What, they didn't like the idea of Big Pat hangin' by his lonesome?"

"Like you said, they're numbskulls. Thing is, I'm not so certain anymore that Big Pat killed the girl."

Jeffry Donn looked at him sharply. "What?"

Hench shrugged. "Got some work to do, yet, but— well, let's just say I got me some doubts now."

"Come on, Hench, Big Pat must'a done it. His knife was in the room!"

"That's part'a the work I gotta do. Figure some things out."

Hench went up the stairs of the Satin Perch brothel to the room where Delilah had been killed. He barged in without knocking. The room was occupied. The man grunted, "Busy here!"

"Out," said Hench, grabbing the man's clothes off one of the chairs and tossing them into the hall.

The dove, Henrietta, started cursing at him. The man, atop her, craned his neck and looked with growing anger at Hench. "If you don't leave right—"

Hench grabbed the man by the arm and yanked him off the dove. The man stumbled to his feet and then took a swing at Hench, who evaded it and then slugged the man in the face. The man looked confused for a second or two and then his knees buckled and his manhood wilted. Hench grabbed him before he keeled over and pushed him out into the hall naked.

"Henrietta, I'll let you get your slip on, but get the hell out."

She stopped cursing and hurried into a white slip with pink flowers around the neck. Hench slammed the door shut behind her. It had been cleaned, of course, but he looked around nonetheless. The broken china pitcher had been replaced and sat in the china basin beneath the vanity. The blood had been cleaned off the wood frame of the bed and from the floor. Both had shellacked finishes and there was no blood left to see. But he noticed several fresh cuts in the headboard. Either made when the killer missed Delilah entirely or perhaps the killer drove the knife in with such violence that the knife tip protruded from her back. Then he noticed other cuts along the edge of the headboard. The killer had lost all control, stabbing and swinging the knife wildly. Most of the cuts in the wood had dried blood in them. Seven of them all total.

He bent closer. Make that eight cuts. One of them was filled and had been hard to detect.

Madam Felicity stormed into the room. "Goddamn it, Terrance!"

Hench spoke calmly. "Shut the door."

"You can't kick out a customer like that."

He took his knife out and used the tip to dig at the eighth cut. She moved closer and her voice returned to a conversational level and tone. "What the hell are you doing?"

Hench dug a little more and a little wedge of metal popped out of the cut. He held it up to Felice. "Big Pat didn't kill Delilah."

She froze for a moment. "But—are you saying Bertram did it?"

"More'n likely. This is the tip of the knife what killed her." He took Big Pat's knife from his gun belt. "Big Pat's knife ain't broken."

"Holy Mother Mary. And we were ready to hang the poor stupid asshole."

"Oh, he's probably still gonna swing," said Hench, putting Big Pat's knife away and then taking a handkerchief from his pocket. He set the knife tip in the middle, folded it back up and stuffed it back in his pocket. "His gang tried to bust him out tonight. Shot Utley pretty good. If the sheriff dies they'll all swing."

She cocked an eyebrow at Hench. "What made you want to come back here in such a tizzy to search the room again?"

"Did you know that Delilah was Big Pat's sister?"

Felice just stared at him, too dazed to comment.

"You didn't know?"

She shook her head. "You sure?"

"Can't be entirely sure, but I left Big Pat bawlin' like a baby back at the jail when I described Delilah's death— and I might'a exaggerated it a tad bit to try and get a reaction outta him. I knew somethin' was wrong, but I didn't know what. Well, I got a reaction, but it sure as hell weren't nothin' I was expectin'."

"That poor stupid asshole."

Hench nodded. "Even I feel almost sorry for the man."

"What are you going to do?"

"Gonna arrest Bertram."

CHAPTER TEN

Hench woke early and went over to Doctor Rousseau's place. Deputy Jacob was there, Tyler had gone home and was going to spell him later.

"How's Utley doin', Doc?" asked Hench.

The physician gave a little shrug. "He's still in danger. Lost a lot of blood, but I got both bullets out. We won't really know for a day or two if he'll pull through."

The deputy said, "Should we keep someone here, y'think?"

"Definitely. Until we got the gang round up or in the ground, I want someone with Utley all the time. Where does Tyler live? I'm gonna need his help."

"Boarding house couple blocks away. But he's up at the jail. We thought it'd be better to sleep there, just in case."

Hench walked over to the jailhouse. The front door was locked. He knocked and called out, "It's Hench!"

Manuel opened the door looking tired and wrung out.

"You get any sleep?"

"Not much," said the deputy.

"Where's Tyler, he get any sleep?"

Manuel shrugged and stepped back from the door. Tyler was sitting on the edge of one of two cots thrown up on one side of the office. "You need me?"

"I'm goin' to arrest Bertram Richardson."

"What? What for?" asked Manuel.

"I'm convinced Big Pat didn't kill Delilah. That leaves Bertram. Want someone to watch the back door of their place, assuming they got one."

Tyler nodded. "They do." He stood up and stretched, slipping his suspenders up over his shoulders. "Let me take a piss and I'll be ready."

The Richardson's lived in a small cottage a couple blocks to the east of the jail. It couldn't have had more than two or three rooms in it. There was a small fenced-in yard with a garden strung with chicken wire to keep out a dozen chickens and three goats.

"Go 'round back," said Hench. "And be careful. If he killed her, he might decide another murder ain't nothin'."

Tyler nodded and took off. Hench waited until he saw him in position, then he approached the front door and knocked. A few moments later, Becca Richardson opened the door. She didn't look like she'd slept much, either.

"Ma'am, I need to see your husband."

"He ain't here."

"Know where he went?"

Her eyes shifted. She was about to lie. Something was wrong. "Headin' over to the Bixby Ranch. He works there. Be back tonight."

She started to shut the door, but Hench pushed it open, sending her scuttling backward a few feet. "What the hell you doin'? Just said he ain't home."

"I'm sure you wouldn't mind me lookin' 'round some." He didn't wait for an answer. The place was neat and tidy. Only two rooms. The main had a cast iron stove, a table and chairs, a large chest of drawers, and other odds and ends. Bertram obviously wasn't there. Hench ducked his head into the bedroom. A brass-framed bed with an overstuffed comforter on top, a small vanity set up in a corner.

"Where's the Bixby Ranch?" asked Hench, turning toward the woman.

"I want you outta my house."

"Ma'am," said Hench, touching the Colorado Ranger badge on his faded blue shirt. "I'm the law. I ain't leavin' 'til you answer my question."

She stared at him for a few moments then shook her head and shrugged. "I got no idea. Never been there." Then she folded her arms and kept staring.

Hench stepped closer, but not to try and get an answer out of her. He looked at her right hand, no longer bandaged. Her knuckles were swollen and bruised, as if she'd hit something hard. She immediately ducked it under her arm.

"Thought you burned it, ma'am. That's what you said the other night at the brothel."

"Did I? I don't remember."

"Don't remember much, do you?"

"Are you finished?"

He moved past her and went over to a makeshift counter adjacent to the stove. It was little more than a shelf attached to the wall at waist height. There were cooking implements on it. Beneath it were a couple of pots and pans. To the right was a block of wood with the handles of five knives sticking out. Hench took out one of the knives. A small carving knife. He put it back and then ran his fingertip over an empty slot.

"Mind me askin' where the sixth knife is?"

"I don't remember."

He looked around the large counter/shelf and poked through several hanging shelves of smaller kitchen items. He crouched down and pulled out the pots and pans. Standing, he went to the back door, opened it, and stepped out into the yard. If you wanted to get rid of a knife you wouldn't hide it in the house. He turned slowly and stopped when he saw a mound of trash—a slop pile, probably for the goats. Freshly turned. You'd get the knife out of the house.

"Tyler? Come on over. Find a shovel and dig through that pile. You're lookin' for a carving knife."

"You serious?" asked the deputy, a look saying he hoped Hench was joking.

"Get to it."

The deputy sighed and started looking around the yard until he found a spade. He used it to dig through the pile. "It stinks," was all he said.

"What the hell you doin'?" said Becca, stepping out into the yard.

Hench ignored her. "It'll probably be at the bottom."

Tyler nodded and kept digging to the immense curiosity of the three goats who kept trying to get in the way of the spade. Hench casually glanced at Becca. Her eyes were riveted on the pile as if it were the most important thing in the world.

Despite the goats trying to help, Tyler managed to clear off the slop. "Huh," he finally said, having dug past the pile and clearing away a small pit of dirt beneath it. "Somethin' shiny here, Hench."

Hench approached. Something shiny indeed. He picked up an eight-inch long carving knife, shaking the dirt loose from it. He pulled out his handkerchief and opened it. He set the knife next to the broken tip. Perfect fit.

Hench turned toward Becca. "Where the hell's your husband?"

She didn't say anything, her face drained of color, her body shivering. To Deputy Tyler, Hench said, "You can head back now. Thanks for your help."

"That the knife what killed her?" he asked.

Hench nodded, folding the tip back up in the handkerchief and putting it back into his pocket. He slid the knife into his gun belt next to Big Pat's. He was getting quite a collection. He went back into the Richardson's house and found a jug of water. He poured some into a metal basin he pulled out from under the counter and washed the dirt from his hands. He turned for a towel, there was one thrown on the kitchen table. Becca probably threw it there on her way to answer the door when Hench knocked. Drying his hands, he noticed a small stack of gray cloth on top of the chest of drawers. A color of gray that looked familiar. He picked up a Confederate tunic and trousers. He looked over for Becca, but she was still outside. He folded them proper and set them back where he'd found them, then he left through the front door.

Hench got back to the jail house just after Tyler. Manuel unlocked and opened the door for the two of them. Behind him, the heavy door to the cells was open. A tray of food sat on Utley's desk.

"Marcie brought Big Pat's breakfast. Was just taking it in when you knocked. Then thought I'd head over—"

"Do either of you know where Jeffry Donn lives?"

"That old guy?" said Tyler, shaking his head.

Manuel nodded.

"Good," said Hench. "You're comin' with me."

"What's going on?"

"I think Bertram might be hidin' out there. Do you know if Jeffry Donn is close with the Richardson's?"

Tyler said, "Sure. Becca's father and Jeffry Donn were close. When he passed, Jeffry Donn looked after her for a spell. I mean, she was grown by then, but he kinda looked after her. Gave her away at the weddin'."

"Get yourself a rifle, Manuel. Don't know how dangerous Bertram, or Jeffry Donn, might—" Hench stopped talking and looked at the door leading into the cell. There was a metallic scraping sound. "What the hell's he doin' in there?"

Hench looked in. Big Pat's cell was in the far-left corner. He had moved his bed to the bars opposite the back wall. He had it up at an angle and was crouched behind it, under his mattress. Hench stared at him for a second and then spun around. "Get down!"

At the same time the back wall exploded.

CHAPTER ELEVEN

"Hench! Hench!"

He opened his eyes, squinting at the bright light. His head thundered in pain. He felt the back of his head. It was wet. Looking at his fingers, they were covered with blood.

"Praise the Lord," said Tyler. "We were afraid you might'a been killed. You must'a taken that chunk of wall to the back of the head."

It hurt to turn his head. There was a fist-sized stone from the back wall lying a few feet away. He said, "What about Big Pat?"

"We got knocked down by the blast. By the time we got to our feet and in back, Big Pat was through the hole. They shot at us."

Manuel said, "We ran out front, but they took our horses. Then we came back in to see if you were alive."

"How long was I out?"

"Maybe five minutes."

"Help me up," said Hench.

Tyler started for the front door. "I'll go get Doc."

"No. Get a rifle. Both of you, and plenty of ammunition. We're ridin' after 'em."

Manuel and Tyler exchanged glances. Manuel said, "Should you—"

"Get some horses at the livery stables. Move it!"

The deputies left. Hench felt woozy and nauseous. He stared at the ceiling for several moments before trying to sit up. The room spun hard. He put a hand on Utley's desk to steady himself then slowly pulled himself onto his feet, grimacing throughout the process. He waited for the world to calm down. Took a few deep breaths.

"Okay," he said out loud, and pushed off the desk to the front door. His head still spun but it was calming down. He waited it out and then started back to the Satin Perch where Speck was tethered. He stopped once to throw up his breakfast, wipe his mouth, and then continue on. It was slow going, but he made it to the brothel. He opened the front door and then leaned against the doorframe.

"Hello!"

After a few moments one of the doves, Millie, came out from the back of the house. They were probably all in the kitchen eating breakfast.

"Can you go get my rifle and saddlebags? Hurry."

"You don't look so good, Hench."

"Thanks."

She went upstairs and disappeared down the hallway. Felice came out from the back. She was in a light sundress. Maybe the first time Hench saw her in anything other than one of her tight satin dresses and corsets.

"You look like shite, Terrance."

"Feel like it, too."

"What's happened?"

"Big Pat escaped, Bertram's disappeared, and I gotta go after 'em."

"Which one?"

"All of 'em."

"Maybe you should rest first." Her eyes narrowed. "Is that blood on your collar?"

"Probably."

Millie came down the stairs, his Spencer carbine in the crook of her arm, his saddlebags slung over a shoulder.

"Want me to put it on your horse?"

"Much obliged," said Hench, thinking he might need to throw up again. He followed behind, forcing himself to walk without a wobble, and pulled himself up onto the saddle. He felt a little better sitting down, though something still tried to break its way out of his skull using a sledgehammer.

He met up with the deputies at the jailhouse. They'd found horses. The three of them rode east out of town, moving at a trot—which did nothing for his head—then angled north toward the Arkansas River. According to Manuel, Jeffry Donn's place was nearly ten miles east. Hench kept a look out for Big Pat's gang. He had no doubt Big Pat overheard them at the jailhouse and was on his way to seek revenge for his sister's murder.

Like most of this part of eastern Colorado, the land was flat, save for a few low rolling hills or little ravines. Hench could see for quite aways, but he didn't see anyone else. The area looked completely desolate, and for the most part it was. Even with the Arkansas River twisting through the land there just wasn't much plant life. Shrubs grew more densely by the banks, but there were few trees. It was as if they just couldn't muster the gumption to grow that tall in a place like this.

"You two see anything?" asked Hench. He wasn't about to rely on his own eyes, which were a bit fuzzy.

"Nothin'," said Tyler. "Maybe they decided to just keep ridin'. Head for Kansas."

"Don't think so," said Hench. "Did either of you know Delilah and Big Pat were relations?"

Both deputies looked at Hench in surprise. Manuel said, "Cousins or something?"

"Brother and sister."

Tyler whistled softly. "You think he's goin' after Bertram no matter what?"

"No matter what."

Manuel said, "Why didn't Big Pat say anything?"

"Well, I think when I first told him about Delilah he was too shocked to say anything other than he didn't do it. Either that, or as soon as I told him he decided he was gonna kill the murderer. He didn't want anyone to know, maybe afraid we'd assume that's what he'd do. I don't know. Hard to get inside the head'a someone like Big Pat."

"But how come neither of 'em, Delilah or him, ever let on they was brother and sister?" asked Tyler. "Why the secret?"

"When you thought about Delilah, when she was alive, what did you think?"

"Sweet girl," said Tyler.

"And when you think of Big Pat?"

Both deputies said together, "Asshole."

Hench shrugged. "Big Pat appears to have had a tiny noble streak in him and they kept it secret so that his reputation didn't wreck her own."

"Huh," said Manuel.

They rode on in silence. Still no sign of Big Pat and his gang. No large group of men had ridden over this trail anytime recently. It was over an hour since leaving town when Manuel pointed.

"See it?"

Hench's eyes were still blurry, but he saw a small log cabin maybe twenty yards from the Arkansas River. It was nestled in high shrubs and even a couple dozen fir trees. Smoke snaked up through a stone chimney. The cabin was up off the ground a couple of feet, built on stilts; Hench assumed to keep it from flooding when the river broke its banks during a big spring runoff.

"Looks like they're home," said Tyler. "Should we rush 'em?"

Hench shook his head. "I don't want us all inside if Big Pat shows up. You two go hide somewhere, a ravine or something, and keep your ears open. If Big Pat shows up, use your smarts. Don't just attack him. Let him and his gang get settled in. Let them feel safe. Then after we've engaged, and their attention is on the cabin, flank 'em."

The two men nodded and Manuel said to Tyler, "There's a gully a couple hundred yards over here I think. Should be deep enough for the horses."

"Hold up," said Hench, easing himself off Speck, taking his carbine and slinging his saddlebags over his shoulder. "Take him with you. Don't want him gettin' shot."

Hench watched them ride off, then he made his way to the cabin. When he got close he could hear the two men talking. The idiots weren't even keeping watch. The front door faced away from the river. Hench went up to it, gritted against the jolt of pain he was going to get in his head, and kicked it in with the flat of a boot. The men gaped at him and the cocked black Schofield revolver in his hand.

It was a one-room cabin. A single small bed was jammed into a corner. A stone fireplace was built into one of the log walls. A fire was going and something almost good-smelling was cooking in a cast-iron pot hanging from a hook next to the fire. A small table was in the middle of the room with two chairs, which sat atop a small rug.

Hench shut the door behind him.

"How the hell you know where to look?" said Jeffry Donn after a couple of moments.

"You left your field grays at Bertram's cottage in town."

"I did?" He looked around the cabin. "Well, dang."

Bertram didn't say anything, just stared at Hench like a child waiting for his punishment.

"You takin' him in?"

"That's the plan," said Hench. "But it ain't that simple. Big Pat escaped. I'm pretty sure he overheard me talkin' about you hidin' out here."

Bertram finally spoke. "To get even 'cause I said Big Pat done it?"

"You picked the absolutely worst person in this whole town to pin for the murder. You'd have had better luck claimin' Sheriff Utley did it."

The men looked confused.

"Big Pat was Delilah's brother."

Bertram's jaw dropped and Jeffry Donn looked only slightly less surprised. The old man said, "Well, dang."

"Exactly. Now I didn't see trace of 'em on the trail out here, but he was pretty beat up about his sister's murder. I can only guess they went somewhere first, maybe got supplies, before headin' this way. If we head back to town now we'll be sitting ducks."

"Shouldn't we run the other way?" said Jeffry Donn. "We're sittin' ducks here, too."

Hench nodded. "True. But at least we're in a defensive position and have good cover. There's extra ammunition in the saddlebags. Jeffry Donn, go on out and let the horses run. No reason to get 'em killed."

As the old man headed outside, Hench said, "And don't think I'll hesitate to kill you if you try anythin' stupid."

The old man nodded and went around to the back of the cabin to open the gate of a crude fence. He shooed the horses out of the fence and away from the cabin, then he hurried back inside. He shut the door and picked up a solid roughhewn board, laying it into hooks mounted to either side of the door.

He turned toward them. "There's a plume of dust maybe a mile away. They're ridin' fast."

CHAPTER TWELVE

Hench used the butt stock of his carbine to break the glass out of all the windows. He made sure his Spencer carbine and Schofield revolvers were fully loaded. Jeffry Donn had a Richmond single-shot rifle and a Spiller & Burr five-shot revolver, both from the war—but they looked clean and well-oiled. Hench turned toward Bertram and pulled out a pair of handcuffs from a saddlebag.

Jeffry Donn said, "You can't be serious."

"The man's a murderer. And despite us bein' in dire straits, he might see a situation where he thinks he can plug me in the back and get away from Big Pat."

Bertram didn't say anything. He seemed accepting of his fate since Hench first broke into the cabin. Jeffry Donn, however, wasn't as accepting. "We're gonna need the extra gun, Hench. That's just plain foolish."

"We'll be okay," said Hench. "We ain't alone. Tyler and Manuel are out there waitin' to flank 'em."

"And how many men does Big Pat got?"

"We'll find out soon enough."

He handcuffed Bertram and had him lie on the floor of the cabin to keep him from getting shot. Then he took up a position at the front window while Jeffry Donn set up to Hench's left at a side window.

Jeffry Donn said, "What if they sneak around back? We could use a pair of eyes back there."

"It's early in the day. We got plenty'a sunshine to keep track of 'em all."

Jeffry Donn huffed, but he took his position. Then they waited. All day.

After it became clear that Big Pat wasn't going to attack until sundown, Hench uncuffed Bertram and let him get off the floor.

"Now what we gonna do about the back?" asked Jeffry Donn as dusk descended and crickets started chirping.

Hench shook his head and said, "I'm gonna give him one of my revolvers and set him up at the back window. So help me, if you shoot me I'm gonna blow your head off. Even if you kill me."

"I ain't gonna shoot you," said Bertram.

It didn't make Hench feel any better—though his headache *was* getting slightly better. But anytime he bent over, even slightly, his head hammered with his heartbeat. Jeffry Donn went to the fireplace and made sure that even the glowing embers were extinguished.

They didn't light any lamps. It would be difficult to see them in the darkness of the cabin.

Just after sundown, the moon rising in the east, they could see Big Pat and his gang moving toward the cabin, taking up positions. Jeffry Donn took careful aim with his Richmond, held his breath, and squeezed the trigger. Less than a second later a man cried out in the darkness. Jeffry Donn grinned.

Hench said, "Good shootin'."

"You was lucky at Glorieta Pass, son."

Hench nodded and turned back to the window. The men had disappeared, now flat on their stomachs. "I counted nine before you shot—not countin' Big Pat, who must be out there somewhere."

"Me, too. Now what?"

"We'll wait until they feel comfortable," said Hench, "then we'll start shootin'. We need them focused on the cabin so the deputies can come up behind and take 'em by surprise."

"What about me?" asked Bertram.

"Don't fire unless you see someone. Your job is to protect our flank. There ain't much room between the cabin and the river, so if they come 'round back, they're gonna be in close. A shot or two should keep 'em at distance."

It was an hour after sundown when someone in Big Pat's gang fired their first shot. They heard the explosion of the cartridge followed almost instantly by the thud of it into the thick timber of a cabin wall. Another shot and thud followed by a third.

"Sounds like they're comfortable," said Jeffry Donn.

Hench started firing his carbine and Jeffry Donn fired his rifle. The gang out front shot back. It wasn't non-stop shooting, but Hench figured they were keeping the gang's attention. He didn't know how soon Tyler and Manuel would attack so he fired slowly, not wanting to use up all his ammunition—the night could be a long one even with the deputies' help.

"I—I think I see somethin' movin' out here," called Bertram.

"Not so loud, son," said Jeffry Donn. "Go ahead and take a shot. Let 'em know we're watchin' the back."

"Gun won't fire!" he whispered in a voice almost as loud as if he were yelling.

"Got to cock the hammer back with your thumb for each shot," said Hench.

"Oh." Bertram fired once. There was a pause, at least ten seconds, then he fired five more times. Hench turned to scold him, but Bertram said first, "I got him! I just shot a man. He—he was runnin' at the cabin with a torch. Think he was gonna throw it."

Hench looked over at Jeffry Donn who moved to the back of the cabin and peeked out the back window. He turned to Hench. "Sure enough. Someone's down out there and they got a torch next to 'em." He clapped Bertram on the back. "You done good, son."

Bertram held the gun out to the old man. His hand shook.

Jeffry Donn said, "That the first man you shot?" He eased the gun out of Bertram's hand.

Bertram nodded.

Jeffry Donn broke the Schofield open, making sure Bertram was watching, dumped the spent shells on the floor and reloaded. He handed back the gun. Bertram still shook.

"Keep your finger off the trigger 'til you're ready to shoot," said Jeffry Donn.

Even in the dark, Bertram looked like he might throw up.

Hench turned back to the front window. There was movement. They were staying low, but they were coming closer. At least he had something to aim at other than puffs of smoke in the dark. He hoped his bleary eyesight wouldn't betray him. He fired and a man screamed. The rest of the crawling shapes dropped to the ground.

"They're up to somethin'," said Jeffry Donn, back up front. "Where the hell's your deputies?"

"I'd kinda like to know that myself. They seem like good men, can't imagine them runnin'."

The two men took aim with their rifles and fired more shots, but no more obvious hits. Hench could sense Big Pat and his gang crawling closer in the dark. They could be in some real trouble if the deputies didn't show up soon.

"Anything more out back?" asked Hench.

"Nothin' I can see," said Bertram.

Hench then aimed his carbine to his far right. "'Nother torch." But the man lay low in the brush.

"Over here, too," said Jeffry Donn.

Then three more torches lit up the night.

"Can't believe they're this smart," said Hench. "Get ready."

"For what?" asked Bertram.

Neither Hench nor Jeffry Donn answered him as they waited for the attack. It came a few seconds later. Four of the men opened fire, unloading their guns at the cabin. Jeffry Donn and Hench had to duck, but not before Hench saw the man on the far right pick up the torch and sprint forward. Hench kept his head down, but poked out his carbine. The man zigzagged erratically during his ten-yard sprint. Hench fired and missed. The man flung the torch high into the air at the cabin and then he dropped back to the ground, disappearing into darkness. The torch hit the roof. Jeffry Donn and Hench looked up and waited.

"Didn't roll off," said Jeffry Donn.

Then, after the gang had time enough to reload, the next barrage started. Another man, to the left, ran forward and heaved a torch at the cabin. Jeffry Donn missed the shot. The torch hit the front of the cabin.

"Well, dang," said the old man.

They heard the crackle of dry brush.

CHAPTER THIRTEEN

The brush fire spread, lighting the area in front of the cabin. Hench and Jeffry Donn were more cautious with the light coming in through the windows. Jeffry Donn moved over a few steps and put his hand against the timber of the inside of the front wall.

"It's gettin' hot."

Smoke wafted in under the door.

Bertram said, "We can climb out the back window."

Jeffry Donn said, "There was only five out front with the torches, so there's at least two of 'em on the sides, waitin' for just that. Maybe more now. They shoot you before you could get through the window. We need them damn deputies to show themselves."

Hench looked up. Smoke was coming in through the rafters. The torch on the roof was doing its job.

"We're gonna go up quick," said Jeffry Donn. "This wood is nothin' but kindling."

"We're gonna burn up?" asked Bertram, looking plenty rattled.

Hench shook his head. "Naw. Smoke'll kill us before then."

Jeffry Donn chuckled and went to the table in the middle of the room. There was a metal pitcher on it. He took out a handkerchief and dunked it inside. It came out dripping. He tied it around his face. Hench followed suit, then Bertram.

"Let's see if we can shoot a few snakes in the grass first."

Hench nodded and returned to the window. As soon as he poked his head up, three rifles went off outside, one of the bullets splintering wood in the windowsill. He stood his ground and took aim. They were lit up inside now, but so were the men outside. He fired and one of the men bucked like a rat caught in a trap. The other men immediately started to pull back. Jeffry Donn fired from his position. More shots hit the cabin. Hench fired back while Jeffry Donn reloaded.

The smoke from under the door and from the rafters was swirling through the cabin. The windows would slow it, but not for long. Hench kept firing. Maybe they'd get lucky and take out enough of them for them to stampede out the front door. Hench started coughing even with the wet handkerchief over his nose and mouth. His eyes watered, making it even harder to aim with his already bleary vision from the hit to the head earlier. The pounding in his head grew worse.

"Hench!"

He looked at the window to his left, but Jeffry Donn wasn't there. He turned. The old man sat on the edge of a cutout in the floor, a trapdoor open at his side. The table, chairs, and small rug where pushed aside.

"Keep 'em busy," said the old man. "And when you come out this way, head west." He disappeared beneath the cabin.

Bertram said, "Shouldn't we follow him? We can get away!"

"Not yet. Stay at your post. We'll buy him some time."

Bertram looked incredulous. Hench pointed at the back window. "Do it!"

Hench turned back to his own window and started firing. His eyesight was so bad now that there was little chance, except through sheer luck, of hitting anyone. But he kept it up. Big Pat's men fired back in return. Hench called over his shoulder. "Start shootin'."

Bertram complied as the smoke swirled around them. Then Bertram ducked. "They're shootin' back!"

"Keep shootin'!"

Hench reloaded four times, spacing out his shots to keep Big Pat's gang interested but to not go through all his ammunition. It'd been at least fifteen minutes since Jeffry Donn left. The smoke was getting much worse.

"I can't take it!" said Bertram, falling to his knees, coughing.

Hench was going to yell at him, but then he had to bend over as he coughed, putting his hands on his knees to anchor himself. He got even woozier by dipping his head like that, the headache hammering away at the inside of his skull. His knees wobbled. He forced himself upright. A wood splinter struck him in the face. He flinched, but he didn't back away. He fired another seven shots through the window.

As he reloaded, he felt heat from above. Flames roiled inside the rafters. The heat was intense.

Bertram yelled something from the back of the cabin, but the flames were too loud for Hench to hear. The man pointed behind Hench, to his left. Turning, flames were spreading to the inside wall of the cabin. He picked up his saddlebags and backed away from the window, staying low and waved Bertram over. The man scrambled to the cutout in the floor.

Hench yelled over the fury of the fire, "Let me lead the way! We're going northwest, toward the river. Stay on your toes, no tellin' if Jeffry Donn cleared a path for us or not!"

Bertram nodded and Hench lowered himself through the cutout to the dirt below. It was cleaner underneath than he would have guessed. Only a few cobwebs and no grass, just dirt. As he bent under the floor, getting himself on all fours, he was shocked at the pain in his head. He didn't think it could hurt that much. He pitched forward, his face plowing into the dirt as his arms gave out. Bertram dropped down behind him.

"You okay?" he asked.

Hench pushed himself up. "I'm fine. C'mon."

He forced himself forward. Light from the raging fire in the cabin lit the space. At the edge of the cabin, they pushed their way through the brush, giving them some cover. He motioned for Bertram to get on his stomach.

Here on out they'd be crawling on their bellies. There was a loud whoosh from behind and fire erupted through the cutout in the floor. They'd gotten out just in time. The roof must have collapsed.

Hench pulled out his other Schofield revolver, holding it in his right hand, and kept his carbine in his left, his saddlebags over his left forearm so he could lift it to drag it along. After they'd gotten a dozen yards away from the cabin, Hench looked back. The front half of the roof was gone and flames roared twenty feet into the air. He wondered what Big Pat and his gang were thinking right about then? Were they assuming everyone had perished in the fire? Were they celebrating their victory—letting their guard down?

Bertram tapped him on the back then pointed toward the river. A pair of boots, toes down, could just be seen through the brush. Hench motioned for Bertram to stay where he was. Hench let go of his carbine and saddlebags and slid forward. They weren't Jeffry Donn's boots. He moved so he'd come in about waist-level on the man. As he got closer, thanks to the huge bonfire behind them, he could clearly see the blood covering the back of the man's coat. Then he saw the dead eyes of the man, his face turned toward Hench. He crawled closer. Jeffry Donn had used a knife on him.

He waved back to Bertram, who suddenly ran past him. He saw the reason. The dried brush behind them was on fire and racing their way. Hench pushed himself up and followed behind. He reached the rocky scrabbled bank of the river, free of brush, which sloped down to the water's edge, before he remembered his saddlebags and carbine. But there was no going back. The fire had already reached that far.

"Damn."

Then he turned toward Bertram, who crouched right at the edge of the river—Hench's saddlebags over the man's shoulder and his carbine in one hand, his revolver in the other. Hench took the saddlebags and dropped them farther up the bank, then took both weapons, holstering the Schofield revolver and laying his Spencer across the saddlebags.

The brush fire reached the bank of the river ten yards away. Ash and smoke billowed over them. Hench motioned for Bertram to lie down. Hench did the same, head toward the river. He removed his hat and dunked his head into the cold water. He left it there for about half a minute, the cold feeling so good, pushing the headache back a bit. Then he lifted his head and drank deeply. Bertram lay beside him, also drinking. Hench put his hat back on and rolled over. A swirling tornado of flame reaching greedily for the sky marked the cabin. He crawled to his carbine and cocked and levered it, rising into a crouch. He didn't see anyone through the brush fire, which was already dying out as the fire had eaten the dried grasses surrounding the cabin.

Hench pointed to a stand of four fir trees to his right, farther west from the cabin. The brush fire had died out before reaching it. The two men, keeping low, made their way there. Hench stood up behind a tree and looked out.

The cabin, what was left of it, still burned fiercely, lighting everything in the area. On the far side, south of the fire, Hench saw Big Pat standing there with maybe four men. The dunk in the river had also helped his eyesight a bit, but it was still too bleary and the smoke too thick to make out the men clearly. They were dim shifting phantoms to him—though Big Pat was a damned big phantom.

He crouched next to Bertram, who sat with his back to a tree, breathing hard, looking worn out. Pretty much how Hench felt. He pulled out a revolver and held it out toward Bertram. As the man reached for it, Hench slipped a handcuff over the man's left wrist, snapping it shut. During Bertram's confusion, Hench yanked hard, pulling Bertram sideways off balance. He put the other cuff around the base of a thick tree branch, closing it tight so Bertram couldn't side it down and off the branch.

"What are you doing?" Panic was in Bertram's eyes.

"Can't have you runnin' off and you'll just get both of us killed if you tag along." He held up the revolver until

Bertram finally focused on it. "I'm gonna let you have this. I doubt they'll come over here, but I ain't gonna leave you unarmed. And, again, if you shoot me—or try to shoot me—there won't be enough of your head left for your wife to recognize at George's. Got it?"

"But they're gonna kill me!"

"Then you better hope I get 'em all or drive 'em off. And I'd stop shoutin'. You don't really wanna draw attention to yourself. I'm gonna set this down on the ground. You reach for it before I'm gone and you're dead. Got it?"

Bertram stared wildly at him.

"You gotta answer me, Bertram. You gotta tell me I can trust you with this."

Bertram finally nodded. "Won't pick it up 'til you're gone. You ain't gonna just run off and leave me here, are you?"

"If I don't come back it means I'm dead. So I guess you better also hope I don't die."

Hench backed out of the fir trees, making sure Bertram didn't grab for the gun. But the man didn't move. "Don't go nowhere," he said, and moved off farther west, circling wide to get himself around to the front of the cabin.

CHAPTER FOURTEEN

As he circled west and south, to eventually put himself behind Big Pat and his gang, he came across the second man Jeffry Donn killed—knife wounds tearing up the man's gut, one of his eyes gouged out. The man was also partially burned from the brush fire. If Jeffry Donn hadn't killed these two men, Hench figured he and Bertram would have been in a world of hurt right then. Both men had been in good positions to pick them off as they scrambled away from the brush fire.

The smoke from the fire was tracking north. The farther Hench moved south, the clearer the air. By the time he'd moved past the cabin, at least a hundred yards west of it, he could see fairly well, though his eyes were still a bit blurry from the hit to the head. The cabin fire was dying out by this time, the wood of the cabin consumed.

He jumped a small ditch with running water from the Arkansas River. That's where he found two more bodies tangled up together. He knelt next to the ditch and pulled up on the top body, revealing Jeffry Donn beneath it. To get Jeffry Donn out of the ditch, he had to first pull the top body clear. Jeffry Donn's knife protruded from the man's side. He let him fall as soon as he was clear of Jeffry Donn. Then he pulled out the old Confederate. At first he didn't see any wounds on the man and wondered if he'd drowned beneath his victim, but out of the water for a bit, blood seeped from a wound in his chest. A bullet hole. Whether the bullet or the water killed him, Hench couldn't be sure.

He pulled the old man toward thicker brush, the brush fire hadn't jumped the ditch, and laid him there. Hopefully Jeffry Donn was out of sight if Big Pat or his gang came looking for their men.

"Thanks, old man," said Hench in way of eulogizing him before moving on.

With the cabin fire dwindling, night pressed forward again. That was good for Hench, letting him move in the open country without being detected. Big Pat and his gang were barely outlined from the mound of glowing embers that used to be the cabin. He eased closer until he could hear them.

Big Pat was speaking. "—leavin' before I know Bertram's dead. We're gonna look through them ashes."

"It's too hot still," said another man. "We'll have to come back in the mornin'. Be easier to see then, too."

Big Pat said, "I guess. I just don't want him sneakin' off free."

"What 'bout the deputies? We can't leave 'em alive, can we? They seen us and all."

"Gotta kill 'em. Dump 'em in the river after."

Big Pat said, "Yeah. After what we done two more bodies won't matter much I reckon. We can sell their horses over in Lamar. None of us can stay 'round here no more anyways."

"What 'bout the rest of our boys? Shouldn't we go look for 'em? Maybe they're hurt or somethin' and need our help."

"We could split up and —"

"Hell, no, I ain't goin' out there alone. What if that lawman made it out? Naw, we gotta stick together."

Hench moved on swiftly while they discussed the situation. He tried to take a bead on the gully where the deputies had hidden. In the dark, he wasn't as sure about where it was. When he thought he might be close, he whistled low, so low he could hardly hear it himself. Speck huffed at him in the darkness. Hench hurried forward. The moon was sliding toward the horizon in the west, but he could see enough. Manuel and Tyler were hogtied on the ground by the three horses. Hench put a hand back against the incline and shuffled and slid down to the bottom.

"You two okay?"

"We've been better," said Tyler.

"They got the drop on us," said Manuel.

"You think?" said Hench, taking out his knife. He cut through the ropes. "We gotta hurry, they might be comin' back here right now. Did they drop your guns somewhere or—"

"Took 'em with 'em," said Tyler.

The men tried to stand, but couldn't.

"I can't feel my feet," said Manuel.

Hench helped Manuel first, dragging him and shoving him up onto his horse. Then he did the same for Tyler. Hench pulled himself up onto Speck.

"What 'bout that old Reb and Bertram?" asked Tyler.

"Jeffry Donn's dead. I'll circle back around after you two are away and pick up Bertram. Now move."

"Can't feel the reins," said Tyler.

"Just don't fall off." Speck climbed the gully deftly. The other two horses followed and the deputies managed to hold onto the reins. "Head back to town. Go."

The deputies kicked the horses into action. Hench went with them a half mile, then pulled up and waited until he couldn't see the two men and the horses anymore. He and Speck went due north until they reached the Arkansas River, they rode alongside it until Hench felt they were close enough. He dismounted.

"Stay here," he said, moving off into the dark.

It was a couple hundred yards to the four fir trees. He snuck up quietly, not wanting to get shot by a panicked Bertram. But Bertram was asleep, his left hand dangling in the air by the handcuffs. Hench went right up to him and took his revolver back and even managed to uncuff the man without waking him. He pressed his hand firmly over Bertram's mouth and pressed his head back against the tree. Bertram's eyes flew open and looked wildly around. Hench didn't move his hand, slapping away

Bertram's attempts to grab that hand, until Bertram was fully awake and seemed to recognize him.

"We're gonna go get Jeffry Donn, okay?"

Bertram nodded behind Hench's hand. Hench removed it and stood up, attaching the cuffs to his gun belt and moving off toward where he'd left the old Confederate.

"Be quiet. Big Pat and his boys are still 'round here."

Bertram nodded again. The men walked back through burnt brush. The thick sharp smell of the ash filled Hench's nose, causing his headache to pound again. He held a hand up and showed Bertram the ditch, which was hard to see now that the firelight was gone. The two men jumped it. Big Pat's man still lay where he'd left him.

Bertram stopped in his tracks, staring at Jeffry Donn's body. "He dead?"

"Help me carry him. We gotta hurry, Big Pat could be right along."

"He was a good—"

"Gotta move!" hissed Hench.

With a bit of tussle and stumbles, the two men got Jeffry Donn back to Speck. It was much harder getting him up and over the saddle face down.

"How we all gonna ride that horse?" asked Bertram.

"We ain't. Jeffry Donn gets a ride. We walk."

"But it's ten miles back to town."

"Yep." Hench started walking and Speck followed at his side.

CHAPTER FIFTEEN

They kept off any trails, not that they couldn't still be seen by sharp eyes in the dark, but they never heard any riders. Maybe Big Pat and his gang moved on to Lamar after finding the deputies gone. The land around them turned gray, then pink, then an orange-yellow as the sun broke through the crust of the world. The town was just ahead of them by that time.

They stopped at George's first to drop off Jeffry Donn. Hench paid for the casket and burial. Then they walked to the jailhouse. The front door was unlocked and Jacob was inside cleaning debris from the office that had blown through the door connecting it to the cells in back. The deputy looked almost refreshed. The only one of them who'd gotten any rest lately.

"Tyler and Manuel went home to sleep. We figured Utley was probably safe now."

Hench decided not to disagree with him. "How's he doin'?"

Jacob nodded. "Doc says he should be okay. He even woke up once and talked normal—you know, knew who he was and where he was."

"Good. Any cells in back not got a hole in 'em?"

Jacob nodded. "Tyler said you'd be bringin' Bertram in. Cleaned up one of the front cells. It'll be a might bright and sunny, but it'll hold him. Assumin' the roof don't collapse."

Bertram looked panicked again. "You can't lock me in there if the roof's gonna fall on me!"

Hench said, "I'm more'n willin' to take that chance."

Hench woke up in a feather bed at the Satin Perch. The sun was still up, but his headache was more distant now. Juanita sat at her vanity applying makeup.

"You got blood on my satin pillowcase," said Juanita.

"Gettin' ready for the evenin'?"

"Sí. Though I don't think it's the same evening you think it is."

"You lost me."

"You slept all the way through yesterday and last night."

Hench blinked at her. "I been asleep for over a day?"

"Sí."

"No wonder I gotta piss so bad."

Juanita pointed to the door. "Take it outside!"

"Yes, ma'am."

Hench still felt a bit sluggish, but so much better than the day before. Was that right? Two days before? Wasn't worth thinking about. He headed to the jailhouse. Jacob and Tyler were packing up the front office. Bertram and Manuel weren't there.

"What's goin' on?"

"Hey, Hench," said Tyler. "Movin' over to the mayor's offices. Manuel's over there keepin' an eye on Bertram. We wired the county surveyor. He'll be here in a couple'a days to check out the jailhouse. Told us we should move out as it could fall on our heads. Said we'll probably have to bring the whole buildin' down and rebuild it. Got the Lobato brothers workin' on a temporary place 'til what time we get us a new jailhouse."

Doctor Rousseau entered the sheriff's office. He had a small gash on his forehead, dried blood outlining the right side of his face.

"It's Big Pat. He's taken Sheriff Utley hostage."

"You okay, Doc?" asked Hench.

The doctor nodded. "He hit me when I wouldn't let him near the sheriff. Then he sent me over here. Some of what he said didn't make any sense. Said there weren't any bones in the ashes. Does that mean anything?"

Hench nodded. "Anything else?"

"When they snuck back to town, one of his men heard about Bertram being in jail. Big Pat wants a straight trade of Bertram for the sheriff. Says he'll kill the sheriff if he doesn't hear from you within an hour."

"How many men did Big Pat have with him?

"Two that I saw, but I got the feeling there were a few more hiding out somewhere nearby. Couldn't swear to that, however."

"You're probably right."

"You gonna give him Bertram? The man's gonna die one way or other," said Tyler.

Hench pressed his lips together as anger surged through him. After a moment, he said, "Anyone else gettin' tired of this asshole? Doc, is Utley in any shape to move? Can he walk?"

"He shouldn't."

"Okay, you two go over to the mayor's office and get Bertram ready to move in an hour. Doc, go with 'em and stay safe."

As the men walked away, Hench cocked the hammers back on both of his Schofield revolvers and walked to the doctor's office and house. It was a two-story building with an office and examination rooms on the ground floor and the doctor's residence above.

Hench pounded on the front door. A man opened the door a crack, a revolver in his hand. "Yeah?"

Hench fired through the door with both of his guns and then kicked in the door. The man spilled backwards, falling to the ground, writhing and yelling in pain. Hench kicked him in the head with the flat of his boot. The man went quiet. Hench took the man's guns and tossed them out the front door and followed behind them, running around the corner of the building into a side alley, a grocer's building on the right.

Utley had been in one of the upstairs guest rooms. Unless Big Pat had moved him, Hench assumed he was still there. But right now, Big Pat and whoever else he had in there, were scrambling in a panic.

He ran down the alley as fast as he could, skidding around the far corner and coming up on the back door, which he kicked in. It led to one of the exam rooms. No one was guarding it. He moved through it out into the hall that went straight up to the front door. A man who had been bent over his fallen comrade spun and fired wildly. Hench fired both pistols, re-cocked, and fired again. The man fell.

Hench then ducked back into the exam room and waited by the side of the kicked-in back door. Footsteps ran his way. That would be one of the men who had been "hiding out somewhere nearby." The man blundered into the room, a double-barrel shotgun in his hands. Hench brought his right fist and the butt of a revolver down hard on his head. The man went to his knees, trying to turn. Hench coiled his body and then uncoiled, whipping his other hand forward from behind his back and smashing the bottom of that fist, along with the butt of that revolver, into the side of the man's face. Teeth and blood flew from the man's mouth and he thudded to the floor of the room.

Hench picked up the man's shotgun and flung it out the back door, doing the same with the one revolver the man had in his holster. Hench then reloaded his revolvers while keeping an eye on the front door. He didn't expect anyone else through the back as there just couldn't be too many men left in Big Pat's gang. At most he had five men plus himself. Three of them were down. There'd be at least one more outside who was supposed to be watching the front. Hench had gambled that none of them would be expecting such a swift and direct attack from a single man. They'd probably been lax, waiting to get word about when the trade would happen, not expecting anything to happen anytime soon.

Well, Hench was fed up with all of them.

As he finished reloading, Big Pat yelled from the upstairs. "I got Utley up here! Come up unarmed and we'll talk about tradin' for Bertram."

Hench ran down the hall to the front of the building. A man stood in the middle of the street, a rifle in his hands, trying to peer inside to see what was happening. Hench fired both revolvers out the front door, the man dove to the side, and then Hench turned sharply to run up the stairs, taking them two at a time. The room Utley had been in was down the upstairs hall at the far end to the left. As he bounded up into the hallway, both guns cocked and leading the way, he turned to see Big Pat standing in the doorway holding Utley up as a shield. He held a gun to the sheriff's head. Hench never slowed down. He charged straight ahead hoping for the reaction he got. Big Pat let out a yell of shock and instead of pulling the trigger and killing the sheriff, he backed up a step and pointed his gun at Hench, firing a shot. Hench took the bullet in his side and grunted.

Utley lashed out with his elbow, clipping Big Pat in the chin, then he dropped to the floor and Hench fired both revolvers.

CHAPTER SIXTEEN

Big Pat wasn't dead, nor was he likely to die from his wounds. The other doctor in town, Doctor Phillips, was patching up Big Pat in another room, Deputies Tyler and Manuel standing over him, guns drawn. Doctor Rousseau worked on Hench. The bullet had gone all the way through below the ribs.

"Ain't this the second time you been shot since gettin' to town?" said Utley, sitting in a chair on the other side of the room. His bandages showed fresh blood from his actions, but he waved off the doctor until Hench got sewn up.

"Shot myself the first time; not sure that counts." Hench sat on the edge of the examination chair.

"It counts," said Doctor Rousseau, drawing thread through his skin. "Especially since I have to restitch your arm."

Hench grimaced and drank a big slug of rye from a half-full or half-empty bottle.

"That should do it," said the doctor, applying a bandage over the front hole in Hench's side. "Switch places with the sheriff."

Hench rose from the examination chair and started to lift his arms up over his head to stretch them out.

"Stop that!" admonished Doctor Rousseau. "Keep your arms down. No fighting, no shooting, no anything for at least a week."

"Can I at least take a piss?"

"No!"

Sheriff Utley smiled and slowly eased himself up out of the chair. The sheriff looked gaunt—more gaunt than usual from all the blood loss. He walked slowly the few feet to the examination chair and the doctor helped him sit down, then began to remove his bandages.

Hench, helping Utley, walked into the other examination room. Doctor Phillips glanced over his shoulder. He was an older man with a rim of erratic white hair around his bright pink-skinned skull. It looked like his scalp had been spit-shined.

"He wake up?" asked Utley.

Manuel said, "No, not yet."

Big Pat murmured, "I'm awake."

The doctor paused, thread pulled tight through his skin. "Don't this hurt?"

"Like a son of a bitch."

"He gonna pull through?" asked Hench.

"Sure. One bullet went through and I dug out the other. Were you awake for that?"

Big Pat gave a slight shrug. A tough man—stupid, but tough. Big Pat opened his eyes and looked at Hench and Utley. "Y'all gotta promise that Bertram Richardson hangs for what he done."

Utley started to nod his head, but Hench said, "I don't think he killed your sister."

Everyone, including the doctor, turned and looked at Hench.

"Horseshit," muttered Big Pat.

Hench shrugged. "I'm just tellin' you what I think. We'll find out soon enough."

"We will?" said Utley.

"Yep."

"It's Bertram, ain't it?" said Becca. "I heard Big Pat took the sheriff. But you sent for me. That mean Big Pat got to Bertram? Is he dead? Tell me!" The woman was in a small office for an assistant of an assistant to the mayor. Her eyes were red from crying, her pale face covered with a sprawl of red blotches.

Utley sat down behind the small desk in the room, easing himself into the chair and grimacing in obvious pain. Hench sat on a corner of the desk. He said, "Your husband's spun us a wild tale, Mrs. Richardson."

She looked confused. "Is he still alive? You gotta tell me—"

Hench nodded. "He's still alive. But he's decided to come clean."

"I don't understand."

"Yes, you do. It wasn't Big Pat who killed Delilah. And it wasn't your husband."

"What are you sayin'?"

"It was you."

The red blotches on Becca's disappeared as her color drained away. She trembled. "What? No!"

Hench nodded. "I've been confused about this ever since the start. First, I couldn't figure out why Big Pat would want to kill Delilah in the first place and then why so violently? Not only that, but he does it in front of a witness that he leaves alive? The man's dumb, but he wouldn't leave a witness. Which begged the question, why was your husband still alive? But then I found out. It was because Big Pat didn't do it."

"'Course he did!'"

Hench shook his head. "Big Pat and Delilah were brother and sister."

Becca gasped.

"Yep. That's been a surprise to everyone. And that's when the whole case against Big Pat started to crumble. So I looked at it more closely. Found a knife tip stuck in Delilah's bed frame. Big Pat's knife wasn't broke. Then you know I found the murder weapon at your cottage."

She nodded. "Yes. My husband—"

Hench shook his head. "No. That didn't make sense either. Your husband was a regular at the Satin Perch. You probably knew that, didn't you? Or you suspected it, I'd wager. But I had the same problem about your husband. Why would he kill her? And why attack Delilah with such fury and violence? The person that killed her lost control. So when your husband finally admitted that you were the killer—well, it all made sense."

"How can you believe that? He was havin' relations with her in that room. He was there, not me!"

"Wanna know why I believe him? That first night when you showed up at the brothel. Why weren't you more upset? And I don't mean about your husband being injured. But why weren't you angry at your husband for bein' there in the first place? Sheriff even made mention of his own wife and the fit she would'a had. We all took it that you was more concerned over your husband's injuries than his regular transgressions at the Satin Perch. But it did make me wonder at the time. Were you some kinda saint? But now I understand. When you came back the second time—the first time bein' when you took out all your anger on Delilah—you'd had plenty of time to calm down. Set your emotions straight. But earlier? Well, you butchered that girl like a pig to market—hell, worse than that.

"How did it start? Were you already suspicious of your husband? Or just curious where he went when he snuck out at night? I'm thinkin' this particular night you followed him and seen him go into the Satin Perch. I bet when you seen him walk in you was crushed. Horrified. Angry." Hench watched her face. Small ticks and tremors moved like insects beneath the surface of her skin, all of them wanting to get out.

"You must have been near mad. I can imagine it. Your face didn't even look like you. I bet your husband was scared'a you in that moment. Terrified. This wild woman, so obviously off her wagon, your eyes wide and a snarl on your face. I bet you looked like a mad dog right then."

Becca's eyes suddenly glistened with tears and she said in a low voice, "It wasn't like that at all."

"Had to be. You see—"

She shook her head, jostling the tears, spilling them down her face. "I wasn't a wild dog. After he went in there I walked around the whorehouse, lookin' in the windows. Seen him up in the second floor undressin'. I pushed those empty crates over to the window and climbed up. And when I snuck into that room and Bertram was astraddle that whore, pushin' into her like a ruttin' animal. I was—I was *cold*. I felt like the dead'a winter. I picked up the china pitcher and smashed it over his head. Like it was nothin'. Wouldn't'a mattered if I'd killed him with it. The girl saw me then, but she didn't see the knife, so she's kinda confused. Kinda angry, until I stabbed her in the stomach. She yelled, I think, or maybe screamed. She tried to hit me, but she was too slow. I stabbed her again and again. I couldn't stop myself, you see. It wasn't until Bertram pulled me off that I stopped. I think if he hadn't done that I might never have stopped. Hacked her to bits."

Hench nodded. "Then I'm guessin' your husband came up with the whole Big Pat thing?"

She looked up at him. "Sort'a. He got me out the window and followed behind me. I wasn't thinkin' of nothin' right then. Everything was, was hazy. I barely remember it. Like a dream. I think he just wanted us to get home without no one seein' us and hope for the best. But then we come up on Big Pat dead drunk and face down in the alley. That's when Bertram got the idea. He rolled Big Pat over and then forced me to roll on top of him, to get blood on him. Then he had me hit him in the face a couple'a times—my husband's face that is, not Big Pat's, so it looked like they fought each other." She held up her bruised hand and smiled, a quick quivering thing like a rabbit fleeing before the dogs. "I liked doin' that. Hittin' Bertram."

"Then you went home and cleaned up, your husband took Big Pat's knife and went back to the brothel."

"Close enough."

"Merciful Heaven," breathed Sheriff Utley, shaking his head slowly.

"I can't believe my husband said anything," said Becca.

"He didn't."

Becca looked confused.

Hench shrugged. "It's just the way I figured it played out. But you admitting it to me and the sheriff? I think that'll be enough for a judge and jury."

BLOOD HOARD

Book Two

CHAPTER ONE

Hench stared at a ghost. He saw her across Larimer Street in Denver and froze, unable to breathe. His heart pounded. She was twenty years old wearing a blue calico dress with some kind of yellow pattern on it, black riding boots, and a well-worn Stetson in one hand as she used the sleeve of her dress to wipe her forehead. Her long auburn hair was braided and fell down the middle of her back.

The ghost didn't just resemble his deceased wife, Gloria, she looked just like her. That *was* Gloria. She disappeared behind a horse-drawn Denver City Railway trolley car with LARIMER STREET emblazoned on its side. The trolley came to a stop on its tracks in the middle of the wide dirt street. People got on and off. Hench knew he should go after the girl, but he couldn't move. The trolley passed on but the ghost was gone. He was overwhelmed. Gloria had died sixteen years earlier, but that horrible memory smashed him in the face, causing his head to spin, kicked him in the gut, making him winded.

"Hench?"

He blinked and looked to his right at the grocer, Gerry.

Gerry said, "Good Lord, man, what's wrong?"

He saw Gerry's face. He'd heard his name. But his thoughts tumbled like an avalanche down the side of a ravine. Speck, his cream-colored reddish-brown-spotted Appaloosa, seemed to sense Hench's disarray and nudged the Colorado Ranger in the chest. Hench looked at his horse, then bent his head down, touching Speck's forehead with his own, scratching each side of the horse's muzzle. That connection snapped him out of it. He took a big ragged breath and turned back to Gerry.

"How much?"

Gerry stared at him, confused. "Uh. Three twenty-seven."

Hench went to a saddlebag straddling Speck and took out a coin purse, counting out the grocer fee. He held it out to Gerry who stepped off the boardwalk and retrieved it.

"Carrots?" said Hench.

Gerry motioned to the burlap sack. "They're on top per usual."

Hench ignored Gerry's questioning look and retrieved a carrot, offering it to Speck, who took it happily—huffing and shuffling his back legs. He was a young gelding and still showed he wasn't that far removed from being a pony.

"Okay, boy, let's go after her." He stepped up onto the saddle. "Keep that for me, Gerry. I'll be back in a bit."

Hench had just arrived in Denver. He'd been up in Georgetown when he got word that Gloria's family was in trouble. He still wore his trail garb: a long well-worn tan duster, a broad-brimmed hat of the same condition and color, and old black leather chaps. No spurs. He didn't need them with Speck. Beneath the duster he wore gray wool pants and a faded blue side-button shirt. He had brown hair turning to gray and a scruffy short beard more gray than brown.

Hench guided Speck across and down Larimer to the spot he'd last seen the ghost. He bent low and looked in shop windows as Speck ambled down to the end of the block. She must have turned right at 15th Street. She couldn't have gone far. He dismounted and walked up the street, not holding the reins. Speck followed at Hench's side.

On his right, the block was lined with four- and five-story gray and white buildings made of Colorado stone. The first building housed the M. J. McNamara Dry Goods Company. If she'd gone in there, he probably wouldn't see her from the street in such a large store. They walked a little farther on. Denver was bustling and the girl could have easily slipped from sight among the crowd and still been on the street.

Up ahead, a woman yelled, her voice full of anger though Hench couldn't make out the words. Then a knot of people formed at the end of the block, other people yelling and a general commotion breaking out. Hench hurried forward. Suddenly the knot scattered, as though a gale force wind blew the seeds from the head of a dandelion. As the crowd scattered, Hench entered the void. Two men held the ghost between them. She struggled, calling them names most women didn't use in public. The cause of the crowd dispersal presented itself as a third man holding a revolver.

Hench turned to Speck and lifted a hand, palm out to the horse for him to stay. The young gelding stopped in the street. Hench turned back, cocked both of his Smith & Wesson Schofield Model 3 revolvers, but left them holstered. No point in provoking the man into shooting.

He then took his silver Colorado Ranger badge from his pocket and cupped it in his left hand. He approached, hands out from his sides.

"What's the trouble?" said Hench.

The man with the gun turned toward him. The other two men momentarily froze. The ghost looked startled, then smiled broadly. "Uncle Hench!"

The ranger didn't take his eyes from the man with the gun. "What's goin' on, Rose?"

One of the men holding Rose muttered, "Damn!"

The man with the gun said, "Stay right there. We ain't gonna hurt her. We just need to borrow her for a short time."

"They're kidnapping me," said Rose. Her voice was full of emotion, as Hench would expect, but she didn't sound scared or panicked, just mightily angry.

"You're not takin' the girl."

"I'm a woman now, Uncle Hench."

"Stay outta this," warned the man with the gun, glaring at Hench.

Hench smiled sadly. "You have certainly grown." Even this close she looked so much like Gloria. The ranger lifted his hands chest-high and took a step toward the man at the same time.

She said, "People tend to do that when you last saw them when they were ten. I'm twenty now, Uncle."

Hench shook his head slightly. "Hard to believe it's been that long. The trail takes me—"

"The trail takes you to Denver plenty of times, Uncle."

Hench felt the kick in his gut he'd carried with him for sixteen years now. "You're right. I wish I could—damn, you look so much like her."

When the man with the gun glanced at Rose, Hench took another step closer. The man was confused. Uncertain what to do.

"Jesus, Patrick," said one of the men holding Rose. "Shoot him already."

"That would be a mistake," said Hench, showing them his badge and taking another step forward at the same time, putting himself within six feet of Patrick. "I'm a ranger, gentlemen, and you're under arrest." He made sure the man with the gun saw the badge. He did, his eyes focusing on it with dawning panic. Hench raised the badge higher and to the left.

Patrick's gaze followed the badge and Hench surged forward. He coiled and unleashed his right arm, driving the lower part of his palm into the man's jaw. At the same time, he dropped his badge from his other hand and pulled his revolver, pointing it at the wobbly man. Patrick stumbled back a step and then fell on his ass on the boardwalk, his eyes glazed, dropping his gun.

One of the men holding Rose released her and reached for his own gun. Before he could clear leather, Hench's second gun was staring him in the face.

"This is over," said Hench.

Rose pulled hard on the other man's grip, freeing herself and stepping to Hench's side.

"Rose, go behind these two gentlemen and relieve 'em of their guns."

Before she could move a man's voice from behind

said. "Take it real easy there, mister."

Hench didn't move, but Rose turned her head. She smiled. "It's okay, it's a police officer."

"Holster your guns nice and slow," said the officer.

Rose said, "You don't understand, he's a Colorado Ranger, officer."

Hench complied, but left them cocked. He didn't turn. It was a bad position to be in, but if the man was really a police officer, Hench would rather keep his eyes on the three men who had tried to take Rose.

The officer said, "You three, move along. Go!"

The two men who'd been holding Rose helped the third man to his feet and then they moved off quickly. Hench finally turned, but the officer was twenty yards away and moving fast. With a sigh, Hench uncocked his guns and retrieved his badge from the ground, fastening it to his blue shirt.

"Why'd he do that?" asked Rose.

Hench said, "The man undoubtedly earns two pay stubs."

"What?"

"Someone paid him off."

"Oh."

"Do you know any of those guys?"

Rose shook her head. "Never saw them before. But it can't be a coincidence."

Hench nodded. "Agreed. They're connected to your father's disappearance."

CHAPTER TWO

Vincent Edwards brought a silver revolver out from his desk drawer and set it softly onto the leather blotter. The man across from him was unarmed, made that way by Vincent's two guards just outside the office door. The man swallowed, then said, "I—what would you like me to say?"

"Oh," said Vincent, placing his hand next to the gun, "it's not about what I want you to say. It's what I asked you to do. And now you're here telling me that you failed."

"But we weren't expecting someone to interfere like that. He was a ranger. Knew how to handle himself."

Vincent tilted his head slightly to the side. "Jason, are you implying that you and your men do not know how to handle themselves? Why is this ranger not dead and the girl in your possession?"

"Well, I—what I mean is, I didn't think you'd want it to get messy. Gettin' the rangers involved by killin' one of theirs."

Vincent sighed. "This is my fault. Obviously, I hired the wrong group of men for this job. My apologies. When you said you could get the girl, when you promised me, I made the mistake of believing you were a man of your word."

"I'll get her next time. I swear." The man was agitated, his eyes staring at the revolver on the desk.

"Did you get the ranger's name, by chance?"

Jason nodded. "She called him Hench, I think."

Vincent looked up sharply. "She knew his name? They were familiar to one another?"

"Yeah. They was talkin' the whole time like maybe they was family or somethin'."

"And you didn't think that was important information to tell me?"

Jason didn't say anything, his eyes never leaving the revolver.

Vincent picked up the gun. "Beautiful, isn't it? Tiffany made it."

"A girl made it?"

Vincent paused for half a second as he marveled at Jason's stupidity. "Silver, of course, and the ivory handle—handle? Is that the correct word? Doesn't matter. A work of art. A show piece. Not really meant for shooting. But I digress. Did you or did you not tell me you could get the girl?"

Jason didn't say anything. Vincent didn't point the gun directly at him, but the man followed its slightest movement like watching the head of a venomous snake.

"Answer me," said Vincent.

"I guess so."

Vincent sighed. "That was my recollection, as well." He pointed the gun at the man and he fired it. He didn't know how other men did it, the recoil always surprised him, especially for such a small thing. He thought perhaps that was one reason he wasn't the best of shots — did he anticipate the recoil and pull his hand away subconsciously? So even though he was only six feet away, a red rose bloomed on the man's shoulder. Vincent had tried to hit the center of his chest. Jason clutched at it and sprang from the chair.

Vincent's two personal guards rushed into the room, guns drawn. Now those men were excellent shots. Jason froze, staring at them and their guns. One of them, Daniel by name, motioned him back into the chair. After the man sat, visibly shaking, which was understandable, the two men moved to behind the man's chair. The two men were dressed nearly as impeccably as Vincent. He didn't want his personal guards looking like scruffy gun hands.

The second guard, Abraham, put away his gun and pulled out a thick two-foot-long leather strap and looked at Vincent. Vincent nodded. Since Jason couldn't see what Abraham was doing, he just sat there as the strap slipped quickly around his throat. Abraham pulled the two ends of the strap in opposite directions. Jason reacted then. He went berserk—again, perfectly understandable. He kicked the chair out from under himself. His arms flailed like he was—well, like he was being strangled. Abraham, however, was a much bigger man, taller than either Daniel or Vincent, certainly bigger than Jason. It looked to Vincent much like a man fighting the pull of a fish. Abraham's large arms jerked with the man's movements, but the man wasn't going anywhere and would soon dangle lifeless from the end of the fishing line, so to speak.

"Pig farm?" asked Daniel, putting his gun away.

Vincent shook his head. "I think not. Leave him where his buddies will find him and make sure they understand what happens to employees who disappoint me."

Vincent waited until dark before heading over to the

house he owned near Cherry Creek at 13th and Arapahoe Streets. He walked up to the front door and softly knocked twice, paused, knocked twice, paused, and was about to knock again when the door opened a few inches. The man inside, Roger, nodded to Vincent and opened the door wider.

"How is our guest?"

Roger shrugged. "Still quiet."

Vincent shook his head. "The man has more resolve than I would have given him credit." He walked through a large front room and down a short hallway to the first door on the right, opening it to reveal stairs. He descended into a dimly lit basement room, the floor hard-packed dirt, the walls roughed in with stone.

William sat in the dirt, leaning against a wall. He was tied securely, ropes around his wrists, around his arms, binding them to his body, and around his calves down to his ankles. The man's face was hard to recognize anymore because of swelling, bruising, and blood—some dried but some still wet. One of William's eyes was swollen shut. Vincent made sure his tormentors—Vincent never laid a hand on him himself—didn't injure the other eye. He wanted William to not only feel the pain, but to see it coming. Anticipation could be just as convincing as the actual pain. Though in William's case, neither was working.

"So, tell me, William, who is Hench?"

William looked at him and Vincent didn't like what he saw. The man opened his swollen and split lips, showing the ragged gaps in his teeth where they'd either been pulled or had been knocked out by bludgeons. But William wasn't opening his mouth to talk. The man was smiling.

CHAPTER THREE

The three of them, Speck walking on one side of Hench and Rose on the other, made their way to the Five Points neighborhood northeast of downtown. They crossed over the steel trolley tracks that ran down Champa Street and walked one more block to Curtis. Hench stopped at the top of the block. Midway down he saw the crabapple trees and the bottom of his heart split open anew. He was surprised that blood wasn't spilling out over the dirt street.

The trees had been tiny twigs when Gloria planted

them out front. Now they were twenty feet tall, their branches spread wide, giving shade to the entire front yard. The house hid behind the trees, a narrow two-story building made of yellow brick. Even from where he was a half block away he could see that the front yard was torn up. Deep furrows slashed the ground in a crisscross.

Rose came abreast and took Hench's hand. "Lord, your hand is freezing."

"Any idea what they were lookin' for?"

Rose shook her head. "No idea. Wait until you see the inside. It's horrible."

She let go his hand and started forward, but Hench couldn't seem to get his legs moving. He stared at those crabapple trees. He tasted the crabapple jelly, sweet and tart, that Gloria made after the fourth year of their planting and the three years after that they'd lived in the house. It'd been sixteen years since he'd last been in it— the last time being Gloria's wake. He left after only ten minutes and never returned to the house, giving it to William and his wife Prudence, and their four-year-old daughter Rose.

But the worst thing of all was that the pain in his chest, in his gut, wasn't as bad as it used to be. That bothered the hell out of Hench. He could never forgive himself for his wife Gloria's death. Ever. He wanted to feel the pain like a fresh wound. It's what he deserved.

Rose looked at Hench, her eyebrows drawing together. "What's wrong? You're breathing like a train engine."

Hench made fists and forced himself to breathe normally.

Rose kept looking at him. He wished she'd look anywhere else. "It can't—you're not still torn up about Aunt Gloria's death, are you?"

Through clenched teeth, he said, "Wish you wouldn't mention it."

"My God, Uncle, that was, what, fifteen years ago—sixteen? How can you still be holding on like this?"

Hench didn't speak.

"You have to let it go."

Hench walked past her. Anything, even seeing the inside of the house again, was better than listening to Rose tell him what he should be feeling. Thankfully Rose stopped talking about it and hurried to catch up to him.

The frame of the front door was splintered around the strike plate. When Hench grabbed the doorknob, it was loose and the latch bolt didn't sit properly anymore, but the door could still shut. He opened it and froze. Rose was right. It *was* horrible. Furnishings were strewn about, walls ripped open, floorboards torn up. It was as if a giant wildcat had been let loose inside, using walls, floor, and even the ceiling to sharpen its claws. It didn't look like anything had escaped its fury. He stepped into the foyer. To the left, hugging the wall, were stairs to the second floor. To the right was a parlor. After that was a dining room with the kitchen beyond that and a small bedroom off to the side. Upstairs was a large master bedroom and two smaller rooms with a living room in the center.

Hench said, "Start from the beginning."

Rose sighed, her face flush as she looked at the house again. Her voice came out strong, however. Full of anger. "Hard to believe it's been only four days. Feels like four months." Her voice quivered slightly and Hench saw the glisten in her eyes. Then she suddenly let loose: "*What the hell did they do to Father?*"

Hench put a hand on her shoulder. She reached up and covered it. Now her hand was cold. She shook her head and sniffed. "Sorry. Sorry. Okay, Sunday night. It's about eight in the evening. We're both in the front room here." She stepped away from Hench and motioned to the dismantled room in front of her. "I heard someone running outside but didn't think anything of it at first. I was reading *Tom Sawyer*. I looked up as the sound came closer, up the stone walk, and then Grandma burst through the front door. She looked scared out of her wits. She slams the door shut behind her and locks it. And tries to tell us what happened.

"Father and I are in a near panic trying to understand her. Grandma's trying to catch her breath and trying to tell us about some men. Grandma moved away from the door, her eyes wild, and pointed behind her as if that would help." Rose, acting as her grandmother Miriam, turned and pointed to the door.

"What happened?"

"I didn't get the whole story right then. Like I was saying, she was out of breath and trying to talk at the same time. Father and I are blurting out asinine questions and telling her to calm down. Then the men showed up. They pounded on the door—I mean, they were trying to break the door down. The whole house shook. Grandma cursed and I don't know what I was doing, it's all a whirlwind in my head, until Father grabs both of us and hauls us out the back door. There's no one there—I mean none of the men who did this. Father tells us to go and hide. Go somewhere safe. We can hear them still banging on the front door. I told Father to come with us. Dear Lord, why didn't I make him come with us?"

Her voice shook. "Well, we hear the front door crash open and Father shoves us both, nearly pushing

Grandma to the ground. He implores us to go. I grab Grandma and drag her the hell out of the backyard and down the alley. Father went back into the house. He was going to try and slow them down, I think. I assume. Grandma and I got away." She vibrated.

"And where did you go?"

Rose took a deep breath and continued. "We ran for several blocks until Grandma couldn't run anymore. Then we walked. It was at least a mile before I realized we had to find a place to stay. I was afraid to go to a friend's house. We didn't know who these men were or what they wanted so I didn't want to endanger anyone. We ended up at the Argo Hotel out past Capitol Hill. I was surprised they rented us a room in the state we looked. No luggage. No money, though they didn't know that at the time."

Hench motioned to the house. "Is anything missing?"

Rose shook her head. "No. I mean, they took a couple of dollars we kept in a small bowl by the front door. But nothing else."

Hench walked through the entire house, fending off painful memories of a happy time and forcing himself to look at the destruction. He tried to see a pattern to it. Make some kind of sense of it. But he didn't.

Back in the front room, Hench asked, "Is Prudence back at the hotel with Miriam?"

"Mother? I guess you wouldn't know, but she left Father nearly two years ago. Moved back to Boston to be with her family. They hadn't been getting along well for a long time."

"Why didn't you go with her?"

"This is my home. I was born and raised in Denver. And, honestly, I never much cared for her side of the family. This is where I belong."

The ranger nodded. "Fair enough. Okay, let's go see Miriam's house."

Miriam Thompson's house was less than two blocks away. Back when Gloria was alive, he got along fine with his mother-in-law. Now was a different matter.

It was a small single-story house made of dark red

brick with large black flecks impregnating it. There was a front window to the right of the door. The door was up four steps from the yard behind a small porch that didn't quite stretch from side to side of the house. The wood shake roof extended down over the porch supported by four robust columns. It was the same house Randall and Miriam had bought together when they moved out to Colorado from Kansas back in 1860 or so with their children, William and Gloria. The same crisscross gouges were in the front yard. The door hung awkwardly against the frame, the hinges torn loose. Hench had to lift the door free of the frame and set it to the side to enter the house. The inside was just as destroyed as William and Rose's house.

"Do you know if anything's missing from here?"

"It doesn't seem like, though I haven't brought Grandma back. She'd know for sure, of course. But I didn't want her to have to make a run for it again if the men showed up while we were here."

"When did you come back to look at the houses?"

"Yesterday. During the day. I figured that would be safer. I sure as hell didn't expect to see this type of wreckage."

"Crickets."

"What is it?"

"Someone was watching the place. Come on, we have to get back to your hotel."

Rose looked confused for a moment than realization dawned on her face. "*Crickets*. That's how they knew where I was when they tried to snatch me."

Speck ran just as nimbly with Hench and Rose on his back as he did when it was just Hench. They rode to within a couple of blocks of the hotel. Hench tied him off. He had Rose go on ahead and he walked far enough behind that no one would assume they were together. He looked for someone paying her too much attention. Two men fit that description.

One was near the end of the block. He'd been sitting on the stoop of a building down the street a little from the hotel. When Rose walked by, he visibly perked up and his head swiveled and followed her progress until she disappeared into the hotel. The other man was in the middle of the block. He wasn't nearly as obvious, but he still watched her walk down the block and into the hotel. Hench followed Rose into the hotel.

She was no longer in the lobby. Hench took the stairs behind the front desk up to the fourth floor and down the hall to 412. Rose stood in the doorway with the door open. She looked relieved. "Grandma, you're safe."

"Of course I'm safe," said Miriam, stepping into view.

"There are at least two men—" began Hench as he came up behind Rose.

Miriam Thompson's eyes blazed with hatred. "What the hell is he doing here?"

CHAPTER FOUR

1863

Twenty years earlier...

Vincent Edwards walked the floor of his Cherokee House saloon at the corner of F Street and Blake Street in downtown Denver City. It was a two-story wood building with hotel rooms upstairs. Vincent made a tidy sum from the drinking, gambling, room rent, and a house fee for the prostitutes. But that didn't mean Vincent was satisfied—that was a word he despised. Men who were satisfied were men who would never amount to anything.

The Cherokee House was raucous with drinking and gambling. Vincent moved through the room, dressed in the finest raiments available in Kansas City and shipped out to this dusty town. But as inconsequential as Denver City was at the moment, Vincent saw potential. The town had overcome its initial mining camp mentality—as short-lived as that was—and had grown considerably in a short time. There was money to be made here and Vincent was ready to grab it with both fists.

Steve, one of his faro dealers, waved at Vincent, who walked over, standing just over the dealer's shoulder. Steve motioned to a drunk man on the playing side of the table. "Our friend, Courtney, here would like to pay in dust."

Vincent held out his hand and Courtney, a young man with a bleary smile, handed over a small tobacco bag that was far heavier than tobacco. Vincent loosened the string and peered inside. It glittered. He poured a small amount of gold dust into the palm of his hand. It was fairly clean with just trace amounts of black sand. Vincent transferred the gold back into the tobacco bag, cinched it tight, and weighed it in the same palm. It was four, nearly five ounces. Vincent slipped the gold into his inside jacket pocket and reached into the chip tray, removing $150 in clay chips, setting them in front of Courtney. The man scooped them up.

Courtney was in his early twenties and wore drab city clothes. Vincent leaned to his right slightly and looked under the table. Courtney wore work boots that had seen better days but were still in decent shape.

Vincent smiled and said, "Courtney, my friend, would it be okay if I look at your hands?"

Courtney looked confused, but the smile never left his face. He held out his hands. They weren't soft, but they certainly weren't worn to the extent of someone digging in riverbeds or scrabbling through rocks.

"So where did you get the dust from, Courtney?"

The young man put a finger to his lips. "Secret."

"You can tell me, Courtney. We're good friends. Is it

payment for a job you did?"

Courtney chuckled and shook his head. Vincent never played games of chance. Ever. But there were times when he gambled. He decided that the young man was worth a small wager. Vincent reached into the table's chip tray and pulled out three green $25 chips and set one in front of each of the other three players at the table who were impatient to keep playing.

"My apologies, gentleman, but this table is closed."

The men didn't look unhappy as they picked up the free money and left the table. Courtney started to stand, nearly knocking over his chair. Vincent put a hand on his shoulder. "Not for you, Courtney. Consider this your private table."

"Really?"

"A good gambler like yourself? You deserve it." Vincent moved around to the playing side and sat next to the young man but looked up at the dealer. "Five hundred, Steve, if you please."

The dealer took five black chips worth $100 each.

Vincent leaned in close to Courtney and whispered. "If you tell me your secret about the gold, you can also have these." He spread the chips out in front of the man, making sure the embossed $100 was clearly visible on each one.

"All that?" said Courtney, his eyes wide.

"All that," said Vincent. "Where did you get the gold from?" It could be that Courtney had simply rolled a miner and stole the gold. But that's what this gamble was all about—maybe it was something more. And if it was, it could be well worth the $500 wager in chips he was giving away.

"Well—" The man looked serious for the first time. "Don't think I can tell you that."

Vincent nodded to Steve and five more black chips appeared on the table.

"Sweet Josephine," said Courtney. "Maybe—well, maybe I can tell you. You won't tell no one else?"

Vincent moved the black chips in close to the young man and nodded solemnly. "You have my word."

Courtney's mouth was practically watering. "Uh. Well. You know the mint?"

Vincent frowned, "Clark and Gruber?"

"Yep. Well, they gotta move, see? The government— the, the, the big government, uh, the *federal* government bought 'em, right? So they're movin'. Well, they still got all kinds of gold there, so one evenin'—"

"You work there, Courtney?"

Courtney barked a short laugh. "Yep. I'm one of the guards."

"Interesting. Please continue."

"Well, there's all this gold whore—" Courtney frowned. "That don't sound right."

"Hoard?"

Courtney brayed a laugh like a donkey. "Yeah, yeah."

Vincent motioned for Courtney to keep it down.

Courtney whispered loudly, "They got their gold *hoard*," he actually giggled, "sittin' in a couple of rooms waitin' to be moved so I, you know, took a little bit." He leaned in close to Vincent. "Just a little."

"Aren't you afraid they'll discover the missing gold?"

Courtney closed his eyes and shook his head a little too vigorously, almost falling off his chair. His eyes snapped open as he caught himself. He looked at Vincent and furrowed his brow.

Vincent said, "You were saying why you weren't afraid of them missing the—"

"Oh, yeah!" yelled Courtney.

Vincent made the same motion for Courtney to lower his voice.

"Oh, yeah," he said more quietly. "Well, there's so much stuff they gotta move real fast that they don't got any idea what all they got. Right? They're not gonna miss a little gold. Heck, a lot of gold could walk on outta there without anyone the wiser."

Vincent smiled at Courtney and stood. He put a hand on Courtney's shoulder and said to the dealer, "Steve, we need to treat our good friend Courtney like a golden ram."

Courtney kept grinning. The dealer nodded. That

meant that Steve should fleece him of all the money Courtney had and then some. Vincent walked away and talked to one of his girls to make sure that his new best friend would not run out of alcohol.

Vincent walked into room 3 upstairs at the Cherokee House holding a full glass of water. Courtney snored on the bed. Vincent was surprised there was no vomit—the young man drank entirely too much the night before. It was now just past noon. Vincent pushed the drapes aside and let the sun in. Courtney squirmed on the bed and clamped his eyes tighter shut.

Vincent walked to the side of the bed. The young man lay on his back, his mouth open and making a horrible noise. "Time to wake up," said Vincent as he poured the entire glass of water on Courtney's face.

The man gagged and coughed and shouted all at once, sitting straight up and flailing his arms as if he were trying to swim. Vincent stepped back. Courtney's eyes were wide open staring around the room before finally fixing on Vincent. Courtney sputtered out water before shaking his head like a dog and then grimacing. Vincent could assume the man's head hurt to quite a degree.

"Glad to see you awake, Courtney."

"Oh, uh. Yeah. Hello."

"My name is Vincent Edwards. We met last night. Do you remember?"

Courtney's eyes narrowed as he stared at Vincent then someone lit the lamp in his head. "Oh, yes sir. You own the Cherokee, right?"

"That is correct. And unfortunately, I have some difficult business to transact with you at the moment. I hate to state something so indelicate, but it would appear that you owe the Cherokee House a considerable sum of money. I have no doubt you're good for it, but I thought I should bring it to your attention."

"I do?" Courtney now looked like he *would* vomit. "I don't remember anything like that."

Vincent reached into his inside breast pocket of his jacket and pulled out a sheet of paper. "Steve kept meticulous details. I believe this is your signature?"

"He did? Uh, who's Steve?"

Vincent smiled thinly. "Surely you remember Steve. He was your faro dealer."

"Oh. Yeah. Right. Steve."

Vincent handed him the sheet of paper with numbers written in a neat and tidy column. A lot of numbers followed by an indecipherable scribble that Courtney may or may not have recognized. Vincent didn't really care.

Courtney's eyes stopped blinking. "This isn't all me, is it?"

"I'm afraid so."

"But I don't got—I mean, dang, that's a lot of money."

Vincent nodded solemnly. "Indeed. But you'll be relieved to know that I've waived the three-dollar rent for the room."

"You did? Well—thanks?"

"You're quite welcome. Now, how would you care to make amends?"

"Amends?"

"How do you plan to pay off your debt, Courtney?"

The young man stared at the piece of paper and ran a hand through his greasy tangled hair. "I'm not—I mean—" His voice trailed off.

"Might I make a suggestion?"

Courtney nodded vigorously then winced.

"I believe you mentioned last night that you are a guard at the Clark and Gruber mint. Am I correct in that?"

Courtney looked up from the paper, his face clouded in confusion. "Uh, yeah. I guess so."

"Excellent. Then I'm sure we can make an arrangement that will be advantageous to us both."

"We can?"

"Indeed."

CHAPTER FIVE

1884

Present day...

Hench expected no less from Miriam than the hatred aimed his way.

Rose said, "You know why Uncle is here, Grandma. We need his help."

"We don't need his help. It'll just get us killed."

"Grandma! What are you talking about? Of course we do." She looked between the two and then Hench saw the realization cross her face. "My God. Aunt Gloria died sixteen years ago! How can you still be carrying so much grief? And here I thought you two were mature adults. You're nothing but whining children."

Neither he nor Miriam made any indication they'd heard her. But he heard her. He just thought she was wrong. Some things you never get over. Unfortunately, she'd probably discover that for herself one day.

"You need to forgive him, Grandma. It wasn't his fault."

In unison, no doubt the only thing the two could ever agree on, they said, "Yes, it was."

Miriam turned away and stalked back into the room. Rose followed, looking stunned. Hench came in last, shutting the door behind him. He said, "You need to pack."

"What the hell for?" said Miriam. She vibrated with her hatred of him.

Rose started to speak, but someone knocked on the door. Hench drew a black Schofield and cocked it. He motioned the women to the other side of the room. With them out of the way, he stepped to the side of the door.

"Yes?"

"Rose, it's me!"

Rose started forward, but Hench waved her back and whispered, "Who is it?"

"A friend of mine. Tobias. It's okay."

"How does he know you're here?"

From outside, Tobias said, "Is everything okay? Hello?" The door handle rattled.

"I told you, he's a friend. He's been helping us."

Hench didn't like it, but he unlocked the door and pulled it open a couple of inches, putting the toe of his boot up against the bottom of the door to keep anyone from forcing it open. Through the sliver he saw an earnest young man, maybe a couple of years older than Rose.

"Let me see your hands," said Hench.

Rose said in shock, "Uncle!"

But the young man raised both hands chest high. They were empty. Hench threw open the door and shoved the young man in the chest, forcing him backward so Hench could see the hallway. It was empty. Hench did not holster his gun—it was the same man Hench had seen near the end of the block watching Rose enter the hotel.

"Keep your hands where I can see them."

Tobias kept them raised chest high as he stared at the barrel of the Schofield. Rose came out into the hall. "It's okay, Tobias is a friend."

Hench used his free hand to block her from stepping in front of him.

Hench said, "He was watching the hotel."

"That's right," said Miriam, "shoot Rose's boyfriend."

The young man blushed, as did Rose. She stammered, "He's not—I mean, we're not—"

"Why were you watching the hotel?" said Hench.

A couple of people down the hall poked their heads out then ducked back inside at seeing Hench with his gun.

Tobias said, "I've been looking out for Mrs. and Miss

Thompson since Mr. Thompson disappeared."

"Why?'

"I told you," said Rose. "He's a friend."

"You're sweet on him?"

Rose blushed a deeper shade of red. "Uncle!"

Tobias looked more intently at Hench. "You're Rose's uncle? I didn't know you had an uncle."

"He's dead to us!" said Miriam, stepping to the other side of Hench

Tobias looked confused.

"Grandma, please."

"Everyone shut up!" Hench poked his revolver toward Tobias. "How long have you been with Rose?"

"Well, I don't know if we're really—"

"How long!"

"Two weeks."

"Almost three," said Rose. "He just moved to Denver."

"I'm staying at a boarding house close to the Thompsons' house."

"He was walking by one day when Father and I were out front and we started up a conversation."

"They invited me to dinner."

"And we've sort of run into each other since."

Hench caught Miriam with a slight smile as she watched the two young people. It turned into a scowl the moment she noticed Hench looking at her. The ranger felt no desire to smile. It was all too pat for Tobias to show up just before the trouble. And since he knew where the women were, it wouldn't be difficult to set up Rose's kidnapping.

Tobias looked at the silver on Hench's chest. "You're a lawman?"

"He's a Colorado Ranger," said Rose.

"He's filth," said Miriam.

Hench could see that the young man wasn't sure how to take Miriam's interjections. Tobias tried to smile but that slipped from his face as he looked between Miriam and Hench.

"I'm not joking," she said.

Tobias didn't say anything.

"Anyway," said Rose. "We're getting ready to—"

"Tobias was just leaving," said Hench. The gun was still in his hand.

"I am?"

"But he could—"

"Leave," said Hench, glaring at the young man.

Tobias was taken aback, as was Rose.

"He's my friend, Uncle. He's staying and—"

"Now," said Hench, his eyes never left Tobias.

Tobias looked like he wanted to protest, but he turned and walked down the hall.

"Wait!" yelled Rose, but Tobias kept walking. She turned on Hench. "Why did you do that?"

Hench waited until Tobias disappeared down the stairs. "I hope I'm wrong, but it strikes me as a bit too convenient him showin' up so soon before those men stampede your houses and take William."

"Oh," muttered Miriam.

"That's a lie!" shouted Rose.

"I hope so. But he knew where you two were, which makes me wonder how those men knew where to find you today, Rose?"

"What?" said Miriam sharply.

"He wouldn't do that," said Rose flatly.

"Some men tried to grab her earlier."

"Dear Lord, are you okay?"

"I'm fine," said Rose. "Uncle stopped them."

"Moving forward," said Hench, "neither of you can tell anyone where you're at. These men are still out there looking for you. For all we know they're on their way here right now. So pack quickly. We're leaving."

Hench took them out the back of the hotel. He crossed the alley and tried the first door he came to. It opened. They found themselves in the kitchen of a restaurant. Hench escorted the women through the hot bustling, sizzling room into the dining area, garnering stares from kitchen staff. They kept walking, ignoring the approach of a man who looked to be owner or host. They exited out onto Buffalo Street, crossed over, and entered a tobacco shop. A man looked curiously at the women. Hench showed him his badge.

"We need the back door."

The man looked relieved at that pronouncement and showed them through a back storage room and to a door to the alley. Hench walked them to the end of the alley to Evans Street.

"Stay close to the buildings and just keep walking." The women did as they were told, heading north on Evans, which was away from the Argo Hotel where they'd been staying. Hench stepped out farther into the street and looked back south. When he was sure no one showed an interest in their direction, Hench turned and followed behind the women, keeping a sharp eye out.

Hench retrieved Speck and they continued to the Bay City House hotel on 4th Street. Hench took the room across the hall from the women. After dropping his saddlebags and bedroll next to the bed, removing his worn black leather chaps and crusty tan duster, he made sure his Spencer Carbine lever-action repeater was fully loaded and took it with him across the hall and knocked on Rose and Miriam's door. He wasn't going anywhere without it—he wanted whoever was after the Thompsons to see him bristling.

Rose answered. Hench stepped into the room and shut and locked the door behind him. "This door stays locked at all times."

Rose nodded and Miriam ignored him, but he knew she'd heard him and she wasn't stupid.

"I need you both to think about what these men could possibly be after. They tore up both houses. Even the yards."

Rose shrugged. "We don't have anything they could want. Certainly nothing buried in the yard."

Hench stared at Miriam until she finally said, "I can't think of anything. We aren't dirt poor, but we certainly don't have anything much of value, except the houses themselves. Though they can't be worth much now."

"Can you think of anything leadin' up to this?

Anyone snoopin' 'round or askin' questions about the houses? Anything odd at all?"

"It's not Tobias, if that's what you're thinking."

She liked him a lot, but Hench couldn't afford to tread carefully where the young man was concerned. Whoever was behind this was too dangerous and powerful, paying off police and willing to stage a kidnapping in the middle of a street in broad daylight. "Has Tobias asked any strange questions? About the houses or about the family?"

"It's not him!"

"Rose!" said Miriam. "You have to at least consider it. Your father is missing, he might even be—" her voice faded and tears glistened in her eyes.

Rose's defiance collapsed as tears spilled from her own eyes. "I—I went looking for Father yesterday."

"What?" said Miriam.

"When you were napping. I checked hospitals and—and the morgues. Where could he be?"

Hench scratched at his beard. "If I were to wager, I'd

say he's still alive. These men are lookin' for somethin' and they haven't found it yet."

"How do you know they haven't found it?" asked Miriam.

Rose looked hopeful. "Because they tried to kidnap me. If they'd found it, why do that?"

Hench nodded but didn't mention that perhaps the men killed William without getting the answer they wanted and that's why they went after Rose. "Has William done anything recently that's been secretive or different than usual?"

The women looked at each other, but they both shrugged. Rose said, "No. But remember they went after Grandma first, not Father."

Hench looked at Miriam. "Did they try to take you? Or were they only interested in the house?"

"Oh, they wanted to take me, all right. I was in the front room sitting by the fireplace when they broke down the door. There were four of them. Scared the bejesus out of me.

"Well, I jumped up, of course, and one of them grabbed me and they talked about tying me up and taking me with them. One of them said that wouldn't be necessary if they found it. Never said what 'it' was. Then they talked about how they would search the house.

"So the other three walked around—looked around. The man holding me was far more interested in what his friends were doing, not paying attention to me. I grabbed the fireplace poker and swung it at his head. Hit him. It didn't do much because I was standing right next to him, he still had a hand on me. But he let go and then I could give it a good swing. Knocked him to the ground." Miriam's face shined with pride. "The door was still open—hell, they practically knocked it off its hinges— and I ran to William and Rose's two blocks over like the Devil was after me."

"Did you recognize any of the men?"

Miriam gave him a look like he was an idiot. "Don't you think I'd have said something if I knew who they were?"

"They could have worn bandanas over their face."

"They didn't."

"Which means they didn't care if you recognized them or not."

"So?"

Rose said softly, "It means they were going to kill you, Grandma. And Father and me, too. So Father might—"

"It's a possibility," said Hench. "But I'd bet on him still being alive, at least until they find what they're looking for, which means we have to find it first. It must have a lot of value or why go through all this trouble? And it's small enough that it could be hidden in a wall or under floorboards."

"But it might not be one thing, right? Maybe it's a lot of little things."

Miriam screwed up her face. "What, a buried treasure? Who the hell would think we had buried treasure hidden in our house? Don't they think we'd have spent it and moved into better houses?"

"They might not know what to think," said Hench.

"But it is curious. If you're up for it, Miriam, I'd like to go to your house tomorrow morning and have you look around. See if anything's missing. Or if what they tore up brings to mind anything."

CHAPTER SIX

1863

Twenty years earlier…

Vincent knocked on the door of the house. It was in the Five Points neighborhood to the northeast of downtown Denver City on Curtis Street. It was dusk, but a light glowed within the single front window. A small horse-drawn wagon moved along the dirt street. Vincent's horse was tied to a post just behind him.

An attractive woman answered the door. Vincent removed his black flat-top derby and bowed his head.

"Ma'am, could I inquire as to whether Randall is home this evening?"

"Sure, he's here. Please come in. Who may I say is calling?" She opened the door and Vincent stepped into the aroma of biscuits and fried chicken.

"Vincent Edwards."

She shut the door behind him and motioned to a chair in the front room and she disappeared through a doorway. Less than a minute later Randall Thompson came through the doorway smiling. "Vincent! What a pleasure to see you. I heard you'd moved out to this part of the country."

Vincent stood and shook his old friend's hand. "Indeed. I like the prospects of this little metropolitan oasis at the foot of the Rocky Mountains."

"Metropolitan?" said Randall with a smile. "That's being generous."

"Give it time, my friend. You'll see. I even opened a saloon over in Denver City called the Cherokee House."

"I think I've seen it. I'll be sure to stop by now that I

know you're the proprietor."

"Please do."

"So, what brings you all the way to the outskirts?" Randall moved to the other chair in the front room, both of which faced a small fireplace. The men sat.

A cozy little home, if Vincent were to be charitable with a description. "Was that your wife?"

Randall looked toward the doorway. "Yes. That's Miriam. We met in Kansas. Decided to move farther West for new opportunities."

"I'm glad to hear that. My visit is all about opportunity. You see, I require someone both trustworthy and with a particular talent—which describes you, my friend."

"Talent?"

"I require your expertise in the smelting and refining of ores. Gold in particular."

Randall raised an eyebrow. "You have some raw gold?"

Vincent looked sideways at Randall. He knew the

man wasn't a stickler for the law, but this enterprise would be further outside the law than the man might be comfortable with. He wasn't sure Randall would go in for it. "Let's say I have access to gold. Most likely dust." He leaned toward Randall and said in a low tone. "I feel confident I can acquire a couple pounds of gold and would like it purified and transmogrified for easier liquidity."

Randall peered at him for a couple of moments and Vincent knew he was weighing his next words. "And would your acquirement of this gold be legal?"

Vincent shrugged. Randall sat back in his chair and pursed his lips, his eyes moving around the small house.

"How many pounds?"

"Honestly, I cannot promise a figure, but I would not consider this opportunity if I did not feel it was worth the effort. And the risk."

"How difficult will it be—"

Voices from the back of the house came closer. Randall smiled as a young man and woman came through the doorway with Miriam behind them. It appeared that they were discussing a job opportunity for the young man. Randall and Vincent stood.

Randall said, "Vincent, this is my son William and his wife Prudence. Miriam you just met."

William looked like a younger slightly heavier-set version of Randall. The young man held out his hand and Vincent took it. Nice strong grip. He nodded to Prudence and Miriam, who both smiled.

"We're discussing future possibilities," said Miriam. "William has been offered a favorable position as a clerk."

Randall beamed. "They offered you the position."

"Yes, sir. I start next week."

Randall nodded. "Very proud, son. Very proud. Glad you could get out of the brewery."

Prudence nodded. "I will not miss the smell of hops in his clothes."

"That goes for me, as well," said William. He looked at his father and his smile faltered. "Of course, there's nothing wrong with the smell."

Randall continued to smile and shook his head. "I didn't want you working in the brewery the rest of your life. I'm very happy for you both."

Miriam said, her smile somewhat sad, "They're talking of renting a room in a boarding house."

Vincent saw the look between Miriam and Randall.

"Well," said Randall. "Let's discuss. It would be good for you to stay here to save up your money. Maybe in a year or two you could afford a house."

William and Miriam smiled, but Prudence looked doubtful—she was ready to get out from under the in-laws. Vincent was glad he was single as he watched the nuances of the relationships that were complicated and compounded by a license. It made him shudder—on the inside. On the outside, he smiled congenially.

"We'll talk," said Randall. "Speaking of which, Vincent and I still have to finish our conversation."

Miriam and the young couple said their goodbyes and disappeared into the back of the house.

"Nice family," said Vincent, trying to sound sincere.

"Thank you." Randall walked to the fireplace then turned back, his voice lowered. "So how difficult will it be to get the gold?"

"It should not be difficult at all. We walk in light of foot and we walk out quite a bit heavier."

"We?"

"The two of us could carry more gold than myself alone."

Randall nodded and was silent for several moments. Finally, he said, "What quality of gold are we talking about?"

He was interested. "I've been told its gold dust from Pikes Peak."

"And someone has excess dust just lying around?"

"As it were. Shall I explain?" Vincent drew closer.

Randall looked him in the eye as if studying him. Vincent told him about the Clark and Gruber mint shutting down and moving. About a room brimming with dust.

"And this guard who gave you the information. Is *he* trustworthy?"

Vincent shrugged. "I wouldn't wager my life on the man, but I would be willing to let him hold a door open for us as we carry gold from the premises."

"And when would this venture begin?"

"Soon, as the move begins shortly."

"And where would I refine?"

"I have a storage room in the basement of the Cherokee that is being cleared out as we speak. If you know where we can purchase the equipment you need, we're in business."

Randall pursed his lips and sucked in a deep breath through his nose before holding out his hand. "We're in business."

CHAPTER SEVEN

1884

Present day...

Vincent stood on the small balcony that overlooked the gambling floor and bar of the Palace. Behind him was his office, below and behind him was the Palace Theatre. Above were three floors of hotel rooms. So much bigger than the Cherokee House of twenty years ago.

"Excuse me, sir?"

Vincent turned to his secretary Owen.

"The mayor wants to talk to you."

"About?"

Owen gave a slight shrug. "Best guess is the public works law you're sponsoring in the council. Wants to make sure some of his important constituents are well represented when contracts are handed out."

Vincent nodded. "Very well."

Owen looked down at a notebook open in his hands. "You're free tomorrow morning at 10:30."

"No. Make him wait a few days."

"Thursday?"

Vincent nodded and Owen scribbled.

"When is the next city council meeting?"

Owen said, "Next Tuesday at the Field House. Ten in the morning."

"Send Daniel in."

Owen left and a few moments later, Daniel appeared on the balcony. He wasn't any taller than Vincent but the man had an imposing presence about him. He was obviously quite sturdy beneath his tailored suit and there was an ominous cast to his face, which Vincent knew was well founded.

"Find out anything about Hench?"

Daniel nodded. "Terrance Hench. Colorado Ranger for over twenty years. And was, once upon a time, William Thompson's brother-in-law. Hench's wife died back in 1868 and the ranger took to trails after that, coming back to Denver infrequently."

"Reputation?"

"No one I talked to would want to cross the man."

"And since he's here for family," said Vincent, "or ex-family, as it were, I would be quite surprised if I could pay him off. Okay then. We still have someone watching the Thompson residences?"

"Yes, sir."

"If the ranger goes by again, track him and have some of our best men take care of him. I don't want him found."

"And the women?"

"Same as before—abduct and take them to the house."

CHAPTER EIGHT

Hench made them walk in a circuitous route to Miriam's house. Two blocks away, he had the women wait within the shadow of a small group of spruce trees on an empty lot. Hench approached the house from behind. He wasn't certain they'd be watching the house, but he would be cautious nonetheless.

No one looked out-of-place in the alley. There were a couple of men in the backyard of a house down from Miriam's huffing and puffing over a stubborn tree stump. A man and woman were in another yard tending to chickens. Hench stopped in the alley and watched the house. He didn't see any movement inside. Cocking the hammer of his Spencer Carbine, he approached the back door. He opened it a crack and pushed it open with his foot. He didn't see anyone.

The back door opened to a narrow set of four steps leading up into the kitchen and a full set of stone steps leading down into the dugout basement. Hench stepped lightly up into the kitchen. From here he could see through to the small dining room and part of the front room. He stopped and listened. He didn't hear anyone in the house. He moved forward and a quick search revealed the house was empty.

He retrieved the women. Miriam looked sick as she walked through the torn-up backyard and into the house itself. She made little moaning noises as she proceeded farther into the house. They had to watch where they walked as strips of floorboards were torn up. The entire contents of cupboards and closets were strewn across floors. The beds in the two small bedrooms were overturned, the mattresses slashed. The soft moans turned to quiet sobs. She returned to the kitchen. "Who would do this?"

Hench stood in the dining room. Rose and Miriam were in the kitchen.

"Is anything missing, Grandma?"

She shook her head. "Nothing."

She bent and picked up a round white-enameled burner plate and set it back into one of the round openings of the cast-iron stovetop. The stove was covered in ash, but it was still a beautiful stove and oven. There was the black cast iron, but there were white-enameled parts: all four burner plates, the oven door, the broiler door, the feed door, and the backsplash. The contrast between the black iron and the white enamel was attractive. Gloria had dropped more than a few hints, as in asking Hench directly if they could buy a similar stove and oven someday. That day never came.

The ransackers had pulled apart the metal chimney and the stove top. What remained of the floor of the kitchen was covered in soot. Hench assumed the only reason the stove and oven still stood was because it was too heavy to turn over or tear apart easily. Rose picked up two other burner plates and set them into the stove. Hench didn't see the fourth plate.

Miriam ran her hand along the top of the stove. "At least they didn't destroy this. It was the last thing your grandfather bought me before he disappeared."

It was assumed that Randall Thompson had perished in the great downtown fire of '63. They never found his remains. Hench and other Colorado Rangers stationed in Denver helped with the search and rescue after the fire. Everyone was shocked that nobody else disappeared that night. No remains—other than livestock—were found. No one other than Miriam reported anyone missing.

In the dining room where Hench stood, looking at the destruction, he wondered what the men had hoped to find? Something caught his eye in the dark recess of a pulled-up floorboard. He picked up the fourth white burner plate. It was about ten inches across and weighed at least six pounds. He returned it to the stove.

"Let's go."

Heading back to the hotel, Hench had them take a different route. Four blocks away he took them through shops and restaurants, going from front door to back door, through alleys. A few shop owners squawked, but Hench didn't care. This route would take them to the back entrance of the hotel.

Two blocks away, Hench stopped in an alley. "You two go on ahead and enter the hotel through the back. I'm going to wait here for a bit and see if we have anyone following us."

The women continued and Hench moved farther down the alley and waited. It took the man fifteen minutes to come through the door, no doubt asking store owners if a small group of people had come through. The man looked at the doors across the alley, starting on his left. When he turned to look at the doors on his right he saw Hench, who stood patiently waiting to be seen. He had his carbine down at his waist, but it was pointed at the man, who jumped in surprise. He started to reach for his revolver and Hench cocked the carbine. The man froze.

Hench said, "Who hired you?"

The man hesitated, then said, "I don't know what you're talking about."

Hench fired the carbine. The report was loud and echoed in the alley between brick walls. The bullet hit the bricks behind the man. The man ducked and covered his head, as though that would stop a bullet. The ranger levered and cocked the carbine.

The man yelled, "Daniel! His name is Daniel."

"Look at me."

The man stood a little straighter but seemed afraid to stand fully upright.

"Daniel who?"

"I—I swear I don't know. Just called himself Daniel. Hired me and some other men."

"Take me to him."

"He comes to us. I got no idea how to find him."

"Horseshit." Hench fired again, levered, and cocked. "Next one goes in your leg."

"I ain't lying. I swear."

Hench raised the carbine to his shoulder and aimed at the man's thigh.

"No!" The man turned and ran. Hench decided to shoot him in an easier target. The bullet hit his left butt cheek. The man screamed and dropped to the ground, clawing at his ass.

Hench walked up to him. "Shut up."

The man was yelling incoherent things.

Hench pointed the rifle between the man's legs. "Shut up."

The man quieted down with only occasional groans, his face stretched in a terrible grimace. After several moments of Hench standing there, his carbine aimed at the man's groin, the man finally said, "We go to the Navarre saloon and leave a message with the bartender. He gets word to Daniel who then comes and sees us.

That's the only way we can contact him."

"And where is William Thompson being held?"

"Who?"

Hench kicked the man in the face. Blood poured from his nose.

"Where's the man who was kidnapped four nights ago?"

"He's—he's in a house over by the creek."

"Cherry Creek?"

The man nodded, turning slightly to let the blood drain from his mashed nose. "If that's the creek. I ain't from Denver. I think it's Arapahoe between 13th and 14th. Red brick house. Middle of the block."

Hench reloaded his carbine, removing the magazine tube from the butt stock and slipping in three cartridges, before he headed to the house. The man might be lying, but he'd find out soon enough. He'd thought about waiting until night when he could more easily sneak up on the house, but he wasn't going to kill the man in the alley in cold blood, and he wasn't about to drag him to jail. That meant going to the house now before the man was found and could warn anyone.

All the houses along the block were made of red brick as were many houses in Denver because of the large amount of red clay in the soil. The man said the middle of the block, but that could mean a couple of houses. He couldn't just go up and knock. But he had to get up close and see what he could see.

CHAPTER NINE

1863

Twenty years earlier...

Randall approached the front of the large building at the corner of G Street and McGaa Street. A sign spanned the top of the building: BANK & MINT. Below that, above four white columns, was another sign: CLARK, GRUBER & Co.

It was hard to breathe. He'd done some dishonest things in his life—a few petty things here and there—this was so far beyond any of that. If they got caught it would mean years in prison. He shivered despite the warmth of the night. His hands were ice cold.

"You ready?"

Randall jumped and he would have cried out, but his mouth wouldn't work. His heart thundered in his chest. After a couple of moments, he said, "By jinks, you scared the ghost out of me."

"Let's hope not literally," said Vincent.

The man smiled! He didn't look nervous in the least. Randall realized this was fun for him.

"Shall we?"

Randall followed Vincent to F Street, where they turned down the alley behind the mint. They moved along the dirt about twenty yards and stopped in the deep shadows where they could see the loading bay and a smaller side door at the back of the building.

They didn't wait long before the side door opened and Courtney stuck his head out, looking in both directions. Randall forced himself to move into the moonlight. It took three tries to emit a low whistle, his lips felt like blocks of wood. Courtney waved back.

Vincent walked quickly past Randall, who had to convince his legs it was okay to move. When they reached the mint, Randall felt his heart trying to crawl up his throat. He looked up and down the alley. All was quiet. Courtney held the door open for them. Vincent went past and Randall took a deep breath and followed. No turning back now.

Courtney shut the solid metal door. He looked as nervous as Randall felt.

"We gotta call this off," he said, his eyes moving wildly like a scared horse.

Vincent tipped his head slightly. "And why would that be?"

"The Clarks hired Pinkertons to help with the move. We found out today. Sweet Josephine, they could show up any minute."

Vincent nodded. "Then best we hurry."

"No, seriously," said Courtney, swallowing hard. "They might be on their way here right now."

Randall stepped back as Vincent pulled out a silver revolver and pointed it at Courtney's head. "Take us to the gold."

Courtney's legs wobbled and Randall thought he heard the man whimper, but the young man moved off down a hallway. Vincent followed behind and Randall shook his head, cursing himself for getting involved in something this dangerous.

Courtney practically ran down the hall as if the Pinkertons were pounding on the door behind them. Oil lamps stuck in wall sconces every ten yards lit the way. They turned a corner and Courtney stopped at the first closed door. "Some of it's in there. The room's got gold dust from Pikes Peak."

"Unlock it," said Vincent.

Courtney grimaced but fished through the dozen or so keys on his keyring. He unlocked and pulled the door open. Vincent put his revolver away, but paused, looking at something on the floor. The man bent down and came up with a small gold coin.

He smiled at Randall. "Our good luck piece," he said, holding it up between his forefinger and thumb.

It was a twenty-dollar gold coin. Vincent pocketed it and entered the room. Randall stopped in the doorway behind him, his eyes going wide. There were haphazard stacks of bags full of gold. There was little order to the room, except that along one wall were small two-foot square wood crates that he assumed were full of those same bags. The lust overcame his fear. He wanted that gold.

It was dim inside, but the light from the hallway provided enough to see by. "You okay with dust?" asked Vincent.

Randall nodded before realizing Vincent wasn't looking at him. "Gold dust is fine," he said, his voice calm and even. His heart still beat fast, but now it beat with excitement and desire.

Vincent went to one of the crates. He picked up a side and then set it back down. Then he lifted one of the bags and nodded. "Randall, grab two bags." Vincent bent and grabbed another bag.

Randall picked up two bags close to the door. "About twenty-five pounds each?"

"Feels like," said Vincent.

Randall did the math in his head: one hundred pounds of gold was worth around $40,000—maybe $45,000. He made less than $900 a year at the brewery. The bags suddenly felt feather light.

"You know what? I could carry at least a hundred pounds if you load me up."

Vincent raised an eyebrow and grinned, picking up a bag and laying it sideways in the crook of Randall's arms. With the third bag set in his arms Randall wondered if a hundred pounds was overly optimistic, but he figured he could bull through it. The fourth bag caused his arms to ache almost immediately.

"Okay, we gotta hurry. Not sure how long I can hold them like this."

"Courtney, get your arse in here, if you please," said Vincent.

The young man, looking pale, appeared at the door. "You gotta hurry!"

"If you please, Courtney."

Reluctantly, the guard stepped into the room.

"Stack four bags in my arms."

"We don't have time for that!"

"You are the one wasting time. Step to it!" Vincent's voice became stern and full of threat.

Courtney stacked the bags. Randall and Vincent lumbered out of the room and the guard locked it up behind them. Then Courtney looked down the hall. "Did you hear that?"

Randall shook his head, all he heard was the sound of his own inner voice contemplating what he'd do with his share. Vincent, however, nodded. "Move it," he whispered.

They moved around the corner and down the hall as fast as their legs would carry them. Randall was afraid to go much faster without stumbling and losing his load. It wasn't that a hundred pounds was heavy—not that it was exactly light, either—but it was the awkward way they had to carry it, with their elbows and forearms together. His arms were not happy.

Behind them, Courtney kept muttering, "Goddammit," over and over.

Randall got scared again. "What is it?"

"Someone's coming this way," said Vincent, his voice tighter than it had been before, but still not sounding scared.

Then Randall heard it. Men's voices, the sound of several pairs of boots walking in their direction over the stone floor. Randall made himself move a little more quickly and nearly tripped. Courtney hurried past them and opened the heavy outside door. Randall was happy to be outside. Courtney then shut the door behind them.

"Lock the door, Courtney!" whispered Vincent.

The guard struggled with the keys but managed to get the correct one into the lock and turn it only a moment before someone pounded on the other side. Vincent awkwardly crouched and lowered his arms and let the four heavy bags slide and roll off his arms into the dirt of the alley.

When Courtney turned toward him from the door, Vincent laid him out with a wallop to his face. After Courtney collapsed to the ground, Vincent leaned over him and struck him hard in the face two more times. Vincent stepped back a couple of feet, swung his right foot back, and then he lunged forward, kicking the guard hard in the side.

Vincent knelt next to Courtney. "You were overpowered by two strangers. Got that?"

Courtney moaned and sucked in air, but he nodded. Vincent took the keyring and flung it into the darkness of the alley.

"I can't hold these too much longer," said Randall.

"Go! I'll catch up." Vincent dragged Courtney in front of the door, then he tried to pick up the bags of gold dust by himself. Randall walked backward, watching him, curious as to how he was going to get all four bags. He couldn't. He got two bags onto his arms, but the third one wouldn't cooperate in the least.

"Drag them," said Randall.

Vincent clutched two bags in each hand and started walking backward, dragging the four bags and leaving stark furrows in the dirt. Randall turned around and moved more quickly. His arms shook from the stress and pain of carrying the bags, though a lot of that might have been the fear that had returned.

"Dammit!"

Randall turned back around. One of the furrows glittered in the moonlight. A bag had ruptured. Vincent let go of it. With one bag in that hand, he managed to scoop up the other two and still hold on to the third. His face was set in a grimace and was slick with sweat. Randall doubted he looked any better.

Randall's heart thundered again, the weight causing him to sway and nearly lose his balance. But he turned, righted himself, and moved forward, though it was almost impossible to breathe. At the end of the alley, Randall turned right, but Vincent hissed at him. Vincent went left to a small two-seater buggy and set the gold on the floor of the riding compartment.

Randall stared, unmoving. "But the Cherokee is just a block away."

"We can't go directly there. Please do hurry." Vincent stretched out his arms and waved them in the air.

Randall staggered forward, the gold feeling like a ton. He was relieved to drop them next to Vincent's and scramble up on the buggy's bench. He waved his arms to stretch them out. Vincent untied the single horse from a post and climbed up next to Randall, flicking the reins. The horse cantered off down the dirt street as Randall turned to watch the alley.

"For God's sake put a hand over your face."

"What?"

"Do it!"

Randall covered his face, looking through his fingers as three men came running out of the alley looking in all directions. One of them exclaimed, "There!" and the other two turned. They looked right at Randall and he nearly ducked back around before he remembered he was covering his face.

"Are they following us?"

"They've turned and run back into the alley."

CHAPTER TEN

1884

Present day…

Hench observed the houses in the middle of the block. Was William Thompson even in one of them? The man he'd shot in the alley could have lied. Didn't matter. He had to make sure. He removed three houses from his list of possibles. Their curtains or shades were open—these men would have them drawn. That left two houses that were somewhat in the middle of the block.

He went up to a house two down from one of the

possible ones. An older woman gaped at him from her front window, her eyes fixed on the Spencer Carbine in his hands. Hench tapped at his silver star a few times before her gaze finally lifted to see it. She disappeared and a moment later locks on the front door rattled.

The woman finally got her locks solved and the door opened. "You the law?"

"Yes, ma'am."

"It's about time. Are you here to do something about them boys in that house?"

Hench got interested. "Which house would that be?"

She waved down the street. "Three houses down. Those boys come and go all day and all night. Sometimes they sit out back and drink and talk, interfering with our peaceful habitation. You need to have a good talking with them. Get them to be more considerate of their neighbors."

"Are they a family?"

She was thoughtful for a moment. "Don't think so. They's all about the same age, so couldn't be brothers.

And there ain't been no women that I seen."

"Have they lived in that house for long?"

"Sake's no. Moved in maybe two weeks ago."

"Have you talked to any of them?"

"I wouldn't call it talking, exactly. If they's being too loud at night I'll go out back and yell their way. Tell them to be respectful and all."

Hench walked toward the street and beckoned the woman to follow. "Could you point out which house?"

She sighed like Hench was an idiot. "That one right there."

"With the curtains drawn?"

She nodded. "That's the one. And that's another thing. Them curtains is always drawn. That's just not—" she seemed at a loss for the word.

"Respectful?"

She glared at him. "You just do your job, lawman!" She stomped back to her house and slammed the door, peering back out her front window at him. The ranger tipped his hat to her and then walked by the side of her house to the backyard. There he moved cautiously toward the house she'd pointed at.

"What the hell you doing back here?" she yelled from her back porch.

Hench wondered what she'd do if he fired a warning shot her way. If she yelled again he'd let her know that *she* wasn't being respectful.

A man about Hench's age appeared on the back porch of the house next door to the one in question. He scowled at Hench and opened his mouth to say something. Hench put a finger to his lips and moved closer. He said in a low voice, "You see anyone come or go lately from that house?"

"You here about them?"

Hench nodded.

"Well," he pursed his lips for a moment. "Haven't seen anyone in at least an hour, but I also haven't been paying it any particular attention. When I do see them, it seems like it's just whenever. No set times, seems to me. I haven't seen them leave the house at the same time in the morning or get home at the same time in the evening, like they don't have regular jobs. They just come and go whenever. I've tried talking with some of them, but they like to keep to themselves."

"Do you know how many there are?"

He scratched at his nearly bald head. "Oh, well, let's see. I've seen at least four different men. Maybe five?"

"And do you know if they're all home right now?"

The man shrugged. "I seen two of them leave about an hour ago, but they could have returned and I didn't see them. What'd they do?"

"Maybe nothin'. Just checkin' on 'em. But I'd stay inside for a bit if I was you."

That seemed to interest the man, but he stepped back inside. There were waist-high shrubs hugging the corner of the man's house. Hench crouched behind them and looked next door. It was quiet. There were two windows, curtains drawn, and a door facing the backyard. On the side of the house were two more windows. The second floor held a mirror-image of the windows along the first floor. One of the upstairs windows facing the back was open, the curtains doing a slow dance from a light breeze.

Would they be watching out the back? Would they be watching at all or would they be thinking no one would know about the house let alone what was in it? Even still, the men inside would be armed. And even if they weren't expecting someone snooping around they would be on edge. He found that men, even men used to doing bad things, couldn't relax when they were in the midst of their illegal activity. It gnawed at their nerves like a dog gnawing at a bone.

Hench jogged from the shrubs up to the corner of the house where he hoped William was interred. He waited several moments, listening hard. All he heard was a dog barking down the block and the water in Cherry Creek burbling close by. The creek was about thirty yards away, marked by tall cottonwoods and elm growing along its banks.

Hench moved to the closest window at the back of the house. He removed his hat and tried to peer between curtains without luck. He went to the back door and ever so slowly, turned the knob. A push and a pull did no go. It was locked. He continued to the next window, but still couldn't see in. He backed away from the house a few feet and craned at the open window on the second floor.

With a sigh, he moved back to the neighbor's house and knocked softly on the back door. The bald man opened it. "Can't get in?"

"Do you have a ladder that can reach the window on the second floor?"

The man nodded. "Around the other side."

The ladder lay on the ground against the side wall. It was a twelve-foot wood ladder. He looked down at his carbine. It just wasn't prudent to carry it and the ladder. He leaned it against the wall, then balanced the ladder in one hand and pulled out and cocked a black Schofield revolver in the other.

He headed back knowing he was very foolish to risk being in the open carrying a stupid ladder. But he didn't want to kick down the door and charge in. They might have a standing order to kill their prisoner if it seemed like they were being raided. If he could sneak in and find William without alerting them, that would be best.

At the house, he set the ladder down and kneeled in the grass and listened. Still nothing from the house. He watched the two first floor back windows, but saw no movement—no one furtively pushing a corner of a drape aside to peek outside. Well, stupid or not, he holstered his revolver, stood, and carefully set the ladder against the house. He moved quietly up the ladder and paused beneath the window. He pulled out his revolver again and rose to see inside the room. A man stood grinning on the other side of the window pointing a revolver at Hench.

"Climb in the window slowly," said the man.

CHAPTER ELEVEN

1863

Twenty years earlier...

"Here we are," said Vincent in the alley behind the Cherokee House.

"Here we are where?" said Randall. There were some crates and trash in the alley. Some of the crates were stacked against the back of the Cherokee on either side of a door.

Vincent stepped between the crates. "You're smelting room or refining room, whatever you call it." There was the sound of metal on metal and then Vincent stepped back, pulling open a heavy door.

The door opened into the basement of the Cherokee. An oil lamp or two were lit below.

"I replaced the old wood door for better security. This is where we used to store deliveries with a dumbwaiter inside to carry it to the saloon. Go on down."

Randall stepped down the flight of stairs. It was a large basement room, the walls and floor made of smooth stone. Above, floorboards creaked beneath numerous boots and the muted roar of people conversing in the saloon. It was almost cold in the basement, but that wouldn't last long once he had the furnace lit and running.

The room held the smelting equipment he needed: the small stone furnace with bellows, a couple of tables, several small crucibles, tongs, heavy gloves, chemicals, and forms for pouring the purified gold into small bars. Against the back wall were the seven bags of gold dust they'd walked, and dragged, out of the mint.

Randall grinned, feeling a bit giddy. "Can't wait to get started."

"Good. How long do you think it'll take you to refine it all?"

Randall frowned and looked at the bags of dust. "It'll take some time. One man, a small furnace."

Vincent nodded. "Then best you get started."

Randall grinned again.

It was dusk when Randall dragged himself home. Miriam stopped pacing the front room when he walked in. He was in trouble.

"When were you going to tell me?"

Randall had no idea how to answer that so he remained quiet. She couldn't have found out about the stolen gold—could she? He shrugged slightly and waited for her to continue.

"How could you quit your job at Zang's without telling me? And where have you been all day?"

Randall was relieved this was only about his old job

at the brewery. But he was still confused. "How did you find out?"

She put her hands on her hips. "I'm not supposed to *find out*! You're supposed to tell me such things."

"It's okay, sweetheart, I got a new job. No need for worry. But how *did* you find out?"

"I was going to surprise you and take you lunch. Well guess who was surprised? And embarrassed! I should not have to find out like that."

Randall shook his head. "Now what's the chance you taking me lunch the day after I quit? I mean, when was the last time you took me lunch?"

She stabbed a finger at him. "Don't you dare put this on me."

Randall held up his hands. "I'm not!"

"So, what's this new job you have?"

"Remember Vincent? He came by a couple of weeks ago? He has some investments in ore mining and he's hired me to refine metals for him. You should know I wouldn't just quit my job without something else lined up. What's for dinner?"

Randall expected her to look relieved, but instead she looked even more concerned. "You're working for Vincent? I don't much care for him. He looks like a slicker. Can you trust him?"

"We're old friends. Of course I can trust him." The words weren't true. When he thought about Vincent, "trustworthy" did not come to mind. But Randall was in control of the refining process. Vincent needed him. It would all work out. "It's okay, Miriam. This is a good job."

She was still angry, but he was pretty sure he'd filed off the worst edges of it. However, he waited for her to either continue her rant or— "Come on, let's eat. I made cabbage soup and biscuits. I didn't know if we'd have money for anything else. Jerusalem crickets, Randall John, how could you let me worry like this?"

Randall smiled and shrugged. "You weren't supposed to find out."

She swatted his arm, but she let him settle it around her waist as they moved into the small dining room.

CHAPTER TWELVE

1884

Present day…

As soon as Hench saw the man with the gun inside the window, he dropped below the frame. Another man came out the back door, a shotgun in his hands. Hench fired at him. The man dove to the side, losing his shotgun in the process as he hit the ground and rolled. This really had been as stupid as he'd feared. They'd been watching him the entire time.

He raised his hand and fired blindly into the room

and was about to start down the ladder, but a loud thump from the room stopped him. The man might be playing 'possum, but Hench would risk it. He fired two more times at the man in the backyard who kept rolling, which was fine by Hench as it was away from the shotgun.

Hench leaned as far as he could to his left and risked looking in the window again. The man was gone. Hench stepped up higher on the ladder. The man was face-down on an area rug, a large ragged hole in his back where the bullet had left his body. Hench holstered his gun and pulled himself inside a moment before lead pellets blew away part of the window frame behind him. The man outside had recovered his shotgun.

Hench picked up the man's gun from the floor of the bedroom, emptied its cylinder of bullets, then tossed it to the side. Footsteps pounded up the stairs. Two men if he had to guess. Hench drew his other revolver and moved quickly to the door. It was half closed. He crouched and flung the door open wide.

Two men rushed around the corner from the stairs. They were shocked to see Hench. The man in front fired before taking the time to aim. Hench fired in return, hitting the man in the shoulder as he tried to dive to the side. That gave Hench a clear view of the man behind. Hench fired two more times. Both men writhed on the ground.

Hench went down the hall and kicked the men's guns out of reach. Then he took the time to crack the top of both of his revolvers and reload. Holstering them, Hench knelt next to the first man who was shot in the shoulder. He pulled him up off the ground, slapping him hard to get his attention. The man grimaced in pain, his eyes wild.

Hench slapped him again and said, "Who else is in the house?" The man didn't respond quickly enough and Hench raised his hand

The man turned his head. "Just us. Just us."

"Give me a number." He looked back through the bedroom and watched the window in case the man with the shotgun came up the ladder.

"Uh. Dang. Uh. Me, Harvey, Jim, and, and, uh, Tom! Four of us. That's all. I swear."

If he was telling the truth, that left just the man with the shotgun. Hench pulled out his revolver and the man tried to pull free of Hench's grasp, but Hench just pulled him in closer and brought the bottom of his fist, and the butt of his gun's grip, down hard on the man's head. The man closed his eyes and stopped squirming. The second man was still writhing in pain. One bullet in his gut, the other in his left bicep. Good chance he wasn't going to live through this. Hench hit him in the head in the same manner. The man went still.

Hench stood up and listened. He didn't hear anyone inside the house. Was the man with the shotgun waiting for him to come down the stairs? The ranger thought about exiting through the window, but he didn't like the idea of being an easy target clinging to the ladder. He'd done that already. He moved to the top of the stairs and tossed down his hat, hoping to set off an itchy trigger finger. No such luck.

The problem with the stairs was that his legs would be exposed as he descended. If it was him, he'd shoot the legs out from under anyone coming down. Then it'd be easy to kill him as he tumbled the rest of the way. Crickets, the ladder outside the window started to sound better.

He frowned and looked back into the bedroom. Maybe the ladder *would* work. He went into the bedroom and grabbed the dead man under his arms and pulled him past his buddies to the top of the stairs. He pulled a revolver and fired twice then heaved the dead man down.

As soon as he heaved, Hench moved quickly—and quietly—back to the window and crawled out, feeling like a foolish ass. He set the inside of his boots against the outside rails of the ladder and used his hands as brakes and slid down. He'd seen a fireman come down a longer ladder than this one. Of course, the fireman wore gloves. The rough wood of the rails tore at his hands, embedding several good-sized splinters into each hand. But he got to the ground fast and drew and cocked both guns.

He ran to the back door. It was ajar and he stood to the side and pushed it open with the barrel of a gun. Right inside was a mudroom and then a hallway leading straight to the front door. The stairs were halfway on the left. The dead man lay in a heap at the bottom. Still no sign of the man with the shotgun. Had he fled? Only one way to find out. Hench stepped inside.

Through the doorway he saw an open room on his right with a large archway. To his left was a closed door and farther on were the stairs and the dead man. Hench doubted the man would be behind a closed door. He'd have to check out the room with the archway first.

He holstered the gun in his right hand and crept close. The ranger crouched low and grabbed the edge of the ornate wood that framed the arch. Getting his weight forward, he pulled hard and dove onto his left side, sliding slightly on the wood floor, pointing his revolver where he thought the man would be standing. There was no one in the room.

The door across the hall creaked opened. Hench turned as the man emerged, shotgun at his shoulder aimed right at Hench. The shotgun went off—

CHAPTER THIRTEEN

1863

Twenty years earlier...

Courtney had a pretty good black eye and a split lip when Vincent saw him next. The two met near a pig farm northeast of downtown. The smell was truly spectacular on that unseasonably warm March evening.

The young man grinned and rubbed his side. "Think you broke a rib."

"I tried to, it helps with the verisimilitude, after all."

Courtney looked confused. "Oh?"

The man was an idiot. "What's Pinkerton doing about the theft?"

Courtney chuckled. "They're not sure there *was* a theft. They got so much stuff to move that even with three different men keeping track of it on long sheets of paper, they don't got any idea what's what. Those three men are always yelling at each other all the time, right?"

"Weren't the Pinkertons curious about your injuries?"

"Sure they were," said Courtney. "But I told them what you said. A couple strangers jumped me. Those three men with their long lists are still trying to figure out if anything's actually been took."

"Taken."

"Yeah."

Vincent nodded. That was very good news to hear. "I assume you're ready to be paid?"

Courtney's good eye lit up then squinted. "Yeah. But, y'know? I didn't think you'd take—taken?—so much gold. I mean, that was two hundred pounds, right? So maybe I was thinking you could pay me a little more.

Right?"

Vincent reached under his jacket and sighed. "Courtney, we had an agreement. It troubles me when a gentleman reneges on his word."

"When he what?"

Vincent pulled out his silver revolver. "When he gets greedy."

Vincent fired three times. He wasn't the best shot, but Courtney was only a few feet away. The young man fell after the third shot. Vincent stood over him, cocked the revolver, and put a bullet in his head. Men moved out of the shadows. Courtney would soon become pig feed.

CHAPTER FOURTEEN

1884

Present day...

Hench flinched, waiting for the lead pellets to tear through his body. But they didn't. He stared at the shotgun in the man's hands. It hadn't gone off. Instead, the man's eyes glassed over and he collapsed to the floor. The shot came from a handgun. Someone else was in the house. Hench rolled farther into the room and up onto his feet, drawing his other gun. Footsteps came down the hallway.

A young man's voice called out, "Don't shoot!"

Hench frowned. "Tobias?"

"Yeah. Can I come around the corner?"

"Slowly. Hands up and empty." What the hell was going on?

Tobias stepped into view, both hands raised. His left hand, however, was not empty. A silver badge in the shape of a shield gleamed dully in it. Hench recognized its design and knew without reading it that it was engraved with: PINKERTON NATIONAL DETECTIVE AGENCY.

"The hell you say," said Hench. "Let's see identification."

Tobias grinned and, slowly, pulled a slim wallet from the front pocket of his wool pants. He flipped it open and pulled out a Pinkerton identification card.

Hench still found it hard to believe and he kept his guns out. "Why are you here?"

Tobias shrugged. "Followed you. I'd been waiting at Miriam's house hoping you all would show up. And sure enough. When you left, I tagged behind the man who followed you. When you fired shots in that alley, it was easy to catch up to you. Then you led me here."

"I'm not sure I'm buyin' what you're sellin', but first we need to look for William."

"You think he's here?"

"I hope he's here. You lead the way. What's inside that door?"

Tobias cautiously poked his head through. "A basement."

"You can pull your gun. Go on down."

Tobias pulled out a nickel-finished Colt Single Action Army—a Peacemaker—and eased down the unfinished wood stairs. Hench appreciated the young man's courage, heading down into an unknown space as he was. Hench let him get most of the way down the stairs before he followed.

There were two lit oil lamps on shelves up against one of the walls. Even with two lamps, the place was dark and foreboding. The walls were stone, the floor was packed dirt, and it was easily ten degrees cooler than the upstairs.

There was just the one room. William was naked on the ground, propped up in a corner. He was almost unrecognizable. One eye was swollen shut, blood smeared across his face, his lips disfigured and split open in several places. His face was covered in bruises and welts ranging from yellow to dark purple. His right ear was gone, a trail of dried blood running from it down over his shoulder. Dark bruising clouded most of his body. One of his hands was curled and caked in blood. Hench suspected one or more of his fingers had gone missing.

Tobias stood slack in front of William and holstered his gun. "Jesus," he said softly.

Hench kept one of his guns out and hurried to William, kneeling next to him. He leaned in close to William's face. "He's breathing. We need to make a stretcher and get him to a hospital."

Tobias said, "Maybe one of the beds? We could—"

"The ladder. It's out back. We'll break it in half, lay a board or two along the rungs. Wrap William in sheets. Let's go."

They stood outside the County Poor House Hospital in the Whitsitt neighborhood. Hench stared at the young man. He still wasn't sure how much to trust him. Even if he was with Pinkerton it didn't mean he was on the Thompsons' side.

Hench said, "Can I assume that you meeting William and Rose was no coincidence?"

Tobias sighed and nodded. "You're right. I was hired by someone here in Denver to dig into the affairs of Vincent Edwards."

"The gangster?"

"Yes, and city councilman."

"Figures." Hench knew the man from when Denver was little more than a mining camp. He had run a saloon out of a tent in those early years before building the Cherokee House, which notoriously was where the fire of 1863 started. People still went back and forth between blaming temperance people and drunk patrons.

"Not that Mr. Edwards is the only local politician working both sides of the aisle, as it were."

"So why Vincent Edwards?"

"The Pinkerton client is hoping for enough information on Mr. Edwards to either get him kicked off the council or kicked into jail. That's all I can say."

Hench nodded. More than likely the client was someone as corrupt as Edwards. "So why William and Rose?"

"To be honest, I have no idea. I started this case nearly four months ago. Got myself hired on as a messenger for Mr. Edwards. Hoped that would get my fingers into the various pies that Mr. Edwards has baking in this town. I've seen enough to know that the man is thoroughly corrupt—as you say, he's a gangster—and I've gathered some evidence for the client. However, with that said, Mr. Edwards is quite adept at keeping a buffer between himself and the actual dirty work. I don't have anything on him that would land him in jail.

"Then about four weeks ago he tells me to try and get close to William and Rose Thompson. I had no idea who they were and I still don't know what Mr. Edwards's interest is with them. He had me rent a room close to the Thompsons and try to get in their good graces. I was successful with that."

"You're going to break Rose's heart."

Tobias looked rattled. "Lord, I hope not! I—I truly care for her."

Tobias told the truth about that or he was quite the actor. "Did Edwards have William kidnapped?"

"I think so. I mean, that's what I figure, but I have no evidence about that. Nothing's been said by those in his hire. If I hadn't met William and Rose I would never have known about his disappearance." Tobias looked sideways at Hench. "Are you going to tell Rose?"

Hench scratched his beard. "Not yet. But I can promise you that if you're toying with her heart or if I find out you had anything to do with William's kidnapping and torture, well, Rose's hurt feelings will be the least of your worries."

"Understood."

Hench doubted the young man understood at all the extent to which Hench would protect the Thompsons, even Miriam.

"So why were the houses ransacked?"

The young man looked slightly ill and didn't say anything.

"Four months with his organization?" said Hench. "How can you know so little of what's goin' on?"

"I also said I did have *some* evidence about his activities, just nothing where it concerns the Thompsons."

"Do better."

"Excuse me?"

"You heard me. Find something about why Edwards is interested in them. Get me something to link Edwards to the Thompsons. I don't want to find out I killed the wrong man."

"Yes, sir."

Hench stared at him for a moment. "Now."

"Oh." Tobias left.

CHAPTER FIFTEEN

1863

Twenty years earlier...

Randall checked his pocket watch. Almost nine o'clock. He turned slowly inside the basement of the Cherokee House. It looked like a lot of men had been there searching the place. Randall held a heavy crowbar he used to make it look like the men had been none too gentle. Satisfied and terrified, he climbed the steps to the door, unlocked it, and moved out quickly into the alley between the two stacks of crates hiding the door on both sides.

He leaned out and looked up and down the alley. It was empty. He turned back to the door and used the crowbar to pry the door open, damaging the door as much as possible. He stood back. It looked like someone broke in.

He shoved both stacks of crates over, dropped the crowbar onto the dirt, and sprinted out of the alley. He'd timed it well. Vincent was a block away walking in his direction. He ran as fast as he could toward the man. He wasn't worried about how to act panicked as he was already there—petrified of what Vincent would do to him if the man ever found out about his ruse.

Vincent saw him coming and stopped, looking perplexed. "What's going—?"

"We were raided!" said Randall, out of breath and bending over to catch it.

Vincent looked past the man, suddenly concerned. "What? The Cherokee House?"

Randall shook his head and stood upright. "They

knew—they knew about the refining room in the basement. They broke down the door."

"How'd you get away?"

"I wasn't down there. Was just returning to the Cherokee when I saw them coming down the alley. I hid and watched. They, they carried stuff out of the basement. I don't know, maybe eight or even a dozen men. They were wearing badges."

Vincent looked confused. "Couldn't be the police. I have them paid off."

Randall spoke carefully. He didn't want to say something that would alert Vincent to his sham. "Yeah, I don't think it was the police. Might'a been Pinkertons. We should probably talk to Courtney and see what he's heard."

Vincent seemed to think for a moment before he nodded. "I'll talk to Courtney."

"Any chance he might have said something?"

"I doubt it. Maybe someone upstairs said something. Mentioned something about the basement."

Randall relaxed a little. Vincent seemed to believe him. "You think one of your own would do that?"

Vincent sighed and started walking. "For the right price. Come on, let's take a look."

Randall didn't move. Vincent stopped after a half-dozen steps and looked back. "Come on."

Randall tried to look concerned. "What if they're still there? Or what if they're watching the alley—see who goes in there?"

Vincent pursed his lips, then shrugged. "They'll be coming to talk to me sooner than later. I own the goddamn building, they'll assume I knew what was going on in its basement. Come on."

Randall followed him. Despite Vincent's own words, the man did slow down as he approached the alley and took a good look around. A lot of men were on the street heading to various saloons. "See anyone?"

Randall shook his head. "Just the usuals."

Vincent stopped at the entrance to the alley. "Door's open."

"They don't know me—I don't think. Want me to look?"

"Good idea."

Randall walked slowly, looking around as if expecting someone to jump out of the shadows at any moment. He hoped he wasn't overdoing it. But he was scared, so he let himself act the way he felt. He stopped at the open door and crouched to look down into the basement.

He stood and walked to the other end of the alley, as if checking it out just to be sure. He returned to the open door and stopped outside again and stood there, pretending to work up his courage. Then he took a deep breath and started down the steps.

He waited in the basement for a couple of moments, then realized it wouldn't take him more than a second to see no one was in there. He hurried back up the steps, back to Vincent.

"It's gone."

"All of it?"

"Looks like. You want to see?"

"Yeah. Let's go."

Vincent walked around the room. He ran his fingertips along the table where the small gold bars had been stacked. Shaking his head, he muttered several curse words. He picked up an overturned lamp that was still lit. He sighed. "We were so close."

He looked up at the wood underflooring to the building above them, then he swung the arm with the lamp, as if he were going to—Randall gasped as Vincent threw the lamp up and away from himself. The lamp exploded against the heavy joists, flames greedily eating the wood.

"What the hell are you doing?" asked Randall.

"Destroying evidence," he said, turning toward Randall, his shiny silver engraved revolver in his hand.

Randall stared wide-eyed as his heart tried to break through his chest. "What—what—"

"It was a good plan, but can't have any witnesses who might want to turn on me later."

The first bullet went through Randall's right cheek. The fear that rushed through him blocked the pain. He charged. The second bullet hit him in the chest. "No." He felt that one and knew he was in trouble as his legs tumbled out from beneath him and he fell forward onto his face. This wasn't happening.

Vincent stopped at the bottom of the stairs to make sure the flames were going to take. He could build another gambling hall—what he didn't want was to get sidetracked with prison. He hoped with Randall dead and the evidence in the basement of the Cherokee House burned to ash, Clark and Gruber wouldn't have a case against him.

The flames spread quickly. He realized the flooring above was soaked with alcohol. He hurried up the steps and to the end of the alley. The light from the flames danced in orange and red colors against the grimy wooden wall opposite the Cherokee. A few minutes later, flames appeared in the basement doorway, climbing the outside wall. He finally heard yells and screams from inside the building. People poured out the back of the building. He assumed the same exodus was happening up front. Vincent walked away.

1884

Present day...

Vincent sat in his office at the Palace thinking about the fire he'd started back in 1863. It spread so quickly. Shocking, really, but not a bad deal in the end. There *was* a wind that night pushing the flames along. He thought he'd stand at the end of the alley and watch his building burn, but within a couple of minutes the buildings around the Cherokee were burning. The flames were so intense that cinder filled the air and the fire jumped streets. Vincent had to leave downtown to get clear of it. By the end, over seventy buildings burned to the ground. And most miraculous, not that he cared at all, no one died in the fire. Vincent's mouth twitched in a smile. Not even Randall, as he died before the fire.

And, honestly, Denver wouldn't be what it was today without that fire. New buildings were built of brick and stone. The city gained a permanence after the cleansing flame wiped out almost all the wooden structures. He knew he'd never be thanked for the fire, since no one knew he'd started the fire and no one ever would, but there should have been a plaque somewhere honoring him. He chuckled at the thought.

CHAPTER SIXTEEN

Hench rode up to a boarding house on Lawrence Street. It was a dusty old building, one of the few left in the city proper that was still made of wood after the fire in '63. He'd been to the boarding house before and made his way through the dilapidated foyer, down the main hall with cracks in the walls, to room 4, and knocked. "Captain, it's Hench."

"Who the hell? Hench? I suppose you can come in."

Hench opened the door. The room smelled strongly of onions. It always did even though Hench never once saw an onion in the room. There was an empty bottle of rye on a chest of drawers. Hench set down a full bottle next to it.

"That don't do me no good over there."

Hench handed Captain the bottle. He was a ragged man in his seventies sitting in a ragged leather chair rife with cracks. The sun-worn face of the man and the worn skin of the leather chair matched perfectly. Captain wore threadbare white long johns buttoned to the top and a pair of blue wool pants held up by red suspenders. There was a large stain of something on the front of his underwear atop his ample gut. His white hair was in its usual disarray on his head and face, his long jutting beard putting Hench's to shame.

Captain took a long pull from the bottle then handed it back to Hench, who did the same before setting it on the chest of drawers.

"Was just ruminatin' on that time we run down Mountain Bill and his gang up toward Leadville. That'd been some hard ridin'."

Hench nodded. "Was that Philip's horse got shot out from under him?"

Captain scowled for a moment. "Thought it was Michael's."

"That's right, we left Michael there for two days before we could come back for him."

"He was a might angry at us for that."

Hench shrugged. "Nothin' we could do. Not until we got Bill and his gang—and that was only 'cause they run out of ammunition."

"We spent a fair number of cartridges ourselves. I surely miss ridin' trails with you boys."

"Well, that's good to hear 'cause I got a job for you. You haven't hocked your shotgun, have you?"

CHAPTER SEVENTEEN

Vincent lived in a Romanesque two-story mansion of roughhewn gray stone with arched windows and an arched front door. A small castle that glared down upon the city proper from its perch on Capitol Hill. A man hustled down the red dusty flagstone walkway from the front door of the mansion to greet the carriage. The sidewalks were the same large rectangular red flagstones as the walkways up to the front doors of each of the mansions in the neighborhood.

All the mansions were recent. The city itself was little

more than twenty years old. Those made rich from mining or by provisioning miners were eagerly building monuments to themselves throughout Capitol Hill.

Jared, the man racing down from the front door, went up to the horses and took hold of a horse collar, holding the horses steady. It was an open carriage with Abraham upfront behind the reins and Daniel beside him. In the back seat, Vincent read through invoices from the Palace that Owen gave him to review and sign. Vincent tamped the invoices into a neat pile and stepped down from the back of the carriage. Abraham and Daniel stepped down from the front seat.

Jared took the reins from Abraham. "Cook says dinner's almost ready."

Vincent nodded absently and started toward the front door while both guards followed, each casting a look around them. Vincent heard a horse canter down the hard-packed dirt of the street but didn't pay attention until his two bodyguards turned. Vincent paused when the horse stopped in front of his mansion. It was one of his messengers. A young man named Tobias, who looked distressed.

He leaned over his horse and talked to Daniel, who nodded a few times. Tobias then moved off back down the street. Vincent couldn't read Daniel's expression— the man was not one for emoting. He approached Vincent.

"One of the men set to tailing the Thompson women and the Colorado Ranger was found with a bullet in his ass and his nose kicked in. The ranger did it."

Vincent sighed. This ranger was quickly becoming too large of a thorn. But Daniel had more. "The ranger found the house where William Thompson was interred."

Vincent shook his head. "William is no longer in our hands?"

Daniel nodded.

"Anyone left alive?"

"Out of the four in the house at the time, two are still alive. One of them isn't expected to live much longer. The other should pull through. You want to talk to him?"

Vincent wanted to tear the man's head off. He was more than a little disappointed by the incompetence of these men. How could four men, within a highly defensible location, have failed him like this? "How did the ranger know where to find Thompson?"

Daniel shrugged. "Best guess is that the man with the bullet in his ass told the ranger during questioning."

Vincent said. "Get what information you can from the surviving men and then get rid of them. Also find out which hospital they took Thompson to and send somebody to get rid of him, as well."

Daniel motioned to Jared, who came over. "Go around to all of the hospitals and find William Thompson."

The man nodded.

Vincent shook his head at all the chaos since finding out about the gold. "I guess I should have left the dead buried."

"Sir?" said Daniel.

"Nothing."

CHAPTER EIGHTEEN

Tobias rode away from Vincent Edwards and his two bodyguards, Daniel and Abraham. It was a huge risk to deliver the information about what Hench had done. Not only did no one in Vincent's organization know about it yet, but he wasn't positive that Edwards had been behind William Thompson's kidnapping. If his guess had been wrong he'd probably be dead. Daniel and Abraham were killers and good at it from the rumors he'd heard. But by the simple delivery of the message, he confirmed his suspicion that Edwards was behind it all.

Now if he could find evidence linking Edwards to the kidnapping, that wouldn't only get Edwards kicked off the Denver City Council, that would get him carted off to prison for quite some time. But that would be some difficult evidence to find. Maybe they could get the men who had survived Hench's attacks to turn on Edwards and provide evidence of his misdeeds at trial. That was worth considering. And why was Edwards interested in William Thompson at all—or rather, what might be hidden in the Thompsons' houses? Would Edwards have a record of something in his office? It was a good place to start with Edwards at home for the time being.

Once Tobias was out of sight of Edwards he spurred his horse into a gallop, heading straight to the Palace. The building took up nearly the entire block and looked palatial with a smooth white granite facade and columns bordering the large front door facing Wasoola Street. Tobias left his horse at the livery stable two blocks away and moved quickly to the entertainment emporium, as Edwards liked to describe it. It was early evening but the crowds were starting to gather. The theatre had a separate entrance around the corner.

Tobias was well-enough known that employees, dressed in striped silk shirts of red and gold and either black pants or puffy black skirts flowing down to the floor, greeted him as he made his way through the bar and gambling hall.

He wasn't afraid of anyone questioning him being there. He moved between various locations controlled by Edwards all the time. As long as no one caught him rummaging through Edwards's office, he had nothing to worry about. He just had to finish before Edwards returned for the evening.

At the back of the large gambling hall was a door marked PRIVATE. Behind it were the stairs leading up to Edwards's office. The guard outside the door, his name was Ernie, smiled and said, "Evenin', Tobias."

Tobias just nodded in return, not wanting to make any impression on the guard whatsoever. The young man entered the door and hurried up the stairs. At the top was a hallway with rooms along its length. Opposite the top of the stairs was the big office of the boss. Edwards's secretary, Owen, had his own office next door to Edwards. Then there was a counting room, a storage room, a private suite decked out with all the amenities for entertaining, including its own opulent bedroom.

Edwards's office door was large, bigger than any of the other doors on the floor, and made of a shining dark mahogany. A forbidding door that was locked, but Tobias had Pinkerton skeleton keys. He could have broken into the office earlier in his investigation, but his original plan was to move conservatively—don't tip his hand and give Edwards any reason to wonder about him. His clients were content to wait many months, if not a year even, for the information they desired as long as it was concrete and would do real damage to the gangster councilman. But Tobias was on a new mission to help and protect the Thompsons. Edwards had to be taken care of now before he could do further harm.

The door opened and he stepped in and locked it

behind him. There'd been a light coming from under Owen's door. He probably should have waited until early in the morning when the Palace was closed and Edwards and his secretary would both be home, but he felt an urgency—aided in no small part by Hench's directive to find information "now."

There was a commanding presence about the man and Tobias felt compelled to oblige him. Though, he had to admit sheepishly, regaining Rose's admiration was foremost in his thoughts rather than the ranger's mandate.

The office was large—almost as much floor space as Miriam Thompson's entire house. It was lined with rich dark woods and adorned with gilded-framed paintings. One wall was a bookcase lined with books but also small expensive-looking knickknacks. Across from the door was a large window overlooking Wasoola Street letting in enough of dusk's gray light for Tobias to see the interior of the office.

To his left was a door leading into Owen's office. He

grabbed a straight-back chair, one of four sitting about the office, and carefully set the top of the chairback under the doorknob to keep Owen from barging in. He took another chair and did the same to the main door, even though he'd locked it. There was one other door, but that led to a balcony that overlooked the bar and gambling hall.

Feeling somewhat secure, Tobias concentrated on the beast of a desk that nearly spanned the width of the office with a large red leather chair crouched behind it. The top of the desk was orderly, as was the office.

Tobias went behind the desk and pulled the red leather chair away quietly so that he had easy access to the drawers. He tried the flat middle drawer first that was directly in front of him. It was locked. The young Pinkerton took out a different set of skeleton keys and got the drawer open in less than a minute.

He pulled it out as far as it would go and scanned the contents that were just as organized as the desk top. The first thing that caught his eye was a beautifully engraved silver revolver with an ivory grip. He began to reach for it, but stopped himself.

He didn't have time to admire a gun. Instead, he grabbed a sheaf of paper and quietly sifted through them. The handwriting was neat and straight. There was nothing related to the Thompsons, however. He pulled correspondence from several envelopes. There was a thump from Owen's office next door. Tobias froze, even held his breath as if that would help. There was no other sound. Tobias went back to work, flipping through an appointment book. There was nothing of interest. The rest of the drawer held new and old dip pens, a small reservoir of pen nibs, several wood-handled stamps, a small pile of matches, and one $20 gold piece.

He picked up the coin. He hadn't seen the type before. On one side was stamped a triangle that he assumed was supposed to be Pikes Peak because the coin read: PIKES PEAK GOLD TWENTY D—with a smaller inscription of DENVER. On the other side was an eagle clutching an olive branch with one foot and arrows with the other.

The writing on this side read: CLARK GRUBER & CO. 1860. He was tempted to pocket the coin just to vex Edwards. But that was childish. Tobias smiled and put the coin into his vest pocket.

He tried one of the bigger side drawers next, but by the third drawer he hadn't found anything and it was getting too dark to see. Should he risk lighting a lamp? He glanced toward the secretary's door. Light still shown beneath it. He had to risk it. If they couldn't find evidence they couldn't arrest Edwards. He took a match from the middle drawer and, lifting the glass chimney, lit one of two oil lamps on the desk.

With the light, he continued going through the remaining drawers. He had yet to find anything. Granted, it was a fast search, but what had he expected, a piece of paper in Edwards's handwriting with a title reading: My plan against the Thompsons?

He was partially through the last drawer, looking through Palace invoices, knowing they were of no value but doing it nonetheless just in case some other paper had slipped in, when the secretary's doorknob turned.

CHAPTER NINETEEN

Hench returned to the hotel room after visiting Captain. It was early evening and both women looked angry and scared when he entered their room.

"Where the hell have you been? You left us hours ago!" yelled Miriam, her eyes aflame.

"Is everything okay?" asked Rose, looking only slightly less aggravated than her grandmother.

He'd been busy during those hours, but he simply said, "I found William."

Both women erupted in joy and questions, moving

close—even Miriam.

Hench held up his hands. "It ain't that rosy. He's been hurt terrible. I took him to the hospital, but he hasn't woke up yet."

Miriam scowled. "You never were one to sugarcoat."

Hench shrugged.

She said, "That's a compliment you horse's ass."

Rose's eyes rimmed with tears. "Take us to him."

Miriam also cried, dabbing at her eyes with a kerchief she pulled from the wrist cuff of her dress.

He said, "We can't stay long. It's too dangerous out there until I get the people who are behind this. If you agree to stay for no more than, let's say an hour, then I'll take you. Agreed?"

Miriam said sternly, "I'll be staying with my son until he's better!"

"I can't leave Father."

Hench said, "Then we don't go. Your choice."

Both women seethed, then in unison they looked at one another and said. "Let's go."

"I need to hear it," said Hench, looking between them.

Miriam looked ready to punch him in the face, but she said through clenched teeth. "Only an hour."

Rose nodded, not looking any happier than Miriam. "Fine. Only an hour."

Hench moved out into the hall, looking both ways, then beckoned for them to follow. They took a cab to the hospital to keep the women hidden from view.

Miriam exclaimed as they pulled up to a side door, "The County Poor House! We aren't *that* poor."

"Closest hospital. And let me warn you again—"

"We know," said Rose. "He's not doing well."

"They beat him badly."

"I still don't get why anyone would do that to William," said Miriam, her voice hitching.

"That's what I plan to find out," said Hench.

"You better."

They entered through the side door. The hospital was a squat building of pale yellow brick. There were only a couple of doors down the long hallway. Through the open doors were large rooms with a dozen or more beds spaced out and lined up against a wall. At least half the beds were occupied. Hench led them up to the second floor, down another hall to a room with a closed door with the painted label: STORAGE. Hench knocked and called out, "It's me."

"Then come in already!" yelled Captain.

Hench opened the door.

Captain sat in his leather chair. He had on the same blue pants but now wore a rumpled button-up shirt with his silver Colorado Ranger star on his chest. A shotgun lay across his lap. Next to him, in a bed covered in white sheets and a white blanket, was William. Miriam pushed past Hench and went to her son's side. She cried and spoke trembling murmurs to him, obviously wanting to hold him but afraid to touch him. Rose went to the other side of the bed.

Hench looked at Captain. "Anything?"

He shook his head. "Quiet as a cemetery. Uh, sorry," he said, looking sideways at the women.

Rose looked over at Hench. "A storeroom?"

"The place doesn't have any private rooms. My commanding officer pulled a few strings and got the hospital to clear space in here for him so it'll be easier to keep him protected."

The room was partially cleared. Next to Captain and his chair were shelves against the wall loaded with various supplies and equipment. But the hospital had done a good job of clearing it out and getting a bed in the room in quick order.

The women then ignored him and Captain as they talked to the unconscious William and comforted each other. Hench was glad as he'd do a terrible job of trying to comfort them. Rose might be grateful for his efforts, but Miriam would be repulsed. Instead, he stayed back by Captain, taking a long pull from the bottle of rye Captain offered him.

"Any leads?" asked Captain.

"No, but I have someone lookin' into a person of interest. I had rangers visit the house where they were keepin' William, but it was cleared out by the time they got there."

CHAPTER TWENTY

Tobias quickly put the invoices back into Vincent Edwards's desk drawer, closed it, then blew out the oil lamp. He heard Owen insert a key into the door's lock and turned it and then jiggle the brass knob. A muffled "Huh?" came from the other side.

Tobias moved quickly to the main door of the office and moved the straight-back chair to where it had been. Then he went to the secretary's door and waited. The key turned again and then more turning of the doorknob and what sounded like a shoulder hitting against the door.

Tobias held the chair firmly in place beneath the doorknob. He had no idea what he would do if the secretary caught him in Edwards's office.

Owen's muffled voice said, "Well, hell."

There were footsteps walking away from the door. Tobias quickly moved the chair from the door and then grabbed the handle without turning it as he looked at the main door. A few seconds later Owen inserted the key into the lock. Tobias opened the secretary's door and slipped through, shutting the door quietly behind him. He moved on tiptoes to the open hallway door and listened. Edwards's door opened and he heard Owen step inside.

Tobias moved into the hall and waited. When Owen opened the door to his own office and grunted, "Huh," the young man moved quickly past the open door of Edwards's office, glancing in to see Owen halfway into his own office. Tobias got to the stairs and went down them as quietly as he could.

Back out in the gambling hall, as he approached the

main doors, Tobias glanced back over his shoulder. Owen was standing on the balcony outside Edwards's office. Tobias couldn't be sure, but it seemed as though the secretary looked at him as he exited the Palace.

Vincent entered his office and frowned. Why was his chair pushed back almost against the wall?

"Owen!"

His secretary opened his office door. "Yes?"

"Were you at my desk?"

The man shook his head. "Is something missing?"

"My chair's out of place. Have the cleaners been in?"

"Not since you left."

Vincent pursed his lips and moved his red leather chair back into position and sat down. Everything on his desk looked undisturbed. He opened his flat center drawer and looked at the contents. Everything was there, but it wasn't quite where it'd been, as though someone carefully looked through the contents and put it back, though not quite getting it right. Then he realized his $20 gold piece was missing.

"Someone's been in my desk." He opened other drawers. It was the same feeling, more than a certainty, that contents weren't quite where they had been before.

Owen frowned. "Strange. Earlier, maybe an hour ago, I tried to come in here through my door but I couldn't. I tried unlocking it, I even put a shoulder to the door, but the door wouldn't budge. I walked around and came in through the hallway door and my door worked fine—it wasn't jammed or anything."

"Did you see anyone up here?"

Owen hesitated.

"What is it?"

"Well, I don't want to get the boy in trouble for something he didn't do, but after I came into your office I went out onto the balcony, which was my intent from the beginning, and I saw Tobias walk across the floor and out the front door. I can't swear to it because I didn't see him actually exit the stairs," Owen motioned to the stairs outside Vincent's office, "but I had the feeling that the stairs are where he came from. Did you send him over here for anything?"

Vincent shook his head. "But that doesn't mean anything—by itself. But it's interesting. He delivered a message to me not too long ago. I had just gotten home for dinner and he came up on us in the street. Told me about William Thompson being rescued from the house."

Owen jerked back. "Someone got William Thompson?"

"Again, interesting. You didn't know, so you're not the one who sent Tobias to tell me. Who else would know about William Thompson and send me a message via Tobias?"

Owen didn't hesitate. "No one. What's Tobias up to?"

"I would like to find that out." He looked back at his desk. "Other than the coin, nothing is missing as far as I can tell with a cursory look."

"Do you want me to go through it and make sure?"

Vincent sighed. "I guess you'd better. I'll be

downstairs. If Tobias comes up here, detain him."

Owen nodded.

CHAPTER TWENTY-ONE

The women were quiet. Somber. Neither spoke on their way back from the hospital. Miriam unlocked and opened the women's hotel room. Hench stopped by his door. "Do you want to rest up a bit before dinner? We'll have it brought up to the room."

Rose sighed, looking as despondent as Miriam. "I could use a little time."

Miriam didn't respond and entered their room. Rose turned to enter but then her face lit up. "Tobias!"

The young man walked toward them from the stairs.

He grinned back at Rose.

She said, "How did you find us?"

Tobias glanced at Hench, who said, "I told him."

Rose looked even more delighted, which caused Hench consternation. He didn't want to hurt his niece. Should he tell her about Tobias? He had no idea how she would react—though waiting would be worse. Right?

Hench pushed that aside. There were more important things to worry about. He looked at Tobias with raised eyebrows. The young man gave a small shrug.

Miriam came back to the open doorway and looked between the two men. "What the hell is going on?"

Hench said, "I had Tobias look into something for me."

Tobias glanced toward Rose then away. He looked like a man resigned to a distasteful fate. "I—I work for the man who had William kidnapped."

Rose's face clouded. "What?"

"You're sure?" asked Hench.

"I'm sure," said Tobias.

Hench spread out his arms to usher them into the women's hotel room. "Let's get out of the hall."

Rose said, "What the hell is going on?"

Hench shut the door. "Tobias is a Pinkerton detective. He was hired to look into the affairs of Vincent Edwards."

"Vincent Edwards?" said Miriam, a strange look on her face. "That's who hurt my son? I'm going to kill him."

Hench paused, curious about the look. "Do you know him?"

"Knew him. I want a gun."

"How did you know him?"

Miriam looked impatient. "He was friends with Randall. Haven't seen him in—well, last time I saw him was shortly before Randall disappeared." Her eyes widened. "And you say he kidnapped William?"

Hench was floored.

Tobias went to Rose. "I'm so sorry. I wanted to tell you earlier but—"

Rose slapped him hard enough that the sound echoed

in the room. Tobias stepped back in shock and pain.

She said, her voice cold. "When did you know Vincent Edwards kidnapped my father?"

"I—I just found out an hour or two ago. I swear. I wouldn't do anything to hurt you or your father!"

"Except lie to us."

Hench said, "He does care for you, Rose."

Rose glared at him, shutting him up, before returning her severe gaze to Tobias. "Start explaining."

Tobias looked like an animal caught in a trap.

"Well?"

"Tell her everything," said Hench.

"Shut up, Uncle, I don't need your help."

"I do care for you," said Tobias.

Rose glared, not saying anything.

"I was hired by a party to investigate Vincent Edwards," said Tobias. "I've been doing that for a couple of months now."

"Then how could you not know about my father?" Rose's eyes flashed with such intensity that Tobias grimaced against it. Miriam stepped closer, as well. The young man was hemmed in. But he stood tall, even if his face was flushed.

"Edwards never talked about your father. I had no idea."

"Enough of this twaddle," said Miriam. Then she looked at Hench. "I want to know where Vincent Edwards lives and I want you to give me a gun."

Rose said, "How could you work for that man and not know about Father? You didn't have some inkling of a suspicion?"

Tobias looked stricken. Rose turned away.

The young man said, "Yes, I did wonder if Edwards was involved in William's disappearance and, please believe me, I tried to find information. In fact, I just now searched Mr. Edwards's office at the Palace. Went through everything in his desk. There's nothing there to tie him to the kidnapping." Tobias pulled something small and dull from his vest pocket. A gold coin. He idly moved it between his fingers.

Hench said. "What about other crimes?"

Tobias shook head. "Nothing. If he has papers, something connecting him to corruption or crimes, he has them somewhere else."

"We still have no idea what Edwards is up to. Miriam, tell us about Vincent Edwards's and Randall's friendship."

Miriam looked like she wasn't going to say another word, but then finally, "I only met Vincent once maybe twice. He came over to the house to talk to Randall about working for him."

"What kind of job?"

She didn't answer for a couple of moments before shrugging. "I don't recall. Honestly, I don't think Randall said. But it was twenty years ago, after all. The first I knew about the job was when Randall quit his job at Zang's brewery. That I remember because he didn't tell me he was going to quit."

Hench reached for his own memories, brushing away the cobwebs as best he could. "I seem to remember something about that. You came over and talked to Gloria about it. You were pretty upset."

"Hell, yes, I was upset! He ups and quits without telling me and starts working for Vincent. We always talked about big things like that. He'd asked my opinion, we'd go back and forth until we were both at peace with whatever decision we had to make. But this time, all because of Vincent, he's suddenly secretive. I never liked that man. Now I'm going to kill him."

"And Randall never said what the work was? Nothing at all?"

Miriam bit at her lip and slowly shook her head, her eyes moving about the room. Hench knew she was seeing a different place and a different time. "I know we talked about it a bit after I found out he quit Zang's, but I just don't think he ever told me what it was. Or if he did, I've—"

"Holy hell," said Hench, also seeing another time and place. "Randall disappeared the night of the big fire in '63."

They looked at him, waiting.

"The fire started at the Cherokee House."

Rose gave a slight shrug and Miriam looked impatient.

"Vincent Edwards owned the Cherokee House."

"Give me a goddamn gun, Hench. I'm going to kill the son of a bitch!"

Tobias looked stunned. "That's—you mean you think Edwards killed Randall and now, twenty years later, kidnapped William?"

"It sure as hell looks like it."

"But why?"

"Where does he live?" said Miriam. "Tell me!"

Hench ignored her as his mind churned through possibilities. "There's gotta be a connection between Randall working for him, the houses being ransacked, and William's kidnapping. That's too big of a coincidence to ignore. Randall must have taken something from Edwards. Hid it away—or at least that's what Edwards thinks. Did Edwards ever meet William back then?"

Miriam didn't look at him. Her eyes stared at the wall, her face contorted with rage.

"Miriam!"

She blinked, then looked at Hench. "Give me a gun."

"Did William meet Edwards back then?"

"Who cares? We know he kidnapped William and," her voice caught, "beat him. That's enough for me. What the hell else you need?"

"Evidence would be good," said Hench.

"He isn't going to jail," said Miriam. "He's going to his grave."

"Don't you want to know what this is all about?"

Miriam turned on Tobias. "Do you know where Vincent lives? Give me a gun and take me there."

Tobias raised his hands chest high. "I'm sorry, I can't do that, ma'am."

"What good are you two?"

"Grandma," said Rose, "let's try to help them, okay? If they can find evidence, then they can go after him. If they go after him before then, they could get in big trouble."

Miriam wasn't happy, but she calmed down enough to say, "Don't you think I'd know if Randall hid something in the house?"

"Well, you said he was being secretive."

"I'd know!"

"Of course," said Tobias, "it might not have been something big. It could have just been some papers. I mean, it could have been anything, really. Money or just some documents Edwards doesn't want found by anyone."

Rose said, "Whatever it is, it seems to be big enough that they thought they might find it by digging up the yard. I don't think it's just some paper."

Tobias shrugged. "What did Randall do for Zang's brewery? Was he an accountant? Maybe he kept Edwards's books and hid those away. Big leather-bound books could be big enough."

Miriam shook her head. "He didn't have the head for

numbers. He worked with his hands. He did different jobs at Zang's. Just before he quit he was," she made a stirring motion with her hand, "mixing the grain."

"Mashing," said Hench.

Tobias put his hands up chest high again. The coin fell to the floor. He ignored it as he said, "Not to be crass or disrespectful, but could Randall Thompson have, um, simply stolen from Mr. Edwards? Grabbed a bag of money or something from him?"

Hench picked up the coin. "I haven't seen one of these in years. Where'd you get it?"

Tobias smiled embarrassedly. "I might have snatched it from Mr. Edwards desk, just to twist his rope."

Hench turned the coin over in his hand. He looked up. "Gold. Back in Kansas, Randall refined gold."

"He did," said Miriam, her face clouding with memory. "He smelted and refined raw metals coming from—well, from here. From the Rockies. That's how we heard about Denver City in the first place and decided to move out here. I wanted to see mountains."

"What would Edwards want with a refiner?" asked Tobias.

Hench handed back the coin. "Back then there were still a lot of miners in town. Maybe they paid with gold — dust and nuggets. Maybe Edwards had a stockpile of it at the Cherokee House that he wanted refined. Decided it'd be cheaper to hire someone to do it rather than ship it off. There was quite a bit of theft with ore shipments from Colorado to the smelters back east."

Miriam looked surprised. "Well, dip me, I think you're right. Now I remember. Randall said something about Vincent having some gold. I don't remember where he got it from. Yes, I think Randall *was* refining gold for Vincent."

"And he stole some of the gold?" said Rose.

Hench shrugged. "Certainly possible. And the refining would require a furnace. If he was doing the refining at the Cherokee House, maybe there was an accident. Those buildings were nothing more than kindling back then. Maybe the fire, and even Randall's death, was an accident."

"Doesn't matter," said Miriam. "William's kidnapping and beating wasn't an accident. Vincent's going to pay for that."

"He will," said Hench. "But let's figure out if Randall stole gold from Edwards. And if he did, where did he hide it? Edwards doesn't know and that's why he destroyed both houses and kidnapped William. So," he said, looking at Miriam, "where would Randall hide gold?"

"You can probably discount the houses, right?" said Tobias. "I mean, they tore them apart so there's nowhere left where a large amount of gold *could* be hidden."

Miriam muttered, "He would have told me." She looked up at Rose. "He would have told me, right?"

Rose frowned. "But he wouldn't want you to know he stole the gold. Maybe he planned to tell you later, but Vincent found out about the theft."

"Something's not sitting right," said Hench. "If Edwards knew the gold was stolen why wait twenty years to look for it? Why now?"

Rose said, "Maybe Vincent didn't know. Maybe there *was* an accident at the Cherokee House. Everything burned up and Vincent thought the gold was gone. Then something happened recently that changed his mind."

Everyone went quiet looking between one another.

Miriam finally groused, "This is fruitless. We may never know. We need to get Edwards for what he did to William regardless of what he might have done to Randall. You two either take care of it or I'm going to take care of it."

CHAPTER TWENTY-TWO

Several months earlier...

Vincent Edwards sat in the smoking room of the Carlyle Club talking with Milton Clark—former gold trader, mint owner, bank owner, and now financial broker.

"Sometimes I think we keep Pinkerton in business by ourselves." Milton Clark referred to himself and his brother Austin.

"Security is neither easy nor inexpensive," said Vincent, sitting back in the comfortable leather chair. "You've had Pinkertons in your employ for quite some time now."

Clark nodded.

"I'm reminded of when you owned the mint. I've heard whispers here and there over the years that when you were moving operations—"

"1863—hard to believe that was twenty years ago already."

Vincent nodded. "I'd heard rumors that some of your gold went missing. But the Pinkertons reclaimed it for you."

Clark chuckled softly, finishing the last of his cognac. His fourth such drink. "You have part of that correct."

"Oh?"

Clark sat up and leaned toward Vincent, who did the same. In a low tone, Clark said, "We never found the gold. Hell, the Pinkertons never made any progress on the theft at all. Of course, we never mentioned the theft. Still won't—so you never heard this."

Vincent froze. "Pinkertons didn't find the gold?"

Clark shook his head. "Not even an ounce of the stuff.

Just disappeared. All we knew was two men jumped a guard and made off with—well, no reason to go into details of a time so far removed. I'll just say it was more than a trifle of gold. Could have ruined our banking operations if people knew we'd been robbed and never recovered it. I'm surprised you heard anything about it."

"Me, too," said Vincent, his mind reeling.

Dear Lord. Randall Thompson faked the whole thing. Made it look like they'd been raided. Vincent sat back in complete disbelief. Randall stole the gold. He'd always felt lucky that no one ever came to ask him about the gold the Pinkertons found in the Cherokee House. He'd managed to convince himself that the fire that burned down so much of downtown had distracted everyone away from the robbery. What an idiot he'd been.

Then another thought percolated up. Was the gold still out there? He'd have to consider that widow of Randall's. What was her name? Something with an M if he remembered correctly. And didn't they have kids? Time to find out all he could about the Thompsons.

CHAPTER TWENTY-THREE

Present day…

Tobias was worn out by the time he got home to his boarding house. He clomped up the wood steps to the porch, pulled out his key to the front door, but it was unlocked. Stepping in, he didn't hear any voices coming from the parlor but lights were on. Maybe they'd simply forgotten to blow out the lamps before turning in or, most likely, one or more boarders were in there smoking quietly before bed.

He had no intention of joining them, he was exhausted and ready for sleep, but the wide entryway to the parlor was on the way to the stairs in back. As he walked past, he glanced inside and saw Lilly Jean, the proprietress of the house, and Winchell Davis, an older boarder who had come to Denver as a miner back in the day. They both stared at Tobias with wide eyes, fear stamped on their faces. Lilly Jean's eyes darted to the side of the entranceway.

Tobias reached for his Peacemaker but the barrel of a gun dug into his back.

"Easy now, Toby. Don't make me decorate this nice parlor with your innards."

Tobias froze. He recognized Percival's voice—a man who worked for Vincent Edwards and who would have no trouble pulling the trigger. Two other men stepped into view from either side of the parlor's entryway, revolvers drawn.

Tobias said, "What's going on, boys? Why the iron?"

"Boss wants to chat with you."

He'd been found out. Maybe Owen had seen him leave Edwards's office after all. Or Edwards figured out

Tobias couldn't possibly have known about William's rescue unless he'd been there himself. But they hadn't shot first, so he held out hope he might talk his way out of it.

Percival took Tobias's Colt Peacemaker from his holster then said, "Let's go."

Outside the boarding house, Percival said, "So what the hell did you do, Toby? You steal something from the Palace?"

Tobias shrugged. "I haven't done anything. It's gotta be a misunderstanding."

Percival chuckled. "You better hope so or you'll be visiting the hog farm."

Tobias sat in front of the huge desk in one of the straight-back chairs. Daniel and Abraham stood on either side of him. The young man felt itchy hot but tried to look unconcerned. Tried not to fidget. Vincent Edwards sat behind his desk and set his hands palms down on the leather blotter. "What were you looking for?"

Tobias shook his head. "I don't understand."

"Of course you do. You went through my desk. I assume you were looking for something. What was it?"

"I didn't go through your desk. I swear."

"So then why were you in my office?"

"I—I don't understand. I came by the Palace, but I—"

"Ernie!"

Tobias glanced toward Owen's office door as it opened. The guard who'd been stationed outside the door to the stairs came in. Tobias was sunk.

Edwards said, "Are you sure it was Tobias who entered the downstairs door?"

The guard nodded. "Yeah. No mistake of that, I seen him a hundred times."

"I just said I was here. But I didn't go up the stairs or anything. Just stayed on the floor. Honest."

"Ernie?"

The guard shook his head. "It was him. Even said 'hi' or whatever. No way was I mistaken. I mean, he was—"

Edwards waved for him to shut up. He looked back

at Tobias. "Again, I ask: what were you looking for?"

Tobias tried to look confused and scared, which was half right. "Ernie must have mistaken me for someone else, it wasn't—"

"You callin' me a liar?" yelled Ernie, stepping toward Tobias.

Edwards held up a hand, but the guard didn't notice, his face red as he glared at Tobias. Edwards glanced at Daniel, who immediately stepped between Ernie and Tobias and said, "Calm down."

"I wasn't confused," he said, looking back at Edwards.

"I believe you. Again, Tobias, why did you come up here? What were you looking for? My patience has worn thin."

Tobias wondered if he could make a break to the balcony. It was only the second floor, he might not break anything if he jumped, and Daniel and Abraham would probably take the stairs, giving him time to get out of the Palace. He almost missed the glance toward Abraham.

Something, a strip of something, flashed before his eyes and he suddenly couldn't breathe. He reached up and felt a leather strap tight around his neck. He heard Abraham give a little grunt as the big man lifted him free of the chair.

CHAPTER TWENTY-FOUR

Tobias tried to yell, but no sound came from his mouth. He flailed madly, trying to reach Abraham who stood behind him, holding him aloft with a leather strap tight around his neck. He got his feet under himself, but that didn't help, the strap was too tight. He was surprised at how quickly the room began to dim. He still had breath in his lungs, but he was already blacking out. He tried to reach Abraham's hands to scratch and claw at them, but the leather strap was too long.

Then he felt the wooden seat beneath his ass and he

could breathe again. It sounded like a gale force wind rushed through his ears as the room spun. He was alive, but the leather strap was still around his neck. He bowed his head and breathed deeply, twisting his neck to try and loosen the strap further. He could see Abraham's boots behind his chair.

"Well?" said Edwards, looking almost bored.

Tobias figured he had one chance. One very slim chance. He looked up at Edwards and nodded his head. "Okay, okay. I'll talk."

He hoped that would put Abraham off guard. He leaned forward slightly and took a deep breath, looking up at Edwards. Looking as scared and earnest as he could before he lurched toward the desk, getting his hands on the edge and his weight forward. He pulled his legs off the floor, curling them toward his chest and then kicking back like a mule as hard as he could. The soles of his boots caught Abraham just below his chest.

The large man huffed out air and doubled up, stumbling backwards, his hands empty. The leather strap fell free onto Tobias's shoulders. He pushed off from the desk and ran to his left, to the balcony door, praying it wasn't locked. He flung it open at the same time he heard a gun fire. It felt like someone thumped him in the right shoulder. He flung himself over the balcony's railing.

Either the bullet in his shoulder or just his mad dash over the balcony carried him ass over teakettle. He spun in a slow somersault, his arms and legs kicking as though he was trying to swim. He turned far enough in the air, almost a full revolution, that his boots came down on the roulette table first, followed almost immediately by his back. There was a tremendous *whomp!* and clay chips flew into the air around him like confetti. People scrambled backward.

Tobias rolled from the table onto his feet and stumbled toward the front door hoping they wouldn't shoot into the crowded gambling hall. Then he felt the bullet in his shoulder as though someone jabbed him with a hot poker.

He stumbled and he couldn't see well, his eyesight fuzzy. Someone, he couldn't see who it was, though he wore a red and gold striped silk shirt, appeared directly in front of him. He veered sharply to his right and lowered his left shoulder, driving it into the man's chest. The man sprawled backward, yelling out. Other people, patrons, moved out of the way. Ahead he could see the front doors, though they were blurred.

Then strong arms went around his waist and dragged him to the ground. Someone else, all he saw were legs, jumped forward from the crowd and a boot swung, catching Tobias in the gut. He doubled-up on the ground and couldn't breathe, then something hard hit him in the side of the head.

"Damn," said Vincent, looking down at Tobias's still form. He didn't care about the welfare of the young man, Vincent frowned at the Pinkerton identification paper.

Tobias, the Pinkerton detective apparently, was still alive but had a large welt on the side of his face. They had him on the floor of Owen's office because of the blood coming from the bullet in his shoulder. Vincent didn't want that on his expensive rug. Tobias's neck looked none too good either from the marks of Abraham's leather strap.

"Pigs?" asked Daniel.

Vincent pursed his lips and leaned against the edge of Owen's desk. He wished he *could* make the boy disappear. "We have to play it smart. His working for me was at the behest of a client of Pinkerton. Which means the agency knows he's here. If he disappears without a trace that'll just make them more interested in me. His death will have to look like something else. No way to make it look like an accident with all these injuries."

Vincent dropped Tobias's wallet and the Pinkerton paper onto the desk next to the Pinkerton badge they'd found and his gold coin. He picked up the coin. "We do know that he was definitely the one in my office. But, no, we can't just kill him. Not yet. Go lock him up until I figure this out. If nothing else, we can force him to write

Pinkerton a letter to tell them everything is A-OK." He looked up at Daniel. "Find out if he actually works for them. If the badge and paper turn out to be fictions then we'll feed the hogs."

Abraham bent and lifted the young man in his arms almost as easily as lifting a baby. "Here or—?"

"Here for now. Down the hall."

Abraham nodded and left the office, Daniel followed behind.

Owen said, "How much do you think Tobias knows?"

"The real question is who else knows?"

CHAPTER TWENTY-FIVE

The orderly smiled then coughed self-consciously and tried to look serious. There was blood smeared on the man's white coat. Jared thought the man looked like a ghoul and could have been digging up bodies at a cemetery. Then again, carting out dead bodies at the hospital would fit the man, as well, he supposed.

"I can't get his name," said the orderly. "It's some kinda big secret. But he's beat up real bad. I saw him through the door as I walked by. His face is a mess. And he's the only person in a room by himself. I'm thinkin' maybe it's the guy you're lookin' for."

It certainly sounded possible. "Has the man had any visitors?"

"I don't know, my job keeps me runnin' all over the hospital."

"Thank you for your help," said Jared, holding his hand out as if to shake the orderly's hand.

The man completed the ruse, taking the money and laudanum from Jared and slipping it into the pocket of his white coat. "If you need anything else, you know you can count on me."

Jared wondered if the man would be so eager if he knew how Vincent Edwards dealt with those who disappointed him. Jared turned to his partner Simon. "Shall we?"

The two entered the County Poor House Hospital. It was late morning, almost noon. It'd been easier finding William Thompson than Jared thought it'd be, but then there weren't that many hospitals in Denver. After visiting two others earlier in the morning, this hospital was next on the list. It made sense because of its relative proximity to the house where they'd been holding William Thompson.

The place was busy. Men in white coats and women in white dresses moved down hallways. People in street clothes came and went, some of them crying. The two men made their way to the second floor, following the orderly's instructions. They had to do some searching, it was a big hospital, but they found a closed door marked: STORAGE.

Simon glanced at Jared, who nodded. Simon opened the door but didn't enter. Jared leaned to look past his comrade. An old grizzled man in an old battered leather chair frowned back at them, a shotgun in the old man's hands, the gun pointed at Simon's chest. Jared saw a bed with a man in it swathed in bandages.

Simon said, "I thought this was a storage room?"

"It ain't," said the old man, the shotgun held steady. There was a silver star on the man's crumpled shirt.

"I see. Sorry." Simon closed the door.

They moved off down the hallway some distance. Jared whispered, "That has to be Thompson."

Simon nodded. "How do you want to deal with the guard? Come back in the middle of the night?"

"Yes. See if we can catch the guard sleeping. Plus, fewer witnesses when we kill him and William Thompson."

They left the hospital, returning to the Palace to inform Vincent Edwards of their progress.

Hench went downstairs to the archive of the Rocky Mountain News offices. It was a closed-in musty basement with narrow passages between shelving going from floor to ceiling. In a small clearing sat a small man amongst several large leather-bound volumes of what appeared to be old newspapers. He squinted up at Hench as though having a difficult time focusing on the man after peering at the small print of a newspaper. "Yes?"

"How far back do your archives go?"

"To the beginning of the newspaper." There was a

note of derision in his voice as though that answer would be obvious.

"Which is—?"

"1859. What years you looking for?"

"April 1863, from the fire on back maybe as much as a year. Not sure."

"And what in particular are you interested in?"

"Information about the Clark and Gruber mint. Were they robbed of gold during that time?" The gold coin Tobias took from Edwards got Hench to thinking. Edwards was already doing well in 1863, so where would there be enough gold to get him interested in stealing it and the kind of gold that would need refining? The gold hoard of a mint might be enticing to a gangster.

The man shook his head. "Clark, Gruber, and company were never robbed. Least wise that it was reported."

"And you're positive about this?"

"Wouldn't say it if I wasn't. Robbing the mint would be a big story. Now they did sell the mint to the federal government in '63—were forced to. After that they opened the First National Bank of Denver. That was in '65."

"They sold the mint in '63?"

"Funny you should mention the fire. The sale and the fire both happened in April 1863. But the fire started at a place called the Cherokee House—which now would be 15th and Blake. The mint building survived. Made of brick. It's still there over on Holladay and 16th."

"They were only a block apart?"

The man smirked. "Closer to two blocks, but yes. So you think someone stole from the mint? And, what, covered it up by setting fire to the whole damned town?"

"Wouldn't surprise me. But, no, if the theft occurred it would have been earlier. How did the mint get their gold? Did they bring in gold bars or were they working with dust and nuggets?"

"A lot of dust and nuggets. That's why the Clark brothers and Gruber started the mint. To save on shipping and insurance. There was enough trouble sending raw gold east that they opened the mint in Denver City to refine the ore and strike the coins."

"Of course," said Hench, more to himself than the newspaper man, "if someone stole a large amount gold and it was never recovered—that's not exactly the kind of news the Clarks or Gruber would want getting out. Especially if they were opening a national bank."

The man frowned. "Hold on a second." He pushed himself up and disappeared down a narrow passage of looming shelves. It was nearly ten minutes before he returned with a large leather-bound volume of old newspapers. He dropped it with a loud thump onto the table.

Without speaking, he started paging carefully through the yellowing papers. After another couple of minutes, by which time Hench was ready to walk out on him, the man said, "Ah," and pointed to an article.

Hench stepped closer and bent to look at the paper. It was also from April 1863. It was a story about a number of Pinkerton detectives descending upon Denver City in the employ of Clark, Gruber & Co. The article claimed the detectives were to help with the move of raw gold from the mint building.

"Probably a lot of raw gold," said Hench.

The man nodded and flipped forward nearly four weeks and pointed to another article. It told about how the Pinkertons, at least eight of them, were still in town helping the Clarks and Gruber.

The man said, "The move was long over by this time."

"So why such a strong force of Pinkertons?"

"Exactly."

CHAPTER TWENTY-SIX

Jared and Simon stepped through the side door of the County Poor House Hospital dressed in white longcoats that Jared hoped looked enough like the hospital coats that doctors and orderlies wore. It was almost two in the morning. The hallway was dim with about half of the oil lamps along the walls lit. A nurse came out of one of the rooms, glanced their way, frowned, but continued down the hall away from them. The rooms had even fewer lit lamps. Most of the patients slept.

Jared kept a hand in the side pocket of the coat to hold

the shotgun hidden beneath. Simon did the same. Their boots seemed loud and out of place against the tiled floor in the eerie quiet of the hospital. Jared smiled thinly. It wouldn't be quiet for long.

Moving to the stairs, they saw only one other person, an orderly who didn't glance up from the patient he leaned over in the twilight of one of the rooms. The two men had already made their plans and so neither spoke as they went up the stairs. At the top, they paused to make sure the hallway was empty.

The storeroom was on their left. Simon stopped in front of the door. Jared went on ahead and checked the side hallway. It was empty. He looked back to his partner and nodded. Simon kicked in the door, fast and violent, and fired a round in the direction of where the old man had sat earlier. But his frown told Jared something was wrong.

"The room's empty."

A shotgun blast came from somewhere and Simon gasped, looking down at blood suddenly appearing on his white coat. A second shotgun blast nearly cut him in half. It came from the room behind Simon. He looked at Jared with utter disbelief before he collapsed to the floor.

"Damn." Jared turned to run down the side hallway, but a man stood in his way. An older man, maybe in his forties, with a graying beard, a blue shirt, tan pants, and two black revolvers in his hands.

"Don't even breathe," said the man.

After the first shotgun blast, Hench stepped out into the hall. A man in a white duster stood in front of him looking back toward the storeroom. Hench had both of his Schofield revolvers drawn and cocked, waiting for the man to notice him.

Another shotgun fired. The sound was different from the first. It was Captain's shotgun from the room across the hall from the storeroom. The same shotgun barked a second time. Hench waited. The man turned toward him, ready to run, before he saw Hench and froze.

"Don't even breathe." The ranger stayed where he

was for a few seconds, giving Captain time to reload, then Hench started forward. "You there, Captain?"

"Sure enough," called the old man.

The man at the end of the hall glanced in the old man's direction.

Hench said, "We're gonna have a little talk. I want information about your boss."

He didn't like the look on the man's face. It wasn't one of resignation. He was calculating his odds. Move against Hench or the old man? Hench fired both revolvers the moment the man swung toward Captain, pulling something up from his white duster — a shotgun. Three shots fired simultaneously, both of Hench's revolvers and another from Captain's shotgun. The man never had a chance.

Hench walked up and kicked the man's shotgun away from him, then he scanned both hallways, but no one else showed up.

Captain grinned. "Good thing they showed up when they did, I was ready to fall asleep." Behind the old man, the door of the room across from the storeroom had a large hole in the middle of it. Captain hadn't bothered to open the door, shooting through it blind.

Hench looked over at the first man that Captain had shot. He was obviously as dead as his partner. "Guess there's no askin' them questions about Vincent Edwards."

"You can ask, but I don't think you'll get much of an answer."

Hench holstered his guns and knelt next to the man he'd just shot and went through his pockets. He found some money, which he left for the undertaker, but otherwise his pockets were empty. He flipped the white duster wide to look for inside pockets. He found nothing.

Hench stood. "You go home and get some rest. I'll stay here with William."

Captain nodded. "I'll let 'em know we're done up here."

CHAPTER TWENTY-SEVEN

Vincent dipped the thick strip of bacon into an egg yolk. The bacon and yolk never reached his mouth. Daniel came in looking dour.

Vincent dropped the bacon to the plate. "Now what?"

"Just talked to an orderly downstairs who works at the hospital where the Thompson man is holed up. Neither of our men survived. The orderly heard they were gunned down by Colorado Rangers."

"Multiple? How many?"

"Two. Description of one sounds like the same who

rescued Thompson from the house."

"Hench," said Vincent.

Daniel nodded. "The other was simply described as an old man with a badge and a shotgun."

"I want you and Abraham to take care of Hench. Now."

"What about Tobias?"

"He can sit and stew. We can find out later if he's really Pinkerton. The ranger's caused far too much trouble. Put him down like a rabid dog."

The office for the Colorado Rangers was in a building in Auraria, just west of downtown Denver. The rangers took up only the second floor of the five-story building. Daniel entered the main double doors. There were some desks in the office and four men. One was in a uniform, the others looked like clerks. Daniel cleared his throat.

A sallow man with greased back hair, one of the clerks, glanced up. "Yeah?"

"I'm looking for Ranger Hench. Heard he was in

town. I'm a friend of his."

The man frowned at Daniel for a moment, then he turned his head. "Vernon, did Hench ever check in?"

A fat man with a thick head of reddish hair pursed his lips. There was something wrong with his face. It took Daniel a little while to realize he had no eyebrows.

Vernon finally nodded. "That's right. Yes. He stopped by to get some help searching that house, remember? Let's see." The man pushed himself up from his desk with some effort and shuffled over to a wall of small cubby holes. He reached his hand into one and pulled out a piece of paper. "Yes. Here it is. He's over at the Bay City House hotel." He turned the paper over a couple of times. "Don't see a room number."

"That will work perfectly," said Daniel. "Thank you, gentlemen."

Captain came back to the hospital around noon. Hench had gotten a little sleep in the big leather chair, but he was tired. He headed back to the hotel for rye whiskey and rest. He got a bottle of rye in the small tavern next door to the hotel. He had a quarter of it gone by the time he got to his room.

Miriam and Rose's door opened and Rose came out looking worried.

"What is it?" he asked.

"Tobias is missing. He never showed up yesterday."

He noted the concern in her voice and painted across her face. Thinking him imperiled, her anger toward him had disappeared—or at least retreated a bit. But Hench was now also concerned. Tobias was supposed to keep watch over the women while he watched over William at the hospital. Something had happened to the young Pinkerton. He wouldn't have missed being near Rose if he could have helped it.

Hench took a last pull from the bottle and handed it to Rose. Turning, he took only a few steps when he heard her swallow hard. He glanced back as she lowered the bottle from her lips.

CHAPTER TWENTY-EIGHT

Hench came down the stairs of the hotel. First thing was to go to Tobias's boarding house. See if the Pinkerton was there last night. As he walked through the lobby, a large man—not fat, but imposing—glanced back down at his dime novel. Hench caught the man looking at him when he came through the lobby not more than a couple of minutes ago to go up the stairs. The ranger then noticed the clerk behind the counter glance at the big man. Something wasn't right. Hench diverted his path. Instead of heading out the back door of the hotel, he went into the kitchen. A couple of men working the kitchen glanced up.

Hench tapped the silver star on his chest. "Best you all go take a smoke break."

They looked confused.

"Leave the kitchen. Now!"

The men shuffled out the back door of the kitchen and into the alley. Hench took stock. To his left was a row of cast-iron stoves and ovens. The stove on the far left, closest to Hench, was partially dismantled, the round burner plates stacked on a counter, the oven door hanging open. He'd interrupted the kitchen staff cleaning the stoves.

Along the back wall were large wood and metal ice boxes big enough for a man to walk into. Next to that were shelves of canned and dried foods. In the back corner was a doorway probably to a cellar pantry. A half dozen large tables spaced out evenly in the center of the kitchen were strewn with raw meats and vegetables in various stages of preparation. Above the tables dangled various pots and pans for easy access. Below the tables each had a shelf stacked with more utensils and cookware.

A little more cluttered than he would have liked if his arrest didn't go smoothly, but a better place to ambush the man than out in the lobby, where a bystander might get hurt, or in the alley where the man's compatriots might be waiting. Hench pulled one of his black Schofield revolvers and waited.

Daniel stood across the street from the hotel keeping an eye on the people coming and going. He also kept an eye on the front window, waiting for Abraham to give him a signal. He assumed that Hench would use the back entrance of the hotel and he'd much rather be standing outside the alley than in the front, but then there would be no way to signal Abraham, or vice versa. It was boring work, though no more boring than standing at the ready for Mr. Edwards—except the last couple of weeks with the kidnapping and now with the advent of the ranger made life far more exciting than usual.

He and Abraham were both glad to be out in the field, as it were. But even still, standing outside a hotel or sitting in a lobby waiting on the possibility of the ranger showing his face was a slow, if necessary, part of the job. To help keep both on their toes, Daniel had them switch positions every hour or so; it was too easy to become drowsy sitting in the soft-cushioned chair in the lobby that afforded the best view of the stairs.

Outside, however, it was easy to get distracted. Daniel watched several boys caterwauling as they gamboled down the street in a mad dash. A slight smile ticked the corners of his mouth. He'd once been a boy like that roaming the streets of Kansas City as a youth, fending for himself and looking for ways to survive and, when the means revealed themselves, get ahead.

He learned early that it all came down to determination. When fighting another boy for a scrap he was amazed that he could see the other boy's determination wither beneath the onslaught of someone who simply wanted it more. And that determination is what led him to Mr. Edwards as a teenager. He fled Kansas City when the display of his bold persistence, as it were, resulted in the death of a man who got in his way over a scrap he coveted.

Mr. Edwards recognized and admired the teenager's fearless doggedness and took him under his wing. And as Daniel also learned as a youth, you had to recognize when luck favored you and strike out after it with the same determination one would use for a carefully crafted plan. He immediately recognized the great fortune that presented itself in the guise of Mr. Edwards and instead of chaffing at the education the man afforded him, he sunk his teeth into it with the relish of a dog going for the throat of a rival.

Daniel watched the boys round the far corner of the street heading off into adventures unknown when he heard a sharp whistle. Abraham leaned out the front door of the hotel across the street, two fingers curled in his mouth for another whistle. His partner looked slightly peeved at Daniel as he made the hand signal to indicate the ranger had left the hotel through the back door. Daniel sprinted in the same direction as the group of boys, but rounded the corner in the opposite direction, pulling to a stop at the corner of the alley. He risked a quick look, but the alley was empty. Was he too late?

He looked up and down the street but didn't see the ranger. He thought about running through the alley to the next street but that would be stupid. The ranger might come out the back door any second now. No, he'd have to wait for Abraham to emerge and the two could make further plans.

After a minute went by, the alley still empty, Daniel bit at the inside of his cheek. Where was Abraham? Maybe the ranger had doubled back into the hotel. He hated when the situation changed and he was stuck in a position of not knowing what was going on. After another full minute, which seemed so much longer as his worry grew, he moved into the alley, pulling and cocking his revolver. If he ran into the ranger, so be it. He'd shoot first and then find out what had taken the man so long.

He stopped at and eased open the hotel's back door. The hallway was empty. He slipped inside and moved down past a couple of doors marked as offices. Was it a trap? Had the ranger spotted them and was luring him into an ambush? He forced himself to relax his grip on the revolver. A tense hand was crud for aiming.

He got to the end of the hall and opened the door into the lobby. No ranger. He stepped out. He could see the entire lobby and Abraham wasn't there either. He started for the front desk to ask the man they'd bribed what had happened, but then he heard a gunshot come from the hotel's kitchen.

Hench began to wonder if he'd been mistaken about the big man in the lobby. If he was keeping tabs on Hench wouldn't he have entered the kitchen by now? Of course, he could have simply been a look out. Or Hench was mistaken about him entirely. Nevertheless, the ranger stayed where he was, gun in hand. If he was wrong about the big man, the wait wouldn't hurt anything.

But the big man did finally come through the door into the kitchen by himself. The man was over six feet, a half-dozen inches taller than Hench. The expensive suit the man wore bulged at the seams. He came through the door slowly, wary, a cannon of a revolver in his hand. Hench couldn't identify it—probably a custom design to better fit the man's large grip.

He didn't want to shoot the man and risk killing him. He needed to get one of Vincent Edwards's men alive to turn on their boss and give evidence at trial. Before the big man saw him, Hench said, "Don't move! Don't even twitch that gun hand." Hench cocked his Schofield.

He was surprised by the man's poise. Hench suddenly calling out like that would have made most men jump at least a little. The big man simply stopped and holstered his gun before turning and raising his hands.

"I'm taking you in," said Hench.

"What charge? Walking into a kitchen?"

Hench removed the handcuffs attached to his gun belt. "Put a bracelet around your right wrist." Hench tossed the handcuffs over.

The big man caught them and did as he was told.

Hench moved toward him. The man stood between two of the tables. "Turn around. Both arms behind your back."

As the big man turned, the back door opened. Hench tensed. But it was just one of the kitchen staff. "Can we come back—"

The big man kept turning, grabbing a large cast-iron frying pan hanging near his head. The man was smooth and fast and Hench was too close. The ranger started to duck. The pan glanced off his head, knocking him into the next row of tables. His Schofield revolver fell to the floor. The big man got behind him, shoving the ranger up against a table. Something flashed past Hench's eyes. A leather strap tightened around his neck at the same time one of the big man's knees pressed hard into his back. Wedged up against the table, the ranger couldn't twist away. Or breathe.

Hench shoved against the big heavy table, moving it forward several inches. The knee fell from his back, but the big man pulled up hard on the leather strap, nearly lifting the ranger from the floor.

Hench drew his other gun and got the reaction he hoped for. The leather strap went limp as the man grabbed for the gun. The ranger spun, raising his other arm and smashing his elbow into the big man's face. The man didn't stagger back as far as Hench thought he would. The man leapt forward, grabbing the thick strap still tangled around the ranger's neck, pulling it tight again.

Hench had no choice. He fired.

CHAPTER TWENTY-NINE

Tobias woke up to pain. His head didn't just throb, it felt cracked open wide. A broken egg. He was thankful that the room was dark. Light would have killed him, he was sure. He tried to reach up to see if his head was, in fact, still in one piece, but his hands were tied behind his back. His ankles were also tied. His facilities slowly, painfully returned. This took several minutes or maybe hours, he wasn't certain if he was staying conscious or fading in and out.

He felt a somewhat muted pain in his shoulder and

remembered being shot. The pain was muted only because the destruction of his skull so far outstripped it.

The room was a dim gray, like dusk just moments before night truly falls. He turned his head, which was a mistake of pain, and found a solid strip of light coming in from under a door. Tobias turned away from it as that solitary strip was blindingly painful.

Turning caused new explosions in his skull. He waited for the pain and the after-image of light to fade, then he looked around once more. There was nothing to see. It was a small room with a table and two wooden chairs. He lay on a wood floor.

He was surprised he was still alive and had to assume that situation would be remedied sooner than later to his detriment. Escape was imperative. He strained his arms, moving his hands to his side. That woke up his shoulder, sending a sizzling sting of pain radiating out from his bullet wound. He hissed and grimaced, but didn't stop. He had to reach his Pinkerton badge in his front pocket. He kept one edge sharpened so that he could use it as a blade when needed.

His wrists were tied crosswise, leaving his hands relatively free. He hooked the edge of his front pocket with his fingers and pulled to bring his arms farther to the side. A groan escaped his lips from the searing pain in his shoulder. He stopped for a few seconds to regain his senses, then twisted his legs sideways to bring the pocket closer. But when he felt the outside of the pocket to locate his badge, his pocket was empty. They'd taken it, which meant they knew he was Pinkerton. He was even more surprised he was still alive.

His wrists would be difficult to untie so he focused on his ankles. His boots were still on. He twisted his legs, concentrating on moving his ankles back and forth. Pulling one leg up while keeping the other stiff. Reversing that. Twisting again. Working on them until sweat trickled from his brow. Working on them until his legs pulsed with fatigue.

He stopped to rest his legs. Concentrating on the rope had eased the pain in his head, but it came rushing back, a flash flood down a bone-dry creek bed. He gasped and lay as still as possible waiting for the flood to ebb. A whine escaped his lips before he realized he was doing it.

After several moments he whispered, "Ow."

But he couldn't stop for too long. He pulled his left leg up slightly, enough to clear the heel of his right boot. He slipped that beneath the heel of his left boot, using that leverage to slide his right foot a fraction toward the back of the boot.

He put all concentration into feeling what his foot was doing and how the heel of his left boot caught the right boot. He squirmed and pulled. A gap formed in the bottom of his right boot. He pressed the heel of his left boot into that gap and kept working his foot until, like the birth of a calf, it suddenly slipped from the boot, past the rope. He pulled his leg out of the boot and then rolled to his knees and stood up.

His head swam and he fell onto one of the chairs, barely keeping from tumbling off to the floor. He sat without moving for at least a minute as the pain cascaded from his head down his arms and back. He didn't know how much longer he could go without collapsing, but he forced himself to his feet and put his back to the table. It was a small wood table. He moved along its edges, running his fingers over it. The roughest edge were the framing pieces on which the tabletop lay.

Using his thighs, he pushed the table up against the wall, then he turned, slowly crouched, trying not to pass out. He grabbed a table leg and stood until the table pitched over. He cringed at the sound it made as the leading edge scraped down the wall and struck the floor.

Gasping against the pain, he eased to the floor and scooched backward over the top of a table leg, to hold the table in place. He moved back until he was up against the underside of the table. Finding the rough edge, he sawed the rope against it.

He had no idea how long he'd been at it. He fell asleep at one point—though saying he passed out would probably be more accurate. But when he jerked awake he went back to sawing at the rope. Someone walked down the hall. He didn't stop. What would be the point? If they came in they'd see what he was doing whether his arms were moving or not. The footsteps faded. The next time he woke up his wrists were free, his arms dangling at his side.

He finished removing the rope from his other ankle and put his boot back on. He used a chair to help him stand. Staggering to the door, he almost laughed when it opened. They hadn't locked him in. He squinted against the blinding daylight in the hallway and thought he might throw up. The pain was a red-hot poker thrust into his eyes. But the worst of it passed.

He peered out of the room. It was the first time he knew for sure he was still upstairs at the Palace. Down the hall, Owen's and Edwards's office doors were open. The stairs at that end of the hallway were less than ideal. Even if he got past the offices, he'd be out in the gambling hall where any number of employees who might know about his situation could stop him. And he was in no shape to fight back.

He eased out of the room and went in the opposite direction. There were, of course, back stairs leading down to the alley. But unlike the stairs that led to the gambling hall, there were doors at the top and bottom that were always locked. However, he tried just in case. The door *was* locked and they'd taken his skeleton keys. He'd have to sneak past Owen and Edwards to get out.

CHAPTER THIRTY

The big man grunted and went down to one knee, covering the bullet hole in his side. At least he hadn't killed him. Hench kept the man covered and went around a table to get behind the man. "Okay, face-down on the floor, hands behind your back."

"I'm bleeding."

"Lie down."

With more grunts, the big man complied. Hench put a knee into the man's back, putting all his weight into it, before he holstered his gun. The man groaned, but kept his arms behind his back. The ranger reached for the cuffs around the man's right wrist when the murmured voices from the lobby suddenly got louder. Someone had opened the kitchen door. Hench looked up, but couldn't see the door through the tables and all of the kitchen items stacked beneath.

The big man moved his arms apart and now the ranger couldn't cuff him. Hench pulled his gun and bent lower, keeping his knee in place and putting the barrel against the back of the man's head before looking again toward the door. He thought he made out trouser legs through the stacks. The sound cut out as the door closed.

The legs turned one way and then the other. After a few moments, the man stepped slowly down the middle of the tables right toward Hench. The ranger lifted the gun.

The big man yelled out, "Careful, Daniel!" as he bucked.

Hench fell sideways and the man twisted, swinging his arm wildly. The arm missed, but the free-end of the cuffs slashed the ranger's face. Hench couldn't fight both men. He fired again. The bullet went in through the big man's side toward his chest. The man gasped, then fell back to the floor.

Daniel called out, "You okay?" After a couple of moments, he said, "Abraham?"

Hench couldn't see Daniel's legs anymore. The ranger moved backward, away from the big man's still form. When he was past the tables, up against the stoves, he moved to his right until he could see down the front length of the kitchen, past the door. There was no sign of the other man. Hench reached up and plucked the top burner plate from the stack on the counter.

He stood just tall enough to throw the cast-iron plate toward the other end of the kitchen and hunkered down. The plate crashed into pots and pans. Hench moved toward the back of the kitchen, looking down each row as he went. He still couldn't see Daniel, but hopefully the man didn't know where Hench was, either.

The ranger stopped moving and listened. Daniel must

have done the same. Looking through the stacked cookware beneath the tables was like trying to peer through long thick grasses for an enemy you knew was near. Your eyes played tricks on you. You saw movement everywhere. Every sound was a threat. It was tempting to stay in one place and wait for Daniel to show himself, but Hench didn't have that luxury. He didn't know if reinforcements were coming.

His knees complained as he stayed crouched and eased down the row, his head constantly turning. He stopped at the end of the table, which put him at the center aisle. He wanted to cross over, but he had that itchy feeling that he'd provide a perfect target. That Daniel was waiting patiently for the ranger to show himself. But the man couldn't have that kind of vantage point, could he? Hench turned slowly, a full circle. No movement from the man, not a glimpse. He risked it, scooting across the open space. No shot was fired. Where was he?

Hench wondered if somehow Daniel had exited the

kitchen. Surely he could see the man by now. The ranger lay flat and looked beneath the small space below the table shelves. He still didn't see Daniel. How could he not be in the kitchen? Then a shadow past over him.

Daniel was on the table!

Hench rose high enough to pitch into the stacked cookware beneath the table, using a forearm to clear a path. At the same time, Daniel fired from above. The ranger felt the bite in his side. Under the table, he turned over and fired up through the tabletop. The wood wasn't thick enough to stop the bullet from his Schofield.

Daniel cussed and danced. His shadow flew across the tiled floor. He struck the next table over with a loud thud. Hench rolled out onto the floor and scrambled to his feet. Daniel raised his gun, but the ranger blocked it with his left arm. The man rolled toward Hench and something flashed in his hand at the same time the ranger brought up his Schofield. A wicked boning knife sliced through Hench's right bicep, throwing off his aim. He fired, but the bullet hit the table. Daniel pulled the knife back and stabbed at Hench's chest.

The ranger deflected the knife as the man swung his top leg, kicking Hench in the side of the head. The ranger staggered to the side as Daniel spun off the edge of the table. The gun was gone from his hand and he grabbed Hench's arm, pulling the ranger down to the ground with him.

Both men cussed as they fell. The barrel of the ranger's gun hitting the floor and bouncing free of his hand. Hench landed on top of Daniel and blocked the man's forearm, preventing him from slashing with the knife. Hench hit him with his other hand. Daniel hit back, jarring the ranger's jaw.

Hench grabbed for Daniel's arm, to trap the knife hand, and the man hit the ranger again. He flashed the knife sideways, but Hench reared back, avoiding it. Then he dove forward, smashing a fist in Daniel's face and trapping the arm with the knife crosswise across the man's chest. He hit Daniel again, then grabbed for the knife with both hands as the man tried to transfer it to his other hand. Hench got hold of it and raised it above Daniel.

The man pulled free his trapped arm and used both hands to grab Hench's wrist. The ranger grabbed one of Daniel's wrist, letting him leverage his weight above the man.

"Stop fighting."

"You can't beat me."

The ranger rose up, so only his toes were touching the ground. The knife wavered and inched toward Daniel's throat.

"Give up!"

"I'm going to kill you."

Hench jerked his upper body up then down, and the knife slid into Daniel's throat. Blood welled up around the blade. The man sputtered, blood spitting from his mouth. But what Hench remembered for the rest of his life, was the look of utter shock and confusion on Daniel's face. It seemed to say that the man never thought he could lose.

Hench pulled the knife free and threw it across the floor. Daniel covered his throat, blood flowed around his fingers. The ranger pulled himself up. From the table he grabbed a large cotton cloth stained with food.

He got Daniel to move his hands and he pressed the towel down over the wound, but the ranger knew it was already too late. The man's face was ashen and he had no strength when he tried to hold the cloth over his throat. Hench held the cloth in place, but it was only moments more before Daniel's eyes glazed over.

The ranger sat back and looked at his side. There were two holes in his shirt, entry and exit, along with blood, but it was little more than a flesh wound, just grazing his side. He stood and grabbed another cloth, tying it off around the cut in his arm.

Among all the utensils and cookware he'd pushed out from under the tables, he saw the burner plate he'd thrown. He picked it up, curious about its weight. It didn't seem heavy enough—just over a pound. The door in the back of the kitchen opened. Hench whirled and remembered too late that his guns were on the floor.

But it was the same kitchen worker as before sticking his head in. "Is it over?"

Hench nodded. He lifted the plate a little higher. "What's this made of?"

The man looked confused and shrugged. "Iron. What else would it be?"

"Huh." Hench tossed it back onto a table and headed for the door that led to the lobby. He had to go upstairs and check on the women in case this had been a multipronged attack and they were in trouble.

The man croaked out, "You're leaving?"

Hench looked back. The man stared wide-eyed at the kitchen.

Hench said, "Go over to the Colorado Ranger's office and tell them to send some men over here. Make sure you get rangers, not the police. And you'll also want to get the body wagon out here from the morgue."

Hench left the kitchen with the man saying a drawn out, "Uh—"

The ranger moved quickly through the lobby to the stairs. People gaped at him. He must have looked pretty—well, pretty beat up. He turned the corner at the stairs and stopped; Rose hurried down, her face tight with emotion.

"Are you okay?" asked Hench, thinking that someone had been upstairs after the women.

"It's Miriam. She's gone."

"They took her?"

Rose stopped a step above Hench and looked confused. "What?"

"Somebody took her?"

Rose shook her head. "No, no. I think she's gone after Vincent Edwards. She railed against him all morning. Asked if I knew where there was a pawn shop. Then just a couple of minutes ago I went down the hall to freshen up and when I got back she was gone." Then she really saw Hench for the first time. "My God, what happened to you?"

Hench shook his head. "A run-in with more of

Edwards's men. Listen, you go back up to—"

Rose shook her head vigorously. "I'm coming with you. There's no way you'd be able to reason with her."

Hench opened his mouth to protest but realized she was right. And, besides, Edwards knew they were here and maybe more men were on their way. "Okay, let's go. We'll look for her at the Palace."

CHAPTER THIRTY-ONE

Vincent sat at his desk, alone in his office, thinking about the whole damned mess. And all over gold he didn't actually need. True, it was a lot of gold, but it wasn't worth the trouble the ranger had dealt him. But that would soon be over when Daniel and Abraham dispatched the man. Then he could eliminate the Thompsons and forget about the entire sordid affair.

His main door opened. He glanced up, a bit miffed that the person hadn't knocked and was shocked to see a woman of about his age standing in the doorway with a gun pointed at him. It took several moments for his brain to finally land upon her identity. He kept himself from smiling. "Miriam Thompson, isn't it?" One Thompson down, only two more to go.

The woman shut the door behind her and took several steps into his office. "Surprised you remember me, asshole."

"How did you get up here?"

She waggled the revolver in her hand. It was old and ill-used, but it would probably fulfill its duty if she pulled the trigger. "I reasoned with your guard."

"Of course." Vincent smiled thinly. "You know, you're just as lovely as you were back when—"

"Did you kill Randall?"

Vincent was taken a bit off guard by that accusation. How could she possibly have figured that out? "Has the ranger been filling your head with fantasies? I did not kill your husband. If you recall, we were friends."

She scowled at him. Despite that, she really did look quite attractive after all these years.

"Were you two friends even after Randall stole the gold from you?"

Vincent started. "How did you—?" He stopped before he said anything condemning of himself. She couldn't possibly know. Could she? What all had that ranger figured out?

"I didn't until right now. What happened? Randall took some of the gold so you killed him?"

Owen's door cracked open behind the woman, his secretary's eye peered through. Miriam hadn't noticed. Vincent gave the slightest of nods. Owen disappeared and then one of his guards from the Palace threw open the door and grabbed the woman in a bear hug before she could move. Owen came around the two and pulled the beat-up revolver from the woman's hand.

The guard let her go. She stood there and glowered at Vincent, who smiled in return.

"Jimmy, thank you for your help. You can leave us now."

The guard nodded and left through the main door.

After the guard was gone, Vincent opened his center drawer and pulled out his Tiffany revolver. "Beautiful, isn't it?" He set it down on his large leather desk blotter.

Miriam didn't look frightened, which was a pity.

She said, "If you're going to kill me, will you have the courtesy of telling me what happened to Randall?"

"Well, I do have a question, since you already know about the gold. Where the hell did Randall hide it?"

Miriam rolled her eyes and shook her head. "Don't you think I would have spent it by now if I'd known? Are you that stupid?"

Vincent sighed and chuckled softly. "Apparently. Owen, if you could move out from behind Mrs. Thompson."

Before his secretary could move, Vincent's door opened again and Jimmy re-entered.

Vincent said, "What is it?"

A man pointing a revolver at Jimmy's back stepped into the doorway. From the relieved expression on Miriam's face, along with the star on the man's blue shirt,

Vincent assumed that this was the mysterious and dangerous ranger who had caused him so much trouble. The ranger looked like he'd been dragged through brambles behind a horse. But he should have been dead. Where were Daniel and Abraham?

Vincent forced himself to stay composed. "Tough day, ranger?"

"Not as tough as it was on the men of yours I just killed."

"Killed?"

The ranger nodded. "Two of 'em. A big man named Abraham and I believe the other was called Daniel."

Vincent went cold. Surely this man couldn't have dispatched Daniel and Abraham. He was lying. Wasn't he?

"You killed Daniel and Abraham?" said the secretary, his voice as full of the disbelief that Vincent felt.

Behind Owen, through the side door, a beautiful young woman stepped through and took the gun from his secretary, who was too astounded to even register the theft.

Hench shrugged. "Let's not worry about them scoundrels. They're on their way to the morgue by now. Let's take care of the current situation. Vincent Edwards, you're under arrest for the—"

Vincent wasn't really paying attention anymore, his mind reeled at the thought that Daniel and Abraham could be dead. He almost missed seeing his guard whirl on the ranger.

The guard tensed, so Hench was ready when the man spun and lunged at him. He could have shot the man but couldn't bring himself to shoot someone who was probably just working a day job and thinking he was defending his boss.

The guard was clumsy. As he lunged, Hench stepped to his right, which let him line up his left fist with the man's face. The man blinked, as though confused by the matters at hand, and then his knees wobbled and gave out. Hench raised his gun hand and brought the bottom of his fist along with the butt of his revolver's grip down hard on top of the man's head. The guard went to sleep. The crusted-over slash in Hench's arm no doubt re-opened.

Behind the unconscious guard, Rose jammed the revolver into the back of the prim-looking man she'd taken it from. Then from out of nowhere, Tobias appeared next to Hench. The young man looked all but done in—but at least he was alive. Tobias opened his mouth to speak, but Miriam lunged for Edwards.

She dove and scrambled up onto his desk and then fell off. At first Hench thought it was a terribly ungainly and unsuccessful attempt to get at the man, but as she fell to the floor, silver flashed in her hand. She had Edwards's gun.

The gangster first jerked away from Miriam, into the back of his large red leather chair, but as she fell, he must have realized her true intent. He dove for the gun but swiped at air. He then clawed up over the top, looking as blundering as Miriam had, and threw himself off the desk.

Tobias started forward, but Hench held up an arm and stopped him.

As she landed, Miriam kicked backwards and tried to raise the gun, but Edwards was over the top and descending. She fired a spastic shot that was far too low. The bullet went under Edwards and under his desk. The gangster crashed into her and she screamed. But it wasn't a scream of fright. It was the scream of a banshee engaging in battle. With her free hand, she clawed savagely at Edwards's eyes. The man cried out and smashed a fist into her face.

Miriam snarled in return, her nose pushed to the left, her upper lip split. Her right arm, with the gun, was trapped beneath Edwards. Most of his weight was on that arm, there was no way for her to free it, so she continued her attack with her other hand, gouging and slashing at Edwards's face.

The gangster arched backward, trying to get out of her reach as bloody scratches appeared across one eye and down his cheek. His face contorted with rage and total loss of control. Hench had seen men completely lose their composure before. Go insane, if only for a short time. That was Vincent Edwards at that moment. He flailed one arm to try and block Miriam's savage attack while he swung wildly with the other, striking her but also freeing her gun hand. The man was not thinking straight. He was caught up in a whirlwind of madness.

Miriam shoved the silver gun up against Edward's side and pulled the trigger, but she'd forgotten to cock it. Unlike Edwards, and despite her rage, she had the composure to take his punches, cock the hammer back, and fire. It was as if Edwards was a marionette whose strings were cut. He fell across the woman.

Hench lowered his arm and Tobias moved forward, helping Miriam roll the gangster's corpse off her. The young man used only his left arm to help, the right shoulder of his shirt nearly black from dried blood. Miriam kicked at Edwards as she squirmed out from under. Tobias stepped back to avoid her boots. The woman scrabbled up on her knees and, silver revolver in hand, struck Edwards's face with it.

In a low cold tone, she accented each blow with, "You. Asshole."

CHAPTER THIRTY-TWO

Hench rode Speck to Miriam's house. He wore his beat-up tan duster and black leather chaps. His saddlebags were packed, his bedroll tied down to the back of the saddle. He stopped in front of the house. It looked like she was moving. A lot of the furniture, all of it destroyed by Edwards's men, was out on the torn-up front yard. He dismounted, but didn't tie up Speck. The horse would stay put until he returned. He moved through the maze of furniture and entered the house.

The interior looked markedly better than it had

before. The large front room was bare of furniture. All the smaller broken furnishings were gone, plaster and lath from walls was cleaned up, though the gaping holes still remained. The floorboards were collected into a pile. And there was Tobias on hands and knees hammering floorboards back into place despite his bandaged right shoulder. Still, he'd gotten about half the floorboards put back.

"Hench," said Tobias, nodding to the ranger before returning to the floorboard in hand.

"Looks a helluva lot better. Is Captain here?"

"The old ranger? He's in back helping in the kitchen, I think."

Hench picked his way past the remaining holes in the floor to the dining room. Captain was moving the dining room table out of the way. Rose cleaned up broken china from the overturned cabinet. Miriam was putting the cast-iron stove back together and cleaned off the layer of ash caused by the destroyed chimney.

"Hi, Uncle."

"Looking good in here," he said.

"Trying not to get too overwhelmed. There's still Father's and my house to clean up next," said Rose.

Hench whispered, "Have you forgiven Tobias?"

She shrugged. "I'm getting there. Did he tell you he requested a permanent transfer to Denver?"

Captain asked, "How's that boy doin' in the hospital?"

Hench said, "Oh, I just came from there. William's awake but feeling bad about not being able to help."

Miriam spoke from the kitchen. "I told him this morning he better stay put until the doctors say he's okay to come home. Leaving early would just set him back something awful."

Rose nodded as she tossed broken shards into a large bucket. She looked up at Hench. "You going to stand around or are you going to help?"

Hench sighed, "Unfortunately, I've been called away to Trinidad."

"How soon?" asked Rose.

"Today. Now."

"Figures," said Miriam, her usual venom for Hench in her voice.

Rose stood and stretched her back. "Seriously, Grandma, you have to stop that."

Hench said, "It's somethin' deeper than anger. And, hell, if I can't forgive myself I certainly don't expect Miriam to forgive me."

Captain looked between Hench and Miriam. "You ain't talkin' about Gloria, are you?"

Hench didn't say anything and Miriam just glared.

"Well, hully gee, Miriam, you know Hench loved her. He did all he could to—"

"Don't," said Hench. His throat tightened. He certainly didn't want to relive the horrible event. "Look, I stopped in to say goodbye."

Rose gave him a hug, holding him tight, her face pressed into his chest. "Please, please, don't stay away as long this time."

"I'll try." It was difficult to talk while hugging

Gloria's ghost. Even their smell was similar. He patted Rose's back brusquely and pulled away.

"Families. Darn glad I ain't got none no more," said Captain, looking between them all and shaking his head. "But don't fret too much, ladies, y'know I'll stick around as long as you can stand me to help clean up. Who knows, maybe we'll still stumble on that gold."

Miriam took a deep breath and looked away from Hench. He could tell she was trying to calm down. She finally said, "Wonder what Randall did with it?"

Rose shrugged. "Can't be here or Vincent's men would have found it, don't you think?"

Hench scratched at his beard. "'Nother reason I stopped by was to thank you, Captain, for your help."

"Oh, please," said the old man, looking embarrassed.

"It needs to be mentioned, and I want to pay you for your help."

Captain's eyes flashed with anger. "The hell you will! Don't you even think about it."

"No, no," said Hench, stepping up next to the stove,

causing Miriam to take a few steps back from him. "I insist. This involves you, Miriam." He hefted the largest of the white-enameled burner plates from the stove.

She looked ready to hit him, but she said, "Well, what is it?"

"Can I give this to Captain?"

Her scowl turned to utter confusion. "What?"

Captain got a crooked smile. "This a joke?"

Miriam said, "You're an idiot.

"Please," said Hench. He took a step back from the stove, holding his arm out to force Miriam back a few more steps, as well. He held one end of the plate using both hands and raised it above his head.

Miriam yelled, "What are you doing?"

Similar comments came from Captain and Rose. He turned his face and smashed the smooth flat side of the plate down on the edge of the cast-iron stove as hard as he could. White enamel shattered and flew off in a shower of tiny chunks, a few biting at his cheek. Hench looked at the plate where he'd broken the enamel. The plate winked back at him.

"You asshole!" said Miriam. "Randall gave me—oh, damn."

Hench walked back into the dining room. Captain and Rose stared at him as if he'd lost his mind. He handed the burner plate to Captain. "Please, I want you to have this. And Miriam will want you to keep it. She may hate me to the core, but she's a good person."

"Are you drunk?" said Captain

Hench smiled and walked out into the front room.

Tobias looked up, puzzled. "What's going on in there?"

Hench shrugged and headed for the door. Before he got to it he heard Captain exclaim, "Holy horseshit! There's gold under the enamel!"

Even out at the street, Hench could hear them yelling in shock and celebration. Hench had no idea how much gold Randall took, but if it turned out to be all the enameled pieces, including the oven door and the backsplash, it was a lot. He stepped up onto Speck's saddle. The young horse moved without any command from Hench. The ranger looked back one last time. He could still hear them inside the house.

Hench rode to the cemetery just east of Capitol Hill. He dismounted at the entrance and walked in, Speck by his side. The ranger was shocked by the disrepair. There were few burials in the cemetery anymore and much of the place looked like wild plains with tall grasses and wildflowers. Tombstones littered the field, as though scattered across the earth by a giant hand. How could the city let this happen? But he pushed his anger aside. He had no right to it. This was his first visit since Gloria's burial in 1868. He was as guilty as anyone. That guilt punched him in the gut. He was glad for it. He deserved it.

Despite the sixteen years, he knew the way to Gloria's plot. It felt like the funeral happened last week, maybe last month. Speck huffed next to him, sensing his anxiety. Hench started to reach up to encircle the horse's neck, but the ranger didn't deserve that comfort. He walked the rest of the way with stiff legs and a trembling jaw.

When he entered the cemetery, there were wide lanes between parcels, but the deeper he ventured, the lanes were also overgrown. Soon he found himself on a small path worn by feet through the grass and weeds that grew past his waist. He could no longer see the tombstones. The land had reclaimed it all. It broke his heart to think of Gloria's tombstone forgotten. Abandoned. Speck huffed again and tossed his head.

Hench stayed on the small path as it continued in the direction he wanted to go. The thought crossed his mind that in all this growth he might not be able to find Gloria's tombstone. Or what if it was gone or vandalized after all these years? He'd find out in a moment. If it was still there, it was just up ahead. His chest tightened.

The narrow path went straight but he felt positive that the plot was to his right. Hench pushed through the tall grass, tripping over a small tombstone and nearly going down. He refrained from cursing and kept his eyes on the ground, stepping more carefully. What if he really couldn't find it? But then he suddenly pushed through into a small clearing—an oasis of recently cut grass. The tall growth surrounded the area like a fence. In the middle was a marble tombstone with the name Gloria Hench. Beneath the stone was freshly turned earth with flowers in full bloom. As he approached her grave he saw the small path enter the clearing to his left. Miriam came here often enough—and probably William and Rose—to have created the path.

The ranger knelt next to the grave. His vision blurred. In a trembling voice, he said, "Hello, Gloria."

ALL'S JAKE

Book Three

CHAPTER ONE

The two men eyed him warily as he approached on his Appaloosa. Hench wasn't much for smiling, but he tried one on for good measure. That seemed to make the men more nervous. He let it go, knowing his scruffy appearance with his thick brown hair and beard wasn't one to put men at ease. In his early forties, his brown hair was losing its fight with gray.

"No reason to be alarmed. I'm a Colorado Ranger on my way to Georgetown. Can I be of help?" Hench pulled aside the lapel of his weather-worn duster, the same mottled tan as his hat. His silver star caught the sunlight as it clung to his faded blue side-button shirt. His horse Speck, on the other hand, was a handsome young Appaloosa with a cream-colored coat sprayed with reddish-brown spots.

The men relaxed a little, though still a tad nervous, which wasn't surprising. The reason the ranger rode up to Georgetown was because of a gang of outlaws running roughshod over the mountain towns along Clear Creek Canyon, a valley that wound its way from Golden below up through the Rocky Mountains to the creek's head water near Loveland Pass far above them.

The men were moving a wagon down the mountain along the wide and well-maintained road connecting the mountain towns. Concord Coaches regularly moved up and down the valley, though trains running daily on the other side of Clear Creek now took most of the load.

The tarp covering the wagon bulged two feet above the sides. Supply trip from Georgetown. The men didn't look like prospectors—too clean cut. Domesticated.

Maybe on their way home to a smaller town. The wagon was pulled by two large draft horses.

"We got her fixed," said one of the men, about Hench's age, in his early forties. The man had an Irish accent that was watered down a bit. "Brass insert in the hub busted. We got it replaced and we'll be on our way shortly. But thank you, officer."

Hench tipped his hat and he and Speck continued up the road. Clear Creek growled to Hench's right, swollen with spring runoff. The wagon had stopped in a large natural clearing. Ahead of the ranger, the road cut through the clearing and back into the heavy evergreen forest that covered most of the valley.

The ranger scratched at his beard. It was a tad greasy, even for him. He looked forward to a bath and some clean clothes in Georgetown. Speck would enjoy some time in the livery stable getting plenty of oats and some rest. They were coming from the town of Evergreen, which was down the hill. He'd been called in to help the Evergreen constabulary track down vandals who were causing quite a bit of trouble for a logging company. Turned out to be several ex-loggers who'd been fired for drunken behavior. The locals asked for help from the Colorado Rangers when the vandals set a trap that nearly killed the logging company's owner.

After catching and arresting the men, who were drunk when Hench found them, he'd received a wire to head up to Georgetown. He was to check out reports of a band of outlaws—real outlaws, not drunken loggers—whose raids on the mountain towns were becoming brazen. Two people had reportedly been seriously injured so far. He'd investigate and then wire for more rangers if he felt the situation warranted it.

This part of the Rocky Mountains was covered in spruce and pine with an occasional white slash of aspen. The spring sun was hot, and it felt good to get back among the trees and their cool shadows as the wide road cut back into the forest. He was engulfed in the invigorating aroma of spruce and pine. Hench wasn't much for perfume-y smells, but the smells of an evergreen forest was a thing of comfort.

They'd gone several hundred yards into the forest when his young horse's ears perked up and the gelding raised his head in alert. The Appaloosa heard something he didn't like. Hench tipped his head from side to side, trying to pick up on it, but all he could hear was the roar of the creek.

Speck whinnied and huffed. Something wasn't sitting right with him. Hench pulled his Spencer carbine, levering the short rifle and cocking it. He didn't see any movement among the trees. Off to their right, sunlight sparkled off the creek, dancing among the trees like fireflies who didn't realize it was daytime.

Speck didn't like what he was hearing. Mountain lion? But Hench didn't think so. Something as dangerous as a big cat would have caused the horse to stamp and shudder his warning. No. It was something else. Speck's ears twisted backward. Behind them. Hench turned the horse and continued to peer between trees. Then the ranger thought he heard something. A yell maybe? Down the road. The wagon?

"Let's go," said Hench, leaning forward.

Speck didn't need to be told twice and the Appaloosa surged forward. Trees whipped past them on either side, the horse's ears flat against his head. Hench kept one hand on the reins and the other gripped his carbine. It might be nothing. Maybe a simple dispute between the two men, but the ranger had learned to trust Speck's instincts.

Then the world blinded him for a moment as the horse raced free of the trees. It took a moment for his eyes to adjust. Then he saw four horses ringing the wagon. One of the saddles was empty, the rider standing over the Irishman, who was prone on his back, his hands splayed in the air above him. The Irishman's buddy stood to the side, hands raised.

One of the horsemen jumped to the ground and went to the wagon. Soon after smoke rose. The Irishman surged up, then fell back flat to the ground. A half-second later the sound of a gunshot reached Hench.

"Crickets," he muttered, raising the carbine to his shoulder.

CHAPTER TWO

Hench leaned into the shot, his Spencer carbine tight to his shoulder, his knees holding him in the saddle. Speck drove hard but smooth. Still a young horse, he learned fast and he and Hench could already communicate as if they'd ridden together for a decade. The slightest pressure from a knee or shift in weight, Speck changed course.

Shooting from the back of a horse was difficult, to say the least, but Hench was trained on it from the get-go back in the early 1860s when he joined the rangers. Now, over twenty years later, it was second nature. He aimed for the two men on horseback and fired. Without waiting to see if he'd hit anyone, he levered, cocked, and fired again by the time the sound of the first shot reached the outlaws. One of the men clutched an arm and the two outlaws on the ground scrambled to their mounts. The four took off. As the outlaws passed the second man from the wagon, one of them swung his rifle by the barrel, striking the man in the head. He fell to the ground.

The four men sped away, moving off-trail toward the nearest line of trees. Hench aimed, fired, and repeated, but the outlaws reached the forest. Was this the Hensley gang, named for brothers Damon and Daren Hensley? If so, it was the same group of outlaws he'd been ordered to investigate when he'd been at the logging site near Evergreen.

"Damn," said the ranger, slowing Speck. He wasn't about to ride into the trees by himself. The outlaws could dismount and hide, picking him off when he came close. He turned the Appaloosa toward the wagon. The fire spread quickly. Hench was shocked the draft horses hadn't bolted, but then he saw they were tied to a sturdy pine. The two animals were panicked, however, trying to pull free.

Hench reloaded his Spencer, removing the magazine tube from the butt stock as he and Speck approached. The Appaloosa stopped a respectable distance from the fire, which climbed high above the back of the wagon, crackling and roaring. Reloaded, the ranger dismounted and ran to the horses. He set his carbine against the tree and pulled his knife.

He didn't cut the reins tied to the large tree—not yet. Instead, he went to the wagon and cut the thick leather traces. Careful not to get kicked, he leapt past the back end of one of the horses to straddle the wagon shaft, so he could pull the pin free that held the yoke in place. The horses still tried to pull loose, but the reins tied to the evergreen tree kept them in place. Hench then mounted the horse closest to the tree, pulling himself up by the harness. Leaning forward, he finally cut the reins near the tree. The horses took off down the trail.

Once clear of the wagon and fire he figured the horses would stop easily enough. Hench pulled on the shortened reins, but they were too terrified. Still bound to the yoke, the horses whipped from side to side, fighting against each other without the wagon to keep them stable.

Then the sunlight dimmed as they entered the downstream forest. Hench kept pressure on the reins. He had to slow them soon, the road was too twisting, the trees far too close. As if to emphasize his thoughts, the rump of the other draft horse sideswiped the trunk of a tree. Hench thought for sure it was going to go down, pulling both horses and himself down into a mangled bloody heap, but it managed to find its footing. But even that misstep didn't get either horse to slow down. Hench realized he had to jump clear and let the horses run until they got tired or killed themselves.

Then a streak of brown and cream flashed by on his left. Speck raced out in front, the smaller lithe horse easily outpacing the drafts. The Appaloosa moved in front of the large horses, which steadied them almost immediately, getting them to stop careening off one another. Then Speck began to slow, and the drafts followed suit. After another fifty yards they came to a stop. As smart as he knew his horse to be, Hench was left in shocked awe.

Speck then walked over to him as calm as could be. Hench smiled and scratched the horse's cheeks. "That was the goddamndest thing I ever saw." Speck flicked his ears and tossed his head. He breathed hard, but otherwise looked unfazed. The draft horses breathed like locomotives but were unharmed.

Hench dismounted and tied the wagon reins to Speck's saddle horn and turned the drafts around. He walked between them back up the trail. It was a long walk back, but he hoped it would work out any fear they might have left. After a ways he smelled the smoke from the wagon. He looked at the drafts, but they seemed unconcerned.

It took about fifteen minutes before the wagon was in sight. He tied the horses to a tree a hundred yards from the fire. The wagon was engulfed, the heat so strong that Hench had to give it a wide berth to get around to see to the two men. As he suspected, the Irishman he'd talked to was shot in the chest, his coat flung wide, his white shirt now blood red. Still, Hench knelt next to him and felt at the man's neck. He couldn't find a pulse.

He went to the other man, who was still alive. There was a big gash on his head folding under part of his scalp. A lot of blood, as well. He'd need a doctor if it wasn't already too late. The ranger lifted the man under his arms and pulled him across the clearing in the same direction the outlaws had taken. He needed to get him clear enough that the draft horses wouldn't be spooked by the fire. Hench did the same with the Irishman, then he returned to the horses and brought them up. He put each man belly down on a horse, which was quite a job in and of itself. Luckily neither was a big man. He strapped them in place using the leather traces. Retrieving his carbine, he got up on Speck and rode them up to Georgetown.

CHAPTER THREE

Georgetown, Colorado—the center of a rich silver region of the Rocky Mountains—hugged close to either side of Clear Creek in the narrow valley. Most of the town lay along the east bank, pushing hard against the dense evergreen forest. Tall craggy peaks loomed over it east and west as the creek cut north and south for a short stretch. To Hench's right, on the west side of the creek, a train from Golden huffed and strained up the narrow-gauge track, people peering out the windows. A spiderweb of tracks made Georgetown a hub of train

421

activity surpassed only by Denver 50 miles to the east. It was no tiny mountain town, what with its 3,000 or so residents.

And those residents who were outside that afternoon as Hench entered the town proper, stopped to gape at them, no doubt curious about the bodies strapped to the big draft horses. Hench rode up Main Street to a doctor he knew. He went into the two-story house without knocking, and yelled, "Doc!"

A younger man, mid-thirties and trim, came down the stairs. "Thought it was you, ranger. You shot again?"

"Got a man outside banged up pretty good. Give me a hand."

The doc followed Hench outside and stopped. The ranger pointed, and the doctor hurried to the man with the crack in his head. "And the other one?" he asked.

Hench said, "Dead."

"How'd it happen?"

"They were heading back from Georgetown with supplies. Outlaws stopped 'em and set their wagon on fire."

The doctor felt the man's neck, frowned, then took the stethoscope from around his neck. He listened to the man's back for a moment. "Still alive. Heartbeat's faint, though. Let's cut him loose and carry him inside."

After that, Hench went to a funeral parlor at the south end of town and deposited the Irishman. The ranger gave a few dollars to the undertaker. He'd get it back from the town marshal.

Next, he took all three horses to the livery stable, paying to have them fed and rubbed down. He took his carbine, bedroll, and saddlebags and checked into the Silver Plume Saloon and Hotel. He always chose that hotel—clean rooms, good food, and better whiskey. In his room on the second floor, Hench removed his well-worn black leather chaps, stored his gear, and went downstairs to the saloon. He bought a bottle of rye, took three long pulls, then handed it back to the bartender to keep for him. The man used a black grease pencil to write HENCH on the side of the bottle, then drew a slash to mark the level of the alcohol inside.

Feeling more refreshed by the whiskey, he went down Main Street, stopping in at a hardware store. There were others in town he'd have to stop at if he wasn't lucky. A man a little over five feet greeted him.

"Was wonderin'," said Hench, "if a couple of Irishmen came in recently makin' purchases."

The man's eyes narrowed. "You got something against the Irish?"

"One of 'em was just murdered and the other hurt real bad. I'm tryin' to find where they came from. See if I can't get word to kin. The two were headin' down the hill with a wagon load when they were set upon."

The short man's face went pale. "Was it Jimmy Kirkpatrick and Dylan Walsh? They were—damn. They was just in here earlier today. Which one's dead?"

"No idea. They live in one of the small towns along Clear Creek?"

"Yeah, well, no. It's not a town. A tiny settlement. A bunch of folks, mostly family. Wanted to live some place quiet. I wonder—" The man trailed off.

"What's that?"

"Well, for over a year now, Jimmy and some of the other men from the settlement been complaining about the new silver mine that started operations near them. Said the company men been stirring trouble. Trying to force them out so they could take over the valley to expand the mining town."

"Huh," said the ranger. "That could explain why the outlaws set fire to the wagon instead of takin' it for themselves."

The short man nodded. "Wouldn't put it past them. Jimmy and his friends said the company was starting to get nasty about the situation."

"You think you could get word to that settlement? Let them know about Jimmy and Dylan?"

"Possibly. I'll give it a try, anyhow."

Hench next paid a visit to Marshal Jackson. The office and jail was a small yellow-brick building near the center of town a block off Main Street. Hench clumped into the office and Marshal Jackson grinned widely. "Ranger Hench, been expecting you. Always a pleasure."

Hench shook the man's hand. The marshal was a bit taller than Hench, who wasn't quite six-foot tall in his boots. The Georgetown lawman was starting to go to fat and had a head of thinning blonde hair along with a thick handlebar mustache. The marshal wore green wool pants, a white cotton shirt, and a dark brown leather vest, his star stabbing the leather.

"Got your wire you was coming to town to look into the Hensley brothers."

Hench nodded. "You know 'em?"

The marshal chuckled. "Ain't a lawman in the valley don't know those sidewinders."

"I might'a seen 'em a few hours ago. Was makin' my way up from Evergreen and came across a wagon headin' down the hill. After I passed 'em, maybe ten minutes after, four outlaws set fire to the wagon, killin' one man and badly hurtin' the other. I drove off the four and brought the men up here."

Marshal Jackson looked grim. "Sounds 'bout right for those scoundrels. Only four you say? They have as many as eight in the gang, least ways that's what I gathered from other lawmen up and down the valley. But you might'a just gotten some real luck with this."

"How's that?"

"Just a couple of days ago I became privy to their hideout. Or might have, don't know for sure, haven't had time to check it out. It's not too far from here—a small canyon. It'd be a good place for them to lay low."

"How'd you find out?"

The marshal retrieved a bottle of amber alcohol from his desk. "Silver prospector told me just last week he saw 'em camped out in the canyon. I been trying to figure out what to do about it. You know, making plans with my deputies, then I got your wire." The marshal took a swig and handed the bottle to Hench, who followed suit. The marshal smiled. "Now I figure we can both take a look and make plans. Maybe you can call in more rangers to help. Mean time I'll send some deputies down to take care of the burned wagon."

"Sounds good to me. Can you show me the canyon?" Hench moved around the marshal's desk, setting the bottle on it. Behind the desk on the wall was a map of Georgetown and some of the surrounding area.

"Sure, but it'll be easier to just take you there." The marshal went to the map and pointed. "There's a ravine here that widens into a small canyon. But we can go up this way here. There's a good outcropping and we can look down on 'em if they're there."

"That seems close to where the four men attacked the wagon. Disappeared into the trees about here." Hench pointed at the map. "Wasn't 'bout to follow 'em in."

"Smart. So how about we go in the morning?"

Hench nodded. "It's a plan."

It'd been a cold spring night. There was frost on the dirt roads of Georgetown. Speck's hooves crunched through it as they made their way to the marshal's office. The sun was just peering down into the valley. Jackson was outside on the boardwalk stamping his feet and blowing white vapor from his mouth.

"It's a cold one," he said, moving to his horse.

They rode down the hill, backtracking over the path Hench took the previous day, but before reaching the wagon, Marshal Jackson stopped his horse and pointed. "That outcropping is up yonder aways. Should be able to see the canyon from it. Let's leave the horses here."

The two men dismounted, tied the horses to trees, and started walking. Hench held his Spencer carbine at the ready. He felt edgy, like maybe someone was watching them.

CHAPTER FOUR

Something was wrong.

Hench looked around the forest but didn't see anything. But he felt it. Like an itch on the back of his neck. "You sure this is the way?"

Marshal Jackson nodded and pointed upslope. "Yep. They come through here and go on up to a little ravine cut into the mountain. Follow that a bit and it opens into a small canyon where they hold up."

Hench cocked his Spencer carbine. He couldn't hear much of anything above the furious rush of Clear Creek.

The creek was only a hundred feet away or so. They were surrounded by spruce so thick he couldn't see far with any certainty. But there were shadows and movements along the fringe he didn't like. He pointed the carbine at the marshal.

"What's goin' on, Jackson? They pay you off?"

The marshal froze, looking suddenly ill. "I—what?"

"You settin' me up?"

The marshal's eyes flicked over the top of the ranger's shoulder. Despite the swollen creek, he heard a branch snap. He spun. A man no more than twenty yards away fired a revolver. Hench shot as well. Neither bullet hit. The man stepped behind a tree. The ranger levered and cocked his carbine and backed toward the marshal.

"Stop right there, Hench," said Jackson.

The ranger had expected it. He spun, raising the carbine high, smashing the butt stock into the marshal's face. The man fell. Hench drove the stock into his face a second time to make sure he stayed down. Another shot barked in the woods. It came from a different direction.

If the marshal told the truth about there being eight in the Hensley gang, he was in no small amount of trouble.

He crouched and moved away from the last echoing shot. Movement to his left. He fired, levered, and cocked. Another shot from the woods. The bullet hit the trunk of a spruce next to Hench, small shards of wood biting at his face. He kept moving. The creek's growl drew close. He wanted his back to the creek to make sure he couldn't be flanked.

His near-fatal mistake was in not looking up. As he got closer to the creek, he turned his back to it. A shot from his left moved him to his right—he realized too late, guiding him. The weight of a man fell on his back, driving him to the forest floor.

Hench hit the ground hard, his face smashed into the layer of dried evergreen needles and dirt. He bucked and the man on his back fell away. The ranger twisted and kicked, hitting someone in the gut. The man huffed air and Hench scrambled to his feet. Six other men stood no more than fifteen steps away pointing guns at him.

Hench thought seriously about just opening fire with his carbine, getting at least one of them before they turned him into a colander. But instead he set the rifle on the ground and raised his hands chest high.

The man on the ground rose, scowling, and hit Hench in the face. The ranger staggered back a step or two. The man stepped forward.

"Hold on there, Damon. You can't go hittin' a lawman."

One of the men stepped up behind Damon—they looked enough alike to be brothers. So this was definitely the Hensley gang. Daren must have been the other man, who holstered his gun and stepped up to Hench. He pulled free both of the ranger's black Schofield Model 3 revolvers and tossed them behind him. Then he reached out and ripped the silver badge from the ranger's faded blue shirt and tossed the star behind him as well. "There. Now he's just some asshole. It's okay to be beat up assholes."

"Thanks, Daren." The brother who'd jumped him stepped forward, grinning, while the other stepped back. Damon and Daren appeared to be a couple of years apart in age, both somewhere in their thirties. Hench was about ten years older. The two had long dark straggly hair sticking out from beneath their hats. Their sun-worn faces were covered in a week's worth of scruff. Their clothes dirty from the trail.

Damon swung like someone expecting his target to stand still. The ranger, however, had assessed his chances with these men and he knew his chances weren't good. He had no doubt all of them had killed before and would kill again. Hench was likely their next victim. So he saw no reason to take the hit. He leaned to his right, easily evading the swing, and smashed his fist into the man's nose.

Damon blinked, a look of shock on his face. Hench hit him again and the man crumpled to the ground. Daren charged forward, only a couple steps away, and lowered his shoulder. He plowed into Hench and the two went to the ground. They wrestled and clawed and gouged and hit each other, two wildcats.

Hench managed to get Daren turned and the ranger slipped an arm around the man's throat. Daren bucked and twisted while Hench wrapped his legs around the man's waist and used his other arm to anchor the first. It didn't take long for Daren to slow, his body falling still, his arms slapping lightly at Hench's grip. But the man didn't succumb fast enough. One of the gang approached with a large rock raised in his hand.

Hench let go of Daren to try and deflect. The man first hit the ranger in the forearm, maybe breaking the bone, but at the least causing the entire arm to go numb and lose its strength. The second hit with the rock caught Hench in the side of the head.

The rest was a haze. Hands hauled him to his feet. His vision blurred, and his head swam. The rough men looked happy as they took turns hitting the ranger in the body and the face. One of his eyes swelled shut from repeated hits. There was gruff laughter and talk. Bury his body or leave him for the wolves?

They let go of him and he fell to his knees. The bottom of a boot appeared in his blurry line of sight. It smashed into his face. He fell back. He didn't feel pain anymore. He was too far gone for that. He should have been unconscious but was too stubborn. His "good" eye was now almost swollen shut as well. However, the men stopped hitting him as they clustered together and discussed his fate.

The ranger rolled onto his stomach and pulled himself toward the creek. It was only a few yards away but seemed like a mile. He had to try, though, because the alternative was certain death. He faintly heard voices behind him, but it was drowned out either by the rushing water ahead or the ringing in his ears from the beating. He had no idea which.

He reached the bank of the creek and started crawling the four feet down to the water. His hands pulled against mud and then his front hand was in water. They dragged him back to his feet, turning him.

His head cleared enough that he recognized Damon standing in front of him, a knife drawn, his bloody face with its freshly broken nose a mask of hate and evil. Hench tried to spit on him, but his lips didn't work anymore. Men held him on either side preventing him from deflecting the blade that Damon plunged into the ranger below his rib cage.

Through the haze he felt the sting and jerked back. It wasn't much movement, but the three of them—Hench and the men holding him—slipped in the oozing mud of the bank. They released him to keep their balance and the ranger fell backward. A shock of near-freezing water enveloped him and swept him away. He tried to swim, but his arms were useless. He sped down the creek head first, which was as dangerous as the knife had been.

The rush of water was too strong and pushed him so fast his weak limbs were unable to get his body swung around, though he did manage to turn over onto his stomach just in time to see the large boulder he barreled toward.

CHAPTER FIVE

Speck didn't like what he saw. Strange men approached him.

"There's the horses," said one of them.

Several of the men dragged along another man who staggered and had a difficult time staying on his feet. His face was bloody. They pushed him up onto the other horse where the man weaved and looked ready to fall off. But somehow the man got the horse turned around and moving toward the road.

One of the loud men untied Speck's reins and started walking deeper into the forest. The Appaloosa pulled against the reins.

"Easy now," said the man, tugging on the leather.

Speck didn't like the boisterous noise of the men as they all but shouted to one another and laughed harshly. He tossed his head and tried to turn, but the man growled at him and took hold of the reins in two hands, yanking hard.

The horse reared up, sending the man sprawling and tearing the reins from his hands. The other men laughed, but moved in quickly, putting their hands up, trying to calm Speck, and get him under control. The horse surged forward. Two men in front of him dove out of the way as the Appaloosa galloped into the open where he could run free.

CHAPTER SIX

Speck came to a stop when the shouting stopped. The men's voices receded and then were gone. He started back, sniffing the air, moving toward the smell of *his* man. The smell of the other men was strong, however, which made him skittish. He especially didn't like that he also smelled blood. Then there was the sound of the creek, a roar to his sensitive ears, but he walked toward it. He wended through the trees, stopping often as another sound, another smell, drew his attention, causing him to jerk in fear. His reins, dragging along the ground, snagged often and he had to toss his head to free them and keep moving.

Then he came to a small clearing. The smells leapt at him. Many men, blood, sweat, but also the smell of his own man. Speck snuffed the ground, turned his head from side to side, then moved slowly toward the creek. His man went this way. All the way to the creek, where the smell vanished in the water. The horse turned and retraced his steps. There were faint spores that led him back out of the forest, but his man was not there.

He went back to the creek. The smell was strongest here. Speck walked the area in a loop, over and over until the sun went down.

CHAPTER SEVEN

It was daytime, the sun shining through a window, though he had no idea what time of day it was. He looked at a fireplace, blackened with use. Had there been a fire? He had some recollection of that, though maybe he dreamed it. He was in a cabin—no, it was too nice for that. Someone's house. Painted walls, store-bought furniture, a Sears and Roebuck stove. The fireplace had a mantel covered in knickknacks. He was in what appeared to be a living room that was open to the kitchen, though he was in a bed. The floor was beautifully stained and varnished wood.

A woman's face appeared, startling him. He didn't know her, or did she seem vaguely familiar? She was in her late thirties, perhaps, and attractive. Brown hair tied in a ponytail that flowed over the front of her shoulder and down her chest nearly two feet. She wore a green dress that had seen many a chore. He opened his mouth to speak, but it was dry, and his throat hurt.

"Let me get you some water."

He tried to sit up, but his head swam.

"Don't move. You've been coming in and out for nearly two days now. Just lie there, okay?"

He tried to speak again, but still couldn't. The woman sat next to him and slipped a hand under his shoulders, helping him sit up. In her other hand, she tipped a blue enamel cup to his lips. Water ran into his mouth. Nothing ever tasted so good. He gulped greedily, but she pulled the cup away.

"Easy now. Don't want to vomit again." She placed the cup to his lips again. He sipped. "That's better. It's been difficult getting food and water down. Nearly killed you a couple times these past couple of days. Choked and vomited a good deal."

He managed to whisper, "Days?"

She nodded. "Afraid so. I'm Emma Thornberry. Not that you'll remember, I imagine. I've told you my name several times. But then you pass out and sleep for hours." She eased him back down to the bed. That small movement caused his head to throb as if dynamite was going off every few seconds inside his skull.

"Well," she said, "who are you? And, no, it isn't the first time I've asked you that."

"What did I tell you before?" He whispered, unable to put much force behind his speech.

"You didn't."

Damn. He frowned and squinted at Emma. "I—I'm—" He looked away. Looked at the room he was in, looked back at Emma. But his name wasn't handy. He couldn't find it anywhere. "I don't remember."

"Honestly?" She looked puzzled but amused at the same time. "You pulling my leg?"

He tried to shake his head but winced instead. After a moment, after the room stopped swirling and he was fairly sure he wouldn't throw up, he whispered. "Honest."

"Huh. Never knew anyone who forgot his name. But you have to give me something, I'm not going to go around calling you mister."

Names eluded him. The only one that came to mind was Emma. He looked at her helplessly.

She pursed her lips. "Okay, don't fret. I'll call you—" she looked toward the ceiling as if for inspiration, "— well, how about Jake? That's as good as any and we don't have a Jake in the settlement. Three Philips and two Michaels, but no Jake."

"Jake," said the man. "Okay, that's jake by me."

She smiled. "At least you have a sense of humor."

"I wouldn't know," he whispered, a slight smile on his lips.

"You're more awake than any time since we fished you out of the creek. Maybe this time it'll stick. You hungry?"

Jake grimaced. "Don't think my stomach's up for that just yet. You say I've been here a couple of days?"

"Let's see, this is Saturday. We fished you out of the creek on Thursday."

It should have been a shock that he'd been unconscious for so long, but he had no recollection of what day he thought it should have been, so Saturday was as good a day as any. "What's the date?"

"Seriously?" She squinted at him, cocking her head, clearly not sure if she should believe him. "It's April 25. Next you'll tell me you don't know the year."

"1866, right?" He waited five seconds or so as she frowned at him. "Kidding, I know it's 1884. At least I think I do."

He reached up and scratched his beard, except he didn't have a beard. A little stubble, but otherwise his face was shaved. He reached higher. So was his head. "Was I bald when I got here? I seem to remember a beard."

She chuckled. "Yes, you had hair on your head and a beard. We had to shave it to tend to your wounds. You have some pretty good gashes on your face and head, not to mention elsewhere. You were a sight, not that you're all that mended now, but your eyes are open, they were swollen nearly shut until last night. Still bruised though. You look like a raccoon. A bald raccoon. A couple of big bumps on your noggin. We stitched up some of your cuts. Ginny, that's my brother's wife, thinks the cut in your abdomen was from a knife. She was a nurse back in Pennsylvania, where we come from. Said the wound wasn't too bad. Didn't appear to cut your intestines or anything else vital. Don't suppose you remember being stabbed?"

Jake put his hands beneath the heavy blankets and moved them over his chest and stomach. He found stitches near his nethers. Had he fought someone? That almost sounded familiar, but his memories were vapors, never fully forming and evaporating before he could see them clearly. "Nope. Don't remember a thing. So whereabouts am I? Are we?"

Emma smiled and stood up. "That's a new question. Well, we're nestled in a valley of the Rocky Mountains — of Colorado?"

Jake smiled. "I know I'm in Colorado."

She waved her hand. "Georgetown is a couple of hours horse ride that way. My brother and I fished you out of Clear Creek, which is a little less than a mile past the north edge of the settlement. We built along two meandering tributaries that run through our little valley. But to be honest, we figured we were pulling you out for your funeral until you started coughing and sputtering. We strapped you to the back of Gary, his mule, and brought you home. Well, my home. His house is full up with a wife and two kids."

"And what's the name of your town?"

"We aren't a proper town. We're a group of settlers homesteading this valley. None of us opened shops or a hotel or the like. We're all farmers of sorts, growing small crops or raising animals that we share amongst ourselves. Anything we can't build or grow we buy from Georgetown. On the other end of our valley is a mining town. Silver. Maybe you're a miner?"

Jake pulled his hands out from under the covers and looked at them front and back. "Don't think so. Hands ain't banged up enough." There were scabs on the knuckles of each hand. He frowned at that.

Emma nodded. "Yeah, we noticed that, too. You slugged it out with someone."

"Who proceeded to poke me with a knife and dump me in Clear Creek."

"Looks like." She pointed a finger at him. "You better not be an outlaw. You do anything I don't like I'll smash you in the head with a frying pan."

Was he an outlaw?

"Look," she said, "we forced water down your gullet and even got some broth in you yesterday, but you should try eating. Only way to get your strength back."

Jake's mouth watered at the mention, but not in a good way. However, he nodded. "I'll give it a try." Because she was right. Then a horrible thought crossed his mind.

"I suppose I've been relievin' myself."

"You suppose correctly."

"Any chance your brother cleaned me up?"

"Seriously, you think I'm calling my brother over every time you need changing?"

"I—I can't tell you how mortified I am right now."

She smiled and didn't seem the least bit put out or embarrassed. "On the bright side, because you haven't eaten anything solid, you don't go much. I fashioned a diaper after the first couple of hours when you weren't waking up."

"I'm wearing a diaper?"

"Damned straight."

"And I thought I couldn't feel worse."

CHAPTER EIGHT

"Any chance my clothes survived?" asked Jake.

"Your boots came through okay and that was it. They were soaked through and through so hopefully you can soften and stretch them out again. But I have some clothes that should fit."

"Your brother's? 'Cause I ain't goin' around in one of your dresses," said Jake with a smile.

She raised an eyebrow. "You should be so lucky. And, no, not my brother's, but I have some shirts and pants that should fit you. Let me lay them out. You can change in my room." Emma left the front room, disappearing through a doorway.

Jake pushed himself into a sitting position. The room spun as he did so. He let it pass before draping a sheet over his shoulders and slowly standing. The room tilted a little but didn't spin as much and he managed to stay on his feet. He was weak, but not horribly so. Not like he was going to keel over any moment.

He shuffled into the bedroom. It was a nice room with a big brass bed, an armoire, and a dressing table. Emma knelt inside a closet that Jake could smell from the doorway—it was lined with cedar. She rummaged through a big trunk. She'd taken out the top insert, which was on the bed, and now she carefully dug down deep into the trunk's underbelly. She came up with a wool red plaid shirt and black pants. Even some undergarments and socks. She set them on the bed. Jake looked curiously at them.

"I had a husband once upon a time," she said, her voice suddenly thick. "He passed on a few years back."

She sniffed and chuckled. "Damn, you'd think I'd be over the bastard by now."

"I'm sorry, Emma. I—" Jake felt a memory bubble up, but it wouldn't quite surface.

"What? Did you remember something?"

"Thought I did. It's already gone. But I think I might have lost someone myself. Crickets, what if I have a wife and family somewhere and I've completely forgotten about them?"

"Surely you'd remember something like that?"

Jake's head spun as he thought about a family out there worried sick for him.

She stepped past him, squeezing his arm lightly. "It'll come back to you. Try not to worry." She closed the door behind her.

Jake shook his head as he dropped the sheet and stared down at his diaper. *A diaper!* He slid the white cloth down his legs. It was clean, thank the Lord. He shuddered again at the thought of the woman changing him. Cleaning him! He shuddered and tried to force it from his head. He examined the knife wound. The stitching looked good, the wound clean and free from angry red swelling. It was mending nicely.

The undergarments were a pair of faded red longjohns. Next went on a pair of gray wool socks. Then the black pants, which fit satisfactorily, and finally the red plaid shirt. As he buttoned the shirt he looked around for his boots but didn't see them. Black boots? He thought maybe they were. Tucking in his shirt, he ambled out to the front room feeling a thousand times better just having clothes on. Emma wasn't there, but the front door was open. Two brown hens stood in the doorway and he heard a mess of chickens outside gossiping.

He poked around the front room looking for his boots and found them under the bed. They were indeed black. Had that been a guess on his part or had he actually remembered their color? They were all but done in thanks to the soaking. It took quite a bit of negotiation and a lot of stamping, which drove the hens back outside, before he got them on. They squeezed his feet. It'd take a little wear time to get them stretched out again. But at least he was dressed and felt almost human.

"Don't you touch me!" said Emma, anger in her voice.

Jake walked to the door and looked out. Two men stood in a rutted lane just beyond a split-rail fence lined with chicken wire. A couple dozen chickens wandered the yard. Emma stood at the fence and one of the men held Emma's upper arm. The man pulled on it, dragging her toward the gate. The woman slapped him, but he just grinned.

Jake moved quickly toward them. "Let's see if you grin when I'm done slappin' you!"

All three turned, startled.

The man let go of Emma and stared at Jake. "Who the hell is that?"

Emma held up her hands. "Everything's all right. You move along, Nate."

"Who is he?" asked Nate, anger and suspicion in his voice.

"He's my cousin. Just got up here from Denver. Now, please go. I'll talk to you later."

"Yeah, run along," said Jake, anger seething through him, making him forget how weak he was.

"Looks like you ran into a bit a trouble already," said Nate. "You don't wanna mix with me." He spit a brown stream next to Emma, and then the two men walked down the lane. Jake came up next to her and leaned against the fence as his head did a little twirl due to moving too quickly across the yard.

Jake waited for the men to get out of earshot before asking, "You okay?"

Emma sighed. "Never you mind. Nothing to worry over."

Jake turned toward the house, resting his butt against the fence. "I'm guessin' you raise chickens?"

Emma turned and also leaned on the fence. "You're mighty observant."

Jake looked around the area. They were in a little flat valley, the Rocky Mountains rising around them on all sides. Snow still touched the summits of the higher peaks. This part of the valley was mostly cleared of trees, with wild grasses and shrubs outlining several lanes that wove between at least twenty houses that he could see.

"So Georgetown's that way?" he asked, pointing toward her house.

Emma nodded. "You know Georgetown?"

"Seems to ring a bell."

She hooked a thumb over her shoulder. "That means Denver's down the mountain that way."

Images of the city sprang to Jake's mind. "Well, I've definitely been to Denver. I can picture the streets. All the wood buildings."

Emma chuckled. "That's a stale memory. It's been twenty years since Denver had wooden buildings. Had a huge fire in the mid-60s that burned most of it to the ground. Everything's brick and stone now. Or mostly, anyway."

"The fire sounds familiar. I think. So, how'd you end up here?"

"Well, pretty much everyone living in this settlement are family and close friends. We immigrated together from the old country."

"I hear an accent, but it kinda wanders. Which old country you talkin' about?"

"Ireland. I was a wee one back then. Hardly remember the trip."

"The famine?" asked Jake.

"Yes. We left a small village near Skibbereen." She sighed and shook her head. "So many died, but our elders had the money and wherewithal to get us to America. We originally settled near Pittsburgh. Then twenty years on, a lot of us got tired of the city and even the smaller town we were in.

"One of our church elders by the name of Conor started the talk about moving away from everyone. Find a nice patch of land and settle down away from any bustle. Quinn, another elder who he lives over yonder, heard about this valley from cousins of his who were mining up the mountain farther. So, the mess of us came out here.

"My husband and I built that house together, though we all chipped in to help each other build and get settled. Somehow that was eight years ago already. Hard to believe. My husband passed six years ago. Got cut bad. Infected the blood. We have a few people among us who know medicine, like my brother's wife Ginny, but nothing we could do. Took him into Georgetown. All the doctors there gathered together but couldn't help him. He passed." Her voice faded.

She looked over at Jake and smiled sadly, shaking her head. "Six years and I'm still carrying on like a schoolgirl."

"You're not carryin' on. And everyone carries their torches for as long as need be."

She looked at him more closely. "You say that from experience?"

He frowned and thought on it. "I think I do, but I don't know."

She sighed. "Well, I brought him back here. His grave is in a little cemetery at the edge of the valley to the west there, up the slope overlooking us."

"Well, despite that, it seems you found a peaceful life."

"Yeah, up until some asshole found silver at the back end of the valley. Some prospector we don't even know. Sold his claim to a mining company and, well, it hasn't been quite so peaceful for the last year as they grow the mine and their town. Those fellas who just left work for the mining company."

"Nate tryin' to lay claim to you?"

Emma went quiet and Jake didn't think she'd answer, until she finally said, "I guess, but I'm not interested. And that'd be fine, I can take care of myself, but the company is trying to push their way into our settlement. They have some flat land around the mine where they'd built themselves a company town, but as they get more miners, they keep pestering us into letting them build close by. This is the only good land in the valley. It gets pretty rocky and hilly the farther south you head up the valley toward the mine. We told them to go to Hell, but they're becoming more insistent."

Jake sighed. "Why is it that money turns men so easily from their better nature?"

"Turns them into assholes." The woman had no compunction about cursing—which Jake found rather endearing. "So how are you feeling?"

"Okay, I reckon. Head hurts a might, feel kinda weak in general. Course, I don't have any recollection of how I felt before, so maybe this is an improvement."

Emma chuckled and pushed off from the fence. "Hope you like fried chicken."

"Who doesn't?" Though he still wasn't sure he could eat.

"Think you can manage to carry some firewood? It's around the side of the house. Kitchen bin is running low."

"Yes, ma'am." Hench pushed off from the fence and moved slowly. As he went around the corner he saw

Nate and his friend down the rutted lane staring back at the house.

CHAPTER NINE

Jake opened his eyes. The front room of Emma's house was cast in orange pewter from glowing embers in the fireplace and moonlight streaming through the front windows. He looked around with the distinct feeling that something woke him. But all was quiet. He closed his eyes to settle back into sleep.

"Damn."

He threw the sheet and blanket off and sat up. He had to pee. He wore the red longjohns so he slipped his feet into his boots. He caught himself just in time from stamping the boots to seat them properly and waking Emma. Thankfully they were already easier to get on.

He pushed himself up and was pleasantly surprised his head didn't spin. The meal had helped, though he hadn't eaten all that much. Just one chicken thigh, a small portion of collard greens, and a chunk or two from a large boiled turnip. His stomach already growled from hunger. He took getting his appetite back as a good sign.

He slipped quietly outside, ignoring the outhouse in the back. He walked through the empty yard, the chickens in their roost, climbed the fence without too much pain, walked a dozen or so yards into the field to the side of Emma's house, and relieved himself. It was a cool night. He shivered. The sky was clear and the moon high and bright. He took a deep breath and turned back to the house. He stopped after only a step, turning back toward the sprawl of settlement houses.

There was a yellow glow dancing in the night about a half mile away. A fire. Would someone have a pit fire going this late? Jake didn't know the time, but if he had to pee and his stomach was empty, it had to be past midnight. He hurried into the house and banged on Emma's door.

"What the jink!" she yelled.

"I think there's a fire. A house maybe."

"Holy Hell."

There was rustling and a loud bang. He imagined her twirling into a dress. Banging into the bureau. As she got ready, he pulled his pants on over his boots, ripping the seam of one leg, but getting them on. There was a sharp twinge in his gut. Hopefully he hadn't ripped open the knife wound. With the red longjohns top, he didn't bother with a shirt and headed for the open front door. As he left the house he heard Emma running across the wood floor and she appeared next to him. He pointed.

"Holy Hell."

They ran toward the fire—it was obviously a fire. It was whether it was someone's house or some idiot bonfire—in the middle of the night. Jake ran for nearly fifty yards before his injuries caught up to him. He nearly fell to the dirt lane, his lungs heaving and burning for air.

"Damn it!"

Emma turned.

He waved her on. "I'm okay, just winded. Go, go."

Emma ran on into the night. Jake followed at a shuffling jog, cursing himself most of the way. As he drew close it became evident it was someone's house. He heard a loud banging and Emma yelling, "Fire!"

She hammered the front door of a single-story house. Smoke billowed out from under the door then a window ten feet from her blew out, flames rolling up into the sky. She cried out and jerked away for a brief moment then returned to pounding on the door.

Jake came up beside her. "How many are likely to be inside?"

"Just Conor—but he's pretty old. We have to get him out of there."

Jake swept her away from the door with one arm and kicked it in. Flames leapt at them and they both jumped back, retreating to the front yard from the intense heat.

"Go rouse the neighbors!" yelled Jake, almost doubled-over. He had no doubt he opened the knife wound.

Emma nodded and took off running. Jake stood as straight as he could and moved quickly around the house. Each window showed flames. The fire was worse in the back where it breached the outside walls and shot high into the air. There was no way to get inside. Behind the house was a large barn. It was separated by a good hundred feet, but the front of the barn was also on fire. A man looking to be in his 70s tried to get to the burning doors of the barn.

Jake shuffled over and pulled him back.

"Let go! My animals are inside!"

He had such a thick Irish brogue that Jake wasn't quite sure that's what he said, but by the panic on the man's face, he figured it was a good guess.

"Is there a back door?"

The man nodded, but said, "Blocked from the inside. New shipment of hay. Haven't had time to move it."

"Let's go. You Conor?"

"I am." He then reeled off a list of animals that were trapped inside, which Jake ignored as he looked for tools.

The two men shuffled-ran to the back of the large structure, Jake unable to move any quicker than the old man. Frightened animals cried from within. "Have an axe or sledgehammer?"

The old man motioned to the barn. "Inside."

Jake moved to the back corner of the barn and kicked with the bottom of his boot at a plank several feet above ground. He ignored the sharp pain in his side and kept at it until the board splintered and caved in. Within moments little goat heads appeared, bleating desperately and trying to push through the too-small opening. The old man rushed forward. Jake had to practically throw him back.

"Give me room!" he yelled, kicking at the next board over. When three were broken he pulled and twisted on the bottom of the first plank until it came loose. The goats tried to push through, a few making it. Jake worked on the next broken board and pulled it free. Goats flooded through the opening, surrounding the old man.

"Lead them away!"

Conor moved off, the goats jumping and running around him like frantic moths around a flame. Jake went back to work and pulled free the last broken board, giving him room to crawl in. The air was still fairly clear this low to the ground, but he started coughing. It wouldn't take long for the smoke to fill the structure and kill everything inside.

The front of the barn was a wall of flame. Horses and cows cried in terror from stalls, sounding like terrified people. Jake used the wall to pull himself to his feet and hurry forward to open gates, releasing all four horses and seven cows. The big animals rushed to the back of the barn. Jake had to be quick to avoid being struck. He followed behind, shoving and pushing his way through their churning panic, barely able to avoid kicks from both horse and cow.

Conor's face appeared in the opening Jake had made. "Hole isn't big enough!"

Jake didn't even tell him to get out of the way, he just started pushing on the top of the first plank he'd broken, loosening it further. On the outside, Conor pulled on it. The board, however, was too long to push free. But once it was loose enough, he worked on the second, and then the third, exposing the diagonal wood brace that angled down to the corner of the barn and held the vertical boards in place.

Jake yelled, "Rope!"

Conor, holding up one of the planks, pointed. "Wall behind you!"

Jake grabbed the rope and made a noose at one end. Counting out ten lengths with his arms, he tied the middle part of the rope around the diagonal board. He then waited a few seconds for the largest horse to churn toward him. He lassoed it with the noose and cinched it tight enough that, facing the horse, he could grab the loop of rope on either side just below the jaw and pull the horse toward him.

The horse's eyes were wild, and it jerked its head, but Jake held on tight and the horse moved forward. Jake bent and stepped backward over the diagonal brace and out of the barn. Conor held the planks up far enough that Jake made it outside without the boards scraping against his back. He kept walking backward, pulling on the horse until it managed to clear its front legs over the diagonal brace.

Conor let go the planks and they struck the back of the large horse. It reared up, yanking free of Jake's grip and tearing loose one board and snapping the other. Jake grabbed the rope and pulled as Conor raised his hands and moved in front of the beast to calm it. The horse surged forward several yards, striking Conor squarely in the chest, sending the old man tumbling, but it also got clear of the barn.

Jake pulled on the rope. "Come on, you nag, keep moving!"

The horse moved away from the opening. Jake released the rope and went up next to the horse, slapping it on the rump and yelling, "HA!"

The horse skittered away but jerked to a stop when the rope went taut. A cow's head and large shoulders pushed into the opening in the barn just above the diagonal brace. Jake slapped the horse again. It pulled. Jake grabbed the rope and pulled along with the horse. The cow moaned and fought against the board, trying to get out. The three of them finally snapped the diagonal brace. The cow spilled out the opening, nearly falling to the ground. Right behind it, the rest of the small herd followed.

CHAPTER TEN

There was plenty to eat in the forest, and with the creek, plenty of water. The Appaloosa walked the trail of his man's spore from where he had dismounted just outside the forest, to the creek. Speck walked that trail dozens of times over the next two days. Every time he turned to retrace the trail, he expected to see his man standing before him. But it never happened.

What did finally happen was as he drank from the creek, his reins swam in the water and pulled downstream. He followed the pull, walking along the edge of the creek for a dozen yards. He stopped and looked back. Back there was the spore—the smell of his man. Here there was nothing but the smell of water and trees and the spore of animals that lived here—the squirrels in the trees, chittering at him, the bird droppings, rabbits, fox, and even a smell that caused the skin on his neck and back to tingle with warning. The smell of a wolf.

It was old, faded with time, but still Speck stamped his feet and tossed his head in fear, his eyes and ears searching for the danger, his large nostrils wide as they smelled the air. He moved away from the smell at a canter, moved farther from the smell of his man—moved downstream, following the creek.

The smell of wolf faded and disappeared. Speck slowed to a walk, but his nerves were jangled, and he skittered at every sound that wasn't the roar of water and every movement out of the corners of his eyes.

CHAPTER ELEVEN

Jake took the noose from the horse and it jogged away from the fire. People started running up. Several went to Conor, who was prone and motionless on the ground.

One man said, "The animals?"

Jake said, "They're all free."

There was a horribly loud crunch and *whump!* as part of the house's roof collapsed. Bucket brigades quickly formed to keep the fire from spreading to neighboring houses. The settlement wasn't like Denver, where the downtown wooden buildings were built practically on top of one another. A fiery image surfaced of Denver burning. The heat like nothing he'd ever felt before. But he didn't have time to explore the memory further as he joined a bucket brigade.

Hours later, the fire spent, the eastern horizon turning orange, Jake dropped an empty bucket to the ground. People looked like phantoms in the thick foggy steam and smoke that filled the area. The acrid smell was so strong that it felt like a physical thing, like smoldering chunks of charcoal jammed into his mouth and nose.

The house was razed flat to the ground. The barn was about half burned. They'd have to tear it down to rebuild. Thankfully all the animals made it out.

Jake turned to Emma, "Any word on Conor?"

She nodded. "He's awake and seems okay. What are you looking at?"

Jake smiled and fought an urge to push a lock of brown hair from her face. It wouldn't be seemly, nor did he think she would welcome such a familiar gesture. Her beautiful face was smudged with black, but that somehow made it more alluring. He was startled when she stepped closer and leaned against him. Out of instinct, he put his arm around her shoulders. He felt awkward standing there like that. He was a stranger to the settlement and she was a single woman. But he didn't move an inch, relishing her touch. Unfortunately, the phantoms around them started to move and Emma stepped away.

Despite everyone's exhaustion, there was no going back to sleep anytime soon. People went about retrieving the freed animals and penning them at neighbors' houses. The goats joined the chickens in Emma's yard.

Little more than an hour later, the sun was a swollen blood-red disc that hung over the craggy eastern peaks of the Rockies just visible through the smoky haze. Some men ventured gingerly over the still-smoldering debris of the former house, heat coming off it in a steady wave. They checked to make sure the fire was completely out but also seeing if anything of Conor's could be salvaged. The men poked and lifted using pry bars. Some had thick leather gloves and tossed aside different sized black planks, some crumbling in their hands. One man cursed and threw a thick smoldering post. He clapped his gloved hands together and waited several moments before venturing to grab more smoking rubble.

Jake watched them for a moment, hypnotized by their actions and his exhaustion. Then he roused himself and turned to head back to Emma's. He hadn't seen her for at least a half-hour, no doubt making sure the goats had everything they needed. But before he could take a step, a small two-gallon milk jug made of galvanized metal caught his attention. It was beneath the ashy remains of a shrub that hadn't survived its proximity to the front of Conor's house.

He bent down and touched the jug cautiously, but it wasn't hot. He lifted it by its one remaining handle, there was a hole in the metal where the other handle would have been on the opposite side. The hole was large, at least a third of the jug missing. The jagged metal edge of the hole pushed outward.

Jake stood up and carried the jug to the edge of the burnt house. "Any of you live next door?"

The men, five of them, seemed to notice him for the first time, all of them eyeing him curiously, even suspiciously. One of the men, younger than Jake, nodded. "I live right there." Like Emma, he had the residue of an Irish accent.

"Did you hear an explosion?"

The man looked even more confused and shook his head.

Jake held up the jug. "Something in this exploded."

An older man, his accent hardly touched by America, said, "Boiling milk?"

"Maybe. Where's Conor staying at?"

The younger man pointed to a house. Jake started for it, the men following behind. He entered the front door without knocking, though opening it slowly and peering inside. The front room was empty. He proceeded into the house and found Conor in a bedroom, in bed, flanked by three women. The oldest of the women, about Conor's age, turned toward the door.

She whispered, "Shush!"

Jake stopped in the doorway. The men behind him, who'd been muttering amongst themselves, went quiet.

Her face flashed lightning, but still she whispered. "What in tarnation are you all doing in here? Conor needs his rest."

"I'm sorry, ma'am," said Jake, finding himself whispering, as well. "I just need to ask him a question."

"No!"

"It's okay, Jeanie. What is it, son?"

At least that's what Jake thought he said. He held up the demolished metal jug. "This yours?"

The old man scrunched up his face. "Could be. Use them for my cows."

"Of course," said Jake. "And you had one of them in your house?"

The old man frowned for a moment, then shook his head. "No. I put what I need into a ceramic urn and keep that in my kitchen."

"And you're sure you didn't leave one of these in your kitchen after fillin' your urn?"

"I fill the urn in the barn. What's this about?"

Jake hesitated. He didn't want to upset the old man, but he decided to continue. "I found this outside the front of your house. See how the edge of the metal is blown out? Somethin' inside it exploded. And I'm wonderin' if it wasn't something other than milk. Kerosene, perhaps."

The old man looked confused. "What are you getting at?"

The shushing woman looked appalled, but still whispered, "You think someone set that fire on purpose."

Jake nodded. He looked back to the old man, whose eyes were focused on the ceiling as though thinking through this news. Jake said, "Now if—"

"I wonder if that's what woke me up," said Conor.

"Excuse me?"

The old man looked at Jake. "I was sound asleep and then I jolted awake. Dreamt I was standing next to a copper kettle that suddenly exploded."

The woman held her hands out toward the old man. "You settle down now, Brother." She turned toward Jake. "Okay, you've upset him quite enough. Leave us to peace."

Jake nodded and turned. The five men behind him were bunched up and had to turn and lead the way out the front door.

Back outside, the young man frowned. "Funny about his dream. Something like that happened with me. I just sort of woke up. Maybe ten minutes before I heard people yelling."

"And I hate to say it," said Jake, "but maybe they weren't tryin' to just set fire to the house, but to kill Conor outright with this bomb. Anyone know why someone would want to do that?"

"Who are you?" asked a thin man with smashed-in features, as though he'd partaken in more than a few fights.

"You a lawman?" asked another. "How did you even come up with this idea just by looking at that jug?"

Was he a lawman? He put a hand to his chest, his fingers expecting to feel a badge. "Could be," he muttered. Or was he remembering the badges of the men tracking him down? Maybe the badge of the man who stabbed him. He didn't know.

"Or maybe he's from the mine?" Their looks immediately became suspicious. That thought must have been swimming somewhere in all their heads and now quickly bobbed to the surface.

"Funny he should think to even look for that jug."

"Yeah. Maybe he was the one that did it."

Suspicion turned to anger.

"Do you think I'd say anything about the jug if I'd done it?" said Jake, taking a step back.

"Maybe. Maybe you're just covering up for yourself."

Almost as one, the men stepped closer, their hands balled into fists.

CHAPTER TWELVE

"Get 'round behind him," said one of the men.

They spread out. Jake didn't much care for being trapped like this. He picked out the meanest looking and punched him in the face. The man stumbled backward and fell. He hoped it would be enough to knock one of them to the ground.

It wasn't.

They swarmed him like ants attacking a wasp. As a group, they roiled and floundered across the lane toward the burned remains of Conor's house. They pummeled with hits and kicks. They beat him hard. He was already weak from helping with the fire and still recuperating from his earlier injuries. But he kept swinging. Two of the men fell away, blood gushing from broken noses. For the remaining two, that freed up room for them to land more damaging blows.

From the corner of his eye, Jake saw a charcoal board swing into view. He turned his head to avoid the brunt of the impact. The board thunked loudly, but he wasn't hit. One of the two men fighting him whirled, ready to punch, a cloud of ash engulfing his head. He froze, however, and gaped at Emma. She gripped the board in both hands, cocking it back to swing again.

"What'd you do that for?" the man asked.

The fighting paused at the sudden intrusion.

"What the hell are you doing!" yelled Emma, stepping next to Jake, board at the ready.

The men looked confused. One of them said, "He had something to do with the fire." The others grumbled their agreement, even those with hands covering their faces, blood flowing down their wrists.

"Oh, for heaven's sake, he was asleep in my house when the fire broke out."

That quieted them down, their eyes going wide.

"Jesus H. Christ," she said, "not like that. He's staying in the front room until his wounds heal. Any of you notice he was injured? Did you look at his face? Criminy, the man was stabbed! And you go jumping him, five against one. Such brave men you are. He's the one Liam and I fished out of Clear Creek."

The men looked embarrassed, standing awkwardly like school children caught in mischief by the schoolmarm. The man Emma hit with the board rubbed the back of his head and said, "Uh, our apologies."

"But how'd he know about the jug?" asked another.

"What are you talking about?" said Emma.

Jake motioned to the jug on the ground. "I think someone used that as a bomb to set off the fire."

Emma looked stunned. "You sure?"

"Pretty sure."

"Dear Lord. But why?"

Jake looked at the men. "You think the mining company had something to do with this?"

They looked between them, but it was Emma who said, "That makes sense. It wouldn't be one of our own, so unless it was some stranger passing through."

Jake didn't like the lingering look that Emma gave him as she said that.

He said, "Why couldn't it be one of yours? A love spat. An argument over money. You'd be surprised."

"Sure talks like a lawman," said one of the men.

Jake furrowed his bloody brow. The words just came out without thinking. His fingers returned to his chest.

"We aren't going to figure any of this out right now. Let's get you cleaned up." Emma and Jake walked away, leaving the men to stare after them, still looking confused.

"I didn't do it," said Jake when they were out of earshot.

"Didn't say you did."

"I saw the look you gave me. I'm gonna find somewhere else to sleep 'til I'm healed enough to move on. Hell, I could just grab a mess of blankets and sleep under the stars."

He couldn't miss the pause, but she said, "No. That's foolish. I know you didn't do it."

"You *hope* I didn't do it. Besides, it's not right me stayin' with you, you bein' an unattached woman and all. Don't want your friends thinkin' poorly of you."

"Oh, please, I'm too old to give a damn what my friends think. And they wouldn't be very good friends if me helping a hurt man got them to chirping."

Back inside her house she said, "Need to clean you up. If anything, you look worse than you did when we fished you out of the creek."

He didn't feel good. His head pounded and most everything else ached.

"Unbutton your top, let's see how bad the knife wound is."

He hesitated, feeling a bit reserved about undressing in front of her. But she'd seen him naked—he shuddered yet again thinking about the diaper. He unbuttoned the top to the red longjohns and shrugged out of it, but he kept his pants on. Looking down, he was surprised to see the stitches mostly intact. There was blood and a broken loop or two, but the wound wasn't completely split open as he'd assumed.

She poured water from her kitchen pitcher into a large bowl and came over to him, a kitchen towel over her shoulder. She looked as exhausted as he felt, her hair mostly undone, her face covered in ash. Jake thought she looked lovely.

She sat next to him on the bed and dipped the towel into the water, putting a hand on his chin to turn his face. "I can't believe my friends did this," she said, shaking her head slightly.

"Everyone's spooked about the fire—and everyone's probably been on edge since the mining operations got going."

"I don't know if we're on edge," she said, carefully dabbing and rubbing at the new cuts and abrasions he'd just received. It hurt, but he didn't mind her attention in the least.

"Maybe not outward-like. But somethin' like this gnaws at a person on the inside. Just an uneasy feelin' that maybe you don't notice all the time, but it's there."

She shrugged. "Maybe." Then she made a face, puckering her lips and moving them to the side. He imitated her, and she cleaned up something on the side of his mouth. A strong urge to lean forward and kiss those lips came over him. He had to move out, even thinking about kissing her seemed so inappropriate.

"Face is done. Lie back."

He did as she asked, and she leaned over and examined the wound, gently pressing the wet towel against it. "I'll have my sister-in-law come by tomorrow." She chuckled. "I guess later today and see about tightening up these stitches some."

"Lookin' forward to it," said Jake, sitting back up with

a grimace, Emma putting a hand behind his back. She seemed to hold it there longer than she needed, but he was sure he was just imagining. Hopeful thinking.

After another moment, she stood up. "I'm done in and going back to bed."

Jake nodded. "It's been a rather eventful night—or morning."

She paused in the doorway of her bedroom. "I meant it, you know. I don't think you had anything to do with the fire." Her gaze lingered a moment, then she went into her room and closed the door behind her.

It didn't matter, he had to move on. He sat on the edge of the bed. Now was as good a time as any. He had no belongings to pack. He'd have to take the clothes she'd loaned him, but he could send her money later. He'd head to the mining town and see if anyone knew him, see if maybe he was a miner after all. At the least, there'd be a bunkhouse or tents he could sleep in. New mining towns always needed workers.

"I'll just wait for her to fall asleep," he said quietly, lying back on the bed for just a moment.

CHAPTER THIRTEEN

Wayne Hensley, superintendent of the Sideways Mining Company, looked up as Nate Greer and two of his other men came into his office. They looked done in, like they'd been up all night.

Hensley's office was on the second floor of the mining company building that sat in the middle of the town. Calling it a town was being overly kind, but it was the first seeds of what could become a thriving community. They were finding and digging out enough silver to make the enterprise worthwhile and that would lead to more and more people finding it worthwhile to move here.

Right now, it was nothing more than a main street with the barest of essentials. But Hensley knew that if they kept pulling silver from the mountain, people would come and what was a hard scrabble collection of buildings could become another Georgetown or Leadville. With him as boss. He liked that idea quite a bit. Lord Mayor, so to speak, with his fingers in everyone's pot.

But for that to happen, they needed room to grow. The valley wasn't very large, and the mine and town were crammed into one end. It opened up nicely to the north—except those troublesome settlers had all that land.

Hensley cocked an eyebrow. "Well?"

"Burned his house to the ground."

Hensley nodded. "Good. What about the old man?"

"He's okay. Got out fine."

"And his animals? Did you burn down the barn?"

Nate made a face. "It was burning, but they managed to get the animals out in time. It only took a few minutes before it looked like the whole settlement was there putting out the fire. Maybe next time we set a couple fires. You know, on different sides of the settlement so they gotta split up."

Hensley pursed his lips and ran a hand over his mostly bald pate, pressing down what strings of hair he had. "Not a bad idea. But let's see what that old man does. Hopefully he shows up tomorrow begging me to take the settlement off their hands. Ain't like we didn't offer them a fair enough price."

One of the other men looked confused. "Why not just burn it all down? They can't stay if none of 'em got a place to live."

Hensley sighed and looked at him. "Let's hope it don't come to that 'cause right now there's all those nice houses. Why build from scratch when they already provided? But first we have to get that old man to decide it would be better to move on than to put up with us. The way he leans is the way the rest of them will lean."

CHAPTER FOURTEEN

Jake woke up on his bed when Emma came out of her room hours later. He groggily reprimanded himself for not moving on while she slept. Of course, he could do that now, but seeing her made him hesitate. Neither spoke. He couldn't think of anything to say and he wondered if she was getting up the nerve to tell him to hit the trail. Before their silence could be broken a crier's voice wafted in from outside about a meeting.

The settlement had a common house—a large square structure. Unlike the homes, there wasn't much decoration to it. A front and back door and two windows on each side. The inside was just as plain with only one room. Benches lined it like pews, which is what they were used for every Sunday. The benches were also for students during school. Sometimes they were moved to the walls for celebrations and dances.

They built the place big enough that everyone had a seat with room to grow. It was dusk, sunlight dwindling to purple gray, the smoky haze all but gone. People brought lanterns and there were wall sconces already lit. Near one wall was a podium. Jack was surprised to see Conor standing behind it. His shaggy hair was mostly white, his face ruddy and weathered, and legs so bowed you could see a foot sticking out from either side of the podium. He started the meeting with a prayer. Jake's ear for the man's heavy brogue was improving. He understood much of it.

Behind the man sat several people, one of which was the woman who'd admonished him when he came to see

Conor right after the fire. Jake leaned toward Emma. "Who's she? His wife?"

"Sister."

Behind the podium, Conor held a Bible, though he hardly glanced at it, speaking Scripture for fifteen minutes or so as the room riffled with, "Amens."

"The Lord," said Conor, looking at the room for a moment, then shaking his head. "The Lord has tested us mightily this past week. First, we get word that James and Dylan were attacked near Georgetown. Poor Jimmy killed, and Dylan hurt so badly he's still up there with the doctor. Our wagon of supplies destroyed. And now, my house burned to the ground. Sometimes it's difficult to understand God's plan, but that's when faith is most needed."

Amens moved through the room.

"But along with faith, God expects us to help ourselves. I suggest we send someone up to Georgetown and demand from Marshal Jackson that he come down here to look into these incidents. There are those among us who believe the occurrences are related."

Jake wondered if the man picked up on the irony of saying they needed to help themselves by suggesting they send for outside help.

"Murder was committed!" yelled Conor suddenly, slamming a palm against the top of the podium with a loud *whomp!* "James was a good man. The marshal must tend to it and see justice is done. And while we can all guess where the murderers came from, we need the marshal to ferret them out, find the ones who pulled the trigger, throw them in jail or even, God save us, have them hanged."

Heads nodded.

"Any volunteers want to go up to Georgetown? Maybe it should be several men, for safety. Five or six men, even."

Hands raised and Conor nodded. "Good. No reason you can't go as soon as tomorrow."

That's when Liam, Emma's brother, stood up. He and his sister had a passing resemblance, though Liam was several inches taller with a muscular build. "I don't mean to be disrespectful, but don't we have to do something more than send for the marshal up in Georgetown?"

Conor looked at him curiously. "Such as?"

Liam took a deep breath. The man's face was red. His hands shook. "I'm tired of this, and I know others are, too. You talk as if this just started happening. The mining company's been nipping at us for over six months now. It has to stop. The marshal won't put an end to that even if he finds who killed James. And when Jackson leaves, we'll be back to fretting over what the company will do next."

No one spoke, but some nodded in agreement.

He took another deep breath. "I say we go into that unholy town and find the murderers ourselves. We know where to look. Whoever did it works for Wayne Hensley. We *know* that. He's the one giving the orders. He sent his men down here last night to burn your house,

Conor. Or worse, to kill you. Maybe he figured with you out of the way the rest of us would fold. What's stopping us from going after Hensley himself? Drag him out of that town and treat him to the kind of justice he deserves."

Conor looked shocked. "What are you saying?"

"You know what I'm saying. If we deal with him, it'll be cutting off the head of the snake. The body will wither and die. He's the one behind everything. He runs the mining town for the company. Put an end to him and our troubles go away."

"Dear Lord," said Conor. "It's just the emotions of the moment getting carried away. You don't—you can't mean what you're saying. Now don't think I don't understand. And you're right in that if Hensley were gone, our troubles would be lighter. But we do it the right way. Bring in the law and have them do their job."

"Why? So the blood isn't on our hands? Maybe it's time we bloodied our knuckles. We're not cowards. Let me and some others go after him. We've turned the other cheek too many goddamned times, beg your pardon. We need to push back."

Murmurs ran through the congregation. Jake picked up assent and dissent among the people. The settlement was torn.

Conor raised his hands and the people quieted. "I know you don't mean any of this, Liam. I *refuse* to believe that you would become a—" the older man couldn't finish the sentence.

Liam's face turned an even deeper red. He was furious. In a low tone, he said, "I am willing to kill to protect what's mine. What's ours. This is no different than if men came to my door with ill intent. I would defend my family unto death. Well, the wolves are baying, and we must defend ourselves. Like you said, God wants us to help ourselves. And you know what has to be done to wolves who threaten the flock."

A louder murmur. More people seemed to agree with Liam. Conor slammed his hand down on the podium more violently. "No! We are not murderers! We will not turn our back on God. No!"

Liam didn't back down. "We have to stand up for ourselves. Defend what's ours. And that means going after those who have caused us harm. It's not like we're unsure of who needs to be brought to justice. There's no question who we need to call out."

People started talking to one another, debating Liam's words in a sudden cacophony. Jake looked up at Conor, who seemed sadly resigned to letting it run its course. Emma looked at her brother with worry. Jake asked, "Who is Conor? He your mayor or the like?"

It took Emma a moment to respond, finally looking away from Liam. "He's an elder. One of those who organized the move to this valley. When we gather like this, he tends to be the one people look to. But he doesn't have any formal title. I'm sorry, I have to get out of here."

She hurried from the building. Jake listened to those around him for a few more minutes seeing which way they leaned, then he walked out and looked for Emma.

She was out past her house, walking through the grass meadow, spring flowers surrounding her like fireworks frozen in time.

"What's wrong?"

She sighed and shook her head and Jake didn't think she was going to answer, but then she said. "It's my brother."

"Worried he's going to do something reckless?"

She nodded. "He's no coward. Only reason he and his friends haven't headed to the mining town before this is because of Conor and some of the other elders getting them to calm down. And not just the elders. Liam's married. His friends are married. We don't need a settlement full of widows and fatherless children. But now, with James dead and them burning Conor's house, I don't see how anyone can stop them. Not this time. And I understand—just as I know their wives understand. I want to hurt whoever did this."

"But you don't want it to be your brother?"

"I don't want anyone else to get killed. But, yes, I don't want my baby brother killed. He's good in a fight, but this is different from what any of these men are used to. This isn't a scuffle in a saloon. You don't shake hands at the end of it and buy each other a drink. Wayne Hensley has ten or more men whose job it is to keep peace among the miners. They're roughnecks who aren't afraid to fight, either."

The last visage of daylight disappeared, and the moon reflected off her glistening eyes. "But—I don't know. Maybe we *should* deal with this ourselves. If we send enough men with guns, maybe we can—I don't know. James deserves justice, even if it's a bunch of our men going into the mining town and breaking it apart. Lord knows that whole town is rotten."

"But it's your brother."

"And I don't want him to be found dead in a burning house—along with his wife and kids."

CHAPTER FIFTEEN

The next morning, Emma spread feed for the chickens in the growing dawn light while Jake filled a small trough with food for the goats. The small animals raised a ruckus, bleating and crying in excitement, literally jumping over one another.

Jake said, "It's like they got springs in their legs."

Emma smiled thinly. She still looked tired and he wondered if she'd gotten much sleep worrying about her brother. As he replenished the goats' water he noticed people moving about. The settlement seemed to all be early risers. Then a man approached, "Good morning."

Emma nodded. "Good morning, Angus."

He was a big sturdy man with a wild head of hair and a bushy beard of rusty brown, but no mustaches. "We're starting the cleanup over at Conor's."

"We'll be along shortly," she said.

He moved on. Emma finished throwing feed from the bucket and set it down next to the door, ducking back inside. She reappeared with two pairs of leather gloves in her hands. "Let's go."

They weren't the only ones heading over. A small procession, like early-morning churchgoers, joined Emma and Jake. Ahead of them were Liam, Ginny, and their little girl and boy. A few people were already pulling boards from the charred remains and stacking them in the clearing between the house and the barn. Liam and Ginny joined in, their two children running off with other children to play nearby.

Tools appeared again. The people were like ants

swarming the remains of a picnic, carrying off bits and stacking it into piles. Several wagons pulled up and boards were loaded and hauled off to the town's garbage dump. Conor was among them, helping clean up. The old man was spry and strong. His sister tried to get him to slow down, but he ignored her with a smile.

It didn't take much more than an hour to clear away the solid pieces, leaving the ash behind. Shovels dumped it into barrels that were loaded onto wagons, creating a black cloud and a lot of coughs. In another hour, the land was flat and looked like nothing more than a patch of cleared land singed by fire.

They started on the barn next. About a quarter had burned, so they made two stacks: what could and couldn't be salvaged. Jake found himself up on the roof, ignoring Emma's protests. Liam knelt nearby using a crowbar to pry up shingles. Jake took the shingles and dumped them over the edge.

"They worked you over pretty good," said Liam.

Jake used his tongue to feel the inside of his fat lip. He

also had a cut over his right eye, along with a black eye, and a bruise on his cheek. "Probably doesn't help me get my memory back."

Liam squinted up at him. "You still don't remember anything?"

"Nope. There are times when it feels like a memory is *right* there. That I could reach out and touch it, but then it's gone. But I do want to thank you for fishin' me outta Clear Creek. We haven't had a chance to talk since then."

Liam shrugged, returning to the shingles. They'd cleared the crown and were working their way down the west side of the roof. Another small group of men were on the east side doing the same.

Jake looked down at the man for a moment, then said, "You know it'd be a mistake to head into the minin' town lookin' for revenge."

"That you talking or my sister?"

"Both. But I can't imagine what you hope to gain by marchin' in there. They got a host of men in that town."

"We have to do something. For ourselves. Can't rely on the marshal to do what's right. If he comes down, the mining boss'll just smile and act like it couldn't possibly have been any of his men who did this. What's the marshal going to do?"

"But what are *you* going to do? You willin' to kill a man over this?"

Liam shrugged. "Maybe."

"Okay, but which man? The minin' boss? One of his crew?"

"I'm thinking we take the boss and get him to tell us what happened."

"Then what? Take the boss to the marshal, who'll arrest you for kidnappin'?"

"Then we take care of the men who killed James and tried to kill Conor."

"And what if they get you first?"

He looked up at Jake. "I'm not afraid."

"What about your wife and kids?"

He turned back and smashed the hammer down several times, splintering shingles. He didn't speak again.

Jake and Emma sat at the table in her front room eating a lunch of day-old biscuits and cold ham.

"Talked to your brother," he said after a while.

"And?"

Jake shrugged. "He seems pretty set. Told him there weren't no point goin' into town lookin' for revenge."

"Justice. He'd be looking for justice."

Jake nodded. "Whatever you wanna call it. But I doubt Liam took anythin' I said to heart."

Emma smiled wanly. "I appreciate you trying. He's like father, stubborn and looking to protect his own. Father hated depending on others."

"And you?" asked Jake. "You like your mother?"

Emma shrugged. "I guess so. They're both good people."

"They up here? In the settlement?"

She shook her head. "They're in Wisconsin with my mother's family. Liam and I wanted to head farther west. Neither of us liked the idea of being too settled just yet."

Jake watched the way her hair, piled up on her head, swayed as she talked. She'd had it tied in a bun, but much of it had come loose during the work at Conor's. The strands that fell to either side of her face framed it nicely. She glanced at him and he looked away quickly, as though caught snooping. A genuine smile touched her lips and she put a hand over the top of Jake's. He looked down at it, relishing the touch. He closed his hand around the ends of her fingers and squeezed gently. She returned the affection.

Jake didn't want to spoil the moment with stupid words, so he sat there and enjoyed the touch. After several minutes, he lifted her hand to his lips and kissed the back of it, then slowly pulled his hand away and stood up, stacking their plates.

"I can't stay here in your house," he said.

Emma furrowed her brow. "You have a funny way of wooing a woman."

He smiled. "I'm mended now. Or mostly. Kinda. It wouldn't be right. I gotta find some place to stay. It'd be easier if your settlement had an inn or boarding house. But I gotta bunk somewhere else."

She stood and stepped close to him, looking up into his eyes, taking his hands in hers. "You have to do that right this moment?"

He felt a heat as intense as the fire from the night before. "Well, maybe not *right* this moment."

CHAPTER SIXTEEN

Spring nights in the Rocky Mountains were cold, but Speck had endured far worse, especially out on the plains with the wind howling off these same mountains, pushing freezing rains or blizzards before it. But thus far, the spring days were pleasant for the horse. And there was shelter among the trees when a spring snow dropped several inches one night.

The Appaloosa kept walking down the mountain. Perhaps only because it was easier than going up. He plodded along at a slow but steady pace. There was no urgency.

Of course, he had no sense of time. It was either day or night, and his man wasn't there. That didn't mean there weren't seeds of absence or even fear at times with a longing to see the man. And fear the man wouldn't ever return.

But there were other fears. He was in a forest in the Rocky Mountains. He'd smelled bears, came across their spore and scat, causing him unease. But the worst was the night a wolf howled—and the lonely terrifying call was answered.

CHAPTER SEVENTEEN

Someone pounded on the front door. Jake leapt from bed and when Emma came into the room, he held his hand up for her to stop. He called out, "Who is it?"

"It's Ginny!"

Emma rushed past Jake and opened the door. A small stout woman burst into the house. "Liam snuck out. When I woke up I saw him and three others riding toward the mining town. Dear God, they're going to be killed!"

Jake, already in his longjohns, put on his pants and shirt, socks and boots. Emma looked at him curiously.

He said, "Where can I get a horse?"

For a moment it looked like Emma would fight him on this, but then she said, "Come on."

A half-moon shone over the valley, lighting up a spring snow that must have moved through the valley after sundown. It provided enough light for Jake and, more importantly, the horse. He pushed the horse to speed, despite the slippery conditions, hoping to catch up with Liam and his friends before they got to town. And then? He could only hope to convince them to come home.

But he was too late.

A few lights shone from windows up ahead like lone beacons in a dark sea. Jake slowed the horse. Outlines of buildings solidified. The tracks of Liam and the others' horses in the snow led him to them, tied up to trees. He tied up his own horse and followed on foot. Their footprints disappeared into a muddy mess as he entered the mining town.

Even in the darkness there were deeper shadows. Jake sought them out as he moved forward. His right hand kept moving to his waist. Unconsciously reaching for a gun?

He passed several wood structures and a large canvas tent. None of these buildings had lights on. Even the saloon he passed was dark, no doubt because of a curfew to prevent the miners from drinking all night. If everyone in town was asleep, maybe he could find Liam and the others and get them out before they caused trouble.

The main street of the mining town was wide, with the dirt right up to front doors. Farther on he found the skeleton of a boardwalk, thick beams thrust into the ground framed by stout boards. They were still building the foundation of the walk and didn't look ready to add the planks to the top. The new boardwalk fronted a large building with a large stenciled sign that read: Sideways

Mining Company. The company office. The heart or fist of the town, depending on how you wanted to look at it.

As Jake passed in front he heard the scuffle of boots. He stopped and listened. He turned his head one way and the other trying to pinpoint it. It came from inside the mining company building. That made sense. They were after the local boss. He probably lived in an apartment inside.

There were several heavy boards crosswise on the boardwalk foundation to allow people to enter the building more easily. Jake eased up on to them and moved to the front door. It was ajar a few inches. He heard the squeak of a floorboard from inside. Someone stupidly shushed the squeaker. Had to be Liam and his buddies. Jake still had a chance to stop them. As he pushed open the door, all Hell broke loose.

It started with someone farther inside the building calling out, "Who the hell's down there? Stanley, that you?"

Feet pounded away from the door—Liam and his friends. A light appeared at the top of stairs at the back of a large room. Crazy elongated shadows of the four men in front of Jake twisted across the floor and one of the walls.

CHAPTER EIGHTEEN

Speck bolted before the wolf howls dwindled into faint echoes. The Appaloosa weaved through trees as a cream and brown blur, pushing to move faster. His ears twitched on his head, forced back by his full-out gallop, but he heard the growling barks of the two wolves closing in on him from both sides.

The horse had known fear before, but he always had the calming voice and presence of his man to reassure him. Now he was alone in the dark, a half-moon glowing above that barely touched the lower branches of the forest. Breath chugged steam from his nostrils in the brittle cold. Heart pounded in his massive chest. Head steady as his legs churned beneath him, flinging up snow and mud in a wake behind him. Trees flashed by.

He burst out of the forest into a clearing, the smooth expanse of snow almost blinding after the close-in darkness of the forest. Nearly even with him, one to either side, the wolves flashed out of the forest. Then a third wolf came into a view, a huge silver and black streak that was ahead of him, circling to cut him off. The two other wolves closed in from behind.

CHAPTER NINETEEN

A man appeared at the top of the stairs, gaping at the four below. A shotgun blast went off, outlining Liam and the others briefly in fire, and the man on the stairs ducked and scurried back up. The settlement men pounded up the stairs. Jake slipped inside. From behind, men's voices shouted in the night.

Jake moved away from the door, into a corner of the front room. He didn't want to charge up after Liam and get trapped from behind by men pouring in from outside, which they did. Jake counted seven, most of them yelling questions but not waiting for answers.

A couple of them had lanterns. Another shot sounded from upstairs. The men didn't even look around the front room, rushing across it and up the stairs. A couple of them had revolvers, a few shotguns, and others held what looked to be lead pipes. Liam and his three friends were in a heap of trouble.

As the last of the men started up the stairs, Jake moved to the back of the room, finding a door. He entered and moved through a hallway and found another door leading outside. Before he opened it, the floor above erupted in noise. Men yelling, another gun going off, and then what sounded like buffalo stampeding. It was one hell of a free-for-all.

Jake slipped out the back door and found what he'd hoped to find: another staircase. This one hugging the outside wall. He clambered up, unafraid of making noise. No one inside would hear him. At the top of the stairs was a small landing in front of a locked door. Jake leaned over the railing to look into a window. The room beyond was an office, but most importantly, it was empty. Light from a hallway sliced through it, the light staccato lightning from the melee beyond.

Jake pushed up on the window. It groaned but moved. Opening it fully, he grabbed the windowsill. Getting his knees up on the railing, he pulled and heaved himself into the room.

He hit the floor with his shoulder and rolled to his feet. Every ache and wound flared pain, but he moved quickly to the wall next to the open door. The fight wasn't more than a minute old, but it already started to settle down. Jake assumed the superior numbers of the company men outweighed the vengeance of Liam and his buddies. He risked a quick look into the hallway. Halfway down, three men stood outside another room, all three craning to see inside. There was some shouting, some of it Liam's, his voice angry and distraught.

Jake walked right up to the men in the hallway, positioning himself to get a glimpse inside the room.

There were several lamps providing plenty of light. The room was done up nicer than the rest of the building. Expensive furniture with a couch and several comfortable chairs. A couple of Persian rugs on the polished wood floor. Paneling along the walls. It was like someone's den in a house back East. Inside, Liam and two of his pals were on their knees, their hands being bound behind them. The blood and red swelling on their faces indicated why they only gave a halfhearted struggle.

One of the men in the hallway eyed Jake sideways. "Who are you?"

"I'm Jake. One of the miners. Heard the ruckus and came up to take a peek."

The man stared at him for a moment. "What the hell happened to you?"

"A little roughhousing in the bunkhouse. Over some cards." Jake took a chance saying "bunkhouse," hoping the miners weren't sleeping in tents.

The other two men glanced at him and then returned their attention to the room. None of the three recognized him, which seemed to put to rest the chance of him being from the mining town.

"Who are those fellas?"

"Don't worry about 'em," said the man. "Maybe you should mosey on back to the bunkhouse."

"What'cha gonna do with 'em?"

Another man chuckled. "Nothin' they'll enjoy." The other two nodded.

Inside the room, a man came into view, walking a circle around the prisoners, looking down at them. He was about Jake's age, but gone to pot, his belly spilling over the stressed waist of his wool pants. He had a thick head of graying hair and a bulbous nose that looked like it'd been broken a dozen times. He said, "Any more of you in town?"

None of the three answered. Liam glared with one good eye, the other swollen shut. Was this Wayne Hensley? The man in charge? Jake moved positions to see a different part of the room. Another man, it was Angus from the settlement, sat on the floor, propped against a wall. He grimaced and held a bloody wad of cloth to his arm.

In the hallway, the man who'd been talking to Jake turned toward him. "Seriously, fella, get back to the bunkhouse. Nothin' for you to see here."

Disappointed, but in no position to argue, Jake moved away. There were four other doorways down the hall, which ended at the stairs. He clumped down to the first floor. There wasn't much furniture. A few chairs and spittoons, off to his left was a large desk with more chairs. He thought about going down the back hall again but decided it'd be better to wait outside, with a clear view of the front door.

CHAPTER TWENTY

Wayne Hensley knelt next to the settlement man who seemed to be in charge. He slapped him hard across the face. "Tell me! Are there more of you?"

The man just stared back with one good eye. Hensley stood up with a little effort thanks to age and weight. He went over to the man who was shot. Pointing at him, he said. "How many more are out there?" He put a hand on the wall and leaned over, hitting the bullet wound with a fist.

The man cried out and pulled away.

"How many?"

But the man didn't speak. Hensley stood up and looked at the four men. He didn't like this. Not one bit. The settlers were supposed to be scared and ready to move out. The old man should have come to town today, hat in hand, ready to take up the offer to buy them out. They sure as hell weren't supposed to send men after him. And none of the four settlers, who were trapped like rats, looked particularly scared. Instead, they looked defiant. But maybe that was because they were together. He pointed to the man who'd been shot.

"Grab him and bring him along."

Two men, Nate and Tom, grabbed the large bearded man, standing him up with a little grunting effort, and walked him out of the room behind Hensley. He led them into a smaller room lined with shelves covered in the odds and ends they needed to run the business of the mine.

Nate said, "What you want us to do?"

"Hurt him. Make him cry out. I wanna scare one of the other fellas into telling us what they know."

Tom said, "Scare 'em?"

Hensley sighed. "If they think we're beating the tar outta this guy, they'll tell me what I wanna know to get us to stop hurting him."

"Oh." Tom looked at Nate. "Go ahead."

Nate stepped back far enough to swing a fist. He struck the man in the cheek, but the big man took it without even a grimace. Nate shook his hand.

"His wound," said Hensley. "Hit him there."

Nate nodded and moved toward Tom, who was on that side. The wound was in the fleshy part of the man's bicep, presenting a good target. Nate put his weight into it and hit him. The big man grimaced, but he didn't make much of a sound this time. Not enough to be heard in the other room.

"Cut him," said Hensley.

Tom had a knife, but his face turned pale as he pulled it from his belt. "I'm not so—"

"Nate, you do it," Hensley said impatiently.

Nate didn't reach for the knife, his face suddenly covered in sweat. "I don't think I can." He looked back at his boss, who didn't like what he was seeing from his men. In a feeble voice, Nate said, "Maybe you could do it?"

Hensley looked at the knife in Tom's shaking hand. His stomach turned. The thought of sticking the blade into a man who was just standing there— "Christ. We got anyone who would do this?" Hensley hated the slight smile trying to hide beneath the settler's thick beard.

Tom and Nate looked at each other. Tom finally said, "I don't think so. I mean, we're willin' to tussle. But cut someone up?"

"Dammit," muttered Hensley. "Put that thing away. Okay, this is what you'll do. Tom, you start yelling like you're this big fella. Make it sound like you're getting the tar beat out of you. I'll go back into the other room and see if I can get one of the others to talk."

The smile on the settler's face was now unmistakable.

Tom looked confused. "You mean, like, play act?"

Hensley thought about taking Tom's knife and stabbing both of his men. "Do it!"

Hensley went back into his office where the other three settlers were trussed up. After a long moment, Tom's voice wailed through the doorway. It was pathetic. Like someone playing at being a ghost. Hensley shook his head and left the room without asking a question.

CHAPTER TWENTY-ONE

Speck pulled up, sliding in the snowy mud, his eyes wide in terror. The lead wolf stopped in front of him, growling from deep within his chest, his eyes glowing in the moonlight. The other two wolves didn't slow down, attacking from either side.

The Appaloosa screeched a high whining note as the two closed in. They barked and growled, leaping at almost the same time. The horse skittered and danced before kicking out and catching one wolf in the chest. The creature huffed and tumbled in the air before landing in an unmoving heap, its chest caved in. Its companion crashed into Speck's left flank, biting and clawing at the horse flesh.

Speck cried out and whirled as the wolf fell away. The two wolves filled the air with barks and growls, threatening to drive the Appaloosa mad with terror. The lead wolf surged forward. Speck saw him too late. The wolf looking like huge gnashing teeth rimmed in a halo of silver and black hair. The horse tried to jerk out of the way, but the wolf slammed into him, knocking him sideways, causing him to almost lose his footing in the slush.

As the horse stumbled to the side, the other wolf jumped at his exposed throat. Speck reared back as best he could on his slipping hooves and the wolf's teeth snapped shut on night air with a crack as loud as a gunshot. The horse kicked out with his front legs, knocking his attacker back, but the wolf twisted and landed on its feet, moving in again for Speck's throat.

The Appaloosa tried to rear back again, the ground a

slippery mess beneath him. The lead wolf lunged at his side, taking the leather stirrup strap in his mouth and pulling. Speck's back legs slid out from under him and the horse fell forward with a thud and the crack of bones breaking—the wolf biting at his neck now crushed beneath him.

Speck flailed with his legs, kicking in a frenzied terror, attempting to right himself and get to his feet. The last wolf released the leather and backed away from the flashing legs, which gave the horse time to roll and scramble to his feet. Once standing, Speck slipped and slid through the mud as he tried to run, managing to stay on his hooves.

The lead wolf didn't attack and as Speck moved away, the wolf moved to its companion. The crushed wolf whimpered, legs twitching, unable to raise its head. The wolf looked back at the horse for a moment, then turned to its pack mate and snapped its jaws tight on the hurt wolf's throat.

Speck found his footing and ran into the night.

CHAPTER TWENTY-TWO

Jake slept, hidden behind barrels in a recess between buildings across from the mining company building. He borrowed loose planks from the boardwalk construction to sit on and keep him out of the muddy snow.

Someone on the street laughed and he came awake. He'd meant only to doze, but the sun was up—hours had passed. By the shadows beyond the barrels he guessed it to be around nine in the morning. He pulled himself to his feet, grunting from creaky joints, and soreness from his injuries. His back ached, his side itched from the knife wound, though that was a good sign it was healing, and his stomach growled. He needed food and water.

Stepping out of the recess, he expected to see more activity, but the small mining town wasn't bustling. A few men wandered the main street and that was it. Of course, the miners were working. There were no women to be seen, maybe the town hadn't been around long enough for that.

He felt scraggly, but his clothes weren't too wrinkled. There was a several-day growth of hair on his head and face. He scratched at his neck. Maybe he'd let it grow out. He liked the idea of having a beard.

Two men he recognized from the night before, now on horseback, entered town with five horses in tow. They'd found Liam's horses along with the one he'd borrowed. They took them down the street to a corral. A small wood hut sat next to it. The town's answer to a livery stable. Jake was glad. The horses would get food and water.

Jake crossed the street and entered the mining company building. There wasn't any activity, not like the night before. The desk was occupied. A man sat there yawning and staring blearily at papers. Jake walked up to him.

"You lookin' for miners? Just got up here from Denver. Wanna dig me up some silver."

The man, about Jake's size but younger, squinted up at him. "Well, sir, it wouldn't be *your* silver. You'd be working for the Sideways Mining Company. If you're okay with that, we could use you."

They discussed pay and sleeping arrangements. There were tents and the aforementioned bunkhouse at the other end of town closer to the mine. The man gave him the name of the foreman who would put him to work.

"Now, can you stake me two bits for breakfast?" asked Jake.

The man sighed and reached a finger into a vest pocket. He came out with a dime. "You can get biscuits and gravy and coffee for five cents."

"Much obliged. I'll pay you back. What's your name?"

"Jordan. And I know you'll pay me back as I'll be taking twenty cents out of your first pay."

Jake feigned shock and disappointment. "For a measly ten cents?"

"Think that's bad, wait'll you see the prices at the company store."

Jake cursed under his breath, as that would be expected of him, and left the building. There was a small restaurant a few buildings up the street. He got two orders of the biscuits and gravy and drank nearly a pot of coffee. The food wasn't great, but as hungry as he was, it satisfied.

Afterward, he walked out behind the one-room restaurant, up into a wooded area and relieved himself, then walked through the woods to the back of the mining company building. He stayed hidden in the trees, wondering if Liam and the others were still in there. The window at the top of the backstairs was still open. No reason not to try that route again and see if he could find Liam, but before he could move from the trees, two men came out the back door and headed straight toward him.

They didn't look in his direction, he was pretty sure it was just dumb luck, but he moved quickly back around the restaurant to the main street. He returned to the barrels across from the mining building, cautious no one saw him. He hunkered down to wait for now. The inaction gnawed at him, but he didn't see much choice.

There still wasn't much activity, but he counted seven different men coming and going from the building over the course of a few hours. At one point a doctor came down the street, a black leather satchel in hand, and entered the building. Jake hoped that meant it was for Liam and his friends. Less than an hour later the doctor left. Jake stood and waited a few moments for the feeling to return to his legs, then he followed the man. The doctor headed up the street, past the corral, to a large canvas tent with DOCTOR carved into a rectangle of wood hung over the entrance. Jake followed the man inside.

It was an unappetizing smell of sweet tar and turned meat. Jake recognized the smell—another memory!—as carbolic acid. The turned meat smell, well, he could imagine the type of injuries miners could get. It was not a gentle occupation.

The doctor set down his leather satchel and started putting a cigarette together, obviously not realizing he had company standing behind him.

The tent was large. A couple of cots were set up against one wall. There were two tables. One with medical implements and personal items. That's where the doctor set the satchel. On the other table, by the entrance, were a couple rows of small brown bottles and materials for wounds. Jake edged over to the table and palmed one of the small bottles.

The doctor finished rolling the cigarette, licking the edge to seal it. Jake coughed to get his attention. The doctor turned and raised his eyebrows. "Yes? You here about your face?"

The man reached into a pocket and pulled out a silver engraved tinder box. Opening it, he pulled out the steel striker and holding the box and the flint deftly in his left hand, struck the flint and ignited the tinder. He bent to it and lit his rolled cigarette, dropping the striker and flint back into the box and snuffing the flame by snapping the lid back in place.

It took Jake a moment to realize the doctor was talking about the bruises on his face. "Oh, no, not here for that. I was at the, uh, altercation last night and was wonderin' how the injured men were gettin' on?"

The doctor took a deep drag on the cigarette, holding the smoke for a moment, then released a cloud. "They'll live. You know the men?"

Jake shook his head. "Naw. Ain't them fellas from that settlement down the valley?"

"Appear to be, but they weren't speaking much, or so I gathered. Is there anything else?" The doctor looked terribly bored.

"Oh, sorry." Jake left the tent.

He headed straight to the mining company building. There didn't appear to be more than seven men working for the company, not including Wayne Hensley, the man in charge who'd asked the questions the night before. It would be a fluke if all seven men were there right now, they were coming and going at random intervals.

Jordan, the same man he'd begged the dime from, was behind the desk with another man leaning against it, chatting with him, a revolver on his hip. Jake ignored them and walked toward the stairs.

"What the hell are you doing?" called Jordan.

Jake held up the brown bottle. "Doc grabbed me outside his tent and told me to bring this over for the injured fella what got shot. Said he was upstairs."

The man looked at Jake for a moment, furrowing his brow. "Go get that, Lem."

Lem took a step toward him.

"Ain't no problem," said Jake, starting for the stairs again.

"Hold it right there. Lem, get the goddamned bottle and you, get the hell out of here before I decide to fire you before you have a chance to even start. Why the hell aren't you over at the mine?"

Jake shrugged, holding the bottle up in his left hand, but close to his chest. Lem came over and reached for it, leaving himself open. Jake pretended to fumble the bottle as he tried to hand it over. The man grabbed for it and Jake drove his right fist hard into Lem's face, smashing his nose. As the man stumbled back, Jake jumped forward, grabbing the revolver from its holster. It wasn't a new revolver and didn't look to be particularly well cared for, which told Jake the man wasn't a gunman—just some company man required to carry a firearm.

But for Jake, the heavy weight in his hand, the feel of the wood grip in his palm, his thumb automatically cocking the hammer back. It all felt right, leaving him little doubt he was either a lawman or an outlaw who was handy with a gun.

The man behind the desk rose up and the gun swiveled toward him.

"Don't be stupid, Jordan."

The man froze, keeping his hands in sight. He didn't wear a gun belt. Lem held a hand to his nose. Blood oozed down over his lips and a grizzled chin.

"Both of you lead the way upstairs. Come on, let's go. Take me to the fellas you have trussed up from last night."

The two men moved to the back of the large room and up the stairs. Jake followed behind, keeping an eye ahead but also behind in case one of the other men entered the building.

As Jordan stepped into the upstairs hallway, his head moved slightly left then whipped back forward. Jake grabbed a handful of Lem's shirt and pulled the man back down a step. He pressed the barrel of the gun hard into his back and whispered into his ear, "We're walkin' together, like we're one person, got it? At the top of the stairs, you turn left, or you'll have a bullet through your back."

Lem nodded. Jordan moved to his right, then turned to look at Jake, who stopped before the top step, preventing Lem from stepping up onto the landing.

"Jordan, move down the hall that way," Jake said, motioning to his left with a wag of his head. The man did as he was told.

Jake then pressed Lem forward. As the two took another step up, Lem now on the landing, Jake glanced to his right. The hallway was empty. He then stepped up behind Lem. Over the man's shoulder were were two more men, guns drawn—one with a shotgun and the other a revolver. They looked agitated. Behind them, joined by Jordan, was Hensley, the boss man.

Hensley said, "Move aside, Lem. That man isn't going to shoot. He's just some huckleberry from the settlement."

Jake held tight to Lem's shirt. He glanced down at his hand with the gun. It was steady. Would he shoot? The thought of shooting didn't make him anxious. While across from him, he somehow knew the two men with guns weren't cold-blooded killers. He could see the fear in their eyes, in the way they stood, even in the way they gripped their guns, keeping the barrels down so they wouldn't accidentally shoot Lem. They were hoping Jake would back down so they could beat on him a bit and then tie him up with Liam and the other three from the settlement.

Lem said, a hitch in his voice. "He's got a grip on my shirt. I can't move."

Hensley sighed. "What's your move? You just going to stand there with your thumb up your ass?"

CHAPTER TWENTY-THREE

Jake moved the gun into view, pointing the barrel at the wall, away from any of the men, and straightened his arm.

"That's smart, mister," said Hensley. "Trent, go grab it."

Before either of the men with guns could move forward, Jake whipped his arm back and smashed Lem in the side of the head. He hit him with the bottom of his fist wrapped around the butt of the revolver's grip. The man grunted in pain, then squawked in surprise as his knees gave out and he tumbled down the stairs.

Jake made sure that after hitting Lem, the revolver would be aimed at the two men with the guns. They either didn't have the reflexes or perhaps the wherewithal to raise their own guns.

Jake didn't wait for them to make up their minds. He moved forward swiftly and pointed the gun directly into the face of the man with the shotgun, who flinched a half step back. Jake grabbed the long barrel of the gun and yanked it from the man's grip, then he swung around, putting the revolver in the face of the second man. The man also flinched, dropping his gun and backing away quickly. He'd been right. Neither were gunmen and neither wanted to shoot—or be shot.

Jake poked the shotgun's owner in the chest with the stock of his own gun to get him to back up. Then he pointed the revolver at Hensley. "Your move."

He held the revolver steady. Excitement and even eagerness rushed through him, but he didn't feel any nerves. There'd been some fear that one of the men might actually shoot, but that fear obviously hadn't stopped him from taking action. He was mighty curious about what he used to do in his prior life.

Hensley's face simmered with a mix of anger and fear. "Jordan, go untie his friends."

Jordan hesitated, motioning to a closed door right next to Jake, who took a few steps back. "Open it, then stop."

Jordan did as he was told. Jake spun the shotgun in his left hand like a drum major's baton so that the barrel now faced the right way. He slid the gun forward until his hand found the grip and his index finger slid into the trigger guard. He pointed it directly at Hensley, while he covered Jordan with the revolver.

In the room, Jake saw Liam and one of the other men from the settlement sitting in the middle of the floor. Both looked shocked. Liam said, "I thought that was your voice. What the Hell are you doing here?"

"What the Hell does it look like?"

Liam smiled thinly and shook his head in relieved disbelief.

"Okay, go untie 'em."

Jordan walked toward Emma's brother. As he moved into the room, Jake stepped half into the doorway so that he had a clear view of Jordan as well as Hensley and the others in the hall. From this vantage, Jake saw the other two men from the settlement sitting against a wall. Angus, who'd been shot, had a fresh bandage.

Jordan knelt behind Liam for a moment, then said, "Knots are too tight."

Jake looked at the men in the hall. One had a knife in his gun belt. "Drop your blade to the floor and kick it over."

The man did as he was told. Jake in turn kicked the knife into the room. Jordan retrieved it and returned to Liam, putting the steel up against Liam's neck. "Drop the guns or I swear to God I slice his throat." There was a hitch in the man's voice and his hand shook, but Jake gave him credit for guts.

But that didn't dissuade Jake. He pointed the revolver directly at Jordan's head. "You so much as nick him and your brains decorate the room behind you." His voice was firm, his hand steady. He'd already cocked the revolver, or he would have done that for added effect.

Hensley opened his mouth.

"I suggest you don't say a word, Hensley," said Jake without taking his eyes off Jordan

Jordan and Hensley stared back mutely. The knife started shaking so much that Jake was afraid the man would cut Liam's throat by accident. But Jordan pulled the knife away and cut the ropes. His hands free, Liam twisted and hit Jordan in the face, knocking him down. Liam picked up the knife and went to work on the ropes binding his legs. Free, he rose and wobbled.

"Crud, my legs are numb."

"Angus," said Jake, "how's the wound doing?"

Liam hunkered over the man next to him and cut the ropes and said without looking up, "Angus is fine. Doc removed the lead and patched him up."

Through his thick beard, Angus scowled at Liam's back. "Good? Wait 'til you get shot and I'll tell people you're just dandy."

Liam grinned and stood, stretching his back before moving to cut the ropes on Angus and the last man. The bonds cut on all four, they stood and shook out their arms and legs, though Angus kept his wounded arm still. All the while, Jake kept the mining town men covered out in the hall. He called back into the room, "Ready?"

The men from the settlement came to the door as Jake backed to the top of the stairs. Any hope of getting out of the building without further trouble was banished the moment Liam saw Hensley in the hall. Emma's brother lunged at the man, which caused an immediate reaction from the others. It turned into a brawl. Even Angus waded in with one arm, which happened to be more than enough. He knocked out one of Hensley's men. The other two from the settlement beat on the other company man while Liam and Hensley tussled. Everyone seemed to have forgotten about Jake.

At first, he was content to let the men fight. But then Liam slammed Hensley against the wall, holding him up with one hand and pummeling the man until blood poured free and Jake wasn't sure Hensley was even conscious anymore.

"That's enough!" called Jake.

Liam didn't stop. His face was bright red with rage and his eyes had gone mad. Jake pointed the revolver at the ceiling and fired. It was a loud explosion in the confined space of the hallway. Liam stopped and craned his neck toward Jake.

"That's enough, you're gonna kill the man."

Liam trembled. "He deserves it."

"You don't know that," said Jake. "Now let's get out of this town while we're all in one piece."

Liam started to drag Hensley toward the stairs. The man *was* unconscious.

"Leave him."

Liam glared.

Jake said, "What would you do with him? There's no jail at the settlement and there's certainly no law or judge. The people there, most of 'em, anyway, won't let you kill the man—especially your wife and Emma. Conor, either. So let's get the Hell out of here while we can."

Liam continued to tremble, but he was otherwise frozen with indecision. Angus reached out and took Liam's arm. "Let's go. Jake's right. We're lucky we're still alive. Let's go home before something happens we can't live with."

Liam looked between them, then his shoulders sagged, and he released Hensley, who thudded to the floor.

"Wait," said one of the others. "Our guns." He walked past Jake into another room. He came out a few moments later with guns and handed them out.

Jake looked sternly at the four men. "I'm expectin' you to keep your wits." His look lingered on Liam, who took a moment, but nodded. "Keep your fingers off the goddamned triggers. Don't need anyone to get killed—especially one of us."

Liam said, "They killed James."

Jake glared at him. "You kill someone here, unprovoked, and I'll shoot you. That's a promise. We clear?"

He waited for Liam to respond and finally got another nod.

"Okay, be alert. Fingers off triggers."

Jake led them downstairs past Lem who was in a heap at the bottom. As they crossed the room, two company men came through the front door.

CHAPTER TWENTY-FOUR

The two company men froze just inside the door. They had guns but didn't reach for them. Jake raised the shotgun, which got the men to raise their hands. Like the others upstairs, neither of these men were trained gunmen.

"Get their guns."

Angus and another of the men, Jake thought his name was Sean, but he wasn't sure, grabbed the men's revolvers.

Jake motioned. "Get to the back of the room. Actually, go upstairs and make sure your boss is still alive."

Shock crossed their faces as they hurried past Jake and the others. They looked down at Lem, who was coming to, and then clomped up the stairs.

"Let's go," said Jake.

Outside, he paused for a moment, looking up and down the street. No one was running in their direction. There were only two men in view, and they leaned against a hitching post two buildings down talking calmly with one another.

"Okay. Be casual. You're just four men getting your horses. The stable's up that way. Carry the guns at your sides. Only use them if the alternative is you'll get killed. In other words, try hard not to shoot anyone. If the stable hand gives you trouble, tie him up, but don't hurt him. We just need to get the Hell out of this town. Got it?"

"Why you telling us this? Aren't you coming?"

"Bring my horse—it's one of Conor's—but I'm staying here in the doorway in case the men upstairs get any stupid ideas."

"Come on," said Liam, leading the four up the street.

Jake watched them go as he moved to the other side of the door and waited for the company men. It took longer than he thought it would, which was another good sign they weren't really looking for a shootout. But boots did stomp down the stairs, at least four men, so a couple of them regained consciousness. They weren't in a hurry as they walked across the floor toward the door.

Jake tucked the revolver inside his belt and stepped back a few paces, leveling the shotgun at the door. That would be more intimidating than the revolver. The men came out, still in no hurry. One of them saw him and immediately raised his hands. The others watched Liam's group nearing the stable. They didn't run after them. They all carried guns, replenishing their stock from a room upstairs probably full of company weapons.

Jake said in a calm voice. "Easy now. Turn around slowly."

The other three turned, none of them raising their guns.

"Put 'em down and back away."

Jake got the impression they were happy to do so. There couldn't be a showdown if they were unarmed.

It took ten minutes or so before Liam and the rest clopped down the street on their horses. They eyed the company men nervously, but Jake wasn't worried. He handed up the guns he'd collected from the men and mounted his borrowed horse. The five rode in a cantor out of town. Jake looked back frequently, but no one followed.

After a couple of minutes, Angus cleared his throat and looked over at Jake. "Uh, thanks."

Jake looked at him and nodded. The other two men grunted some kind of thanks, but Liam looked straight ahead. Jake felt as uncomfortable as the men from the settlement looked. He felt certain that in his previous life he did not like the attention of being thanked. The grunts were more than enough. Though when Emma thanked him, well, that was different. It made him feel lighter.

"You think I'm an idiot," muttered Liam.

Jake looked over at him. "You're hot-headed. I don't think you thought this out. But—" he felt strangely awkward, though compelled to say these things because it was Emma's brother "—you, all of you, have guts. And you certainly thought you were doing the right thing."

"Of course we were doing the right thing!" said Liam. His face was red and boiling over. "They killed our friend."

"Okay, let's say they killed James—"

Liam turned and glared at him. "They *did* kill—"

Jake held up a hand. "But then what? What were you going to do? Did you plan to kill them all or just Hensley?"

Liam breathed hard, sounding like a train pulling out of a station.

Jake looked at Angus. "Were you ready to kill them?"

Angus didn't have Liam's certainty. He finally said, "I—I don't know. I was just so mad that—that I had to do *something*."

"I get it," said Jake. "If it were my friend, well, I don't know what I'd do."

The man he thought was named Sean said, "You don't know because you don't remember anything. No offense. But I watched you handle those guns. You, well, you've done it before. You're too sure of yourself. Too steady. If James was your friend, I think the company men would be dead right now."

Would he have killed? "Maybe. But I think I would have been sure they'd done it."

Liam kept seething. "They did it!"

Jake said, "They might have, but that's just it. I don't know for sure. I would like to think I wouldn't kill a man because maybe he'd done somethin'. But those men back there, I didn't see a killer among 'em."

"Horseshit," said Liam. "How the hell would you even know?"

"You're probably right. But watchin' those men. They didn't want to use those guns. None of 'em did."

"They shot me," said Angus.

"Sure, but that was a brawl. Heat of the moment. But when they had to think about it—I just don't think they're killers. Just like you all ain't killers. Would they bash some heads together? Without a doubt. They're willing to stir it up, throw some punches. But I don't know. You could certainly be right, Liam. But don't you think we need to find somethin' that pins it on them? So we're sure?"

"You talking about evidence?" said Sean.

"Yep. When we get back to the settlement, we need to figure out how we find somethin' that points to Hensley and his men. Somethin' we can take to a lawman and a judge."

"What if there isn't anything like that?" asked Angus.

"There might not be."

Liam looked at him. "Then what do we do?"

Jake looked back. "Well, to be honest, it probably don't matter 'cause Hensley is gonna do somethin' after that beatin' you gave him."

"But they're not killers, so we don't have anything to worry about. Right?" Liam said it with sarcasm.

"We need to post guards. Everyone needs to be ready in case they come a'callin'."

"We should have killed him," said Liam.

"Maybe, but then the law would come down on you—don't think for a moment that the mine owners wouldn't have come after you. And then you'd swing by your neck until dead."

Sean whispered, "Sweet Jesus."

"If that were to happen," said Liam, "I'd take some of them with me."

"Even if it's a group of state or federal marshals?"

Liam didn't say anything.

Angus said, "You really think Hensley will come after us?"

"Guaranteed."

CHAPTER TWENTY-FIVE

Wayne Hensley grimaced and swatted irritably at Doc. "Okay, already."

"I'm almost finished."

"You're finished. Go away."

"But—"

"Go away!"

Doc sighed and started putting his medical supplies back into his black leather satchel. Hensley sat in a hardback chair beside the desk in the front room of the Sideways Mining Company building. His head throbbed and felt like it had swollen to the size of a watermelon. He could only see through thin slits that made everything fuzzy. Around him were his good-for-nothing men, none of them worth an ounce of the silver dug from the mountain.

"What now?" asked Jordan, leaning against the desk, a wad of leaf tobacco in his fingers ready to go into his mouth.

Hensley didn't speak for a moment. He was enraged. After the fire to the old man's place he'd expected the settlement to give up. But, fine, they chose to do something stupid, and he'd quashed it. But then one man—

"One man!" yelled Hensley. "He runs roughshod over the lot of you. You just wilted. *Pathetic!*"

His men avoided his eyes, looking like punished school boys. Then Nate cleared his throat.

"What?"

"That man you're talking about," said Nate. "I don't think he's from the settlement, if you catch my meaning."

"I don't! What the hell are you talking about?"

Nate flinched, but he raised his eyes to look at his boss. "He just showed up, I think. Maybe a week or two ago."

Hensley frowned, and Nate looked away. After a moment, Hensley shook his head, only slightly, but he winced in pain. After a moment, after the sudden wave of nausea and lightheadedness passed, he said, "Of course. They done sent for a hired gun."

Jordan said around the wad of tobacco stuffed into his cheek, "Those bastards."

Hensley said, "Well, if they want to escalate, so bet it. Get word to my brothers."

Jordan swallowed and started to cough up the tobacco juice. Hensley glared at him, but after getting his breath back, Jordan said, "You sure about that?"

"What the hell do you think? Them sidewinders hired a gun. You all sure as hell can't deal with him."

Lem said defensively. "We got the others tied up. Even shot one!"

Hensley glared at him until he looked away.

Jordan said, "People could get hurt if they're involved. As in dead. We want to go that far?"

"Piss on them! Get me a map, I'll show you where my brothers are most likely camped. I want riders sent out today. Now!"

CHAPTER TWENTY-SIX

There was fear and anger in the yell, but Jake couldn't understand the words. He stopped chopping wood and listened. It was quiet again—well, quiet except for the normal sounds of a breeze rustling leaves, the songs of birds, the conversation of chickens surrounding him in the yard, and the newly added bleats of goats.

He waited, listening. Everyone was on edge since he, Liam, and the others returned from the mining town nearly a week ago now. The settlement even decided to place guards—volunteers, but everyone, man and woman, volunteered.

After nearly a minute and no follow-up yells, Jake went back to his task and swung the axe, splitting the log neatly as it rested on the flat stump of what once had been a large cottonwood tree. He reached for another log from the pile he'd made and stopped again, bent over and listening. Had that been another yell?

He stood up when he heard footsteps approaching. It was two men about fifty yards off coming around the corner of the lane. Jake recognized one of them as a company man. Both men had revolvers in their hands.

Jake moved quickly toward the house, scattering chickens and goats. The company man stopped, grabbing the other's arm and pointing at Jake, who didn't remember seeing the other one before. They talked with each other, tones far too low to hear from this distance. The familiar man motioned behind them while the other hefted his revolver, as if making the point that they were armed.

Jake stepped inside the house. The gun belt hung on a peg near the door. He strapped it on and edged a look back outside. The men were gone. He stepped completely out, tying the cinch around his thigh as his head swiveled, but there was no sight of them.

Jake moved cautiously toward where he'd last seen the men, his revolver drawn and cocked. He figured one of two things. Either they'd gone back to wherever to get more men or they hid somewhere nearby hoping he'd come blundering past and they could get the drop on him.

The lane was wide enough for wagons. Houses were on either side, none too close to the other. The settlement had cleared most of the trees, which was smart. You didn't want too much vegetation growing up to a house in case of a wildfire. That also meant there weren't many places for the men to hide.

But as he approached the first house, he circled wide, going in the opposite direction from where the men had come. They could have hidden around the side of the house ready to open fire. But as he cleared each corner, he didn't find them. Same with the next house. He was convinced they'd returned to wherever they'd come from, but he still approached each house carefully.

He realized he'd been hearing voices talking off in the distance but only just registered the fact as he drew closer to the common house. The voices were curt. Almost as if someone was giving commands to subordinates.

Jake slowed even further, hugging the side of the house that was on the outskirts of the open area near the southern end of the settlement where the common house stood by itself. When building the structure, they left a large area in front of it for outside social gatherings. In that clearing was a group of men.

He recognized some of them from the mining town. One of the strangers spoke. It was the voice he'd been hearing. He gave out orders, sending the men into the settlement in groups of two. The two men Jake had just seen were among them. They talked to the leader in hushed tones. The man nodded.

"You two," the man motioned with a hand, "go with 'em and get this guy. Kill him if you have to."

Jake looked more closely at the men he didn't recognize—the reinforcements. They had a different look to them, a harder look than the company men. Were they sent by the mine's owner? A group of mercenaries ready to do anything it took to maintain order, as long as they got paid?

At this time, a small group of people returned from the settlement. Two men with guns herded a family of a husband, wife, and small child into the common house.

Jake thought through his options. Should he try to free those imprisoned in the common house or go warn as many people as he could, either setting up a defense or getting them to flee to safety?

His decision was colored by his primary concern: Emma. Where was she? She'd gone off earlier to the Sullivans, a family who lived farther toward the north end of the settlement. Jake doubted the company men had made it that far, yet. Still, he had to put his mind at ease as to whether they'd already taken her prisoner.

Jake backed away and then kept heading south around the last of the houses to where the valley opened up. That put him about even with the back of the common house. He moved toward it.

There were no men in the rear keeping guard—were they not that organized, or were the guards on the inside? He ran to the back wall and snuck a look inside one of the windows.

There were already almost a dozen settlement people inside. None of them were Emma. But he saw why no alarm had been raised by the settlement's "sentries"—they were all in the common house. Jake was actually thankful to see them there, meaning none had gotten themselves killed.

He made his way back through the settlement to the Sullivans. He came across four other duos of men, whom he avoided. Half of them were headed back to the common house with prisoners, the others heading away.

It looked as though the company men had cleared about a third of the settlement thus far.

Past the men, Jake moved more quickly, fairly confident the company men weren't this far. Still, he went behind the Sullivans' house and tried their back door. It opened. Most people in the settlement didn't even have locks on their houses—why bother when you knew every neighbor?

He heard a voice when he entered. He was grateful to hear it was normal-sounding, no stress to it. A casual conversation. Jake moved quickly through the kitchen and into the living room. The Sullivans, Ryan and Beth, looked over at Jake as he entered the room. Ryan was setting a large cooking pot onto a hook by the fireplace. Beth sat in a cushioned chair doing needlepoint. They both smiled, recognizing him. Emma sat at a table, a bolt of green cloth partially unrolled in front of her.

Emma looked up and smiled, but that disappeared quickly. "What is it?"

"Company men are in the settlement. They're imprisoning people at the common house."

Emma shook her head in dismay. "They're looking for you and Liam and the rest of you, aren't they?"

Jake nodded.

Ryan said, "What do they plan to do?"

Jake shook his head. "No idea, but we can't wait to find out. I want you to—" he stopped and looked at Emma. *I want you to run to safety. Get the hell away from here.* But she wouldn't listen to that.

She seemed to know. Standing, she said, "We'll spread the word. You go get Liam."

He nodded, adding, "But don't engage with these men. They're willing to shoot."

Beth stood and crossed the front room, dropping her needlepoint on the table. On the wall behind it were two hunting rifles resting on hooks. She handed one to her husband and took the other.

Ryan went to tall-standing shelves that held plates, utensils, glasses, mugs, and a small wooden box that he grabbed and set on the table next to Beth's needlepoint. It was full of rifle cartridges. He said, "Where should we gather?"

Jake didn't have an answer, he wasn't familiar enough with the settlement. But Emma didn't hesitate. "They're coming from the direction of the common house? Then let's meet at the fold of the gully."

That seemed to mean something to the Sullivans, who both nodded.

"Be careful," said Jake, looking only at Emma.

She nodded and stepped close to him. "You be careful," she said. From the corner of his eyes he saw the Sullivans look at each other and then turn away. Emma reached up and cupped the back of his neck, pulling his face to hers.

With Emma and the Sullivans gone, Jake hesitated. He was afraid getting Liam would be dumping a keg of gunpowder on a fire. But there was no alternative. Liam would get involved as soon as he heard or saw what was going on, and maybe Jake could keep him from doing something stupid.

Liam's house was closer to the common house, meaning it was closer to the company men as they worked their way through the settlement. It turned out that it was so close that he found Liam, unarmed, shielding Ginny and their two kids from two company men pointing shotguns at them. The men were between him and Liam and his family. Even from behind, though slightly to the side, he recognized one of the men from the mining town—it was Lem, the man he'd hit in the head and sent tumbling down the stairs. The other was one of the mercenaries.

CHAPTER TWENTY-SEVEN

Jake couldn't shoot the men, even if only to injure them. They might still get shots off, hurting or killing Liam and his family. And at the least, it would bring people running. A gun fight, maybe a big one, would break out. He decided to wait, hoping Liam wasn't so stupid as to attack the men when they obviously had the drop on him. So he stayed around the corner of a neighbor's house and waited.

Liam shooed his family out in front of him, putting himself between them and the guns, the company men dropping in line behind them. The group started down the wide dirt lane toward the common house. Jake quickly pulled off his boots and moved out. It was still risky. Someone could still get shot, but the alternative wasn't good either, letting them imprison Liam and eventually beat him or even kill him for his attack on Wayne Hensley.

Jake moved forward on stockinged feet over the smooth dirt lane. He gripped the revolver tight, though he kept his index finger off the trigger. Literally on tiptoes, he jogged forward, closing the gap between them while keeping an eye out for more company men.

Without making a noise, he came up behind the man he didn't recognize, the mercenary. Something told him, maybe the way he held the gun or even just in his carriage, that he was the more dangerous of the two.

Jake swung as hard as he could, smashing the bottom edge of his fist and the butt of the gun grip into the man's skull. It connected with an amazingly loud thwack and the man crumpled to the ground. Without hesitating,

Jake dropped his revolver and lunged at Lem. He wasn't about to shoot, so he decided to have both hands free. With one, he grabbed the barrel of the shotgun, pushing it down toward the ground, with the other he hit Lem in the face.

The man cried out, but he hadn't the time to do much more. The gun didn't go off and before Jake could hit the man again, Liam crashed into him, the two flying away, the shotgun yanked free of Lem and still in Jake's hand. He swiveled it around to cover Lem, but Liam beat him until he was unconscious. And to his credit, he stopped as soon as that was accomplished.

Ginny and their kids rushed forward. Looking at her, Jake whispered, "Head toward Clear Creek and then west. Get clear of the settlement."

He handed the shotgun to Liam and went back and retrieved his revolver and then his boots. He looked at Ginny again, "Go. Hurry."

"Go on," said Liam

She wanted to protest, but instead she set her jaw,

grabbed a hand of each child, and moved off quickly, going as fast as the children's little legs would let her.

"What now?" asked Liam.

"Grab an arm, we need to drag these fellas into a house out of view and tie 'em up. Then we find your friends."

Liam nodded.

They went to Angus's house first. The front door was open and a quick search found it empty.

"They already got him," said Liam.

"Who's next?"

Sean was standing out in his yard slaughtering a goat. He looked up as he hoisted the dead animal by its hind legs to bleed it into a bucket set below. "Hey, fellas," he said.

"Get your gun," said Liam.

Sean looked confused. "What's going on?"

"Company men are in the settlement," said Liam.

Jake, revolver still drawn, watched the lane back toward the common house.

"Damn," said Sean.

"And bring any .12-gauge shells you have. We got this off one of the company men, so I don't have any extra."

Liam's friend disappeared inside and reappeared moments later with his own shotgun and a box of shells. Liam grabbed a handful and stuffed them into his pants pocket. Sean did the same and dropped the empty box.

"Now what?" asked Sean.

Jake said, "We go house-to-house. Get men with guns to join us and send their families to the west to hide out. Let's go. I'll take this house."

"Okay, I've got the Delaney's," said Sean.

Liam was about to speak, but someone's gun spoke for him. The shot was close by. Jake whirled as Sean cried out and fell to the ground. Two company men crouched down the lane. He returned fire, causing them to scramble for cover. Jake then grabbed one of Sean's arms and pulled him toward his house. The man screamed in pain, but there was nothing Jake could do about it, they were too exposed where they were.

"Shoot back!" said Jake.

Liam looked surprised and a bit rattled, but he raised the shotgun to his shoulder and fired both rounds. As Jake pulled Sean, he fired his revolver, shooting purposefully slow to give Liam time to reload.

"Keep backing up," said Jake.

Liam reloaded and walked backwards. He was brave or foolish, standing tall as he sealed the shotgun's breach while the company men fired at them. Liam fired twice more, then turned and grabbed Sean's other arm. Together, they moved more quickly to the house. The three men tumbled through the front door. Lying on the ground, Jake rolled so that he could reach the cartridges in his gun belt and reload. Liam slammed the door shut and then reloaded as well.

Jake rolled to his feet and knelt next to Sean. The man grimaced and held his side. Blood oozed between his fingers. Jake looked at Liam. "Get to that window and keep 'em at bay."

CHAPTER TWENTY-EIGHT

Liam broke out the front window with the stock of the shotgun, then knelt at the opening, the barrel sticking out. "Don't see anyone."

"After that flurry, we'll have most of the company men here soon."

"Yeah, but we also alerted the rest of the settlement. Everyone knows now that something's going on."

"And they might blunder right into the middle. Get out the back and stop your people from chargin' headlong into trouble. Your sister's out there now getting people to gather at the fold in the gully."

Liam bolted for the back door.

Jake looked down at Sean. "Bullet came out pretty clean and I think it missed your vitals. You have a fire goin' by chance?"

He looked confused.

"To seal your wound. Gotta stop the bleedin'."

"Blazes," he muttered. "Yeah, fire's going in the stove."

"I'll be right back," said Jake.

"Blazes," said Sean again.

Jake stopped at the broken front window and edged a look outside. Still no sign of the company men so he risked running to the kitchen. He used a kitchen towel to open the fire box and jammed the poker into the orange glowing embers. Out the back door, Liam hadn't gotten very far. People were hurrying toward the sound of the shots. Liam talked to them and they dispersed back the way they'd come.

In the distance, perhaps the other side of the settlement, more shots were fired. This could quickly turn deadly. He pulled the poker out of the fire and ran back to the front door.

"Move your hands," said Jake.

With deft movements, he used the kitchen towel to wipe the front bullet hole clean and set the end of the poker against it with a sharp sizzle. Sean grunted and pounded a fist against the floor but stayed remarkably still. The smell of burning flesh assailed his nose.

"Okay, on your side."

Sean looked at him with a nearly blank expression. The pain had swallowed his rational thinking. Jake shoved the man onto his side. The exit wound was not as small. Wiping the blood away, he pressed the poker against it, skin and blood smoking and popping. He moved the poker to a different position. Sean screamed and thrashed this time.

"Hold steady. Almost done."

He moved the poker again and Sean lay still. Jake pressed a knee into the man's butt cheek and forced him onto his stomach, reapplying the poker. Sean didn't make a sound, passed out cold. Jake removed the poker and watched the man's back for a moment, satisfied the bleeding stopped.

Jake lurched to his feet and returned to the front window. Still no movement or sign of the men. They were gathering their forces. Probably spreading out. They'd try to flank them. He hoped Liam was doing a reasonable job of rallying the settlement. He hurried back to the kitchen, dropping the poker into a porcelain sink. Liam came in through the back door. Three men and two women from the settlement, all armed, stayed just outside.

Jake pointed to two of the men. "Move Sean into a bedroom, then come join us. We'll be out back spreadin' the word."

Liam and Jake hustled outside. Settlement people were showing up in greater numbers, maybe half had guns. Jake let Emma's brother talk to them as he was still the stranger.

But as some started back toward their homes to arm themselves, Jake called out, "Careful, they could be anywhere now, and assume they'll shoot."

It wasn't more than a few minutes later before gun fire erupted to the east of Liam's house. Jake quickly set up a haphazard line of men and women to defend to the west, then he hurried with Liam toward the shooting.

"This all because of me?" asked Liam as they ran.

"Most likely. But this time they ain't foolin' around."

"I don't get it. In town they weren't so—" Liam's words trailed off and he shrugged.

"Brazen?"

"Yeah. Like you were saying, the company men didn't seem to really want to fight. Not with guns, anyway. They beat on us, sure enough, but when you confronted them, they all backed down."

"Did you recognize both men who tried to take you and your family?"

Liam thought for a moment then shook his head. "Just one of them."

"My guess is that Hensley hired mercenaries. And they ain't afraid to use their guns."

"But that'd be awful fast. I mean, we were there a week ago. How'd he find these other men?"

"Don't matter. They're here."

As they continued, small groups of women and children sped past them. Jake told them to head north first, then west. Hug Clear Creek if they had to. Then that exodus petered out and they found the battle. It was small. There were two lines, each trying to flank the other, but no one getting the upper hand as no one wanted to show too much of themselves and get shot.

The settlement's line was just south of, though mostly centered around, a large gully marked with a dozen aspen trees. The rally point. Emma must be nearby. For all he knew she'd acquired a gun and was part of the line, though he didn't see her.

The battle reminded Jake of the smaller skirmishes he took part in during the war. He nearly tripped as he came to a full stop. *He fought in the war.* In Colorado—then the memory wavered and disappeared like so much smoke against the wind. Despite that, it *was* a memory. Another piece to the puzzle of himself. It helped explain at least partly his ease with firearms.

The settlement's line spread out nearly fifty yards, composed of at least seven men and four women that Jake could see, all armed and well-stocked with ammunition. How many bullets did the company men bring? If they could cut off any supplies sent from the mining town, their offensive could be over pretty quickly.

"Liam, keep your people firing, but tell them to play it safe. We just need the company men engaged. I'll go back and see if I can swing the other group around to flank 'em and capture 'em. That'll give us bargaining power to get the settlement folk free who are locked up in the common house."

He wanted to look for Emma, make sure she was safe, but there was no time. Too many lives were in the balance. Jake raced back to Sean's house. He was pleased to find a baker's dozen of armed men and women spread out in a line of cover behind the house. There was no shooting and they were on the verge of breaking toward the main battle, itching to help.

Jake broke them into two squads, though he didn't know the people well enough to decide who should be the leader of the first squad, so he picked who seemed most attentive, but not the most eager. He didn't want someone leading a headlong charge into gunfire.

The first squad shadowed the lane that led toward the common house from Sean's house. They were to engage and pin down any company men coming this way. If they didn't encounter anyone after two hundred yards, they were to turn east toward the gun battle.

Jake led the second squad. They went west initially, moving swiftly, and then looped back to the east. They would clear out any company men who hadn't headed toward the shooting and to make sure that the first squad didn't get flanked.

As they moved, the squad spread out enough to keep to cover behind shrubs and houses. They found no opposition, nor any settlement stragglers. They were far enough west that Jake had them march in sight of the last ragged line of houses, including Emma's, to make sure the company men hadn't made it this far.

They were just starting their swing back to the east when a woman to Jake's right stopped the squad with a low whistle. He ran over to where she crouched. Three men were huddled in a lane over a small galvanized metal tub.

"What're they doing?" she whispered.

Jake knew, and he didn't like it. "Cover me."

CHAPTER TWENTY-NINE

The woman brought her hunting rifle up to her shoulder and nodded. Jake turned and performed military hand signs to the others—*another memory!*—before it dawned on him they wouldn't understand. He beckoned them over, pointed out the men so they'd all be aware, and then held his hand out, palm toward them, to get them to stay. They glanced at the woman next to Jake and they all went to a knee, raising their rifles and shotguns to their shoulders. There was fear on all their faces, but none of them hesitated.

Jake turned and ran toward the men, going wide to give his squad a clear shot if he couldn't control the situation. Black smoke rose from the middle of the company men. Two of them stood, each holding a torch spitting fire. They were just outside the yard of a house. The men vaulted the low fence, causing a small flock of sheep to bleat and scatter.

Jake cocked and raised his revolver. "Hold it right there! Don't even twitch!"

As before, Jake recognized one of the men, who stopped. The other man, a mercenary, raised a revolver and fired wildly in Jake's direction and then started the motion to throw the torch at the house. Jake shot him, and the man crumpled to the ground, the torch falling next to him.

The man at the tub got one shot off with a revolver before Jake's squad opened fire. The man was cut down before he could shoot a second time. The company man dropped his torch and fell to the ground, covering his head. He wasn't shot. Jake motioned for the squad to approach as he moved up and knelt next to the mercenary in the yard. He was dead. Picking up the torch, Jake jammed the flame down into the dirt, extinguishing it.

As he rose, one of the women knelt on the company man's back and tied his hands together. Her knots were swift and sure. She then removed his boots, tied his ankles together, and drew them up behind, close to his hands, to finish the hog tie. She finished his bindings before Jake got to the tub. There were several lamp bases full of kerosene in the bottom.

"Smash 'em on the ground so they can't be used," he said. "Now let's get all three men out of view." They dumped the company man into a shed and laid out the two dead men next to the house, covering them with canvas.

They reformed their line and started back east. The sound of gunfire in the distance was steady. Jake was glad he didn't hear the screams of wounded. Hopefully they could get out of this without many casualties. But as they continued their march, Jake heard yelling off to his right, toward the common house.

A man repeated himself over and over, "Stop shooting or the woman dies!"

It took a little time, but slowly the gunfire ended. Jake had expected this to happen at some point, using their hostages for barter. He led his squad in the direction of the yelling, stopping them short of the large clearing in front of the common house. He cautiously continued forward. Three men were in the clearing. One of them held a woman tight to him, a gun pressed to her head. It felt like a draft horse kicked Jake in the gut.

It was Emma.

His breathing went ragged. He almost propelled him headlong at the man holding her. Jake knew he had affections for Emma, but it wasn't until seeing her like this, in danger at the hands of men he knew were willing to kill, that his deepest truest feelings clawed to the surface like a wild cat. He shuddered but forced himself to take a deep breath.

Two of the men were no doubt brothers, each with the same long oily dark hair, narrow eyes, and sharp chins covered in a week's growth of whiskers. Not twins, but obvious close relations. The third man was Nate. Jake knew then that it wasn't a fluke that Emma was their bargaining chip. It wouldn't have surprised him if Nate stumbled upon her, took her prisoner, and dragged her straight to the brothers, who Jake assumed were in charge of the mercenaries and had the power to barter.

Jake put his revolver away, raised his hands chest high, and stepped into the clearing. They saw him immediately. Fear, which had plainly been written on Emma's face—which was as much of a punch through his heart as seeing her held by these men—melted from her face at seeing him. Her expression changed to relief. She believed in him. And he would do whatever it took to keep her safe.

He started to speak, but hesitated. The two brothers didn't just look at him, they gaped. The mouth of the brother not holding Emma was full open, his chin threatening to scrape the ground. "How the hell, Damon?"

The brother holding his beloved sputtered, "Can't be!"

They knew him. It took Jake a moment to refocus. He said, "You harm her, and I'll kill all three of you. That's a promise."

CHAPTER THIRTY

"Not if you're dead," said a brother, bringing his revolver to bear on Jake.

The other, called Damon, did the same thing, to Jake's relief, pulling his revolver away from Emma. But it also meant he had to find cover fast. He didn't dare draw and fire. Even as good a shot as he was, from this distance, he wouldn't risk hitting her.

As he turned and moved, a bullet pierced his thigh. His momentum, however, carried him around the corner of a house. Hidden from view, he pulled his revolver and held it up, ready for the men to charge him. But they didn't. He checked his wound. The bullet tore a crease along the outside of his left thigh. No real damage. Blood, of course, but nothing major. He wouldn't bother to bandage it at the moment.

He pushed himself to his feet. The wound complained, but he ignored it, there was a far more important matter to worry about. And her name was Emma. Thankfully, no one in his squad had opened fire.

He eased back to the corner of the house and risked a look. All three men, and Emma, were gone. They must have gone into the common house, it was the closest structure. He moved back behind the house and found his squad.

"They take her into the common house?" he asked.

One of the men nodded.

That was bad. It was a strong defensive position, especially with however many settlement folk were imprisoned inside. They didn't dare fire upon it.

Liam jogged up, covered in dirt but unharmed. "We got them. A small group of our own snuck up on them from behind. Once they knew they were trapped, they surrendered. A few on both sides got hurt, but thank God, no one was killed."

"They have Emma," said Jake.

Liam's eyes went wide, and he started to shake. "What? Where?"

"She's in the common house." He turned and looked at the squad. "I need you all to show yourselves out front, draw their attention, but no matter what, don't shoot or you might hit one of your own. And please don't get shot. Hurry, do it now."

As soon as the squad moved out, Jake and Liam hurried off. Jake ignored the pain in his leg. They went behind houses, trying not to be seen from the common house, jogging the entire way. Jake winced at the pain but refused to let it slow him down. They circled wide until they came out of the settlement to the south, then made their way to the where they could see the back of the common house while staying under cover. There were still no company men behind the building but how many were inside?

Jake said, "Let's sneak up on the common house and see what's going on inside. From there, well, we'll just have to—"

"Hold on, look."

The back door opened. A man, one of the brothers, he seemed to be the older of the two, poked his head out for a moment. He looked back into the structure, said something, then opened the door wider and stepped out. A rifle now, instead of a revolver, was in his hands.

The younger brother, Damon, came out. He still held Emma, who looked angry enough to eat a hornet's nest. Behind them, three more armed men emerged, one of them Nate and the other two mercenaries.

The two Jake didn't recognize held oil lamps probably pulled from the sconces of the common house. It was difficult to tell in the daylight, but Jake thought he could make out the lit flames of the lamps and saw spurts of black smoke.

"Crickets," he muttered.

"They're not going to—"

One man stepped back and threw his lamp against the floor of the doorway. Flames rushed up the frame on either side. The other man simply threw his lamp as hard as he could against the back wall. A solid circle of flame erupted and quickly climbed the wall to the roof.

Jake shoved Liam back the way they'd come. "Get around front and make sure everyone gets out okay."

Liam hesitated, he wasn't happy leaving his sister, but then he took off running.

Jake watched the men jog away from the common house, Damon dragging Emma with him. She resisted, and he had to yank on her to keep her moving. Jake shadowed them, staying behind shrubs and trees as they entered the wilder untamed part of the valley beyond the settlement.

Up ahead he heard the snicker of horses. He had to stop the men before they reached them. If they got Emma back to the mining town they'd be in an entrenched defensive position. He had to act now. It was tempting to just shoot the man holding Emma, but he couldn't bring himself to shoot him in the back.

"Hold it right there!" he shouted.

The five men froze. Emma tried to pull free, but Damon wouldn't let her go.

"Drop your guns. Now!"

Two of the men and the brother not holding Emma dropped their guns and slowly turned toward him. But Nate whirled and raised his revolver. Jake fired. The man dropped, crying out and writhing on the ground, a rose of blood blooming on the side of his yellow shirt. Damon dragged Emma close, creating a shield. He put the barrel of his gun against her head, sending a shock of rage through Jake.

"Drop *your* gun, ranger. Right now."

Ranger? An image of a silver star on his chest swam briefly in his mind, but he pushed it away. He cocked the revolver and held it out straight and steady, aiming it at the man's head.

"Like I said, you hurt her and you're dead."

The other three men shuffled nervously. Damon's eyes were almost wild as he looked over at his brother, as though for guidance. Jake's eyes, however, didn't waver until Liam appeared behind the company men.

Emma's brother held a shotgun like a club, both hands on the barrel. Jake didn't like it. Even if he knocked Damon out, the outlaw might still squeeze his trigger finger, but there was nothing Jake could do, other than to help by being a distraction.

"Who the hell are you fellas?" asked Jake. "Weren't none of you in town when we stopped in a week ago."

The four men looked confused. The two who looked like brothers exchanged another glance.

"What you playin' at? You couldn't forget us already," said Damon. He was jittery, his hand shaking a little as it held the gun to Emma's head.

But Jake kept going. "Wasn't sure you'd recognize me. Had my head shaved since last we met." They called him a ranger. He assumed that made them outlaws, not just mercenaries, since they were none too pleased to see him. "So why are you helpin' the mining company? You work for 'em?"

Damon said, "We like to keep it in the family. Right, Daren?"

The older brother said, "He don't need to know horseshit."

It looked like Daren was going to say something else, but that's when Liam struck, swinging his shotgun in a big sideways loop, like Paul Bunyan swinging his ax clear through a giant redwood. The heavy stock cracked against the side of Damon's head. Emma called out in surprise. The man's gun fired.

The two fell to the ground in a heap.

"Emma!" shouted Jake, springing forward.

The older brother intervened, plowing into him with a shoulder. Daren and Jake tumbled to the ground, Jake's revolver flying from his hand. He tried desperately to throw the man from him, so he could get to Emma, but the man held tight. And another wisp of a memory floated up. Their wrestling seemed too familiar. Was that the fight that got him stabbed? Daren smashed an elbow into his cheek and his head rang. Stupid. He needed to concentrate on the fight at hand.

Daren twisted until he was on top. He reared up onto his knees, swinging a fist. Jake turned his head and evaded the worst of the hit, which glanced off his forehead. He then shoved the outlaw in the chest, pushing him back and getting his legs free to kick the man in the gut. Daren huffed and fell back. Jake rolled to the side and heaved himself to his feet. The outlaw sprung up as well, his eyes looking greedily at the guns on the ground.

Over the man's shoulder, Liam fought the other two men and was getting the worst of it. The shotgun was no longer in his hands and the men were content to beat on Emma's brother rather than get their guns. But at some point, they'd realize they were better off armed, so Jake pressed the matter with Daren.

He moved closer and jabbed at the man with his left hand. As Daren went to block it, Jake drove his right fist at the outlaw's face. The man moved enough that the blow skipped off his chin. Daren brought his right fist up, clipping Jake in the side of the head, causing a sharp pain to his ear.

But that left Daren open for just an instant. Jake smashed a fist into the outlaw's cheek and eye. The man's head whipped sideways, providing a nice target. Jake drove his other fist into Daren's nose. There was a crunch and the outlaw grunted, knees wobbled, blood flowed from his broken nose.

Jake didn't wait for him to recover, hitting him again with his left and then his right until Daren staggered back and fell to his knees, his face red with blood, his eyes vacant. Jake lunged forward and slammed his knee into Daren's chin. The outlaw fell back unconscious, no doubt swallowing a few teeth.

The other two men were still gleefully beating on Liam, who was somehow standing, but unable to raise his arms to defend himself. Jake scrambled for his revolver plus Daren's. He fired into the air. The men whirled, their faces feral grimaces. They'd been caught in a bloodlust, but the sight of the guns snapped them back.

Liam, however, stood with a blank and bloody expression. Emma's brother was out, he just didn't know it. A shuddering roar to his left got Jake's attention. The common house's roof collapsed, the entire building engulfed in flame. The settlement's residents were wetting down nearby houses to keep them from catching fire.

A small group of men from the settlement, Angus leading them, approached cautiously, their rifles at the ready. "Everything under control?" asked Liam's friend.

"Cover these two and take care of Liam, he's beat pretty bad." Jake holstered his revolver and tucked Daren's gun, a beautiful black Schofield Model 3, into the waist band of the gun belt. Then with an aching heart, he looked down at Emma's still form. An unreal form of terror shuddered through him. He almost couldn't move, but he forced himself forward.

CHAPTER THIRTY-ONE

Damon and Emma were face down, with the outlaw draped across her. There was a lot of blood and a huge welt on the side of the outlaw's head. And there was blood on Emma, wetting her brown hair. Jake grabbed Damon and threw the man from her, then he fell to his knees, afraid to touch her. Afraid to discover she was dead.

"Is she okay?" asked Angus, who helped Liam to the ground where a little bit of awareness returned.

Jake couldn't speak. He brushed the hair from Emma's face, but he couldn't see it clearly for some reason. It took him a moment to realize that tears blurred his vision. He wiped them away impatiently, and then lowered his head to her back, pressing his ear against it. At first all he heard was the rush of his own blood through his ears, but he closed his eyes.

Then he jerked backward when she whispered, "Damn, my head hurts."

The relief that flooded him caused his senses to waver and he put his hands on the ground to steady himself. She opened her eyes and tried to move but winced instead.

"Hold on," he whispered, unable to speak any louder. "Let me look." He used his fingers to comb her hair back, so he could look for a wound beneath the blood. She was shot, but like his thigh, it was just a short furrow along her skin. There was lots of blood, as head wounds were always big bleeders, but nothing fatal. He bent down and lightly kissed her head above the wound.

All rounded up and counted, there were fourteen men from the mining town. A few of them dead, which included Damon, the hit to his head cracking his skull. The wounded on both sides were tended to as best they could, including Emma. After her gunshot was cleaned and dressed, she looked a bit like a pirate with a white cloth tied around her head, the excess trailing down the back of her neck to her shoulders.

Liam was another matter. He'd been beaten badly and was at home in bed, his face misshapen and most likely concussed. Emma joked dryly that she hoped he hadn't lost his memory. Jake suggested writing his name on his forehead just in case.

Conor surveyed the situation. All the mining town men, dead and wounded, were in the clearing in front of the razed common house. The old man shook his head. "How did it get this out of hand?"

Jake and Emma stood next to him. She said, "But we were lucky."

He nodded. "Thanks to Jake, here."

Jake held up his hands. "Everyone pitched in. It was somethin' to see how quickly everyone rallied and took to the defense of the settlement."

"Aye, we're a hardy breed," said Conor. The old man's face scrunched in concentration. "But now what do we do with them?"

"We'll have to escort them up to Georgetown tomorrow," said Jake. "Turn 'em over to the marshal. Tonight, keep 'em tied up and under heavy guard."

"What about Wayne Hensley?" said Emma. "We have to do something about him."

"Yep. I'll head there and take care of him," said Jake.

"By yourself?" said Emma, her voice letting him know she thought that was a bad idea.

Jake gestured to the company men in the clearing. "This is all his men. He'll be alone. Can't imagine he'll be too much trouble."

Emma stared at him.

Early the next morning, Jake, Angus, and five other settlement men headed toward the mining town. At the outskirts, they drew guns. Two of the men stayed back while Jack, Angus, and a young man named Raleigh continued.

The town looked deserted, but it hadn't been exactly bustling the last time Jake was here. They stopped outside the building for the Sideways Mining Company operations. Angus and Jake dismounted, and Raleigh stayed with the horses. The under-construction boardwalk looked no further along than a week ago. Jake and Angus walked across the temporary planks to the door. He held one of Daren's black Schofield Model 3 revolvers in his hand, its twin holstered. It was a beautiful gun and he liked the way it fit. He let it lead the way into the building.

The first floor was empty. The two men headed up the stairs, walking as quietly as squeaky boards would allow. At the top, there was still no sign of anyone.

Jake motioned to Angus to look down one end of the hallway while he went to the other. Some of the doors were open and others closed. He poked his head in the first door. The room was an office that looked like a twister had blown through. The floor and a desk were strewn with papers.

Jake continued to the next room, which was where Liam, Angus, and the others had been held. He slowly opened the door. The room was empty and also ransacked. As he turned to the last two doors, a figure appeared in the doorway to his left. He spun and crouched, ready to shoot.

CHAPTER THIRTY-TWO

A terrified man held his hands up. "Don't shoot!"

Jake shook his head and stood. "Sweet Jesus, Doc, I almost shot you."

It was the town doctor dressed in a blue big-city suit that looked garish and out of place. The doctor breathed deeply a few times and then lowered his hands. "What's going on?"

Jake shrugged. "We're lookin' for Hensley. You seen him?"

He shook his head. "That's who I was looking for. I

saw all those men leave yesterday and haven't seen anything of Mr. Hensley since then."

Angus came up to them. "No one's down that way. Oh, hello, Doc."

"Ah, hello. Angus, wasn't it? How's the wound?"

"Not too bad. Scabbed over and itching."

"Let me have a look," said the doctor, stepped forward.

Jake moved on to the last door and looked inside. It was a bedroom. He checked the armoire and the closet, both were empty. As he returned to the hall, the doctor was nodding at the bullet hole in Angus's arm. "Yes, that's healing fine. Just fine."

Jake said, "Hensley cleared out. Maybe when none of his men returned last night he thought it best he move on to different pastures."

"What was this all about? Where did the men go?"

"Well," said Jake, "now that you ask. We could use your help in the settlement. There was a bit of a ruckus and some people got hurt. You have a buckboard or the like?"

The doctor nodded. "Yes."

"Good. We'll help you pack up and load everything you'll need."

"Well, I don't know—"

"It wasn't a suggestion."

Confused, the doctor followed the two downstairs. Raleigh was inside holding a gun on Jordan. The man held a large cloth satchel in his hand.

"Hensley's gone?" asked Jake.

Jordan, nervously eyeing them all, nodded.

"Where to?"

The man shrugged. "Didn't tell me. Just packed up and took a pony cart out of town."

"You headin' out, too?"

Jordan looked at the bag in his hand. "Uh."

"Don't blame you. But I'd like you to stay."

Jordan looked confused. "Huh?"

"Need you to send word to the owners of this operation. Let 'em know exactly what happened with Hensley and that I'll be seein' to it that nothin' like that happens again. You make sure they understand that if they cross me, they'll regret it."

Jordan nodded. "Yessir."

CHAPTER THIRTY-THREE

The days following the wolf attack were warm and the ground dried up. The Appaloosa continued his trek down the mountain following Clear Creek. He drank when thirsty and ate wild grasses. Small animals chased each other in their springtime rites, unconcerned about the passing of the horse.

During his long walk there were times that Speck heard humans. He was both curious and afraid, moving deeper into the woods and either passing by them or vice versa. Each time there was a welling in his chest of hope, but he never heard nor smelled his own man. The horse continued on alone, not knowing where he was going or when he would get there.

It was on one clear spring day that he came down a particularly steep and rocky descent, the horse carefully placing his hooves with each step, but still slipping occasionally on scree. At the bottom, the ground leveled off into a small valley. The first thing Speck smelled was smoke, which was heavy on the air. He saw structures beyond the trees with slim gray trails of smoke rising languidly into the air. The horse skirted the area, moving to his right even though it took him farther from Clear Creek.

The valley was an easy walk, filled with various grasses and shrubs and fewer trees. He stopped at a small stream, little more than a ditch that snaked across the valley, and drank. After quenching his thirst, he started following the ditch, but stopped again. There was a familiar spore in the air. His nostrils flared as he turned his head one way then the other trying to pinpoint where the smell came from. He quivered and stamped his feet, a whine escaping from deep within his chest. He leapt the ditch and bolted toward the structures.

It was closing in on noon when they returned to the settlement. During the ride back, Angus filled in the doctor about what happened. As they came up on the clearing, which was visible now from the trail with the common house reduced to smoky cinders, Conor approached them, flanked by several others. All armed.

Angus hitched a thumb at the buckboard. "This is the town doctor. He came to help with the wounded."

"That's good, but aren't you missing someone?"

Jake sighed. "Hensley's gone. Cleared out. No tellin' where he could be by now."

"Interesting," said Conor. "Wonder what the company will do now? Did you talk to the miners?"

"No. Left one of the company men in charge, if he hangs around. Wouldn't surprise me if he sets out as well. But we'll see to it the company knows what really happened here. We can wire the company when we take these men to Georgetown."

Conor nodded. "Sounds good. Angus, show the doctor to Sean's house. He'll be one of the patients so might as well use his place as a hospital. Get some volunteers to clear out his front room and set up extra beds."

"This way, Doc."

Jake dismounted as Emma approached. She looked tired, as if she'd been working, which she shouldn't have been doing with her head injury. He'd escort her to the doctor to make sure the wound was properly dealt with.

"No Hensley?" she asked, folding into his arms and placing her head on his shoulder.

"You ain't overdoin' it, are you? How's your head?"

"Like someone's splitting wood on it and missing the wood. But I'm fine. When you heading to Georgetown?"

Jake looked over at Conor. "Still want us to head up today?"

The old man nodded. "The sooner we get rid of this unruly lot, the better. If you leave within the hour you can be there before sundown."

"We'll start getting ready."

Emma held him tighter. "So glad this is over. It'll be nice to spend some time with you without all this hanging over our heads."

"Yes, ma'am, it will." Then he tensed.

"What's wrong?" Then her head came up. "A horse."

Coming fast. He disengaged from her, put his hand to his gun, and turned toward the valley, but it was difficult to tell the direction of the echoing hooves. Then to his right a beautiful Appaloosa, cream colored coat awash with reddish-brown spots, charged into view. It had bridle and saddle, but no rider.

"Someone must be hurt," said Emma.

A hundred yards off, the horse stopped, nostrils flaring as it stamped and turned one way and then another, raising its head into the air.

CHAPTER THIRTY-FOUR

Hench stared and whispered, "Speck?"

"What?" asked Emma.

Hench ran toward the horse. "Speck!"

The horse surged forward, charging straight for him.

"Look out!" yelled Emma.

But Hench didn't slow down, though the Appaloosa did as he got close. The ranger crashed into his horse, wrapping his arms around the horse's neck, rubbing his scruffy face against the coarse hair.

"Where the hell did you come from?"

Emma came up behind Hench, wincing and huffing. "You know each other."

Hench, wiping one side of his face against Speck and pawing at the other with his hand to clear the tears, turned toward her. "This is my horse, Speck."

The horse huffed at him, smelling him, and then set his chin on the ranger's shoulder, rubbing the side of his muzzle against the side of Hench's face. The ranger scratched hard under each ear.

"Your horse?" There was a strange note in Emma's voice. A sadness that concerned him, but he couldn't bring himself to break from Speck as the horse continued to nuzzle him. He wouldn't move from the Appaloosa until the horse did so first as he realized his horse must have been lost in the wilderness for—crickets, nearly two weeks. A pang of guilt and pity sent a shudder through his body. As brave as Speck was, that must have been terrifying, and it made Hench feel like the lowest of scoundrels to let it happen.

Emma said, "He's hurt." She stood on the other side of the horse.

Hench jerked back. "What?"

"Here," she said, touching Speck's shoulder.

Hench stepped under the horse's neck to stand next to Emma. There were cuts scabbing over, cracks glistening. The ranger stepped back from Speck, who moved to close the gap. Hench put a hand on the side of the horse's neck. "Hold on, boy, let me get a look."

They were animal wounds. Teeth marks. Most likely wolf. A mountain lion or bear would have ripped Speck's side open with razor-sharp claws.

Keeping a hand on his horse to keep him at arm's length, Hench moved to his hindquarters, around behind, finding more cuts on the other flank. Then dried blood matted near his shoulder and smearing the leather stirrup strap and fender. Hench lifted the stirrup clear, but there were no cuts in the area.

He looked up into Speck's eye and nodded, "I bet you hurt 'em pretty good, didn't you? You poor brave boy," said Hench, scratching again beneath the horse's ears. "I'm sorry."

Speck tossed his head once.

Hench then moved to the horse's snout and undid the bridle's flash, noseband, and throat lash. Standing beneath his neck, Hench put his arms to either side of Speck's head and lifted the bridle clear of the ears, then slowly lowered it, letting the bit slide free of his mouth. Hench dropped the bridle to the ground and scratched again behind Speck's ears and down his cheeks. As he turned to the saddle, Emma was already detaching the girth. He moved to the opposite side, pulled the girth through the martingale, then removed the saddle, turning and tossing it a few feet away. Emma removed the blanket.

Hench rubbed the saddle area with his hands, avoiding a sore that had formed on Speck's side. "Any sores over there?" he asked.

Emma said, "Two small ones." There was a strange hitch to her voice. Hench frowned and moved around to her side. Her face was troubled, cheeks rose red, eyes rimmed with tears. Her voice trembled. "You remember, don't you?"

Hench nodded slowly. "Uh, yeah. I guess so. Seeing Speck seems to have knocked it loose."

Neither spoke for several moments. Hench wasn't sure what to say and didn't want to rush her.

"So—who are you?"

They didn't look at one another, rubbing Speck as a distraction.

"Well, turns out I'm a Colorado Ranger. Uh, the name's Hench."

Her brow furrowed. "Hench? Just Hench?"

"I have a first name, but—" he looked at the settlement folk gathered round "—I'll tell you later."

"And what about—do you remember everything that happened here? When you were Jake?"

Hench frowned and said, "Well, let's see. I remember Liam and his foolhardy adventure at the mining town. I remember that you're Liam's sister. Emma, isn't it?"

Her face turned to stone. He moved closer and put a hand over hers, which was ice cold. "And I remember I'm in love with you."

She suddenly breathed—had she been holding it? "You are an asshole."

Hench smiled and nodded, turning her toward him. "Oh, I definitely remember that."

Her beautiful eyes glistened, and he leaned in, not caring about the people around them, and kissed her.

CHAPTER THIRTY-FIVE

Despite the reunion with Speck, and Hench getting his memory back, Conor was still intent on cleaning the riffraff out of the settlement. He wanted the outlaws and the company men gone. Over a dozen settlement people volunteered to go to Georgetown with Hench and their prisoners.

Conor eyed the menagerie. "Think Marshal Jackson will have room for all these men?"

"Jackson," said Hench to himself. "Almost forgot about him."

Unconsciously, he put his hands on the grips of his black Schofield Model 3 revolvers. It was good having them back, compliments of Daren Hensley. And that made him wonder. He went over to the stockpile of weapons they'd taken and sure enough, there was his Spencer carbine.

Angus was one of the men going to Georgetown. He stood next to Hench. "How are we getting all these men up there?"

Hench looked over the motley bunch. "Wagons. It'll be easier to keep an eye on 'em."

The settlement brought in three wagons. They tied the outlaws together in pairs, back to back. They put the dead and wounded into back of the third wagon.

As the rest of the volunteers showed up with their horses, Hench went back to Emma's house. She'd taken Speck there to tend to his wounds. The Appaloosa's head was down in a bucket of oats when the ranger approached. Emma was in the yard washing her hands of the salve she'd applied.

"Looks good," said Hench. Emma had cleaned the wounds before applying liberal amounts of the salve.

"He's a good patient."

Speck raised his head from the bucket and huffed oats over the front of Hench and pushed his nose against the ranger's chest. Hench scratched under his ears.

Emma stepped up next to him. "Beautiful animal," she said.

Hench nodded. "We fit each other well."

"So what happens after Georgetown?"

Hench looked at her. It took her a moment to return his gaze. Her eyes glistened, and he sensed unease beneath the surface. He tried to speak, but found his throat constricted. Finally, he said in a forced whisper, "It's back to the trail workin' for the rangers."

"Goodbye and good riddance?" Her cheeks turned to flames upon her pale skin.

He shook his head. "Of course not. But it's my job. Though to be honest, this is the first time in a long time I'm not anxious to get back to it."

"You coming back this way?"

"I'd like to. You know that."

"Do I? Or is this just a damned fine excuse to be rid of me?"

Everything he thought to say sounded asinine in his head. She turned away and walked stiffly toward her house.

"Wait," he said.

She stopped but didn't turn back. "Why? You'll just tell me you'll be back when you can. But we both know that's horseshit. Just an excuse to make you feel good about yourself."

He *was* about to say that, but it's not what he wanted to say. She started walking again.

"Come with me." Had he said that out loud? He wasn't sure until she stopped mid-stride, one foot just off the ground.

Her voice hitched. "What did you say?"

He thought his chest might explode. He was suddenly light-headed and a bit wobbly on his legs. "You heard me."

She turned.

He continued. "It's probably not right me askin' you. Your life is here. Your brother and his family. And it's not like we're hitched yet or any—"

"Tell Conor it's going to be a little longer before you go."

"What? Why?"

"So I can get a horse and gear. Then we'll come back this way after Georgetown and trade my house and all my goddamned chickens for anything else we need for the trail."

CHAPTER THIRTY-SIX

It was a large contingent that went to Georgetown. Hench rode the same horse he'd borrowed before from Conor. He couldn't ride Speck with his injuries and saddle sores. The Appaloosa was not at all happy about it and kept taking swipes with his teeth at Hench's mount.

The ride took a bit longer than expected and the sun disappeared to the west, though there was still enough gray light for them to see by as they reached the edge of the mountain town.

They got quite the stares from the locals at their spectacle of horse riders and prisoners—a shabby circus. Hench felt a strange sensation. Not quite déjà vu, but it seemed like it'd just been yesterday when he'd last ridden into town, though it was now two weeks ago. He still remembered his life as Jake, but it felt somehow separate, like it was a stage play he watched at the opera house in Central City rather than his own personal memories. He looked over at Emma next to him and smiled. No, not all his memories were like that. He couldn't express how good it felt having her ride next to him.

They stopped the wagons nearly two blocks shy of the marshal's office and dismounted. Hench, Emma, Angus, Speck—because he refused to wait behind—and four other settlers went on foot. Coming up the road from the settlement, Hench had filled them all in about Marshal Jackson's underhandedness.

A yellow light glowed within the office. The street was plenty dark by this time, so Hench went to the opposite side and took a look. It was Jackson with two of his deputies.

He motioned, and Emma nodded, heading for the office door. As she entered, Hench, Angus, and one other man moved toward the door, but waited a few seconds before entering. Hench levered and cocked the Spencer carbine.

Jackson and the two deputies had their backs to him, their attention on Emma who stood at the opposite side of the office. But they heard Hench's gun and whirled.

"Easy now," said the ranger, his carbine leveled at the men. Angus and the other settler fanned out behind Hench, their guns pointed at the marshal and deputies.

The deputies looked a mix of scared and outraged.

Marshal Jackson's face went slack and turned an unnatural pale, detectable even in the yellow light of the oil lamps. The bruising from Hench hitting him two weeks earlier with the stock of the carbine were faint shadows on that forlorn face.

One of the deputies reached for his gun. Angus raised his rifle. The deputy froze.

Emma, now behind the three lawmen, pulled revolvers from their holsters and then moved quickly past them to set the guns on the floor behind Hench. The ranger never took his eyes off Jackson. An anger that he realized had simmered in him for weeks, though forgotten, boiled up. But even so, all he said was, "You're under arrest, Jackson."

A deputy yelled, "You can't do that! What the hell is going on?"

Angus said, "Your marshal conspired with the Hensley gang to kill Colorado Ranger Hench—that's the man to my right, here. Walked him right into an ambush that nearly cost him his life."

Jackson almost whimpered when he said, "You gotta understand, they would'a killed me!"

Hench glanced at the deputies. Either the men were fine damned actors, or their looks of shock and disbelief spoke of their innocence. Hench leaned toward the latter, but the deputies would be interrogated by the county sheriff after Hench wired the man.

"I'm lockin' you up, Jackson," said Hench, nodding to the back of the office and the door that led to the jail cells.

Emma grabbed Hench's arm. "Wait, that's it?"

Hench looked at her, confused.

"Aren't you going to, you know, get even?"

"The man is unarmed and he ain't resistin'."

Jackson raised his hands. "I'm not! Y'all see that right?"

His deputies looked disgusted.

She sputtered, "To Hell with that," and launched herself at the ex-marshal, smashing one fist into his thick handlebar mustache followed in fast succession by the other planted square into his nose. Blood flowed, and Jackson fell back, trying futilely to protect himself from her fury. She pummeled his face as he stumbled all the way to the back wall. She looked every part the fierce pirate with her white bandana tied around her head and trailing wildly behind her.

Hench followed, but waited for Emma to get in a few more licks before pushing between her and Jackson, putting an arm around her waist. She vibrated and breathed like a locomotive.

"Angus, we better put him away before she kills him," said Hench in all seriousness.

Angus grinned and nodded as Jackson, his nose sideways, his lips cracked, blood smeared across his swelling face, groaned and slid to the floor.

CHAPTER THIRTY-SEVEN

Angus, Hench, and Emma sat in the saloon. The other settlers were stuck at the jail watching the prisoners, as Hench couldn't trust the deputies. The four small cells in back were crammed tight.

"You know," said Hench, delicately cleaning the blood from Emma's hands with a wet bar towel, "that was a fine piece of work you did to his face."

"Grade A work," said Angus.

Emma squeezed Hench's hands, then grimaced. "Ow."

The ranger nodded. "You're gonna have swollen hands for at least a week or two, that's if you didn't break any knuckles." He couldn't be sure if any were broken, they were all swollen.

"Worth it," she said, letting Hench go back to cleaning off the blood.

The bartender came over and put a bottle of rye on the table. The label had HENCH written on it in grease pencil. The man asked, "You want some dinner?"

"Steak! Thick!" said Emma enthusiastically.

"You heard the woman," said Hench. "And we don't mind if they bleed a bit."

Emma reached for the bottle and winced as she tried to put her hand around it. "Damn. You might have to tend to me."

Hench looked at her seriously, pursing his lips before saying, "Seems only fair, though I might just have to fit you with a diaper."

She smiled and said, "You're lucky my knuckles hurt."

About Hench

To get a FREE Hench short story
sign up for the Hench mailing list by going to:

JosephParksAuthor.com

Printed in Great Britain
by Amazon